LAST TANG STANDING

LAST TANG STANDING

—

Lauren Ho

G. P. Putnam's Sons
New York

PUTNAM
— EST. 1838 —
G. P. PUTNAM'S SONS
Publishers Since 1838
An imprint of Penguin Random House LLC
penguinrandomhouse.com

ISBN 9780593187814

Printed in the United States of America
4th Printing

Book design by Ashley Tucker

For Olivier

Remember that your relatives are only human—
That means they can be killed.

—~~Andrea Tang~~ *Ancient Chinese Proverb*

LAST TANG STANDING

Part I

SPRING IS COMING

1

Tuesday 9 February

Hope. That's what the Spring Festival, the most important celebration in the traditional Chinese calendar, is supposed to commemorate, aside from signalling, well, the coming of spring. Renewal. A time for new beginnings, fresh starts. Green stuff grows out of the ground. Politicians fulfill their campaign promises, concert tickets for A-list pop stars never get scalped, babies get born and nobody gets urinary incontinence after. And Chinese families all over the world come together in honor of love, peace, and togetherness.

But this is not that kind of story. This is a story where bad things happen to good people. Especially single people. Because here's the deal: for folks like me who find themselves single by February, Spring Festival is not a joyous occasion. It's a time for conjuring up imaginary boyfriends with names like Pete Yang or Anderson Lin, hiring male escorts who look smart instead of hot, marrying the next warm body you find, and if all else fails, having plastic surgery and changing your name so your family can never find you. For desperate times call for desperate measures, and there is no period of time more desperate for single Chinese females over the age of thirty everywhere than the Annual Spinster-Shaming Festival, a.k.a. Chinese New Year.

God help us persecuted singletons; God help us all—spring is coming.

It was noon. Linda Mei Reyes and I were sitting in a car in front of our aunt's house in matching updos, smoking *kreteks* and hunched over our smartphones as we crammed for the toughest interview that we would face this year, the "Why Are You Still Single in Your Thirties, You Disappointment to Your Ancestors" inquisition. Our interrogators lay in wait, and they were legion. The Tangs, our family, were very prolific breeders.

Each year, as was customary on the second day of Chinese New Year, Auntie Wei Wei would host a lavish luncheon for all the Singapore-based Tangs. These luncheons were mandatory Family Time: everyone had to show their faces if they were in town; the only acceptable escape clauses being death, disability, a job-related trip, or the loss of one's job (in which case you might as well be dead). If you're wondering why Auntie Wei Wei commanded such power, aside from the fact that she was housing our clan's living deity (Grandma Tang), it's because she was our clan's Godfather, minus the snazzy horse head deliveries. Many of the older Tangs were in her debt: not only did she act as the family's unofficial private bank for the favored few, she'd basically raised the lot of them after my grandfather passed away in the 1950s and left my grandmother destitute. As the eldest of a brood of nine siblings, Auntie Wei Wei had dropped out of secondary school and worked two jobs to help defray household expenses. That's how her siblings all managed to finish their secondary schooling, and for some of the higher achievers, university, even as it came at her own expense.

At least karma had rewarded her sacrifice. After migrating to Singapore in her late twenties, she had married well, against the odds, to a successful businessman; when he died soon after (of entirely natural causes), she'd inherited several tracts of land, the sale of which had made her, and her only daughter, Helen, eye-wateringly wealthy. Hence her unassailable position as de facto matriarch of the Tang clan, since there is nothing that the Chinese respect more than wealth, especially the kind that might potentially trickle downstream. Posthumously.

Ever since I moved to Singapore from London about six years ago, as the sole representative of my father's side of the family in Singapore I'd been obliged by my very persuasive mother to attend Auntie Wei Wei's gatherings. Since my father was her favorite sibling, Auntie Wei Wei had paid off a lot of his debts when he passed and now she basically owns us, emotionally, which is how real power works. I used to enjoy these gatherings, but since Ivan, my long-term partner, and I broke up nine months and twenty-three days ago, way too late for me to find another schmuck to tote to this horror show, there was ample reason to dread today's festivities. Why, you ask? Because Chinese New Year is the worst time to be unattached, bar none. Forget Valentine's Day. I mean, what's the worst that can happen then? Some man-child you've been obsessing over doesn't send you chocolates? Boo-hoo. A frenemy humblebrags about the size of her ugly, overpriced bouquet (that she probably sent herself)? Please. Your fun blind date turns out to be the Zodiac Killer? Tough. Just wait till you have to deal with Older Chinese Relatives. These people understand mental and emotional torture. They will corner you and ask you questions designed to make you want to chug a bottle of antifreeze right after. Popular ones include: "Why are you still single?"; "How old are you again?"; "What's more important than marriage?"; "Do you know you can't wait forever to have babies, otherwise you are pretty much playing Russian roulette with whatever makes it out of your collapsing birth canal?"; "How much money do you make, after taxes?"

As we've been programmed since birth to kowtow to our elders, we force ourselves to Show (our Best) Face at these events, no matter how damaging they can be to our ego and psyche. So that is why, dear Diary, two successful women in their thirties, dressed in orange floral cheongsams they panic-bought the night before, were trying so hard to get their stories about each other's imaginary boyfriend straight to placate an audience that they will not see again for another year.

"It's easy for mine," Linda was saying. My cousin and best friend, Linda is only half-Chinese (the other half being Spanish-Filipino), so she had some wiggle room with the family, but even the normally cold-blooded litigator was sweating in the air-conditioned car. "Just remember that Alvin Chan, whom you've met before by the way, is not just my boss but my boyfriend, and just, you know, extrapolate from there. Make up the details."

"What do you think I am, an amateur?" I snapped, holding up my iPhone to show her a photo of her and her "boyfriend" at a recent gala. I pulled up a screenshot of Korean actor and national treasure Won Bin—unlike Linda, I did not have a hot boss. "Now *you* remember that my boyfriend's name is Henry Chong, he's a Singaporean Chinese in his late thirties, he's the only child of a real estate mogul and a brilliant brain surgeon, and he looks like this." I held the phone in front of her face so she could be inspired by the perfection that is Won Bin.

"Too many details," Linda said, not even looking at the screen. "It's always the details that trip liars up. Keep it simple."

"Not if you're prepared, like I am. You, however, look wasted."

"I'm prepared. And I'm dead sober," she said emphatically before burping gin fumes in my face. Yet somehow her softly braided updo looked fresh while mine was already unspooling, like my life.

I muttered the Lord's Prayer, or what I could recall of it, under my breath. It was going to be a long day. "Remember, Henry's a partner in a midsize Singaporean law firm. He is currently meeting with a client in Dubai, and that's why he can't be here with us today. Oh, and he's tall. And hot."

"Got it," Linda said, rolling her eyes. She took a deep drag from her third "cigarette" of the morning. "Anything else I should casually drop during the convo? Maybe the fact that he has a massive cock?"

"If you're speaking to one of the older aunties, then yes. Go for it, with my blessings."

Linda sighed, stubbing out her "cigarette" in an ashtray. "Got it. And if anyone asks, Alvin's skiing in Val-d'Isère."

"Val-de-Whut?"

"Val-dee-Zehr. It's in the French Alps, you peasant." She grinned. "Here's another tip: peppering a convo with unpronounceable place names usually deters further lines of questioning. Most people don't like looking unsophisticated."

"Good point," I said. "OK, in that case nix Dubai, make it Ashgabat."

She flashed a thumbs-up. "Ashgabat it is. Anyway, there's a chance that none of the relatives will remember who I am since I've not been back in Asia for over a decade, so I might be safe from attack." Linda's family was somewhat estranged from the clan, one of the reasons being that her mother had married an "outsider," i.e., a non-Chinese; plus, having spent most of her formative years attending boarding school in England meant she was less involved, and less inclined to be so, in clan affairs. That was why she kept a low profile with the Tangs since her move to Singapore last Febuary as part of her firm's new market expansion plan. "I could have skipped this whole do and just stayed home, so remind me why I'm putting myself through this shitshow again?"

"Because you love me?" I said brightly.

She snorted.

I narrowed my eyes. "You owe me, woman. Without the help of my excellent notes and last-minute tutorials you would have failed your final year of law school, since you hardly attended any of the lectures."

"Keep telling yourself that. Anyway, I seem to recall being promised a champagne brunch at the St. Regis if I did well today."

"Yes," I grumbled. "I just hope you put as much effort into Henry's history and character development as I did for Alvin's."

"Don't worry. I didn't graduate top of the class—"

"Second. I was first."

"—*top* of the class for nothing. I've got the whole story down pat. Relax." She punched me in the back. "Straighten your shoulders and try not to look so browbeaten. It's no wonder you haven't been made partner."

It took all my self-control not to stab her in the eye with my cigarette.

Perhaps sensing she was in mortal danger if she didn't change the subject, Linda took out a bottle of Febreze and proceeded to baptize us with it. "Anyway, I have one last piece of advice before we go in."

"What?" I said, between coughs.

She pinched my arm, hard. "Whatever happens in there, do not cry in front of them. Don't give those jerks the satisfaction."

"*You* are hurting me," I yelped, eyes welling with tears.

"I really hope no one gives us *ang paos*," Linda said darkly, oblivious to the suffering of others as usual. "They get extra bitchy when they do. I'd rather they just insult us without feeling like they earned it." She was referring to the red envelopes containing cash that married people traditionally give out to children and other unmarried kin regardless of age or sex during Chinese New Year. For kids it's a great way to get extra pocket money, but getting *ang paos* as an adult in your thirties was a special kind of festive embarrassment, akin to getting caught making out with your first cousin by your grandmother. At least the adult recipient can comfort himself imagining the internal weeping and gnashing of teeth the married *ang pao* giver must undergo as he is forced to hand over his hard-earned cash to another able-bodied adult. In our experience, the intrusive questions and snide put-downs were definitely the giver's way of alleviating the mental agony of this reluctant act.

"Let's not be too hasty," I said, crossing myself in case she had jinxed us. "Last year I made almost six hundred bucks easy, three hundred from Auntie Wei Wei alone."

Two breath mints and liberal spritzes of Annick Goutal later, we were red-eyed and ready to face all the orcs that our family tree could throw at us. Auntie Wei Wei lived in an imposing double-storied bungalow in a quiet, leafy neighborhood in Bukit Timah. The gate and double doors of her home were thrown wide open with no security guards stationed at the gate, no salivating rabid dogs on patrol, and no military booby traps set up on the grounds. You could literally just stroll in. Which we did.

In all honesty, the casual indifference of wealthy Singaporeans to what I would deem basic precautionary measures and, quite frankly, the sheer lack of initiative shown by local burglars never failed to amaze me as a Malaysian. Even *I* could have picked this place clean with no trouble or special training whatsoever. All I would need is a couple of duffel bags, maybe a sexy black leotard, a pair of sunglasses, Chanel thigh-high boots, a French accent . . .

"Are you daydreaming again?" Linda's voice broke my reverie, in which I was back-flipping over a field of laser beams à la Catwoman (circa Michelle Pfeiffer).

"No. Why?"

"You're just standing there, drooling. Get in." She pushed open the front door, which had been left ajar.

I stifled a sigh of envy as we made our way to the reception room. Despite it being the umpteenth time I'd stepped into her home over the years, I was impressed. The mansion, with its black marble floors, high ceilings, and bespoke wallpaper, whispered of entitlement and the power to buy politicians. Auntie Wei Wei had had the place decorated in chinoiserie of the highest order. It was hard not to gawk at the fine detailing on the antique porcelain vases and lacquerware, the elegant scrolls of Chinese calligraphy and ink paintings, or to refrain from touching the dancer–shaped blooms of the rare slipper orchids flowering in their china bowls and the stuffed white peacock, with its diamond white train of tail feathers, perched on its ivory base in one corner of the room. All that was missing were some casually scattered gold bars.

It was apparent that every (official) member of our clan had made the effort to Show Face: man, woman, legitimate children, and domestic help; although it was almost 1:00 p.m., three hours after the gathering had officially begun, the place was still packed with close to fifty people. As per usual with such gatherings, everyone was dressed to the nines with their most impressive bling. You could hardly look around without a Rolex, Omega, or Panerai, real or fake, nearly putting your eye out. Key fobs of luxury cars faux-casually dangled or peeked out from pockets. Most donned red, an auspicious color for the Lunar New Year. Many Tangs were also red in the face from the premium wine and whiskey they were knocking back like there was no tomorrow, courtesy of their host. A free-flow bar can bring out the reluctant alcoholic in any Chinese, Asian flush and stomach ulcers be damned. But for me and Linda, boozing Tangs are not usually the problem: it's the sober ones we had to be wary of, the ones drinking tea as black as their stony hearts, their beady eyes looking for fresh prey. I had vivid memories of being forced to recite the times table or some classical Chinese poem in front of these raptors, their breath bated as they waited for me to make a mistake so they could run and get my parents—that way, we could all be shamed *together.* That's how they get off.

At least the food looked amazing; I would have expected nothing less from Auntie Wei Wei. In one corner of the hall was a long buffet table laden with drool-inducing Chinese New Year delicacies such as whole roasted suckling pig; at least four different types of cold noodles; steamed sea bass; beautifully crispy Peking duck; fried spring rolls; pomelo and plum chicken salad; and *niangao.* On a separate table, the desserts: a huge rose-and-lychee cake flanked by two different types of chocolate cake; assorted glazed mini-cupcakes; macarons the perfect red of cherries; trays of golden, buttery pineapple tarts; bowls of pistachios, cashew nuts, and peanuts; platters of cut tropical fruit; and bright pyramids of mandarin oranges and peaches. It was too much food, but by the end of the evening everything would be gone. Gluttony, after all, is a Chinese art form and we've had millennia to perfect it.

Over the din of Chinese New Year songs blaring from sleek Bang & Olufsen speakers and drunken chatter, Linda and I looked for Grandma Tang so we could pay our quick respects before joining our single, pariah peers. Linda, being a head taller than my five foot three, scanned the room and found a queue waiting to greet Grandma Tang, who was wearing a crimson batik cheongsam and all the imperial jade in the world. Someone had seated her in a thronelike high-backed chair in one corner of the hall on a makeshift pedestal, where she could peer imperiously (but blindly) down at the crowd. She was so old and wizened that when we got to her and wished her the standard Chinese New Year greeting of a long, prosperous (*never* forget the "prosperous"), and happy life, she grunted in derision, which is the old lady equivalent of "hah!"

I get my sense of humor from her, of course.

After wishing her thus, we waited for a few uncomfortable seconds before realizing, to our growing horror, that she had no intention of giving us elder singletons *ang paos*. And so, to the chorus of jeering children, we made our shamefaced way to the other end of the room, where a herd of our similarly luckless-in-love cousins were huddled together for safety. The swiftest path to them, however, brought us by some sober aunts who were stationed by the bar, simultaneously haranguing and groping a terrified waiter. There was no way we would be able to avoid them.

"Walk fast," I hissed, gripping Linda's right palm in mine so that she wouldn't canter off in the direction of the bottles of Johnnie Walker Black lined up on the bar's countertop. "And don't look around." We pretended to be deep in a discussion, laughing maniacally as we scurried by the aunts, but to no avail. One of the women, deep in her seventies and dressed in an ill-fitting burgundy cheongsam, detached herself from the gaggle of vultures, I mean, aunts, and lurched over, grinning at me. It took me a while to recognize her as she had slathered on a Beijing opera mask of makeup, and by then it was too late. Leering at me was none other than Auntie Kim, the tyrant who used to make me recite the times table in front of all the Tangs when I was a wee preschooler. I say "auntie," but to be honest, even though I see her at every single Tang gathering, I have no idea if she's really my aunt or if she is even related to me. In many parts of Asia, it is perfectly acceptable to call anyone above the age of forty, be they relative or not, "auntie" or "uncle" in lieu of ever learning their actual names—the grocer, the taxi driver, the retired accountant who does your taxes, the local pedophile—anyone. Unless, of course, you are about the same age or older. Then you're just asking for a good old slap in the face.

I scanned the room, looking for an open window, a friendly face, or a hatchet, but there was none. I tried to catch the attention of my unmarried cousins, clustered a few steps away. Two of them waved before averting their eyes. Cowards.

"Andrea Tang Wei Ling,* why so late?" Auntie Kim shouted in Singlish to all and sundry as she scanned me from top to toe, ignoring Linda (Linda was right: she had effectively been forgotten by

* In Asia, Chinese naming conventions dictate that family name comes first, followed by the given name (consisting of one or two characters), as befitting our collectivist culture. Here, baptismal or English names are written before the Chinese surname + given name, and not as part of the given name. If a Chinese person is calling another Chinese by their full name, you can be sure their intentions are not cuddly.

our family). "Why you here alone? No one want you issit?" She chuckled. "Aiyah, I just joke only, but maybe also true hor, hahaha!"

Everyone within earshot was smirking. Someone's loser kid chimed in in a singsong voice, "Auntie Andrea doesn't want to get married because she doesn't want to give us *ang pao* because she's stingy!" This outburst was greeted with laughter. The loudest laughs came from my feckless single cousins.

Normally Linda would have left me to die in the proverbial gutter by then, but Linda had KPIs* and she was not one to disappoint. Without hesitation, she shoved me aside and clasped the woman's papery hands in her own. "Auntie Kim, don't you worry about ol' Wei Ling here. She's doing very well. It took some time, but she's finally found herself a man!"

I wished she wouldn't say it with such gusto.

"Really, ah? Who?" Auntie Kim was incredulous.

"Henry Chong. Oh, he's *such* a darling, way too good for Wei Ling, really. Very smart. Very handsome. Very big, er, shoulders."

"Hen-Ree?" Auntie Kim mused, sucking on the vowels like they were her missing teeth. "Hen-Ree where right now?"

"Not here," I said petulantly, my arms crossed to hide my sweating pits.

"Oh, he's always flying here and there, that busy bee," Linda said. "Henry's a partner in a *big* law firm. Very *big*. Two, *three* hundred employees." She leaned close to Auntie Kim and stage-whispered, "He's very, very rich."

"A lawyer?" Auntie Kim exclaimed. "Rich some more . . . good, good. And he is Chinese, right?"

"He can trace his Chinaman lineage all the way to the first caveman Chong to have carnal knowledge of a woman, Auntie," Linda said, poker-faced.

---

* Key Performance Indicator. Self-explanatory, really.

"Wah?" Auntie Kim's grasp of English was as strong as Britney Spears's vocal range.

Linda tried again. "Henry is one hundred percent Chinese, pure as rice flour."

"Oh, like that, ah, good lor. Make sure you keep this one, Wei Ling, don't let him fly away, can!" said Auntie Kim, mollified. Having received all the information she needed, she handed us each an *ang pao* and lurched away, her ropes of gold chains clanking, this time heading in the direction of my terrified twenty-nine-year-old cousin, Alison Tang, who'd just arrived and was about to slink into a corner. The trooper had worn pink lip gloss and styled her hair in pigtails to appear younger. Alas, Auntie Kim, despite her decrepit condition, was not so easily fooled. "Alee-son! Alee-son! Where are you going? Why nobody with you again? Why—"

"Let's go," I said, dragging Linda past a trio of red-faced men exchanging loud and drunken reminiscences till we reached the singles posse. Our presence was acknowledged, barely; nobody wanted or dared to break eye contact for too long with their phones. Most were legitimately working (*Not even the most important holiday for the Chinese can stop me from slaving for you!* was the subtext they were channeling to their bosses), while some were Facebooking or surfing mindlessly. The most brazen one of all, Gordon, was browsing Grindr profiles. I watched him text-flirt with one guy after another and wished I could do the same and put myself out there in all my mediocre glory.

To my horror I realized, when Gordon started laughing, that I had spoken out loud without meaning to, which tended to happen when I was under stress. "Andrea darling, just do it! It's really easy. Want me to set up a profile for you? On Tinder, of course. Or that hot new location-based app everyone's talking about, which is like Grindr but for straight people. You know the one: Sponk!"

I demurred; Tinder and Sponk heralded the death of romance

to me. As if you could reduce the search for the all-important Someone Who Won't Kill You in Your Sleep to a thumb-swiping exercise based (mostly) on photos. And since I had no Photoshop skills to speak of, I didn't stand a chance—everyone knows that you had to have a hot profile photo or at least one where you looked like you hadn't given up in order to get any matches. These days I resembled a slightly melted, sun-bleached garden gnome, no thanks to my punishing schedule at work. Maybe if—

"Why, look who it is, my favorite niece, Andrea!"

I turned and saw Auntie Wei Wei, resplendent in a sunset-orange silk *baju kurung* and dripping in diamonds, striding toward us. My stomach clenched; I knew why Auntie Wei Wei was coming over and it certainly wasn't to praise my sartorial choices or make small talk. She always had an agenda when it came to members of the clan; she stuck her nose in everyone's affairs and gave unsolicited advice or orders, but nobody dared to contradict or stop her.

"I'll pay you five hundred bucks if you come out to Auntie Wei Wei right now," I whispered in desperation to Gordon. When I didn't receive a response, I swiveled my head and saw that Gordon and the gang of smartphone-wielding cravens had somehow migrated to the far side of the drawing room and were all texting as if their lives depended on it.

I turned back around and found myself face-to-face with the matriarch of the family. Behind me, I heard, rather than saw, Linda sidling away like the traitorous lowlife she was, but alas for her, the gin from earlier in the car was already working its dulling magic.

"Linda Mei Reyes!" Auntie Wei Wei said in her loud, commanding voice. "The prodigal niece herself. Now isn't this a lovely surprise to have you grace us with your presence at long last." She gave Linda a dismissive once-over. "Huh. Still as hipless as a snake. Where have you been hiding all this time? Did your father finally decide to cut the purse strings?"

Linda froze. This was the only chink in her armor—her financial dependence on her father, despite what she proclaimed to the world. "I'm the partner of a law firm and my boyfriend skis in Val-d'Isère," she said weakly to no one.

"Well, good for you, working with Daddy's pals. I'll say this for José—he always took care of his children, which is more than I can say about my sister." She shook her head and tsk-tsked. "As for you, Andrea"—Auntie Wei Wei turned her attention to me; the blood in my veins ran cold—"are you sick? You've lost a lot of weight. I can see right through you." She waggled a finger at me. "You need to fatten up or you'll lose what's left of your figure. Men don't want to marry scrawny women, you know."

I gave her a rictus grin to match my loser, non-childbearing hips. Last year I was too fat, this year I was too thin: Auntie Wei Wei could give Goldilocks a lesson or two. "*Gong xi fa cai*, Auntie Wei Wei. You look well," I said, lying. Auntie Wei Wei looked like she had crossed the Botox Rubicon in the dark.

"It's the exercise and regular facials, you should try some—I can park a Bentley in one of your pores. Anyway, did you come with Linda? What happened to Ivan?"

"I have a *new* boyfriend," I said, after I'd successfully fought the impulse to pluck out Auntie Wei Wei's eyeballs. "His name is, ah, is—"

Auntie Wei Wei cut me off. "If he's a no-show, he's not serious. You youngsters these days." She sighed. "You know you're wasting your best years being a career woman, right? The Tang women tend not to age well, I must say, speaking from a personal standpoint only, of course." She gave me a pointed look.

Don't cry! Distract her! Distract her! "What about Helen, then?" I blurted before I could stop myself. I felt kind of low bringing up her still-single daughter, who was turning thirty-eight this year.

"Oh, haven't you heard?" Auntie Wei Wei's frozen eyebrows

gave a heroic spasm of joy. "That's our big announcement this Chinese New Year: Helen's engaged! She's marrying a banker, Magnus Svendsen—isn't that a lovely name? Mag-nus! *So* regal!"

"What?" I squeaked, most eloquently. Helen Tang-Chen, who I knew for a fact to be openly gay to all her contemporaries, was getting married—to a *man*? What sorcery was this?

Auntie Wei Wei couldn't have looked more self-satisfied. "It's a little bit of a whirlwind romance, I must admit, but who am I to stand in the path of true love? We're having the Singaporean reception at Capella in May of next year, just after my big sixtieth birthday bash. That's more than enough time for you, and Linda, to find a date, I'm sure. And maybe"—she gave me another pointed look—"both of you could get a more flattering outfit this time, something less . . . off-the-rack?"

I tried to find my voice but my throat was closing up.

Auntie Wei Wei's tone conveyed the pity her eyes couldn't. "You know, I always thought my daughter would be the last to marry among all the Tang women of your generation, but it looks like that's no longer the case."

A wave of nausea overwhelmed me as the realization broke: for the first time in my life, I would indeed be last at something.

"You traitor," I said for the umpteenth time.

We were sprawled on the couch in Linda's penthouse apartment in River Valley, performing the postmortem on Auntie Wei Wei's party with a little help from a bottle of tequila and a bag of Doritos.

"I had to, Andrea, I had to. You saw what she was like!"

"You *betrayed* me. Just left me alone in hostile territory!"

Linda yawned and stretched. "Oh, quit your histrionics. You would have done the same. Besides, she got her claws in me anyway. I'm still smarting."

"Can you believe she only gave us fifty dollars each as *ang pao*," I said feelingly, "when she was way, way more vicious this time?"

Linda shrugged. Money talk bored her—what excited her was winning. At everything and anything. And status. And designer bags. "I don't get it. When I saw Helen in Mambo last December, she swore to me that she was never, ever getting married until gay marriage was legalized in Singapore. And now she's marrying a man? What gives?"

I was stalking Magnus Svendsen on my smartphone. "Have you seen how hot this Magnus looks in his photo? And it's, like, a photo from an annual report. Nobody is supposed to look hot in those—you can't even openly use filters on LinkedIn." I squinted at the photo. "Look at that face! He's so . . . so . . . *symmetrical.*"

Linda glanced at the offensive photo in question and made a face. "Urgh! How unfair. The very least she could have done was take one of the wonky-looking ones off the market. Maybe he's also gay?"

"Does Auntie Wei Wei know that *Helen* is gay?" I asked hopefully. Not that I was planning to throw her under the bus, of course.

Linda rolled her large hazel eyes. "Of course she knows. Don't you know that she once caught Helen messing around with her tutor in their house? But Auntie Wei Wei just pretended like it never happened."

My stomach growled; I had barely eaten at the gathering from all the pretend-texting and one bag of crisps was not enough. "I'm hungry. Pass me the Doritos?"

"We're out of Doritos."

I fell to my knees in mock despair. "Dear God! Can anything else go wrong today?"

"My Netflix is down," Linda added. She checked the bottle. "And we're finally out of tequila."

I curled into a fetal position on the carpet. Clearly this day could get worse.

"Wait." She disappeared and came back with an opened bottle in her hand and a glass. "Here. Have some of this cooking wine. Not sure if it's still good, it's been sitting in the fridge for about three days since Susan made spag bog for me"—Susan was Linda's part-time help—"but you have plebian taste, so."

"Wine is wine." I sat up, ignored the proffered glass, and took a giant swig from the bottle before passing it to Linda, who guzzled half of it after a sniff and a wince. That's what I liked about her: she might look like Harrods on the outside, but on the inside Linda was straight-up T.J.Maxx—hobo without the chic.

She sat cross-legged on the floor next to me. "You know, I heard what that witch said to you. I'm sorry."

"No biggie," I said. "It didn't hurt at all."

She hugged me. "Shh. It's just me here. You don't have to lie."

My lower lip trembled. "It should have been Helen," I said. "She was supposed to be my fail-safe, the Last Tang Standing." Now there would be no one else (older) to share the burden of deflecting criticism on being single from my relatives.

"There, there." She kissed me and let go. "I really don't know why you still go to these things just because they're hosted by family. I wouldn't have."

I had often debated this, too. Linda didn't understand because culturally she was more Westernized than I was. And she really wasn't part of the clan and never had been; having lived most of her life in the Philippines, she had never grown up within this support system. Auntie Wei Wei and the rest had seen my mother and me through when everything had come crashing down on our family, when we found out about my father's cancer and the bills, and when my mother had her own health issues. They were interfering, they were nasty, but they were still family. For all that they had done for me, I had a duty to show up and humor them, at the very least.

You don't run away from family.

"Anyway, you let your family dictate what you should or

should not do *way* too often. Is this how you want to live your life? What about what *you* want?"

"What are you talking about? I make my own choices."

"So you say. You've been incepted so hard you can't even tell, or rather you don't want to, what's your decision and what's theirs anymore." Linda began ticking off a laundry list of items. "Let's talk about how you live in Singapore instead of London, like you've always wanted to, just so you can be close to your family."

"It's called sacrificial love, thank you very much."

"Sure, but you don't see your mother more often than when you were living in London, do you? And let's not forget how you're an M&A lawyer when you never gravitated to that during law school. Or how every man you've dated since you moved back home has been the male version of your Ideal Self According to Ma."

"I don't have a type," I protested weakly.

"Whatever you say." Linda yawned and began doing yoga stretches. "Anyway, I'm playing devil's advocate here, but since they're harassing you to settle down and you have no willpower to defy them, why don't you start dating again?"

I glared at her. "I make my own decisions, not my family. Anyhow, the way things are going at work, I don't have time to date, not if I'm going to be the youngest equity partner of Singh, Lowe & Davidson."

"An admirable quest! Hear, hear!" Linda said. She swigged from the bottle of wine. "Here's to us, sexy, independent working women!"

"Well, you're independent until your salary runs out. Then you go running to Daddy."

"Shut up."

I gave her a big kiss on her right cheek. "You know I love you. Thanks for coming today, really. It meant a lot to me."

She shrugged. "You're welcome. Oh, and FYI, I booked us our

table at St. Regis for the champagne brunch you owe me." She laughed at my sour expression. "What, did you think La Linda would forget?"

I stared glumly at my lap and shook my head. When it came to collecting debt, the Chinese never forget.

2

Saturday 13 February

Received a call on my mobile phone at the butt crack of dawn (10:35 a.m. on a Saturday), waking me up from a terrifying nightmare where I had dropped my work mobile into the toilet just before an important call, thus losing all the progress I had made on Candy Crush.

I stared at the caller ID, which flashed "Unknown." That could only mean one thing: it was my mother. Even pervert-stalkers and telemarketers know better than to mask their caller ID if they wanted the call picked up.

Knowing she would just hit redial until she got through, I answered the call. "Hello?"

"Where are my grandchildren?" she said without preamble.

I groaned, rubbing the sleep from my eyes. "And hello to you, too, Ma."

"Don't 'hello' me. I don't want 'hello.' I want *grandchildren*, Andrea," she admonished. Really, who needs a biological clock when you have a Chinese mother?

"Well, Mom, if we are to follow the cultural and religious norms that you hold dear, then first, I need to find a man, then we need to date for a sufficient amount of time to ensure that he's not a serial child molester or a substance abuser, then I need to manipulate him into marrying me since there are so many younger, hotter women out there, then—"

"Then why did you and Ivan break up?" she cried dramatically.

I could almost hear the Arm Fling. "Auntie Eunice called me after Auntie Wei Wei's gathering to tell me that you came with Linda, no boyfriend in sight. I had to find out from my *least favorite* sister-in-law that my own flesh and blood had broken up with her best prospect? How could you?"

I sighed. So the cat's corpse was out of the bag. "I'm dating someone new," I lied halfheartedly.

She snorted. "I know what 'dating' means to your generation. It means no-strings-attached sex. If you're giving it away for free, which man will want to marry you?"

I rolled my eyes. If only my mom knew how little action I was getting down south, where a secondary forest was on its way to becoming a primary one. "OK, Mom, I get that I need to meet a man, make him fall in love with me, marry me, and impregnate me. I'll get on it right away. Can I go now?"

"I can't believe that even Helen is getting married," my mother said huffily. "It's . . . it's . . . so—unexpected."

"Why not?" I asked, with interest. I wondered how much my mother actually knew about Helen's orientation.

"She's so flighty," was all my mom would say. "But at least she got her act together in the end, unlike you. Just last week at Auntie Loh's Mahjong Friday—you remember Auntie Loh, my hairdresser from the nineties, the one whose servant ran away with a Bangladeshi man?"

"No." Why did mothers always think that if they recited random details about a person you'd never met in your life, you'd somehow magically know what they were talking about?

"No? Well, anyway, did you know that her youngest daughter, Jo, who's your age, is expecting twins *again*?" Her accusatory tone suggested that getting pregnant with twins was just as easy as walking into a supermarket and picking them off the shelf, *if I would just get down to it*.

I made a suitably noncommittal sound.

A loud sigh on the phone. "Wei Ling,* ah, you have a nice face, nice body, unless you've grown fat like when you were studying in England, a good career—so tell me, why are you still single? Are you too busy at work?" She paused before saying, "Do you need me to help you in that department, maybe set up another blind date with someone's son? What was wrong with the last one, that nice boy, Simon?"

I shuddered at the recollection of the one blind date my mother had set up for me with the son of a "good friend" (by which she meant some rando she had met, once, at church), just before I met Ivan. Simon was a limp rice noodle of a man who made white noise seem exciting. "Please do no such thing unless you want me to light myself on fire," I said. To myself. Out loud, I said, "I don't need help meeting men, thanks."

"I'll start asking around," she replied, ignoring me completely, as usual.

"Ma! I told you I have options."

"So what's the problem? Why haven't you gotten serious with anyone after Ivan? Are you being too picky? You modern girls want too much, that's the problem with this generation. You don't know how to compromise!" said the woman who once told me to drop a boyfriend in college because he was "only a biology undergrad." She ranted on in this vein with great vigor. I grunted occasionally as I let my mind drift. Counterarguments were counterproductive—it was better to just sit back, take a chill pill (sometimes literally), and tune out. I set my personal phone down on the bed, pulled my down comforter over it to muffle her voice, took one of my work mobiles out, crunched a Valium, and launched Candy Crush.

". . . I was already married and pushing out your sister when I was *half* your age. If you followed my advice and locked down Ivan years ago, you'd be married by now!"

---

* When my mother reverts to using my Chinese given name, she means business.

I grunted. It was rich of my mother to talk about marriage or give me any relationship advice at all. They had divorced with decided acrimony when I was twenty-two. Even though my mother had deigned to care for my father when he was sick with cancer, they had done so bickering till the (well, my father's) bitter end. That's what happens when you marry at twenty (the peak of my mother's physical attractiveness); they swiftly found out that aside from being from the same sub-ethnic group and having gone to the same university, they had little else in common. Ironically, my friends' parents who had met through arranged marriages were still happily married, voluntarily going on cruise vacations together, where they partook in cooking classes, senior orgies, etc.

"You really should take my advice and find a man. Every time you disobey or ignore me and do your own thing, you always end up regretting it. There's just no substitute for life experience. 我食盐多过你食米."*

This, dear Diary, is her answer to everything: she's eaten more salt in her life than I've eaten rice, i.e., she has more life experience than me by virtue of being older, hence I should defer to her judgment in all matters, at all times.

"Time is running out, not just for you. I'm in my sixties, as you know. I'm not getting any younger."

A tremor entered her voice. "If I'd been born in Laos or North Korea, I'd be dead by now. Even now my body is breaking down from all the menial labor back in my youth."

Just to be clear: my mother worked as a clerk for a judge for two years. That's the only job she had before she married my father and became a housewife.

"Sometimes I wake up, my heart and bones aching, and I

---

* A Chinese proverb that literally translates to "I've eaten more salt than you have eaten rice, Padawan, so shut the fuck up."

wonder—is this how the end looks like? Dying alone, in Kuala Lumpur—without a maid? And no grandchildren?"

Quel emotional blackmail!

Now she hardened her voice. "I'm a simple woman, with simple needs. All I ever wanted in return for the sacrifices I made for my children is their love, and grandchildren. But what do I get instead? A work-crazy elder daughter, who just so happens to be my *favorite* child, in Singapore that I never see and the other one living in sin with that . . . that"—she exhaled with force—"Malay boy."

Same thing again. She was referring to Kamarul Siddiq, my younger sister Melissa's Muslim boyfriend, a brilliant conservation architect in Malaysia, whom my sister had never brought home for introductions because my mother categorically refused to accept him, which was a crying shame since Melissa was going to marry him anyway.

"And here I thought we were talking about my ovaries," I said, attempting to defuse the tension.

"Don't be blithe," she said. "One Halle Berry success story and you think it's fine to delay having children. Wait, wait, wait! And then one day you wake up and you'll find that your womb has become a prune! And you'll be all alone, you'll regret—"

I took a deep breath and ended the call before she could hear me dry heave. Luckily, I had my inhaler at hand. This was a new development in her approach to my singlehood; she never used to be so direct and so aggressive about it. It used to be gentle, the occasional earnest reminder: "Oh, wouldn't it be nice if you'd come over for dinner with that nice young man of yours, Ivan? Do you spend enough time with him? Work is not everything in life." (She can say that with a straight face because I'm senior enough in my career.) Then two years ago she began to get passive-aggressive—I can still see the texts she sent after I messaged her to wish her Happy Mother's Day last year: **Thanks, but I can't wait till I start**

getting Happy Grandmother's Day texts! followed by **Auntie Ong's daughter just gave birth. She's younger than you, isn't she?**—but even that was still tolerable. Since my thirty-third birthday last December, however, the situation had devolved into outright badgering. For example, before she'd found out that I was single again, she used to demand that I drag Ivan down to the registry and just sign the papers first and plan the wedding later.

Doesn't she have anything better to do with her free time than fixate on her daughter's lack of prospects? you ask. Wouldn't she rather spend her golden years discovering exciting new prescription drugs or the cerebral delights of reality TV? No, Diary, she would not. My mother doesn't have time for leisure, or retirement for that matter—that's for rich white people. When she's not hustling to sell some multilevel-marketing product of the day, she's obsessing over how she will marry me off—the last item left unchecked on my mother's checklist of Life Goals (for me). The rest of them, as established a long time ago (when I was an embryo, essentially), were as follows:

- ○ **Go to a Top School (kindergarten/primary school/high school must be appropriate feeder school for top university) (done)**
- ○ **Go to a Top University (done)**
- ○ **Become a doctor (specializing is very much encouraged), lawyer (attaining counsel or partner level), investment banker, or a millionaire (legit currencies only) businesswoman [this goal is within reach, since I'm a lawyer and am already on track for partnership—only a little ways to go to the top!]**
- ○ **Own a piece of property by the time I turn thirty-five (done—well, almost: only twenty-eight more years of mortgage payments to go!)**

And the one my parents thought would be the easiest for me to achieve, but in reality was anything but:

- ○ **Get married by thirty, so I can reproduce, and the vicious cycle can begin once more**

Before she decided I was not making as much progress as she'd like on the marriage front, my mother used to harp on and on about how important career was, how I had to make as much money as I could and be the best. Then, as soon as I turned twenty-eight, her tune changed completely. Now it was all about the man and the wedding and the babies (in this order, of course). How if I wasn't en route to getting sprogged up I was basically an ingrate, that I was displeasing my ancestors, even those I'd never met. Now my mother was all "focus on the family." Not that I didn't see her point, of course.

You see, most Asian countries are not welfare states; we basically need the little moppets that come after us to be successful so they can in turn feed us. That's why family is so important in most traditional Asian cultures.

I am oversimplifying, of course.

I know what you're thinking: screw that, you don't have to do this. You can just shake it off and do your own thing. Right?

Problem is, you can't just shake off centuries of cultural mind-fuckery that tell you that you are nothing but a sandworm without the benevolence and sacrificial love of your parents, who fed your worthless child self and molded you into the acceptable, if not exceptional, adult that you are, and that the only way you can ever hope to repay them is if you take the hopes and dreams your parents had for you and gently but surely stuff them down your brain hole, make them yours, and realize them, or betray your parents and burn in the special place in Chinese Hell for unfilial children while eager but inefficient Chinese demons disembowel you ad infinitum.

And that, my friends, pretty much sums up the concept of Filial Piety.

To be fair, it's not as though following her Life Goals had caused me harm. In fact, so far, so good. I am disrupting a traditionally male-dominated industry. And I don't *hate* the idea of marriage and kids (to Confucian guilt-trip into taking care of me in my old age, naturally). It's just—I need time to achieve the other goals first. If Sheryl Sandberg, unicorn woman, can have it all, so can I—albeit on a more modest scale.

I just need a strategy to fend off my mom before I make partner. Aside from matricide.

3

Sunday 14 February

2:35 p.m. Today is Day Which Must Not Be Named (it's no coincidence it shares the same first letter with "vomit" and "Voldemort"). Urgh. Bought Linda her stupid champagne brunch today upon her insistence and paid Urgh Day primo rates for it. Hated every simpering couple in sight. Comforted myself with the thought that one out of every three marriages in Singapore will end in divorce. That'll teach them to believe in love.

As a gift Linda got me three boxes of Ladurée macarons and told me to go wild. I got her a card (hey, she was already getting a free alcoholic brunch).

I didn't receive any other V-day presents aside from Linda's, unless you count a five-dollar e-coupon from my favorite patisserie. No cards, either, not even an anonymous one. The only V-day texts I got were from my sister and two of my female colleagues. The only way this day could get any sadder is if I get one from my mother.

4:45 p.m. Got an email from my mom. She only sends me emails when she wants a paper trail for her records (she does not trust messaging apps). I opened it with trepidation.

It said:

Happy Valentine's Day, darling. You remember Auntie Mavis, my friend from church, right? Her son went to Harvard Medical School and is still single. She would like very much if the both of you could get together over dinner next week. Should I give her your number?

I broke out in hives and deleted the message.

5:05 p.m. Speaking of things that make me break out in hives, I texted Helen to ask her out for a coffee. Will casually use the occasion to ask her about her sham marriage. I might glean some useful information that I can use later on, when I destroy her.

6:08 p.m. Helen just replied:

I guess you've heard the Good News lol lol *confetti emoji*

Two LOLs? The smug bitch.

She suggested meeting up the next day, meaning she had probably been savoring this gloating session for some time. I agreed, even though I had to reschedule a couple of client meetings. Nothing is more important than finding out the truth.

6:10 p.m. I take that back, universe. Of course making partner is way more important.

6:15 p.m. Just saw Helen's fiancé, Magnus, being interviewed on local news. Apparently, he's some kind of Iron Man veteran. The lens of the cameraman lingered lovingly on his super fit body. Goddammit, why couldn't he have a SpongeBob body? Why? Why?

7:30 p.m. Took a cab to Orchard Road to buy myself an LV bag because no one else will and it being a classic model means it can totally be classified as an investment, according to some listicle.

8:05 p.m. Louis Vuitton was chock-full of gleeful shoppers, and a goddamn queue of soulless consumers.

8:30 p.m. Left the queue in disgust.

8:55 p.m. Bought Earl Grey and lavender buttercream cake from the kind, e-coupon-giving patisserie.

10:10 p.m. Decided to drink. Discovered a bottle of vodka in the freezer. Well, maybe "discovered" is not quite the right word here.

11:25 p.m. Took Tuppi out. Discovered batteries were flat. Too lazy to go the manual way. Watched *The Walking Dead* instead.

2:20 a.m. Woke up disoriented and distressed from the recurring nightmare of taking my exams and getting a B on every paper and having to explain myself to my very unimpressed mother. Had to calm myself by focusing my gaze on the framed first-class honors degree hanging on my wall as my self-worth slowly regenerated. Tomorrow is a new day.

Monday 15 February

7:10 a.m. Is it Monday already? Urgh, back to work. Wish I was one of those hip children who works for a cool company with bean bags, beer pong, and prescription drugs, but I'm not. I have to actually work for a living in a crappy job like the rest of the world, using 80 percent of my waking hours to eke out a living just so I can enjoy what's left of my week for the remaining 20 percent and not be homeless. Unlike Linda, whose parents are loaded and intent on spoiling her to make up for their absenteeism during her formative years, my parents are middle class and from the "I've-raised-you-till-the-legal-drinking-age-now-please-fuck-off-and-let-me-die-in-peace" school.

7:45 a.m. Rush hour. I plunged blindly into a seething mass of commuters trying to board the MRT.* Managed to squeeze into a carriage by virtue of elbowing someone in the boobs, and now she's left on the platform, fuming. Well, she can comfort herself that it wasn't molestation.

7:50 a.m. Ah, shit. Am now crotch-to-shlong with a poker-faced blond cyborg in cycling gear so tight I could see *inside* him. If the train makes an emergency stop I will fall pregnant. It is not the way I wish to go about it, so have placed an expensive handbag between us as a makeshift condom. Sorry, Prada.

Am trying to think happy thoughts but failing. Hate everyone in sight who managed to score a seat, even the young mother in a sundress carrying a toddler. Especially the young mother in a sundress carrying a toddler. Woman, if you're not rushing to work, why take up rush-hour space?

Some people are so selfish, rubbing their happiness in other people's faces.

8:10 a.m. Arrived at the law firm where I will soon become partner, Singh, Lowe & Davidson. Our office is just an eight-minute stroll from the Raffles Place MRT station. We'd just relocated to this spanking-new building two months ago, as befitting our ambitious expansion plan in the region. I stepped past the plush-

---

* MRT stands for Mass Rapid Transit; it's the transportation network or hell that rush-hour commuters have to brave every day to get to work in the Central Business District of Singapore. It spans most of the city-state and is a major component of the railway system in Singapore. It's a giant but necessary/efficient (mostly) pain in the ass.

carpeted lobby with its soft lighting, minimalist artwork, framed portraits of the founding and senior partners, and hot receptionist, and entered the *real* office, what we called the "Chumpit," which had its own, less glitzy entrance away from the carpeted lobby. That's where the real bowels of the office began: more than ninety lawyers were spread out over two floors in open-concept, junior associates' hell, except for the few of us that had enough seniority to share proper offices until they finish renovating the floor upstairs for the new partners, counsels, and senior associates (the current partners have their own offices, of course).

Luckily for me, I was one of the people who actually had an office, an office I was now attempting to sneak into, because I was ten minutes late, even though technically work starts at nine but nine is for unambitious losers and I am not an unambitious loser but an ambitious, no-holds-barred loser—I mean, winner.

"Morning, Andrea," announced my officemate, Suresh Aditparan, at a decibel loud enough to wake the undead.

I scowled at Suresh, who had probably arrived at his desk just a few minutes earlier than I had, because his computer screen was tellingly blank and beads of sweat coaxed by the unforgiving Singaporean sun were coursing down his temples. Unluckily for me, for the past nine working days I've been sharing my office with Suresh, a hotshot M&A senior associate who's British with some Singaporean roots (a Singaporean Indian mom, my PA tells me).

"Morning, Subhan, I mean, *Suresh*," I said, purposely dismissive in a retaliatory Power Move.

We both turned on our computers and proceeded to Power Type with the vigor of (youngish) people who had not had sex in a very long time (longer in my case than his, I'd imagine, but still).

Suresh joined the firm five years ago, but had been based in London and for most of the last three years was the Singapore-London desk rep for the law firm (in part due to the interest in Singapore/Hong Kong/Southeast Asia from Europe, the increasing cross-continental investment and business relations between these continents in the clients we represent, and the bragging rights in having a swish London address, elevating the overall prestige of the firm, that's my guess). He'd just returned to Singapore at the start of the year and was now my Little Buddy (management's new pairing strategy to encourage quicker integration of "new" joiners into the system, and also to orient them in the new office).

I don't like sharing the office with Suresh, even though he smells like cinnamon. He has a habit of saying annoyingly posh things like "loo," and he's tall and conventionally, boringly attractive (golden-brown skin that will turn ashy if not moisturized, hazel eyes framed with such thick eyelashes he'll definitely have droopy eyelids one day, a rakish mop of silky black hair that will most likely never make it past his forties, and, if I'm held at gunpoint, a rugby player physique, but only like a so-so rugby player whose favorite food is tacos), so now I have female visitors to the office I never had before, such as my nemesis, Genevieve Poo, I mean, Beh.

Genevieve is one of those women who's just perfect. Not because she's stunning—she's not, but she's very well-manicured, and is always clotheshorsing lustworthy designer threads. Her family is pedigreed—her uncle on her father's side is a former minister of foreign affairs, her mother's family are politically connected Chinese. She speaks perfect Mandarin, fluent Japanese, and business Korean, aside from English. And she went to Cambridge, then Harvard Law. On top of it she's married and has two children, with another on the way—that's what she does when she was not putting me down in front of others and trying to steal my files: she reproduces. Her husband, Jonathan Beh, a successful real estate multimillionaire, seems to exist solely to gift her with Hermès bags and impregnate her (not necessarily at the same time or in that order)—big, planned families are trendy status symbols these days. The only thing that made me feel slightly superior to her was the fact that she was still a senior associate despite having worked at the firm for longer than I have, possibly because she was always taking maternity leave. Serves her right.

Anyway, as I was saying about Suresh: I don't trust him. He looks like he cleans between his toes. Every day.

More important, Suresh was a potential threat to my career advancement, since we had about the same amount of experience and seniority, and we were both on the same team working under Mong. Mong (short for Toh Sim Mong) was one of the senior partners at our firm and our boss. He was a legendary M&A lawyer and it was my dearest wish to be just like him, minus the divorce and the kids he had fathered but who knew him not. Typically, only one senior associate per department was promoted each year, hence why I was keeping a very close eye on Suresh's manicured paws. Suresh had just that bit more experience on cross-continental deals (especially with European jurisdictions) than I did, and because of this he'd been tasked with servicing some of my larger clients such as Sungguh Capital and Poh Guan Industries as support, but I have the advantage of having squatted in Singapore longer than him, and being a permanent resident in Singapore makes me a more attractive candidate to promote.

Nonetheless, he's still a formidable threat. I spend a lot of my time glaring at him when he's not looking (our desks are facing each other's). Goddamn Foreign Talent,* coming here and stealing jobs from locals.

At no point during this train of thought did I find it ironic that I was a Foreign Talent myself.

Suresh did have one identifiable weakness: he was getting married. His partner was a third-generation British-Indian ob-gyn. Kai, my PA/trusty spy and confidante, whose services I unfortunately had to share with Suresh for now, told me that they were betrothed. I know why Suresh is keeping mum on his upcoming

* Euphemism for "Job Stealer" or "Disease Spreader" to the locals.

nuptials. He's afraid that people at work would start expecting that he was going to impregnate his fiancée sooner rather than later, even if she was currently still in the UK with no definitive plans to move over. Then nobody will promote him.

It makes no difference to me personally whether he is single and available, or not. Even if he were single, Suresh is forbidden fruit.

Most Chinese parents, no matter where they are in the world, want their kids to bring home a mate of:

- Chinese ethnicity (trade-offs are tolerated in some families, but rare—however, likelihood of acceptance increases inversely the longer the errant offspring in question remains single).
- High earning capacity and/or wealth: MD or similar (Lawyer, Investment Banker, Consultant*). Otherwise, being a rich and successful entrepreneur is also acceptable; legit royalty is, of course, welcome.
- Compatible religious faith (which, unfortunately, tends to mean non-Muslim, as the Islamic faith encompasses cultural practices, customs, and beliefs deemed incompatible or at odds with our traditions and cultural practices).
- Good family background: nebulous, but usually linked to social status and wealth.
- Compatible values or the "Nice Guy" catch-all: Chinese parents prefer conservative, traditional mates, believing that such mates also subscribe to values like filial piety, which can only benefit them; so if you're rocking studded sneakers, wreathed in dragon tattoos, and/or believe that elderly retirement homes are acceptable resting places for your parents/in-laws, well goodbye, my friend.

Despite possessing all other desirable qualities, Suresh fails the

* This list used to include Engineer and Teacher, but these career paths are no longer as desirable as they used to be.

first and possibly the third criteria. Anyway, not that it matters. Suresh is taken. And it's not like I'm *attracted* to him.

Also this is my year to shine. This is my year to make partner, and everything else must come second. Only then, if all goes well, maybe I'll beat Hairy Helen to the hitching post somehow.

3:40 p.m. Dashed out for a "client meeting," but in reality am having coffee in a chic café at One Fullerton with Helen.

3:55 p.m. Arrived five minutes late but of course Helen was not there. Urgh. Power Move. We'll see who pays the check.

4:25 p.m. Helen made an appearance almost twenty minutes late, just as I was really starting to stew, sliding into my booth without a whiff of apology. She looked polished in a long-sleeved black boxy top, black jeans, a navy blue Chanel 2.55, and tons of designer bling, her hair a very cute pixie cut with a silver ombré effect. We air-kissed each other and exchanged perfunctory pleasantries.

"WTF," I said/asked when we were seated.

"So you've heard about the wedding and you're dying to know what gives, am I right?" she purred. She lifted an arm lazily, flashing a huge yellow diamond ring that might also be a weapon, and a waiter materialized so fast with menus it was as though he'd been standing there the whole time, which of course he hadn't been, seeing as I'd not been served. Linda tells me it's because I don't give off the "I-will-tip-you-despite-being-Asian" vibe—i.e., I look cheap.

"Yes, pray explain, and in generous detail."

She laughed. "Let me get my coffee first. What would you like?"

She sneered at my choice ("Cappuccino after ten in the morning? What are you, a peasant?"), ordering two double espressos instead. Typical bossy Helen.

I smiled with as much nonchalance as I could fake. "So, why are you getting married, and in a hetero marriage no less? I thought you were holding out till gay marriage was legalized here. What happened to your *principles*?"

She giggled. "You are so jealous, you should see your face. I don't even have the heart to tease you, you poor, poor thing." When I didn't slap her (not because I didn't want to but because I saw one of the partners in my law firm queuing for coffee), she sighed and steepled her hands. "Seriously though, woman, you know I live large, right?"

I rolled my eyes. "Quite," gesturing to her armful of diamond Love bracelets and Richard Mille watch of the day.

Helen nodded grimly. "Well, Mummy told me that if I didn't get hitched—to a man obviously, this *is* Singapore—by the time I'm forty, she would turn off the money tap. And she would throw me out of the house and take me out of her will. Isn't that insane? Her only daughter! As if any of the other money-grubbing Tangs are worthy."

When I didn't rise to the bait, she continued. "I had to act fast after that ultimatum, so I found myself a willing fish. I'll be damned if I have to start buying Zara clothes by default instead of ironically. You might as well just toss me into a meat grinder and call it a day."

I pressed my lips together in a thin smile—Zara was my go-to apparel store. "It took your mom this long to threaten to cut you off?"

Helen shrugged. "Oh, she's threatened before, twice, but she'd never brought up disinheriting me. This time she meant business. Her lawyer was there and everything." She brushed invisible lint off her watch and flicked a sly look at me. "You know she'll take you out of the will, too, if you're single. All the Tangs of our generation have to be married to inherit. And trust me, you'll want to be in that will."

I swallowed and felt faint. Did I! I'd never have to work again. As for my *tiny* credit card debt situation . . .

To steady my staccato heartbeat, I dug my nails into my palms and changed the subject. "So tell me: is Magnus straight?"

"Yup!" Helen said cheerfully. "Straight as an arrow."

"Is he . . . is he aware of your sexual orientation?"

Helen giggled. "Please, Magnus wasn't born yesterday. Of course he is! Don't feel too sorry for him though: he gets to move into Le Grand Maison Tang in Bukit Timah, he gets an outsize allowance and access to the family pool of luxury cars, and anyway, I have this whole open marriage arrangement with Magnus and we have a prenup, so both of us will be fine." She winked. "But hey, the things that private bankers would do to keep their top clients, eh?"

"He's your private banker?" I gasped.

Helen nodded. "Yup, he's been managing my money for years. That's how I got to know him."

"How is this ethical?" I said, scandalized, realizing how naive I sounded as soon as I'd finished.

"Well, it's not like I'm *forcing* him to marry me. He's a consenting adult." She rolled her eyes and leaned forward to grasp my hand. "You're still single after Ivan, aren't you, poor dear?"

I glared at her. "Yes."

"Are you still waiting for your knight in shining armor?" she said mockingly. That's the problem with family: they know all your sore spots.

"Nope. I'm not looking," I said through gritted teeth.

She held up her hands in mock surrender. "Chill, I just thought maybe I could offer some advice to beat the system, which is still rigged against us women, unfortunately." She gestured to a passing waiter for the bill. "Look, even if you're happy being single, it is very practical at our age to find a partner—there's security and comfort in having someone around, especially if they are your equal. So why not? It doesn't have to be the One, la-di-da—we're past that bollocks. My mother had an arranged marriage, and didn't that work out fine for her! And your parents had a love marriage that went belly-up in the end, didn't they?"

I grunted.

"My point is, waiting around for the One is not sound investment advice, so why not try to be more transactional like me? Think Big Picture. Also everyone knows that in Asia, being married gives you extra cachet. Single women in this part of the world can be slayers and still not command the respect they deserve. *I* should know." She sighed. "It really is the smart thing to do if you want your mother and the world off your back. Take my advice, Andrea: be pragmatic and shop for a man. You can still be a hotshot career woman like me, but at least you'll cover all your bases."

"You make some interesting points. If only I had your money," I said, one eye on passing servers, one hand on my wallet.

She shrugged. "Honey, there are tons of solid men out there who are looking for a good companion. You just need to be intentional and get professional help if necessary. Be open-minded and the universe will provide. Oh, by the way"—a silvery, fake laugh—"put your grubby paws away, old girl, it's my little treat. I gave them my card on my way in."

I took my time to get back to work after Helen's gloating session, meandering along the pristine Singapore River and watching people eye it longingly after a long day of pointless work (I know that look well). Maybe she was right. Maybe I was approaching love and relationships all wrong, ascribing foolish romantic notions to what was essentially a very quantifiable commodity. Maybe I should take a leaf out of her book and just find someone Good Enough. It was, after all, a very Chinese way to go about things. If I cut down on nonessential activities, like exercise, I could maybe carve out some time to manage this aspect of my life. Embrace technology; use the platforms, apps, whatever. The search for a

Good Enough Fella would surely be a breeze if I had a very targeted, simple criteria for a suitable match.

6:10 p.m. Back at my desk. Have no work but must outlast Suresh in time logged in the office. Emailed Linda about convo with Helen. Linda is full of admiration for Helen. Apparently, there is a similar arrangement chez Reyes with Papa. Linda, who claims to have never fallen in love, thinks Helen is on the right track, but she's adamant that it would never work for me because I'm a "big sap with unrealistic expectations when it comes to love." Well, people can change.

11:45 p.m. Back home. Had to wait till Suresh gave up and left the office. I win!

12:55 a.m. Have made a decision. Aside from the fact I stand to lose a chance at inheriting, I don't want to be the odd unmarried one of my generation. It's very much a status thing. If Helen, who's the definition of unconventional (she has taken work sabbaticals, *plural*, on a voluntary basis!), is bowing down to social conventions and getting married, why should I be any different? If you can't beat them—join 'em.

That being said, the prospect of rejoining the dating pool is a bit unnerving. I mean, have you seen some of the men out there? Gross.

The other day I saw a man in his late twenties, a good-looking guy in an immaculately tailored shirt and dark gray trousers, placing his iced *kopi* in not one, but *two* small plastic bags, before daintily carrying the bags by the handles *away* from his pants. I followed him, which is a totally legit reaction. He walked a grand total of 150 meters, then he lifted his drink out of the plastic bags and threw them into a trash bin outside his office block.

You see what I'm dealing with?

I'm not saying I am flawless. I am not. I binge-watch trash TV.

I've eaten cereal for dinner, after having it for breakfast and lunch the same day. And just last week, in order to shave precious minutes of prep time before work, I dumped some talc onto the roots of my unwashed (for the second day) hair, pulled it into an "elegant" knot, washed my grease trap of a fringe, blow-dried said fringe, and called myself fit to show up as such to work. And I did. It was not my first time doing the ol' Just-Wash-Your-Fringe-in-a-Pinch routine. But at least by being a little lax with my personal care I saved water. What's Mr. Turtle-Killer's excuse?

I know it sounds like I'm making excuses so I don't have to put myself out there. I am. I'd been together with my ex, Ivan, for a little over five years after all. That's more than a sixth of my life. The breakup really affected me, even though somewhere along the line we just kind of drifted apart and we eventually decided, after a mature, calm discussion where nothing was broken or hurled at the wall, that we had to Consciously Uncouple.

That's the official version of the story, anyway.

Ivan and I met during my first year in Singapore at a Malaysians-working-in-Singapore mixer. Someone had introduced us, which was a good thing since I was not prone to striking up conversations with random men, especially attractive and articulate ones like Ivan, who was working in a private equity firm. Men like Ivan seemed to favor a certain type that I wasn't: models. Yet twenty minutes after being introduced he was still flattering me with his undivided attention.

I decided that if he was still talking to me then maybe I should try to make real conversation. I was intrigued by him, beyond his qualifications (he'd worked for six years in London with Lazard after graduating from Imperial College with a first-class degree in finance, and was now VP at Warburg Pincus—yes, he'd casually mentioned this, just as I'd casually mentioned my own qualifications. Welcome to Asian Speed-Dating 101.) There was just something magnetic about his confidence. He knew where he was going in life, he loved what he was doing, and he was performing at the highest echelon. Ivan was inspirational, aspirational. I felt like I'd met my match, a kindred spirit.

I was so comfortable around him that when he asked me what brought me back from London, where I had been working as a solicitor at Slaughter & May, I told him.

"My dad passed away two years ago, and my mother hasn't been the same since then. Her health isn't good; she had a mental breakdown, just went into this total fugue state for weeks and scared the crap out of me. I couldn't leave her alone, and my sister was unreachable, taking a gap year in South America." I rolled my eyes to show how silly I thought the concept of a gap year was. I could tell he was exactly the kind of person who would get it.

"Oh," he said, looking discomfited, "I'm sorry to hear that. Were they very close?"

I laughed. "Hardly. Maybe never. My parents are, were, divorced and they parted on terrible terms. They were always fighting, but my mother was still devastated when she heard about his passing. I figure that you can only hate someone so much if you had once loved them in equal measure."

He sighed. "I wish my parents were divorced. All they do is fight when they're in the same room, on the rare occasion when they leave the operating theater to see each other and their offspring." He knocked back the rest of his drink and winced. "I think they love me, but what do I know?"

I think that sealed the deal for me, right then and there—the fact that his parents barely communicated with him. Score!

Naturally, when he asked for my number at the end of the night, I said yes. He was very much the type of man that any Chinese parent would approve of, with his clean-cut looks, impeccable manners, solid career prospects, good family, and legit Chinese ancestry. On paper, Ivan Lim was prima facie perfect boyfriend, even husband, material.

On paper.

Anyway, as I was saying, I am very bad with men. And now, apparently everyone who's single was On The Apps. Linda, for one, had been urging me to try them for some time since the Breakup.

Maybe I should just do it. What did I have to lose? How hard could it be? I mean, I use LinkedIn, and isn't that a goddamn minefield?

I stopped playing Candy Crush ironically and downloaded Sponk, since it was the latest, hence the best. Like Happn, which I categorically refuse to use because of its spelling, it uses location-based technology to something something techy, only with *way* more precision and real-time blah-blah: it's all very stalker-friendly and, more important, time-saving, since you can meet immediately once you're matched, like when people used to meet IRL in bars but without the difficult decoding of body language.

When the time comes, which will probably be next quarter, since I have a couple of nasty closings to deal with soon, I just have to launch it in a crowded area and it will send out a Winky Bat Signal of some sort. Or maybe later in Q3 this year. No rush. Although I should probably set up my profile. Every good Chinese knows the proverb: dig your well before you are thirsty.

Within ten minutes I had uploaded my LinkedIn profile photo (very appropriate and professional, giving out the best vibes to future husband, who will be from Ivy League or at least national top ten university) and created a succinct, well-crafted summary of my personality and achievements, especially my recent inclusion in *Singapore Business Review*'s "40 Most Influential Lawyers Under 40," which is a list even Helen couldn't buy her way onto.

When I was finished I read out loud this gleaming manifesto to my desirability. I couldn't believe no one else was using their LinkedIn profile on dating sites, especially here in Asia. What an oversight. I couldn't wait to be overwhelmed with requests to be Sponked.

4

Wednesday 17 February

2:05 p.m. Worked through lunch. No respite from the flurry of emails, each titled "URGENT" with a varying number of exclamation marks appended, each for a different closing scheduled in the next two weeks. Cannot afford to dash out and grab sandwich but must eat as stomach is now emitting weird hobbit growls that elicit chuckles from Suresh, who has ordered a healthful vegetarian meal before lunch hour. Can't believe that I had to eat a candy bar from the office vending machine again. How is anyone supposed to stay slim in this job once you are past your twenties? Everything just congeals in fat rolls stored in the thighs and around the waist, in internal fat purses that your cells now carry. Briefly fantasize about suing law firm for not providing healthful food and snack options, like Google or similar tech companies with their bean bags and sprawling cafeterias where one can order sea bass or other line-caught and gently massaged fish, with a side of organic [insert name of trendy root vegetable] crisps.

Ooh. WhatsApp message from Linda. I surreptitiously grabbed my phone and tried to read it under a binder of case notes.

Linda:

Ladies night at Little Green Aliens. Up for it?

I typed back:

Who else is coming?

Linda:

Just you, me, Ben the investment banker, Filipino Jason, and Valerie from the art gallery

Whenever lawyers hang out with non-lawyers, they feel compelled to flesh out details of said non-lawyers' occupations, in the manner of someone describing a rare, exotic animal.

Me:

Cool. Am in. C U dere.

Stared at sentence before retyping it to read:

See you there.

Felt very old.

The five of us—Linda, Ben Wallich, Valerie Gomez, Jason Sy Garcia, and I—met after work at Little Green Alien, one of those rare nights when I'm out of the office by 7:30 p.m., surprising even Suresh. Being super competitive, both Suresh and I are facing off in an escalating Office Face-Time Battle, where we stay at work way longer than necessary with no tasks to complete except to score Brownie points with our own overworked and unhappy boss. I think I have a good lead over him, though, since he has a terrible future deficit to make up for in his Face-Time Piggy Bank—Kai told me he had applied for two weeks of leave this September so he can start scouting for locations for his wedding, slated for next August. Which means he must bill like crazy the next two quarters if he wants to beat me for this financial year. Ha! Serves him right for getting married and having someone who loves him!

LGA was one of those hipster "secret" speakeasy cocktail bars with mixologists so sanguinely youthful that you start expressing breast milk at the sight of them. Linda was fond of expensive designer cocktails with exotic ingredients, which obviously cost a lot of money, but since she was able to afford it and doesn't mind extending that privilege to all of us, we graciously allow her to ply us with drinks. Monday night at LGA meant two-for-one cocktails, and despite the fact that I had a closing in four days, I was downing them like there was no tomorrow. By the second round even I, with my hardened lawyer's liver, was feeling a pleasant, will-snog-anyone-who-asks-me high. Well, anyone except the man in the suit over there with the sausage lips. Or his friend with the oily comb-over. Reality can be such a literal buzzkill.

"Challenge for today: name the most unfortunate adopted English names you have ever come across," Jason was saying. "Winner gets a cocktail on me."

Jason was Linda's friend, a paralegal, and one of the six Jasons we knew. If I recall correctly, I think she went into a gym one day and chatted with him at the drinking fountain, and he grafted himself onto her on the way out and never really left; she had that effect on men, especially gay men. To distinguish him from the rest, somehow instead of calling him "Paralegal Jason" we went with "Filipino Jason" and now it's too late and it has stuck as a rather unfortunate nickname (although "Paralegal Jason" was perhaps worse, all things considered—I am quoting Linda here). He's quite a bit younger and single, which is surprising considering that he's gorgeous, charming, cultured, and very well put-together in the vein of a Ken doll or one of the leads from *Suits*, all lean Muay Thai muscles and beautifully tailored clothes. Linda theorized that he's gay or asexual since women are routinely throwing themselves at him and getting rebuffed, but the group as a whole is giving him the space to tell us in his own time, or never—we're not fussed.

"Syphilis Tan!" Linda shouted, unconcerned with decorum.

I snorted. "Urban legend, surely."

"I'm dead serious. My friend from Hong Kong taught an ESL student with that very name."

Jason shrugged. "Meh. Next."

"Colleague in Shanghai once told me about a Milky Chin," said Ben, another drinking buddy of ours who flirted with Linda so shamelessly that it was amusing. Ben was Welsh, mousy-haired, bug-eyed, and a partner in a large investment bank; he was a little bizarre on most days, eager as he was to discuss conspiracy theories on every subject under the sun, but he was entertaining enough that we kept him on as our Token White Friend.

"Ouch, poor woman," Jason said.

"Milky Chin belonged to a *guy*, oi oi oi!" Ben said.

Jason groaned. "That *is* a good one, I'll give you that. Ben is in the lead!"

"I've seen Teorem being used," Valerie Gomez said. "And Gemini!"

"Refrigerator Chan," Linda said, her eyes bulging in competition.

"I've got one," Valerie cried. "Ivanna Wang."

"Now you're just making shit up," Jason said.

"Like hell I am," Valerie said, indignant. Or as much as she could show indignity. Valerie, who is Singaporean and of Peranakan-Indian descent, was in her forties (we're guessing—her real age remains a mystery as tightly guarded as the Vatican secret archives); her main goal in life was to look like a twenty-five-year-old, something she managed to do only under dim, hipster cocktail bar lighting, which was precisely the kind LGA had. The woman was more than a tad addicted to Botox and fillers. According to Linda, Valerie's mom was a former beauty queen and Valerie had been raised to think that beauty was to be worshipped above all, in women *and* men. Other than that, she was a fun person to hang out with, though I'd forbidden Linda from inviting her along for any of our daylight jaunts; it would be too traumatizing, like finding out the pop star you idolized in your teens has become a grandmother. "I swear it on my mother's life."

"Please don't," Jason said, wincing. Catholic and half-Chinese, Jason was extremely superstitious.

"OK, fine, on my future children's lives," Valerie said gamely.

The group pretended not to hear this. It got awkward when Valerie said things like this. She was so excited when Fann Wong, a local celebrity, conceived after forty, and was happier than a dog with two tails when she found out Sophie B. Hawkins had a child at age fifty. The way Valerie saw it, this meant that it was entirely possible that she would be able to replicate that result. It was optimism in its purest form—the scary, untethered-to-reality kind. The kind that can make you a good dictator.

Not having a very good poker face, I made my excuses and fled. As is my fate, the queue to the single, unisex toilet was seven deep and all female. Thank goodness I always gave myself some "wee-way" (yes, I know, I went there). I slumped against the wall, pulled out my phone, and launched Sponk, just to see who was around. I scrolled through the available profiles, chose a few non-serial-killer-looking types without expecting results, then grew bored and began to play Candy Crush, which, by the way, I am in no way addicted to.

"Do you come here often?" someone said, startling me before I could finish a level.

I looked up, annoyed, to find a young man smiling at me. This is how you know you're old: when you see anyone younger than you and you think "this young *expletive*" instead of the standard adjective-free form. Thinking that he had mistaken me for someone else, I scowled and said, "I'm sorry?"

"Oh, s-sorry," the poor sod stammered. "I just meant—I mean, I just . . . I mean, er, we Sponked?"

I looked down at my screen and there he was, my Sponk partner. I froze. I hadn't actually thought it would happen so quickly.

He gathered himself and pointed at the queue. "Do you come here often?" he blurted again.

I raised my eyebrow. "You mean, do I go to the toilet often?" I didn't bother lowering my voice. Several women snickered.

"Ah," said the boy, because that's what he was, a sleek, sparkly eyed kid who looked like he'd been poured into his tight jeans and slim-cut shirt. He had the shaved sides and longish top haircut and ironic clear-lensed, tortoiseshell round glasses all boys seemed to sport like uniforms these days, although I had to admit he was not bad-looking, with a lean, toned swimmer's body. With good height, too. "I see how that can be confusing. Let me try again." Holding my eyes, he took two giant steps back, away from the direction of the toilet. "There. So. Hi there. I couldn't help noticing we matched on Sponk. Do you come to LGA, in the general sense and not the toilet per se, often?"

Ack. So he was really trying to pick me up. One of the girls was not very discreetly pointing her phone in my direction, *filming* the whole thing, for fuck's sake. I turned my back on her and moved directly in front of teenage Casanova to save him the embarrassment of being the unwitting subject of a viral video. "Look, kid, I'm too old for you, so, you know, go find some other age-appropriate target through Pounder or whatever hookup app you people use these days," I said shortly, before dropping my gaze back to my beloved, the phone.

I pretended to scroll through the *Daily Mail*, scanning celebrity headlines intently and hoping he would go away. After several seconds of scrolling, I looked up again to find him still smiling at me in his oblique way. What was his problem? I was old enough to be his mom. Wasn't there anyone else his age to chat up? "What do you want?" I said, with some exasperation. I now needed the loo— I mean, toilet. Badly.

"Can I buy you a drink?" he said through his never-faltering, Edward Cullen–esque smile.

"Not interested."

"Doesn't matter. Let me buy you a drink anyway. What would you like? Gin? No, let me guess. Whisky, single malt. A Highlander." He squinted at me. "No, an Islay. Peaty and smoky."

Ooh, yum, that did sound good. I mentally slapped myself and focused on the task at hand. "Let me get this straight: you want to spend money on an older woman who is not interested in you?"

He shrugged. "I'll never say die* until I'm dead."

"That's just . . . that's illogi— Never mind. Go wait by the bar. Let the lady use the toilet first."

He actually bowed a little before he left. I turned back to face the queue. The women in it were looking at me with respect or jealousy. "Kids, right?" I said to no one in particular, to icy stares all around.

I was whistling as I walked back across the crowded room to the bar when I saw something that stopped me dead in my tracks.

Ivan. By the bar. Wearing a white polo and slim-cut dark-wash jeans. With his arm around what could only be described as someone other than me, a stick figure girl in a bad wig, if that was her real hair.

WTF.

I mean, Ivan *never* wore jeans when he was with me: he considered them an abomination of the fashion industry (neither formal nor casual enough, plus too hot for Singaporean weather).

He looked agonizingly happy.

---

* A Singlish expression, meaning "I'll never admit defeat."

I ducked behind a passing waiter, held his arms to pin him to the spot, and peered around him. "Stop moving," I hissed.

"Erm, ma'am"—which is the polite, formal equivalent of "auntie"—"I have to serve dr—"

"I'll give you twenty dollars if you stay still for five minutes," I pleaded.

He shrugged and stood there, while I observed my prey as nonchalantly as I could.

Fucking H. She was young.

Some of the things Ivan said to me the night we agreed, mutually, to break up, boomed in my head: *You can't tell me you didn't see this coming. How can you blame me when you're never around? I want a fam—*

The Slimy Young Thing touched his arm and I was gripped by an overwhelming desire to pick her up and dunk her into the nearest dumpster. Now I am a pacifist, of course. But try telling that to my heart.

They didn't look like they were on a first date. Who was she? There was no way to know without being a proactive stalker. I had cut all social media ties with him, blocked him on WhatsApp, severed ties with all the mutual friends we had (well, most of them were his), and deleted all his phone numbers (personal, Work 1, Work 2, and Work 3 (landline)). Not that I wanted to know who she was, of course.

Just as I was ready to walk over and casually bump into them, so that I could be introduced, he put his arm around her waist and walked her out of the bar.

"No," I whispered in agony.

"Ma'am, can I go now?" the server said tightly.

"Sorry," I muttered. I opened my wallet to extract the money I owed him, but he waved the bills away.

"You look like you'll need it tonight. That, or a fresh start," he remarked, before walking away.

I heard him through a fog. I couldn't believe it—Ivan had moved on. First. With a rather age-inappropriate palate cleanser of a girl. What about me? Why was I still stuck in some weird, monkish state of celibacy when I had wasted over five years of my life on him already?

There are always winners and losers in a breakup. And I am not a loser, not in any sense. I should get a move on, too. Starting tonight. I'll show him age-inappropriateness, the jeans-wearing bastard.

When I rejoined the others to grab my work bag, the boy who hit on me was still waiting by the bar with an elbow planted on the countertop and no phone in sight, which sort of endeared me to him. He saw me and waved cheerily, the way an innocent child might at a strange man in a stained house robe standing in front of what appears to be a totally normal ice-cream truck (I do realize I am the strange man in this scenario).

"Who *is* that yummy morsel?" Valerie stage-whispered, which was enough to send me to the bar just to get away from her and the creepy realization that Valerie was biologically old enough to be his *grandmother*.

"Let's start again. My name is Orson Leong," he said, offering me a surprisingly assured handshake. "What's yours?"

"Andrea," I said. I motioned the bartender over and gave him my order. "I'd like a Laphroaig, twenty-one years old, neat." I turned to Orson, expecting him to be weirded out by the fact that my drink was older than him. But he was unfazed. He ordered a beer, and when the bartender returned, he took out his credit card and waved mine away. "I'm twenty-three, you know. I can afford to buy a pretty lady a drink."

"And I'm thirty-three," I told him aggressively, probably to cover up the fact that I was pleased that he was not as young as I'd originally made him out to be, which was eighteen. I probably needed glasses, perhaps due to the fact that I was (non-addictively) playing Candy Crush in my free time. "Jesus's age, when he died," I added, before I could stop myself.

"OK, Andrea, now that we have the basics covered, why don't we go to that quiet little corner over there away from your staring clique, and you can tell me more about yourself?"

I nodded, and he guided me by my elbow to a secluded nook by the electronic jukebox. Out of the corner of my eye I saw the dumbstruck faces of my friends turn to follow me across the room; Valerie's looked especially comical since she had long ago lost the capacity to lift her eyebrows. I grinned and gave them a cheery wave. Let them wonder. Let them take lots of photos. That I will definitely post on Facebook publicly later.

I didn't expect to enjoy hanging out with Orson, but I did. Orson was easygoing and had an unassuming way of asking questions with his dimpled smile that made me feel comfortable revealing things about myself that I would usually reserve for closer friends. And even though he was much younger, we conversed across a wide array of subjects with ease. I found out that Orson was working in an advertising firm as a copywriter; he read voraciously and counted Rumi and Deborah Landau among his favorite poets (pro); his favorite tipple was gin (meh); he was a dog person (hmm); and he hated EDM and reality TV (pro!).

Sometime around ten o'clock I made my excuses to leave, even though I was not at all tired but I was dangerously tipsy and considering asking him to come up to my place for a shag (I managed to restrain myself by using the clever trick of thinking of spiders every time I thought of kissing him, something I had learned about from a listicle on Aversion Therapy 101). Being the gentleman that he was he walked me to the taxi stand (a queue almost twenty people long, despite the prevalence of ride-hailing apps). I was starting to feel melancholy as the alcoholic buzz began to fade.

"Will I see you again, Andrea?" he asked, his eyes going full-puppy on me.

"Never!" is what I should have said—he was just not right for me, and I had already taken enough selfies with him to let anyone looking know that I was a hot commodity. Instead, I meekly said, "I can't." Pathetic. No wonder I wasn't partner yet.

"Why not?" he asked. He was standing very close to me and I could smell his cologne and stale tobacco and sweat.

"Not a good idea," I said to his shoulder. I was very aware of the heat emanating from him.

"It's the New Year," was his reply near my earlobe. And then his lips were on mine before I could protest: they tasted amazing, young and perky, belonging to someone who didn't need afternoon naps. It was all I could do not to chew on them, driven as I was by hormones—and hunger.

Then he broke the kiss.

"I'm sorry if I came on too strong," he said. "It just came over me. I'm not usually like this."

I nodded, completely dumbstruck. The queue shuffled forward. It was almost my turn.

"Listen, I'd like to see you again. Can I have your number please?"

He gave me his card, as my phone had died, and I gave him my number, my *real* one, even my surname. Now he can find me on the internet. Shit just became real.

When my cab arrived, he opened the door and I got in. "Good night, Andrea. I'll text you." No games, just a promise. Such maturity, such manliness, such round buttocks. Against my will, I began to hope that I would, indeed, see him again.

11:45 p.m. Home. Charged my phone, turned it on to find forty-plus feverish WhatsApp texts from the LGA crew group chat, with Linda's texts being the lewdest.

"Who's Mr. Hot Stuff?" was the general cri de coeur. I decided to let them simmer. I didn't want to talk to them about the night when I was back to being ambivalent about seeing Orson again. I mean, where could this relationship really go? We were at totally different stages of our lives: he was probably just interested in shagging as many willing people as he could get, while I was interested in finding a suitable man for a life partner, which is difficult enough as it is. Let's be honest: the chances of finding your true love when you're almost in your mid-thirties are a little bleak—most of the good ones are taken, and the ones that are still on the shelf and older than you are often riddled with manufacturing or third-party defects, some so well camouflaged that you could be dating them for ten months before you accidentally find their shoebox of toenail clippings or their collection of vintage porn. I shouldn't waste time on him when I was looking for Mr. Right—the return on investment seemed too low to be worth the outsize risk of wasting precious time—right?

On the other hand, I had spent five years with Ivan, and to what avail?

Ooh, text.

> **Hey gorgeous lunch or dins next Wednesday 24th K? unless u hv plans alrdy . . . *three emojis with heart eyes***

It was Millennial Orson. What to do, what to do.

I checked my calendar and launched Candy Crush, just a quick game thereof; no biggie, it helps me think.

Three in the morning. Oops.

5

Thursday 18 February

Emergency summit the next afternoon, over lunch, with Linda.

"You met him through Sponk?" Linda gasped theatrically. We were seated in Lau Pa Sat, a hawker center located in a large, beautiful Victorian filigree cast-iron structure in the Central Business District. The lunch crowd consisted of both tourists and office grunts, chowing down on local street food.

"Yeah, I'm On The Apps." Yes, I said it exactly like this. "Isn't everyone On The Apps?"

Linda sighed. "Could you please try not to sound like you're ancient? And did you have to choose the worst app to start online dating on?"

"What's wrong with Sponk?" I said indignantly.

"Sponk, my dear, is for furries and swingers." She saw my mouth open to ask a question and said, "You can google that later. NSFW."

"Thanks a lot, Cousin Gordon," I muttered. "On the bright side, I did meet this decent, proper Sweet Young Thing, so."

"No one decent uses Sponk; I should know," Linda responded ominously.

"And how is Tinder any better?" I challenged. "Isn't it a hookup app?"

"It all depends on how you screen the people, how you play the game. I've many, many friends who've met their significant others on Tinder." She smiled beatifically. "I mean, I myself have never used it for long-term commitment, but I'm positive we can replicate Angi's success."

I did a double take. "Wh— So it's just that one friend? I thought you said 'friends.' As in plural."

She waved my questions away. "Potato, potahto. How old is this guy again?"

"Twenty-three," I said meekly.

Linda whistled. "Nice. And here I thought I'd be the first cougar of our friend pack."

"Not Valerie?" I was intrigued.

"Valerie-I'm-younger-than-my-surgeon-makes-me-look-in-the-dark-I-swear-Gomez?" Linda said, doing her best imitation of the Rock's signature eyebrow cock. "No way. She would never be able to accept that she's older than the man she's with. Unlike you, you dirty rascal."

"I get that he's a little younger, but he's so mature." I started drumming my fingers on the grease-slicked tabletop. "Would it really be such a bad idea to go on a date with him? You were just saying I need to date outside my comfort zone."

"Depends on your objectives: a hookup or love? In my opinion, you should nip it in the bud, because you're a serial monogamist and you're looking for the One."

"I don't believe in the One," I protested.

Linda rolled her eyes. "Please. I've known you since you were a toddler, remember? You inhaled Sweet Valley novels. You like all the slow songs from Backstreet Boys. You cry at every wedding, and not just because you're not the one getting married. Face it—you're a sucker for love, and that's OK. What you need, my dear, is to get out there and meet guys your *own* age, preferably older." She took out her phone and started scrolling intently. Her voice took on a dangerous Avon salesperson varnish, one octave higher and chirpier than usual. "Just wait till you see what I've got in store for you!"

She shoved the phone in my face. On the high-definition screen of Linda's latest iPhone was my Tinder profile.

I gaped at it. "What? Wh-when and how did you access my F-Facebook . . . ?" I managed to say. What other accounts did she have access to?

"Easy. Your password was a *snooze* to crack, took me literally twelve seconds, haha: *ihateivan*. I mean, seriously, *still*?" Her laughter died when she saw my face, and she cleared her throat. "But look at how good you look!" she crowed, jabbing a manicured finger at my Tinder doppelgänger. I stared at the zoomed-in view of a full-frontal shot of my face, edited and enhanced till I was barely recognizable.

"What filter is this? I look like I just popped out of the womb," I said, squinting at my alert eyes and plumped-up lips, unmarred by years of stress-smoking and disappointment.

Linda shrugged. "Filter? Pah! This was the work of a Photoshop maestro. No filter alone could have achieved this perfection."

Then she tapped on her screen to zoom out and I saw the body upon which my head had been almost seamlessly grafted; with a gasp I recognized the cleavage-baring black bandage dress I had worn—*for our uni graduation dinner.*

I looked at her and she shrugged. Innocently.

"Show me my profile description," I said through gritted teeth. She grinned and scrolled down. "Andrea T. . . . Hey, that's not my age!"

"Give or take one or two years . . . ," Linda said cheerfully, unconcerned with being a class A, bona fide liar.

"Linda, you listed me as being twenty-nine!"

"So?" Linda's already large eyes were wide with faux innocence.

"I'm turning thirty-four in December!"

"Geez, stop being such a stickler for details."

"That's rich, coming from a lawyer."

"If I list your real age, I'll be cutting down your market by eighty percent."

"I don't want to date ageists!"

"I'm being realistic," she huffed. "Good God, it's brutal out there. Look at me, I don't look a day over twenty-six, am highly educated and gorgeous—"

"—and modest, don't forget," I added dryly.

"Yes, of course, and even then, my swipe-rights only increased when I put my age as twenty-nine. Me! What's more, I'm sorry to say this, *you*!"

"Why am I still friends with you?" I muttered, palming my forehead in resignation.

"Because I'm fabulous and I'm going to get you a man worthy of your lovin'. What's one or two li'l fibs in the grand scheme of things?"

"Lies: always a good foundation for a relationship," I said, giving up.

The rest of the draft profile read as such:

> *Andrea, 29*
> *Bubbly and adventurous salsa enthusiast (*What? *I squeaked, to which Linda said,* Shut up and trust me, you have no choice anyway, I locked the profile and only I have the password!*). I'm interested in yoga, baking, whisky (especially when it's free), and puns. I'm very good at playing ball games, especially hand and ball-striking ones. I love a good shuttlecock.*

I covered my face and rocked back and forth in my seat. "Oh God. Oh God."

Linda beamed. "It's perfect. It's funny and sexy and doesn't take itself too seriously. Win."

"Ignoring the godawful innuendo, none of this even applies to me," I protested. Well, except the free whisky and puns part. I began ticking off everything she got wrong on my fingers. "I don't bake, I've been to all of two beginner yoga classes, and the closest I get to salsa is when I'm making a burrito. And there's nothing here about my work, y'know, *Singapore Business Review*'s '40 Most Influential Lawyers Under 40' and all."

Linda rolled her eyes. "Could you please, for one sad second of your life, not shove down everyone's throat how accomplished you are? Seriously, woman, your insecurity is quite disturbing. You have other things going on in your life besides being good at your job and being a smart cookie."

"Like?"

"Like, ah, how you are very, ah, well-read and very, er, creative in . . . Anyway, just list the accolades on LinkedIn where they belong. Or, if you must brag, do it casually on purpose, the way some people take selfies standing in front of their bookshelf and the shelf behind their face is conveniently lined with books by Chomsky and Sagan and lots of dead Russians, instead of the Twilight saga in hardcover and glossy untouched cookbooks that the person bought because they went to the bookstore when they were hungry." She gave me a pointed look, which I ignored.

"You're right," I said, resigned. "I just thought . . . there's not a lot of truth on this profile."

"Says who?" She leaned forward and winked. "Notice that I said 'enthusiast' and 'interested in.' That could mean *anything*, really, if you think about it. Maybe you just really, really enjoy watching *Dancing with the Stars*. And *The Great British Bake Off*. Meaning you love telly. And what bloke doesn't like telly, eh?"

She sat back in her seat, looking smug as, well, a lawyer who'd just won her case.

"No further questions, your Dastardly Overlord," I said, humbled.

"Good. Because you're live."

"What?" I shrieked. "Since when?"

"Since yesterday, you dork! Don't get mad. Look how many matches you've already accrued. Twenty-seven!"

"What? I never chose . . . How many?" Despite my better judgment I was soon scrolling with Linda through the profile matches. (Apparently, in the few hours since she had hacked into my Facebook and created/linked my Tinder account, thus being able to publish my profile, all without my consent, she had already selected a few crush-worthy specimens who had also swiped right on my profile.) I did this over Linda's shoulder, as Linda was still refusing to relinquish the phone or my new Facebook/Tinder password until I had "earned the right to use Tinder unsupervised, because Sponk."

"You need my guidance. After all, there are a lot of creeps and liars out there," she said, oblivious to the irony of her own words.

"So, uh, how are we supposed to handle twenty-seven Tinder chats at the same time?" I wanted to know.

"Oh, sweetie." She gave me a pitying look, the kind she gave men when they asked her why she wouldn't give them her number. "Fifty-five percent of these guys won't text you beyond the first three messages because they're just not that into you; five percent won't make a move at all because they are too chicken shit or they want the woman to make the first move; ten percent will turn out to be liars, freaks, douchebags, socially inept, and psychos who will show themselves on my superior no-BS radar and who I will eliminate after five text lines; which leaves thirty percent worthy of navigating through, after which we will probably only find half of them deserving of our time, which leaves us with approximately three or four potential dates. I'll have your results by Saturday morning."

She had it down to a science.

"So let me get this straight: in order to sieve out the liars, freaks, douchebags, socially inept, and psychos, you are going to *pretend* to be me?"

She rolled her eyes. "Did I not make myself clear?"

“And you don’t see the similarities between you and the people you’re trying to keep away from me? None whatsoever?”

“Nope.”

“Right.” Oh well. The woman did get me twenty-seven matches. “But what if Orson—”

“No. Repeat after me: Orson is poison. Orson is poison.”

I decided to drop it. What did Linda know? She was Linda; she’d never had to compromise a day in her life. Orson seemed to like me for me. Besides, it wasn’t as though I had any other suitors—not counting the twenty-seven potential Tinder matches who were all expecting me to be some bendy yoga hottie who liked to salsa. This whole thing was doomed. By the time I returned to work I was back to giving Orson a go, *if* he texted again. Hey, a bird in the hand is worth twenty-seven in the bush, every good Chinese knows that.

3:00 p.m. Texted Orson to say I’d be happy to have lunch with him next Wednesday. Why wait? And I definitely didn’t need to be supervised on dating platforms/apps. I’m tech-savvy: I’m a LinkedIn Premium user, you know.

5:07 p.m. Got told off for asking Linda for the umpteenth time what was going on in the Tinder chats. She said that if I text her one more time for progress reports, she’ll start sending me dick pics. From Ben.

7:45 p.m. Orson just texted! He said he’s excited to be going on a date with a top forty lawyer. The boy can flirt! I sent him a couple of smiley emojis and chose a café that I knew Linda would never frequent and told him to meet me there at noon.

Am crushing it. Orson is probably younger than Ivan’s girl (though I wouldn’t know, there’s nothing I can see on his Facebook or his other social media platforms, not that I was looking through a fake account or anything).

6

Friday 19 February

Speaking of showing off, I awoke this morning smiling, awash with fresh purpose in life. At long last, the day I had been planning for had arrived—the day I finally take Suresh out.

For lunch.

But not just any lunch: the Establishment-of-Hierarchy Lunch. Just like the ultra-firm handshake I gave him the first time I met him, where I Showed Dominance, I have, by pretending to be super busy, managed to evade hosting the welcome lunch all Orientation Big Buddies are supposed to arrange for their assigned Little Buddy. But it was now well into his third week and I could no longer pretend that I was busy without being rude, well, ruder than I already was. And establishing dominance must be done in a classy, indirect, subtle way, like farting.

It was time Suresh understood who the alpha in the room was. The orientation lunch is all about Power Moves. For that reason I had been waiting for the right moment to invite him out on one: first of all, I had on a total Power Outfit, an exquisite, expensive tailored pantsuit in gray cashmere wool paired with a white long-sleeved cotton dress shirt (even if impractical and my boobs were melting under the layers) and a burgundy crocodile Birkin bag (that technically belonged to Linda); there'd been a significant lapse of time since his arrival before the Ask, calculated to make Suresh understand that he was very low in priority; lastly, I'd managed to book a very visible table in a quiet and expensive fine-dining Shanghainese restaurant that was guaranteed to make Suresh, Anglophile Indian that he was, swallow hard at the sight of all the bone china bowls and pokey chopsticks. Not to mention the fact that Suresh hadn't had enough time to acclimate to the Singaporean weather and was still sweating profusely even in the air-conditioning, which is not in his favor at all. But this state of imbalance would not last long for men like him: I knew I had to strike soon.

I waited till he looked like he was knee-deep in a difficult file before I took a deep breath and said, "Suresh . . . there's something I've been meaning to ask you."

Suresh looked up from his phone, on which he was actually working, smiled, and said, "Me, too."

In an effort to mask my true evil, I said sweetly, "You first."

"It's been so killer busy since I arrived, but I've been meaning to ask you out for lunch. How does today sound?"

"You're asking me out for lunch?" I whispered, blood draining from my face.

"Yes," he said. "I checked with Kai, who said your schedule was free, and since you were free I thought, why wait?"

I took a steadying breath. "Yes, sure, but where—"

Suresh's dimpled smile deepened. "There's this fine-dining Shanghainese restaurant that Kai said you liked. I'm a big fan of Shanghainese food myself, so I thought we'd go with the obvious choice."

"Indeed," I said. I made a mental note to warn Kai from divulging my schedule to Suresh in the future, even if she worked for both of us. Her loyalties should lie with me, dammit: I lent her money for her gym membership.

2:40 p.m. Just back from lunch, which got off to a bad start. Soon after we were shown to our table, I found out that Suresh had spent a year in Hangzhou studying Mandarin and knew more about regional Chinese food, and tea, than I did. He won food-ordering duties after some haggling, and proceeded to order, among other things, chicken feet in soy sauce, a Power Move in itself as this is a dish rife with possibility for disaster (of the dry-cleaning variety). Worst, when the steamed fish arrived, he looked deep into my eyes and complimented my Power Outfit as he plucked the staring eyeball out of the dead, defenseless fish, popped it into his mouth, and chewed in a deliberate manner, which meant I would have to eat the remaining eyeball.

And the lunch got personal when I least expected it. "So, have you always wanted to be a lawyer?" he asked, his lips still coated with juices from the fish's eyeball, the psycho.

I shrugged. "I was given only two choices: law or medicine. I didn't know there was any other path open to me: my mother basically said it was either one of those or be disowned." I made a face. "I think she threatened to disown me every time I tried to make choices that diverged from what she would have picked for me."

He chuckled. "Sounds familiar. I guess you could be luckier, since in my case it was the threat of dismemberment. Or was it disembowelment? I don't remember. Just thank your lucky stars your parents aren't doctors who could actually carry out their threat."

I laughed, against my better judgment. Laughing at your enemy's jokes is a sign of submission. I dug my fingernails into my palms.

"So tell me, given all that you know now: what would you be if you could be anything else?"

I pretended to think this over. "I did want to be a marine biologist. Or was it a mermaid? One of those. And you?" I was not going to reveal my dreams to my competitor. I mean, once upon a time, when I was young and foolish, I'd wanted to be a writer.

"Writer," he answered immediately.

"What a cliché," I said. "You and every sad lawyer I know."

"Clichés exist for a reason; many a lawyer started out as a wee little lad or lass interested in storytelling," he said. "Although I suppose I'm more of a comic book artist at this stage than a writer. I've got a graphic novel, which I plan to get published one day, lying in my desk drawer."

I hated that I had my own unfinished manuscript of sorts lying in my drawer as well, notebooks full of poems about the dark side of law and single life in Singapore. Not that I was going to divulge its existence to Suresh. No, as far as I was concerned, this secret hobby of mine would stay in its drawer, because that's where hobbies belong in real life. I could hear how disdainful I sounded when I continued, "Aside from your, erm, *graphic novel*, have you written anything?"

"I have," he said, smiling. "I have my own superhero comic strip online."

"Doesn't everyone?" I said disparagingly.

"Erm, yes, erm. But mine is, well, quite successful. Have you heard of *The Last True Self*? About a shape-shifting vigilante who murders to protect the oppressed by sucking their life force out by touch, but is doomed to take on the form of the last person he touch-murders?"

"No," I said. "Sounds super boring."

He leaned forward and whispered, "Well, *I'm the creator.* But don't tell anyone at work, since I don't want people to think I actually have hobbies, or a life, outside of the law." He winked.

"Um-hmm," I said, nonchalant but silently taking notes for future evil reference.

"Also, people have been trying to figure out who the creator of *TLTS* is for some time now, since, you know, I killed so many real-life celebrities and politicians in my comic strip. I've had death threats."

I fought the urge to blurt out, "And now I know your Achilles' heel, sucker!"

He seemed reassured, foolishly, by my silence. "Seriously, though, what drew you to read law?"

I hesitated, then said, truthfully, "I wanted to fight for justice for the oppressed. Like Batman. Or you know, like Atticus Finch in *To Kill a Mockingbird*."

Suresh sipped at his tea. "What area of law did you originally want to practice in?"

"International humanitarian law. You?"

"Criminal law."

We both fell silent as we reflected on how far we'd deviated from our ideals.

I gingerly picked out the second fish eyeball and swallowed the slimy, chalky thing whole, nearly gagging in the process. "Lemme guess, Tiger Mom?"

"Tiger Dad," he said. "Well, Tiger Parents, really."

We smiled wanly at each other in commiseration.

"So, Suresh Aditparan, my next question is: would you do things differently when it comes to your kids? Or do you think tiger parenting is the way to go? I mean, all things considered, we turned out pretty well." Great, now I was drawing parallels between us *and* complimenting him. Some Power Lunch this was turning out to be.

He gnawed on his bottom lip as he thought this through. "I think I'd one hundred percent do things differently. I would tell my children to dream big, that I would support them in anything they wanted to do. Anything, that is, except dentistry and accountancy." He grinned. "One has to draw the line somewhere."

I laughed against my will. It's as painful as it sounds, trust me. I couldn't believe that I was starting to enjoy myself.

Then he leaned forward and adopted a businesslike tone. "Let's cut the bullshit, Andrea. This isn't a friendly orienteering lunch, is it?"

"Excuse me?" I said, thrown off course by the lack of segue.

"I know you don't like me"—I opened my mouth to deny this, but he cut me off with a gesture—"but it's OK, you're not very likable either. You are borderline rude, to be honest, glowering at me like I don't have eyes in my head. I get it, you don't have much competition around here. But we don't have to like each other to work in the same office. You stay in your lane, and I'll stay in mine. And soon we'll be out of each other's hair when the office reno is done."

What a pompous, arrogant jerk!

When the meal was over I tried to pay for it in a last-ditch attempt at a Power Move but was foiled at this because he had already left his card with the reception when he entered. The boy was almost more Chinese than I was!

Clearly, I would have to find other ways to establish my alpha status, and soon. Starting by setting up an anonymous Instagram account and spamming him. Let's see who's rude then!

8:55 p.m. OMG. *The Last True Self* has close to 55K followers on Instagram and 38K followers on Twitter. And what's worse: Suresh is good. The comic bursts with style, satire, and dark humor, and lots of opportunity for catharsis (his vigilante, Water, has killed John Mayer (!), among others).

Water is an absurdly handsome, John Wick-ish mercenary vigilante who gained his deadly powers (life-force absorption and shape-shifting) and lost his wife after a freak accident at the experimental lab where they both worked almost two years ago. Each time he touches someone with his bare skin, he immediately kills them and takes on his victim's new form temporarily until his powers recharge and he morphs back, although with each kill he loses a few more of his memories. So while each kill lessens the pain of his wife's loss, it also takes away more of her, of him. As a result of his powers, he's a bit of a loner and has not been involved with anyone since his wife died. To touch someone is to take that person's life; hence the only time he does any touching, aside from himself when no one is watching except God, is when he is ready to kill. It can get a little one-note; it would be nice if Suresh injected, as a counterpoint to all this directionless murder, a bigger agenda for the killing. Maybe a righteous desire to reduce world population to counter global warming—something controversial but logical. Just so there's narrative tension. And maybe a sex scene or two #justsayin.

Not because I find the protagonist hot, of course. Because he looks a heck of a lot like his creator, and that would mean I find Suresh attractive, which I don't.

All the same, there's enough here to please a casual reader. I'm impressed. Using the anonymous IG account I had set up to spam him, I began to follow *TLTS*. Just to better understand the psyche of my enemy.

11:35 p.m. Looked up from screen, dizzy and ravenous, and realized that I'd finished two years' worth of *TLTS* in one sitting. Now I'm hooked, with no choice but to continue following *TLTS*. I'm contributing to his following and, indirectly, his revenue stream.

Worst of all, dear Diary, was the jealousy. Suresh might not have figured it out yet, but if he ever wanted to take a leap of faith, he could switch careers and do something he was passionate about. He had options, whereas I had none.

11:40 p.m. Urgh. Can feel the downward spiral over life choices beginning.

11:55 p.m. Decided to join Ben for a drink at Boat Quay.

1:20 a.m. Saw Ben in action. He is like a relic of the past, going up to younger women and shouting at them over loud music while they blink at him, unimpressed.

1:23 a.m. Come to think of it, is that how I will look to people when I am out with Orson, a boy who has never used a VHS tape player in his life?

1:30 a.m. Oh God. Oh God. Need tequila.

1:45 a.m. Have had tequila, many. Considered, for a panicked moment, whether I should sleep with Ben. Then for some reason I heard Suresh saying, "One has to draw the line somewhere."

2:38 a.m. Tequilas w why we mustr never have a trade wart with mexivco!1

3:20 a.m. Drunkenly made out with sowmeo who looked lke Ivan befr realize he does nott at all, when car drove by alldey light see.

3:45 a.m. Whaar m I doing? Needa to get my datng life in shipshape like carreer or end up ksssng men in alley.

4:10 a.m. Home.

Part II

TWO BIRDS, ONE STONE

7

Saturday 20 February

Valerie called at 10:30 a.m., violating our group's golden rule: "No calls before eleven on a Saturday, unless you or someone we know is dying."

"Andrea! I'm in big trouble," she said with a megaphone. "I don't know what to do or who to turn to!"

"Whaaaat?" I moaned. Someone inside my head was banging a timpani in tandem with my heartbeat.

"Are you listening to me?" Valerie shouted.

I sat up, very slowly, in bed, and whispered, "Sorry, the line's pretty bad, can you repeat the whole thing again?"

"I need to babysit my niece, and I have *no* idea how to take care of a child! You've got to help! You have a younger sister, weren't you always saying?"

I didn't tell her that Melissa practically raised herself, she was so level-headed. I mean, I turn to *her* for advice, not vice versa.

Valerie said her brother Cameron's helper was on leave and Cameron was in the States on a business trip, and Zi Min, her sister-in-law who was also a real estate agent, had some rental properties she had to show that day. I agreed to come with her after enduring another minute of high-pitched begging. By the time she arrived at my condo, barely twenty-five minutes later, I had downed a bottle of special Korean ginseng energy drink, one coconut water, and two double espressos, and was feeling almost human. Unsurprisingly, after I'd vibrated into Valerie's car, I turned my head and found a prone Linda lying on the back seat. Her face was a particularly vibrant hue of zombie gray.

"Hi, sweetie, thank you so much for agreeing to help," Valerie said. She motioned at Linda. "That one back there spent the night at mine after we had a heavy night out in Clarke Quay. Between you and me, I can't believe she's still alive."

Linda groaned and unleashed a cloud of mint-veiled alcohol breath. She should really have been sleeping off her hangover at Valerie's place, but since Valerie and I were the kind of friends who had never hung out alone, it made sense that even her hungover ass was a good buffer against awkward small talk. "Keep your voices down, will you," she pleaded.

I turned my attention to Valerie, who, under the world's largest sunglasses and a cap, looked bright and hard-shiny in the daylight. "How come you're totally fine and she's half-dead?" I asked.

"I'm not an alcoholic," Valerie replied.

We arrived at the condominium in Tiong Bahru where Valerie's brother lived. Valerie was begging us to hurry as we were already nine minutes late and her sister-in-law was a stickler for punctuality. "She's going to freak," she said in a panic.

Which was exactly what happened.

"You're late," Zi Min barked, her arms crossed. I eyed her warily, since the apple never falls far from the tree and we were supposed to take care of her daughter. Zi Min was classically attractive: tall, porcelain-skinned, and thin but B-cupped, she was dressed in a flowy long-sleeved white silk top paired with dark blue jeans and matching denim Chanel ballerina flats and bag. There was no doubt in my mind that she was a conventional pain in the ass.

"Sorry," Valerie said meekly, seeming to shrink into herself. I felt bad for her; she really needed to toughen up.

Zi Min jerked her chin at our direction. "So. Who are these people?"

"These are my friends from, ah, work. They are here to help

me take care of Lilly. They have a lot of experience with, uh, children." I nodded on cue, the enthusiastic smiley nod of a Jehovah's Witness. I had my arm slung companionably around a sunglassed Linda (mostly to prop her up). Linda had already been Febrezed, but we stood a little ways back, just in case.

Zi Min was in too much of a rush to bother vetting us in the care of her only child; she let us in without further debate. She motioned down the hallway. "Lilly just came back from ballet and she was supposed to be having chess lessons but her coach canceled." She scowled. "Make sure she doesn't watch TV. She has to complete her homework, then practice her piano drills for *two hours* for her piano class tonight. For a treat, she may complete *four* advanced Sudoku puzzles before you drop her off for her piano lesson at five o'clock."

"For a treat," Linda repeated in disbelief, jolted out of her hungover stupor.

"Y-e-s," Zi Min said. "Just *four* puzzles. There's lunch in the kitchen, some quinoa salads I got delivered, but if you're still hungry, there's leftover oat and quinoa porridge in the fridge. Lilly is on a gluten-free diet as she is getting super fat. OK, I *really* have to run. I'll try to be back by four thirty in order to send her to piano class. Sometimes she fusses and I have to smack her."

"Where is she now?" Valerie asked as I watched Linda turn a magnificent shade of pukey indignation.

"In her room, studying chess openings. Please watch her!" She had a change of mind and kicked off her ballet flats before shoving her feet into a pair of towering Charlotte Olympia platform pumps. Maybe she intended to intimidate her clients into signing the lease. "All right. Goodbye. Have fun."

The door slammed shut behind her. We heard her heels clattering down the hallway as she ran. A flurry of swearing, then blessed silence. All of us breathed a sigh of relief. Almost immediately, one of the bedroom doors creaked open and a girl's head peeked out. "Is she gone?" Lilly whispered.

"Yes, sweetie," Valerie said, smiling as much as the Botox would allow.

"Oh, thank God!" Lilly stomped out of the room, slammed the door, and threw herself onto the couch. "I *hate* her."

"Now, now," Valerie said, awkwardly petting the girl's head, "she is your mother."

"I know, Auntie Val," Lilly said. "But she's mean and controlling. I never get to do anything *I* want, and you follow her every instruction." She looked around and pouted at me. "Would *you* let me watch TV, please?"

"Well, now . . ." I looked at Valerie. "I'm not in charge here, sweetie. Your aunt Val is."

"Hold on," Valerie mouthed. She sidled to the TV console table and parked her handbag directly in front of an insidious-looking stuffed rabbit with exposed teeth, the only incongruous object in the minimalist living room, which had obviously been decorated by a Scandinavian monk with expensive taste.

"Now you can," she said with a grin.

Valerie turned the TV on and the three of us joined Lilly on the couch without further ado, Lilly gripping the remote control with both hands, her eyes trained on the TV on which five nubile Korean girls were gyrating to techno music and alternatively rapping and yowling. She had the slightly gormless look of an entranced gopher. Poor kid. Valerie explained that every minute of the child's day was scheduled, down to the second. Piano lessons, creative writing, coding, drama therapy, chess lessons, and because Zi Min had hopes that Lilly would excel at a sport, ballet and kiddie golf. Of course, you must understand that these were just after-school enrichment classes designed to gild Lilly's academic CV—God forbid that the kid actually decided she wanted to be a ballerina, a professional athlete, or a violin teacher. Every Chinese parent knows that those extracurricular activities were just that—extra.

I'll have to admit I don't think I had it this rough: what Lilly was experiencing was next-level Tiger Parenting. Val's brother, Cameron, was a high-flying investment banker, and Zi Min was a senior director of a large real estate agency: they had big dreams and only one offspring, so the poor child was essentially hostage to her parents' wishes forever.

But for now the little monster was just hanging loose, her legs splayed over the glass-topped coffee table as she munched on yellowing breath mints that she had salvaged from the bottom of my bag. "I *never* get to eat candy," she confided. "You aunties are the best. I wish all of you were my mommy."

I looked over at Valerie, who was beaming despite having just been called an auntie.

We watched four hours of TV, Linda, Valerie, and I taking turns napping while Lilly watched music video after music video and ate all the breath mints we collectively owned. When she was hungry she asked for McDonald's, which I was only too happy to oblige. You should have seen this kid's eyes when she saw the food arrive—I don't think I've ever seen anyone that excited to see gluten. Linda revived soon after the Big Mac and Coke and she brought out a stack of cards and taught Lilly how to play poker. We were all sorry when the time came to drop Lilly, whose eyes had now crossed from watching almost six hours straight of music videos, off at her music school (her mother had called at 3:00 p.m. to say she had an "emergency errand" to run and would be late, but reminded us to "use all force necessary to get Lilly to her lesson").

And then Lilly's vacation from the real world was over.

I pulled up in front of the music school ten minutes late and did the very Malaysian thing of double-parking with the hazard lights flashing. Lilly refused to leave the car. She threw an epic kicking-and-screaming tantrum, stopping only when Valerie said she would have to call Zi Min and tell her that Lilly wouldn't go to class, at which the child almost immediately stopped fussing, fear evident in her eyes. When Valerie and I finally managed to usher her to her class, Lilly was in tears. To be honest, I was almost in tears myself—who knew a child could bite so hard?

Later, as I drove us back in the car, Valerie said quietly, "I want one."

Linda, who'd once said that Halloween was great because that was when you could poison the kids you didn't like with the sweet justice of candy, turned to Valerie and said, "I think you'd make a great mom, Val."

As for me, having survived today, I went straight to my neighborhood pharmacy and bought a pack of extra-thick, dolphin-friendly condoms, which were helpfully on sale. Score!

9:45 p.m. Val video-called me to thank me for my help. "You're awesome, and I'm going to do something very special for you," she said. "Linda filled me in on your, um, quest, and I think I know just how to help you."

"What do you mean?" Who knew what Linda had been blathering on about in her state last night. And I have many active quests: I've always wanted to find out Beyoncé's real age, for instance.

"I'm going to open my social circles to you. We're going to go out, hunting, the old-fashioned way!" She then added somewhat unnecessarily, "For men."

I was both terrified and intrigued. "What? How? Where?"

"There's an event I've been *dying* to go to and to which I've just been put on the guestlist, so we can try that. I can't divulge any details yet since I need to ask permission from the hostess, but I'm sure you'll be able to meet eligible age-appropriate bachelors there." Her voice took on a steely tone. "But if you are accepted into the fold, you must promise me never to bring anyone else, *especially Linda*, to the club I'm about to bring you to. It's my watering hole. *Mine.*"

And then, against the laws of Botox, she glared at me.

Dear Diary, I am scared.

8

Monday 22 February

10:07 a.m. Orson just sent me a weird-cute GIF of his face superimposed onto a gigantic mandarin orange to wish me Happy Chap Goh Mei. "Chap Goh Mei" in the Hokkien dialect refers to the fifteenth night of Chinese New Year; it marks the drawing to a close of the Lunar New Year celebration. It is also celebrated as the Chinese Valentine's Day for many Malaysians and Singaporeans (because one day of torture was not enough). In this part of the world, there exists a "fun" Chap Goh Mei tradition, where single Chinese ladies throw perfectly good mandarin oranges with their names and phone numbers written on the fruit into a body of water, where they would usually be scooped up by eager gentlemen who may or may not be looking to score a free supply of vitamin C. The origins of this custom are obscure—to foolish die-hard romantics. There is little doubt in my mind that some crafty Southeast Asian mandarin orange cartel came up with this idea as a means of getting rid of their surplus stock at the end of the festivities for profit instead of letting them rot in a landfill; certainly it also makes their lives easy should they wish to pick out the single womenfolk for their trophy wives. Sleazy capitalist bastards.

Anyway, what was I saying? Ah, yes. Orson and the Giant GIF. I thanked him and he immediately messaged back to say that he was in Jakarta on a work trip and couldn't make Wednesday for lunch but hoped to reschedule our date to the following Thursday, and that he would miss me.

I was disappointed that we wouldn't see each other this week, but flattered. The last person who told me they missed me was my online grocer. Who says you can't find nice ones on Sponk.

Thursday 25 February

8:20 p.m. Urgh. Am finally done with another bloody closing.

When I had sent all the documents to the client, I shakily stood up from the desk I had been crouched over for four hours straight and took stock of the damage: my eyes were burning and out of focus; I think I lost a tooth in my coffee; something smelled of warmed kimchi and I was pretty sure it was me (maybe that was why Suresh had taken to working in the library today?). My rib cage hurt from the too-tight sports bra I was wearing instead of a proper one, because I'd run out of clean lingerie. I've been eating takeaway salad (OK, fine, so they were fried spring rolls and not salad per se, but there's radish in there so that counts toward my five-a-day) for lunch and dinner from that Vietnamese deli downstairs for three effing days straight and have slept a total of sixteen hours in the last four days, in my office.

On days like this I fantasize so hard about quitting that I actually have heart pangs. Just like Suresh, my plan wasn't to go to law school to become a corporate lawyer. I had ideals once. I was passionate about human rights. After graduation I paid my dues and put in some time at Slaughter & May, but just as I'd begun a new position as a legal adviser for a small nonprofit helping trafficked women in the UK, my father got really sick and I had to get what my mother called a "real job" to help defray their living expenses, instead of "wasting my expensive legal education." So I did what I had to do: I went back to Slaughter & May, cap in hand, and got my old job back. Some of that money went toward paying part of Melissa's tuition, since she was in the middle of an expensive British degree in architecture and needed to get the best grades she could instead of working part time and getting just a second-lower-class or third-class degree. No way were we going to do that to her.

I guess I'm the reason she was able to meet Kamarul in her third year. This has always made me feel a little guilty toward my mother, not because I condone her casual racism ("You can be friends with them, but you can't date them!"), but because, since I'd borne the full brunt of the financial fallout (cancers are expensive when you don't have good insurance!) and downplayed my mother's mental breakdown after my father's passing in the misguided belief that Melissa shouldn't suffer remotely any more than could be helped, my sister never knew the full extent of how bad things had gotten. My mother recovered thinking Melissa hadn't cared enough to return home after her degree was done a few months after my father's death, embarking instead on a gap year with Kamarul. They've been inseparable since.

Anyway, the rough patch my family found itself in, emotionally and financially, is somewhat over and I could quit and work somewhere else as I had intended to before I had to move back—only I can't. I don't know how to anymore. The money at my job is more than anything I'll make elsewhere; I have little savings in my bank account because of my father's illness and a mortgage I can barely afford (I might have been a little *too* aspirational with the posh address I'd chosen), which is fine, just as long as I have a job. Plus, I can't give up now: I've half-ruined my eyesight on pages of document review, sucked up to too many people, sacrificed too much of my youth and identity, listened to far too many lectures from my mom about languishing in the purgatory of mediocrity. It's no longer a choice; too much hangs in the balance. I *have* to become partner.

9

Monday 29 February (Leap Day!)

6:25 a.m. Goddammit, it's Monday again.

7:20 a.m. Why are people sending me Leap Day memes? It's a goddamn extra day of work.

7:45 a.m. On train. Got elbowed, groped, and stepped on several times.

8:10 a.m. Ooh, Suresh just emailed me and told me he's bringing chocolate croissants to the office.

8:12 a.m. Must not eat croissants from the enemy. Revealing fondness for carbs and sweets is a sign of weakness.

8:20 a.m. Hmm, actually I eat sweets in front of him all the time. I even have a pot of raw sugar on my desk that he uses for his chai. He's already heard the noises of pleasure I make when I have cake, once in a blue moon.

8:22 a.m. I'll just have one croissant.

8:25 a.m. Or two. When he leaves the kitchenette.

9:40 a.m. Poor Suresh got schooled today. We were loafing around in the kitchenette having morning chai and croissants when he told me that he was going to the wedding of an acquaintance from his school that weekend and was planning to put a token sum in the red packet because he didn't know her that well anyway.

"How much is token to you?" I asked, curious.

Suresh seemed uncomfortable with the line of questioning, maybe because I was leaning over him like a horny grandmother. "Er. I don't know. Fifty?"

"What kind of reception: lunch or dinner? Which hotel is it? Four or five stars?"

"Dinner, and, er, I don't know, some fancy-sounding hotel; no doubt it's going to be expensive since she's marrying a senior partner of a Big Four audit firm, but seriously, why does it matter?" He shrugged. "I barely know her. I'm only going because she and Anousha are distantly related and she courtesy-invited me. I'm sure whatever I give will be fine."

"Are you insane? This is social suicide." I stuck my head out of the kitchenette. "Kai, get in here!"

Kai entered wearing a crisp white linen dress and suede pumps, looking flustered. "Is everything all right?" she asked.

I explained the situation and she burst into loud hoots of laughter. "Oh, you're never going to live this down. You should just pack your bags and leave Singapore now," she said.

Suresh raised an eyebrow. "I don't understand what the big deal is. It's a huge wedding with a gazillion people. Everyone will be contributing gifts or money, so why does it matter what amount I put into an *ang pao*? No one cares."

"No one cares!" I exclaimed. "Are you fresh off the boat? Oh wait, you are, because let me tell you something, my friend, *everyone* ca—"

"What's all the commotion?" a sinister voice said from the doorway. Without warning, Genevieve Beh glided into the room in her cloud of dead forest rat secretions, her interest piqued.

I rolled my eyes, which started streaming from an allergic reaction to her perfume, but held my tongue; no one was better suited to emphasize how serious Suresh's situation was about to get if he proceeded as planned. Genevieve was the perfect example of a money-worshipping, soulless, calculating wraith that I wanted to showcase to Suresh. I quickly laid out the pertinent facts.

"Suresh, were you born yesterday? You can't just *give any sum you want*—there are *market rates*!" she exclaimed as though Suresh had just mentioned that he was going to attempt skydiving in his undies. "Has no one here told you about Genevieve's *ang pao* matrix?"

"Er, no. Please enlighten me."

Genevieve's voice trembled with emotion. "It's the Excel spreadsheet containing years of painstaking research and distillation of data on the appropriate amount one should give at any special occasion in Singapore, depending on the venue, the setting, the status of the host, the guests, and whether you are going alone or with a plus-one. I sent it out last year with a link to the shared drive, so the whole office could get educated! Never be caught unawares ever again! It's foolproof!"

"It really is very complete. She covers Chinese New Year, weddings, funerals, special occasions, and she updates the rates yearly," Kai chimed in.

Suresh gave her a blank look.

"So you've *not* heard of my matrix?" Genevieve asked incredulously.

"Er, no," Suresh repeated. I could tell he thought we were all off our rockers, but he was a nice British boy with public school manners, so he asked the only open-ended question that one could ask given the aforementioned facts: "Special occasions? Such as?"

"Chinese bar mitzvahs; second marriages; tooth fairy visitations. Everything." Genevieve was smug.

"Right," Suresh said. "And, ah, what happens if you, ah, deviate from the market rate?"

Genevieve patted his arm. "My friend, let me tell you a horror story of my own. Three years ago, my first child, Gwendolyn, lost her first milk tooth. She still believed in the tooth fairy then, so my husband and I put five dollars under her pillow."

"Wow, that's a lot," Suresh said. "All I got from the lousy English tooth fairy was fifty pence."

Genevieve tittered darkly. "Oh, Suresh, Suresh, Suresh. We both thought it was a good amount of money for a rotten bit of calcium, too, *but we were wrong!* Turns out that when Gwennie went to school the next day and told her friends what the tooth fairy had given her, she was laughed at by Aspen, the granddaughter of some Tan Sri* in Malaysia. It seems that the going rate for tooth fairy payouts in Gwennie's private school is now *twenty* Sing dollars! And Aspen, that little brat, got three hundred *American* dollars for her piggy bank! What a way to spoil the market.† Gwennie was simply devastated. It took her *weeks* of therapy to get over the shame of being known as the poor kid in school." She shuddered. "Anyway, Suresh, heed my words: respect the market rate, if you wish to be respected."

Later, safe in our office, Suresh turned to me and said, "I never thought I'd hear the word 'payout' being used in the context of a tooth fairy's visit."

"Just wait till you see her full moon and baby shower tab and you'll understand why more and more Singaporeans are not reproducing," I said.

"Decent people like us should be the ones reproducing instead of Genevieve," he said offhandedly, but that throwaway comment was enough for my romance-starved imagination to start cranking out scenarios where we . . . never mind.

God, I need a new distraction.

---

* "Tan Sri" is the second most senior federal title in Malaysia. Basically, if you have one, you're minted.

† A Singlish expression, meaning to overachieve and raise the bar unnecessarily for others.

3:45 p.m. Ask and the universe provides. Got a text from Valerie. Turns out the weird gathering she was hoping to bring me to has a spot for me, and I've been "preapproved to come as a guest of hers this one time." She told me to keep this Saturday evening free and to "dress nice."

What kind of gathering is it? I asked her with trepidation.

A book club.

That's it? A lousy *book club*?

Look, you totally have to go to this one, she wrote. **Even if you're not into books.**

I made sure to read her text twice, in case my eyesight was failing. Then I replied: **Even if you don't like books? Isn't that the whole point of a book club?**

She called me immediately.

"Look, slowpoke, this is obviously no ordinary book club," said Valerie. "It's the people, the place. It'll be my first time, too, and I had to be pre-screened, wait-listed—"

Pre-screened? What?

She was babbling on. "—and the only reason spots opened up is because someone died from cocaine overdose in Barbados, isn't that great? I mean, not about the death obvs, but because I'm in! And someone else is out of town so I'm allowed to bring a guest, hurrah! Anyways, it's hosted in this mad beautiful house on Jervois Hill. The owner is subletting it to an actress friend of mine who used to swing with a Malaysian prince, you know the one . . ." She named the prince nonchalantly. Just the sort of status-trumpeting factoid you would expect from Valerie.

"Sounds tempting," I said. "Will I be expected to participate in any ritual sacrifices after reading aloud from the Satanic Bible? Or am I the ritual sacrifice? I have to warn you, I'm not a virgin."

"Hardy-har-har," she said dryly. "Well, I can't promise there won't be any devil-worship, considering that crowd. Listen, jokes aside, you have to come. It's like a Who's Who of the Singaporean elite. You'll be hobnobbing with career deciders. Who knows, maybe you'll even meet your future husband." A singles mixer in a sect, nothing fancy.

"Must I?" I said. It was rhetorical though—she had me at "prince's swinging buddy." I could pull a Magnus and marry wealthy.

"I'll pick you up at seven o'clock. Start with some champers in the car."

"Sounds extravagant."

"Oh yeah? Wait till you get there. DeeDee told me they serve vintage champagne and oysters before starting."

I hooted. "Wow! Is this a black-tie event or a book club?"

"This is how they roll, so try not to embarrass me, OK?" she huffed. "Oh, by the way, you're expected to have read *A Little Life* by Hanya Yanagihara."

"Sure, how long is it? I'll Kindle it."

"Eight hundred pages."

"I'll just read the synopsis."

Tuesday 1 March

8:20 a.m. Was distracted at work today by a very loud conversation that Suresh was having with his fiancée, Anousha, the hotshot ob-gyn.

I put in my earphones and turned up the volume to give him some privacy, but I couldn't help overhearing him say, "Five bedrooms? What are we going to do with a five-bedroom house in Chiswick . . . no dogs, Noushie, I can't . . . you said you would move to Singapore . . . *No*, we talked about this. What do your parents mean by . . . well, I told you many times that I *don't care* that you're not Brahmin."

This hushed, agitated conversation went on for another ten minutes before I heard him slam down the phone.

"What's up?" I asked innocently. "How's Nou— I mean, Anousha doing?"

Suresh gave a snort of frustration and started pacing the room. "Anousha's just dropped a bombshell on me. It's her parents. She says that they want to buy us a house in London as 'dowry.'" He used air quotes, quite charmingly I must say.

"Wow. A house as a dowry?" I whistled. "That's a bit much, isn't it? Not that I'd have a problem saying no to a house. And forgive me for being rude, why are your parents still asking for dowry? I mean, you're acceptable-looking and all . . ." I trailed off.

He stopped pacing to throw a pencil at me. "We didn't ask for a dowry; we specifically said we didn't want one. Both my and Anousha's parents are relatively nontraditional, so I thought we were past that. Anyway, as for getting a house as a 'dowry,' if you knew what it meant you'd reject it like I plan to ask my parents to. As a gift, it's way too much, especially since they aren't giving us an investment property but a marital home!"

"What's the reason for such a crazy generous dow— I mean, gift?" I couldn't understand his displeasure. I wouldn't mind me a five-bedder in Chiswick: I hear it's quite gentrified.

He made an impatient noise and continued pacing. "The excuse is, she's not Brahmin and I am, so they are 'making up for it.'"

"Pardon my ignorance, but why does this matter in this day and age?"

"It doesn't, not to me, but for many Indians, even those who have migrated overseas, the caste system still matters when determining the suitability of a romantic partner. And the Brahmin are the highest of the four castes."

"I don't get it. Your parents are fine about her not being Brahmin, right? I mean, they accepted the match after all."

"It doesn't matter too much to my parents, or they would have said something when we started dating. Maybe it mattered to my mother, but as soon as she found out that Noushie was an ob-gyn, she basically said, it's fine, we're just one caste level apart anyway. This is the twenty-first century." He smiled wryly. "I know and she knows what they are really after, which is for me to move back to the UK. Her parents are using this as leverage to keep their precious daughter in England." His voice was rough with suppressed anger and I could see a large vein throbbing in his neck. It was a little unsettling to see Suresh display any negative emotion—he was so *nice.*

"At least you get a house out of this," I said soothingly. "The last time I was engaged all I got was the emotional scars to show for it. Big whoop."

It worked. He stopped pacing. "You were engaged?" he said, in the tone of someone who had just discovered that a rat he had run over with his bike was, in fact, still alive and was now snacking on his bike tires, despite half its intestines lying on the road.

"Yes." It didn't hurt anymore, but thinking about Ivan still rankled.

"What happened?" Suresh asked. "I mean, if it's not too personal a question to ask."

"I need to be drunk to tell the story, so you're going to have to buy me a few drinks first."

Suresh grinned. "It's a date. Anyway, I'm sure it's his loss."

I thought about this. Ivan was definitely doing better than my voodoo doll version of him was. He'd been promoted (according to his latest LinkedIn update) and profiled by a couple of publications as being some hotshot investment guru. No reason to let Suresh know the truth though, since I didn't trust him. I decided to change the subject. "It sure is. But let's concentrate on your problems for now."

"It's a conundrum that shouldn't be, you know? We'd always said that after our engagement, Anousha would move to Singapore and join me. It makes the most sense for both our careers. So here's the thing that worries me: I don't think it's just her parents wanting her to stay in London instead of moving to Singapore—it's her as well. It feels like it's coming from her."

"It's your own fault, you know. You should have married a non-Indian woman. That would have solved the dowry problem altogether," I blurted.

Silence. Suresh was now looking at me like I was the rat he had run over, which had now given birth to a litter of rat babies on his Tod's suede shoes, despite its spilled entrails hardening in the midday sun.

"Er, joking," I said, flushing and dropping my eyes. I began to peck blindly at my keyboard, pretending to be engrossed in an email. Here I go again, becoming too familiar with the enemy.

Just when I thought he'd really taken offense at my comment, he spoke up.

"You know what? It seems strange to hear this, but I've never even given seriously dating a non-Indian real thought," he said. "Don't get me wrong, I love Anousha, but she's quite literally the epitome of a good Indian girl from a good family, and that's what I'd always assumed . . . no, *know* my parents would want for me. I'm sure that if I ever dated anyone that didn't fit this mold, especially if it's someone from another race . . ." He shrugged. "Well, I don't think my parents would be too pleased about that prospect, to put it very mildly."

"My parents would flip out if I dated someone from another race," I admitted. "It's strange, isn't it, how this form of racism is still accepted under the guise of ensuring that the new addition to your family has a 'similar cultural background and value system'?

I have very little in common with an ethnic Chinese who's spent all his life in Vietnam, for example. Yet somehow . . ."

"We're expected to understand each other just because we have the same skin tone and features," he finished. "Look, I don't know you very well, but I think we definitely have more in common than you would with that Vietnamese man."

"True," I said, thinking of Kamarul and my sister.

"She doesn't find my comic strip any good," he said, out of the blue. "Anousha. She thinks it's juvenile."

"Hmm," I replied, storing this tidbit away for further (nefarious) use.

Suresh appeared lost in thought. I looked at my desktop digital counter—I couldn't reasonably bill this last fifteen minutes of conversation to my client, but I could mark it down in my timesheet as "knowledge management" (non-billable but a respectable code). Happy with my genius, I went back to kicking Suresh's ass. Metaphorically.

Wednesday 2 March

7:10 a.m. Woke up this morning to a text from Orson. It said:

> **Hope I din anythin wrong cz I hvnt heard bak abt tat lunch/ diner date tmw, iz on?**

Linda's right. I can't date him; he can barely spell.

9:05 a.m. Texted him back on WhatsApp to confirm our lunch date, which he confirmed enthusiastically (meaning he has absolutely no game, which is awesome). Thank God for instant messaging, which has done away with the whole waiting-by-the-phone nonsense. Nowadays even a delay of thirty minutes in answering an email is enough to set your colleagues' teeth on edge, and not IMing back someone who fancies you when you have your Last Seen time-stamp mode on can be tantamount to mental harm.

When I texted Linda to tell her, she exploded into a screen confetti of disapproving and red-faced emojis in our WhatsApp chat, followed by angry animated feral cat stickers in our Line app. Then she broadcasted her barely coded disapproval to our chat group by captioning a picture of a durian with "It's gonna fucking hurt when it lands on your thick head, Andrea!" just in case I didn't catch her drift. I wished she would pick up the phone and tell me off directly like she used to in the good old days. Whatever happened to direct gladiatorial confrontation, mano a mano, the way we used to do in the noughties?

Anyway, I'm insulted that Linda thinks I'm no match for the crafty wiles of a millennial hipster munchkin. After all, we've survived dial-up internet, '90s television, and the days when shoulder pads were acceptable. We can overcome anything.

11:40 p.m. Have been working nonstop since 6:00 p.m., after a client sent us a panicked email asking us to handle an urgent matter (nothing is ever non-urgent with clients—nothing). Can feel low-level hysteria enveloping me as I contemplate the flood of snippy emails from the London firm representing the other party to the deal—there is probably no chance of seeing my own bed till 3:00 a.m. How am I supposed to plan my outfit?

Thursday 3 March

1:55 a.m. OMG I'M FINALLY HOME WHY THE HELL DID I BECOME AN M&A LAWYER #fmltothemax

5:50 a.m. Woke up in a blind panic thinking I had overslept. No such luck. I'm due back in the office for a conference call at 8:00 a.m. FML!

7:50 a.m. The clients just *canceled* the conference call even though I'd been preparing for the call for hours.

8:15 a.m. Woke up with a start when Suresh gently patted my arm, smirking. Turned out I'd been drooling on my keyboard. Great, sleeping in front of the enemy, how very alpha of you, Andrea. And now I have keyboard face. FML!

10:05 a.m. Can still see faint outline of keyboard on my face. Damn my flagging collagen production!

10:20 a.m. Read online that the most foolproof way to younger-looking skin is to drink at least two liters of water a day.

10:25 a.m. Bought two large bottles of sparkling water and started to chug water like wine.

10:45 a.m. Finished second bottle of sparkling water. Might have overdone it, as now I need to pee badly but am restraining myself as constantly needing the loo—I mean, toilet is a sign of weakness, or at the very least a weak bladder. In any case, the water appears to have filled out my skin cells. Now I can have my date with Orson without looking like SpongeBob SquarePants.

11:07 a.m. It's no use. I need the washroom. The alternative involves a change of clothing I do not have.

11:15 a.m. Peed like a racehorse, or how I imagine racehorses to pee.

11:35 a.m. Peed again.

11:50 a.m. And again. That'll show me to drink water.

12:10 p.m. Lunchtime. Panicked dash out of office. We're supposed to meet for lunch at Quinn's, a (real) salad bar (not my Vietnamese deli) close by. It was a deliberate choice on my part to do lunch. Orson had to see me in daylight sooner or later, and there is nothing less flattering to an older woman's face and neck than harsh noon daylight, aside from maybe the fluorescent lighting in prisons and the restrooms in petrol stations. All the Crème de la Meh will not make a bulldog look like a Chihuahua, is what Linda likes to say (but not in Valerie's hearing, because Valerie does believe that she can indeed freeze time with her potions, if not turn it back half a dial at the very least).

2:15 p.m. Just back from fun lunch. As usual I was running late, thanks to work. When I arrived, panting and disheveled, I saw that he was already seated in a booth. I took a steadying breath and walked in with the confidence of a woman with a thigh gap. Orson grinned when he saw me and we exchanged air kisses.

"Sorry I'm late."

"No worries," he said, waving my protests away. "I just got here. What would you like for lunch?"

I remembered that he had bought me drinks at LGA. "No, it's my treat today," I said firmly, waving my purse in the air.

"But—"

"Let me." I repeated, narrowing my eyes before I could stop myself. Dear God, I was scary. He held up his hands in mock surrender and gave me his order.

Anyway. Soon I was seated in front of Orson and his sleek black hair.

"So . . . ," he began. "Er, you look nice. I like your watch and shirt. Very chic."

"Oh, thanks," I replied. "I like your, er"—I gave him a desperate once-over, looking for some article of clothing I didn't have to lie about liking: I don't get male fashion these days, and he was a walking poster of trends—"Invisalign," I finished feebly.

I tried hard to find a good conversation starter. Now that I was sober, for the life of me I couldn't think of anything safe. Here's the thing about dating without alcohol at my age: it's pure agony.

You lose the ability to lightheartedly banter as you age; instead you worry about sounding intelligent (but not in an intimidating fashion), being current without trying too hard, while being politically correct. Plus I could clearly see one of the partners from my law firm seated just two rows away from us, munching on an anemic-looking salad, looking morose and clearly hoping that someone would walk up to him and blow his head off or at least give him an encouraging hand job. God, why did I choose the busiest salad bar in the freaking CBD* for a first lunch date?

Oh right. I had a conference call right after and it's close by the office. Priorities.

Somehow Orson came to the rescue. "So, what about this wrap, huh? Don't you wish we were having *nasi lemak* instead? Speaking of which, being a Malaysian, how do you find Singaporean food?"

And just like that, we were off to the races. We pitted Malaysian and Singaporean cuisine against each other and dissed each other's national claim to having invented Hainanese chicken rice. We talked about our favorite hawker stalls, casual and posh eateries, our secret holes-in-the-wall, all the obscure little places where we would never bring anyone other than family, close friends, and bosses we wanted to bribe with nonsexual favors.

I ended up having way more fun that I was supposed to. It's strange how much Orson and I have in common. Maybe it's fate, moving in mysterious ways?

---

* Central Business District, for the uninitiated.

Friday 4 March

12:25 p.m. There was a huge commotion earlier today at work because Mong fainted in the pantry. At first we thought he'd had a heart attack, which in his case would be expected, but he came to a few seconds later, looking bemused. He was about to go back to his office when his secretary and one of the senior partners intervened and marched him off to the hospital. They ran some tests and turns out the man had contracted dengue. With that diagnosis, he now has no choice but to stay home for two full weeks.

The doctor was apparently surprised/horrified that he was able to get to the office this morning and work since, you know, he was running a fever and his white blood cell count was so low it was life-threatening. But that's Mong; he's nothing if not dedicated. #workgoals #restecp (to quote the great Ali G).

Suresh and I have been tasked to cover his files, the few he would never delegate, preferring to work on them directly with the help of his lackeys/junior associates, Olivia and Yu Han. I will never leave the office. Never.

9:35 p.m. Left the office with Suresh. Yu Han and Olivia were killing each other to distinguish themselves to us and were unwilling to leave the office before us, so when Suresh asked if I'd like to grab a drink, I surprised myself and said yes.

Made beeline to a tiny little pub that is popular with the after-work crowd in our building and finished a tower of beer and a bottle of sake. At first the drinking took place in silence (we were tired), then we began to talk. We talked a lot about our families. His mother was now convinced that he and Anousha were never going to get married in time for Anousha to bear children without the helping hand of technology. He showed me a bizarre WhatsApp conversation with his mother where she started sharing articles about how important it is for women without clear romantic prospects to freeze their eggs after hitting thirty, how sperm and egg quality decrease with age, what diseases geriatric-egged babies were more prone to get, etc.

"What?" I said, or perhaps shouted. I was very drunk. I was also very outraged. "What gives these goons the right to . . . the right to tell you where to put it? Where were they"—my voice rose higher—"when you needed to know where babies came from and they told you to ask your high school biology teacher, because that's what they're paid to teach? Where? Nowhere, the cowards!" I slammed the tabletop for emphasis, passion rising, spittle flying. "You know how to dissuade them from sending you stuff like that, right? You just need to send them detailed texts about all the sexual positions you use with Anousha and ask them for tips on how to get each other in the mood. That should make them stop the passive-aggressive 'suggestions' about your sex life, the nosy jerks."

He looked at me and said, "Andrea, stop talking or we might become friends."

11:05 p.m. Home at last. We ended up spending the last two hours strategizing on how best to thwart annoying attempts at matchmaking/speeding up marriage and babies by our respective parents. Surprised by cross-cultural similarities in Asian parents across the spectrum. Also vindicated that I was not the only one who started out a virgin at uni. I don't know how we got to sharing something so personal, but Suresh is very easy to talk to. And maybe the drinking helped a little.

Anyway, speaking of sexual inexperience, I wonder how things would be in the sack with Orson; nowadays, the younger generation are so blasé about sex. They've seen all the mind-boggling stuff with one click that you had to dig through dodgy bookstores to get an idea of (not speaking from personal experience, of course). They know how a threesome works before they've even gotten to first base with another person. For young people these days, porn is not something to be consumed in a dark corner, with shame and peanut butter and jelly sandwiches (again, not speaking from personal experience).

Hmm. I wonder what kind of dodgy stuff Orson expects me to do. Maybe it'll involve food. Mmm. Food.

11:25 p.m. This is what Val texted to remind me of our plans:

> **Tmw be at Swissotel pickup point by 7pm for Sexy Book Club and dress NICE or else.**

Really knows how to sell a fun date, that one.

12

Sunday 6 March

2:07 a.m. Back from Valerie's shindig with both my kidneys and my soul intact, so that's a relief.

At 7:00 p.m. sharp, Valerie rolled up to Swissotel in Bugis. My jaw dropped when she popped out of a black Mercedes-Benz S-Class, dressed in a black one-shoulder dress and making me look completely dowdy in comparison in my gray slacks, cap-sleeved cream silk blouse, and safe, gold ballerina flats.

"Sweeeeetheart!" she said, tottering out in silver heels tall enough to make a supermodel out of a gnome and holding two glasses of bubbly. Everyone was staring at her. I scrambled into the back of the car, dying to get away. "Why are you dressed so fancy?" I asked, flabbergasted.

"DeeDee, my friend the ex-actress, told me to dress nice!"

I shut the door as Valerie got in on the other side. "And you went straight for cocktail attire? What if she meant business casual?"

"When DeeDee says 'nice,' she means 'fabulous.' These people don't work! We're talking thin air, high altitude here, not your *working poor*!"

"Oh, excuse me," I said sarcastically. "I'll just go back to my corporate hovel with the gold-plated taps and the Molton Brown toiletries, and shit while overlooking the sea."

Valerie patted my arm as though I were a troll with coal for brains. "Hush. The point is, you have to work. Ergo, poor."

Valerie had no nuance. How she ended up eking out a comfortable living as a curator at one of the poshest, most respected art galleries in town, I had no idea.

"Well, if I'm poor, so are you," I shot back.

"I'm not poor!" Valerie said in a deeply offended tone. She had been briefly married to the heir of a very wealthy Indo-Chinese family who, as it turned out, was gay. The dude was so deep in the denial closet that he was all the way in Narnia. Valerie literally had to catch him in the act of hoovering chauffeur dick for him to admit that, maybe, just maybe, he was gay. Heartbroken but not stupid, Valerie whipped out her phone and took as many photos of her husband and her naked chauffeur as she could before storming out of their marital home, intending to use them to secure a great divorce settlement. Not that her quick action made a big difference to her fortunes in the end: unfortunately, thanks to an iron-clad prenup, she divorced the man with little more to show (by billionaire divorce standards, that is) than a large River Valley penthouse and eighteen thousand dollars of spending money a month. Add that to the fact that she had had very little sex for the almost nine years that she was married, I thought she had done very badly for herself.

"It's all a matter of perspective," Valerie was saying. "I don't need to work for a living if I don't want to. I *like* my job."

We decided that we would stop arguing in favor of drinking the champagne, a delectable 2002 Pol Roger rosé, which was fizzing dangerously flat. Priorities and all.

We each downed two glasses in quick succession, which was unusual for Valerie.

I soon found out why. "You know, I was joking about the devil-worship the last time we spoke, of course, but to be honest, given DeeDee's swinger reputation, anything is possible tonight," Valerie said as we wove our way through rush-hour traffic. "We could find ourselves in an *Eyes Wide Shut* situation later."

"That's exactly what I'm worried about," I confided. "If this turns out to be some kinky swingers event, I'm going home. I have on underwear so old that it can shrink an erection, and I'd rather nobody saw it tonight."

"And the closest I've ever gotten to any group action was watching a National Geographic special on snakes!"

"What have we gotten ourselves into?" I said wildly. "We should turn around and go back now."

"You can't," the Grab driver cut in.

"And why not?" Valerie demanded.

"Well, you have to reenter your destination into the app, plus I'm not turning around until I've seen this crazy hot party house. And also, we've arrived."

So we had.

After we had passed through security, we were deposited in front of an imposing oak, ushered into a reception room by a maid in an actual uniform, and given a flute of champagne each. Then DeeDee Halim, former beauty queen, model, ex-actress, and alleged orgy buddy of a prince, greeted us herself at the door in a jeweled kaftan in flamingo pink and gold and an armful of gold Cartier Love and Frey Wille bangles, interspersed with bright turquoise bead bracelets. It was a breathtaking vision. She was still beautiful, with full, sensuous features, a shock of graying hair swept into a bun, and large, limpid eyes the color of sand.

"Darling," she said, air-kissing Valerie. "Don't you look *adorable*." Even her voice was velvety.

"Don't *you*!" Valerie cooed, not seeming to mind smashing her carefully honed, Janet Jackson–esque waxen cheekbones against DeeDee's real ones.

DeeDee turned the full blare of those doe-like eyes to me and we exchanged air kisses. "And you must be Andrea, Valerie's good friend."

"I sure am," I said in an unnatural high voice. I had to fight back the impulse to say "ma'am" like a school child.

"Pleased to meet you," DeeDee said. "Follow me." She sashayed away.

It was hard not to gawk as she led us past room after well-appointed room to the living hall. We were like Alice entering Wonderland—an extremely tastefully executed, designer Wonderland. You know those achingly beautiful houses you find in *Architectural Digest*, *Home & Design*, or Pinterest? Those gorgeous homes that have custom everything and never had an Ikea anything? This was that house. Hardwood floors, tasteful lighting, a brutalist chandelier that threw amber-gold light everywhere. Walls done in washes of ecru and pearl, hung with quiet art; a dining room with porcelain vases, brass sculptures, and a crystal chandelier almost as long as a table.

The living hall was the most colorful room in the house so far, thanks to the owner's interesting collection of brightly colored, eclectic art: a trio of Mirós, what was maybe an Alphonse Mucha, framed Persian miniatures in dazzling detail, beautiful collages from an artist that neither of us knew, and a large, show-stopping centerpiece by an artist called Ashley Bickerton that made Valerie gasp. Bouquets of burgundy tulips and lilies in crystal vases dotted the room.

I looked around, intimidated, as I understood what Valerie had been trying to tell me: I was underdressed. A dozen or so beautiful people in cocktail-appropriate attire were fanned out around the room, chatting gaily as two waiters in linen pants and white shirts circulated with flutes of champagne and platters of hors d'oeuvres. In one corner of the room was a large island of food: iced trays of oysters, mini quiches, an assortment of mini toasts, two different salads, bowls of olives, gorgeous platters of macarons and chocolate truffles, next to a bar where a smiling chef stood behind the counter, slicing sashimi that no one seemed to be asking for.

I tried to act nonchalant. Beside me Valerie's eyes were glazed with desire and wonder, and she was possibly low-grade hyperventilating. "OMG, that's Wilson Lam!" she whispered excitedly. I had no idea who she was talking about, but before I could reply she had dashed off, Road Runner–style, to a man in a white suit with silver hair and more work done on his face than Valerie's. A white suit! I shook my head, amused. But then I saw a good-looking man in his forties in a brocade *bleu de france* suit with a Hermès orange bow tie and matching pocket square walk in with a poodle on a monogrammed leash, followed by a woman in ripped acid-green jeans, a black long-sleeved top with large paillettes sewn into the collar and carrying a neon yellow patent leather bag, and that took all the wind from my sails. Maybe I was the one who was out of place, not them.

For a few minutes I stood there alone, sipping on champagne, unsure of what to do. All the guests were engaged in intimate conversations with unwelcoming body language. Twice or thrice, with different groups, I tried to insert myself into a conversation and was politely but so cleanly rebuffed that I gave up and wandered over to gorge on oysters. But when I saw that I was the only person eating I felt uncomfortable and stopped. I looked down at the table where nine empty oyster shells, mine, lay on the bone white porcelain bowl and I felt exposed by my peasant gluttony.

The living room's glass sliding doors were open. I slipped out onto a sloping lawn with a long, lit oblong pool and an unobstructed view of the city. I spied a hillside deck on the edge of the manicured lawn and made my way toward it, eager to take in the magnificent view of the city with its blinking neon eyes. As I strolled I took in the large rain trees bordering the lawn, old, majestic, framing the starless night sky with their stark black boughs. Someone had strung fairy lights in the trees to make up for the missing stars; they needn't have bothered. There were fireflies in the bushes and darting through the frangipani-scented night air.

I stepped gingerly onto the timber deck, nervous to be this close to the edge of a hill. But the view was worth it. Here was Singapore's CBD, skyscrapers slashed with light. Standing there on the deck I could hear the rustle of bird wings and the song of crickets. Crickets!

Tears sprang, unbidden, to my beady, plebeian eyes. That so much beauty was possible in the heart of this stone-and-concrete city, that it should be owned by one person, while I paid almost half my salary and almost all my waking hours for not even a hundredth of this space—it hurt. How could this be what my life had become about?

"Is this spot taken?" someone said in the darkness behind me.

Startled, I whirled around. Behind me was one of the waiters, leaning against the deck railing in a creased white linen shirt and an equally rumpled pair of tan linen khakis. He was older, in his late forties or early fifties, and had a kind face with intense eyes. "Not at all," I said. "There's enough deck space for a harem of dancing hippos."

He chuckled. "Cute imagery." He gestured at the view. "Isn't this something special? I mean, the Singapore skyline is nowhere near as grand as Hong Kong's and Shanghai's, but I prefer it. It's more . . . approachable, if that makes sense."

"Hmmm," I managed, noncommittal. I totally got what he meant.

I could feel him studying my profile. "You don't sound very enthused. Are you not enjoying yourself?"

"It's just . . . so . . . much, you know? These people." I pointed at the beautifully rich cluster, visible through the glass doors. "This place. It's a dream. I feel like I've just walked into a snow globe of magic rich-people glitter. It's just a little too fabulous. But what do I know, I'm just a poor everyman." I laughed a little self-consciously—what must this older man think of poor li'l entitled me moaning about life in my relatively pricey clothes and champagne and $350 cologne. I leaned toward him and adopted a conspiratorial tone. "Anyway, between you and me, I can't figure out this evening. I mean, I know it's supposed to be a book club, but come on, we all know it's really just an excuse for a bunch of super rich, obnoxious people to fellate each other's egos, am I right?"

His eyes twinkled at me. "I've heard it said that 'There are only two things wrong with money: too much or too little.' I suppose you think these people have too much."

"Yes. And I know where that quote's from, that's by Charles Bukowski." I was full of admiration; he'd quoted it word for word. "Are you into poetry as well?"

"A little. I like the greats: Li Bai, Bai Juyi, Li Shangyin. Do you read Chinese poetry?"

I quoted a Meng Haoran poem in response.*

"Beautiful." He was studying me; I blushed. "I think an appreciation of poetry is a good foundation for any relationship. If you're bored, you can just hang out with me. I promise I won't talk about my fleet of Lambos or my watch collection. We can just talk about you." He offered his right hand. "I'm Eric." He had an unusual accent, unplaceable, with a raspy smoker's voice.

"I'm sorry, where are my manners? I'm Andrea." I extended my hand to shake his and he pressed it against his lips before releasing it gently. It was an unaffected, graceful gesture. It was then I realized that he wasn't a waiter—he was one of the guests. Judging by his wrinkled clothing and his Apple Watch, this was a fellow interloper, one of the working poor, perhaps a friend of a richer friend.

We chatted comfortably for a bit until we were summoned by

---

* If you must know, it was the Tang poem "Spring Dawn":
春眠不覺曉，
處處聞啼鳥。
夜來風雨聲，
花落知多少。
In spring sleep, dawn arrives unnoticed.
Suddenly, all around, I hear birds in song.
A loud night. Wind and rain came, tearing
blossoms down. Who knows few or many?
(David Hinton's translation)

a little dinner bell. I shook my head at Eric and made a face, which he chuckled at.

"The overlords await," I said wryly.

"Come, fellow serf," he said, taking my arm. "Let's go eat some more *atas*★ mollusks."

"A man after my own stomach," I said, ecstatic. "What's the point of having primo seafood if everyone is on some kind of diet? And those desserts!"

"I'll ask Hiro to pack all the cupcakes and macarons to go. Most of the people in there are gluten intolerant anyway."

I nodded, half-listening, my eyes on the island of food, especially the glistening ice tray of oysters. I was ready for action, but it was not to be. DeeDee was motioning for the group to be seated. Reluctantly, I strode past the beckoning food and took my seat with the rest of them on the large leather couches. Eric and I sat ourselves next to Valerie and a tall, emaciated blond woman in a silvery dress. There was an expectant buzz as copies of *A Little Life* were fished out of bags. I appeared to be the only one with a Kindle, which was surprising. I didn't care. I turned the Kindle on and pulled out a two-pager cheat sheet of the book. Now, Valerie had told me to read the book, which obviously I hadn't, but I had read the summary and made clever shorthand notes for each character; I had even taken down some choice quotes in case things got seriously granular. I knew how anal retentive the ultra-rich could be from dealing with them at work. When you're not working, you probably have time to memorize quotes.

DeeDee began. "Welcome once again to the Baca Buku club. I believe we have two new guests tonight"—she smiled in Valerie's and my direction—"so can everyone introduce themselves to the

---

★ Singlish for "posh" or "sophisticated," or, when applied to a person, "arrogant"; it's derived from the Malay word "up."

room with your first name and a few words about yourself before we start the discussions?"

One by one, we complied. The introductions were pretty sober; no one made any jokey quips (the group knew each other too well, I supposed), so I was obliged to swallow mine about being an alcoholic desk-bound paper pusher. Instead I said, "Andrea, lawyer and oyster fan," to the mirth of Eric, who followed with the simple, "Eric, entrepreneur."

"I hope you've all read Hanya Yanagihara's new tome, *A Little Life*, the book we will be discussing tonight. It's such a gem and Michiko darling says—"

"Michiko who?" I whispered to Eric.

"Kakutani, the literary critic," Eric whispered back. "You know, of the *New York Times*."

"Ooh, are they friends?" I was dead impressed.

Eric smirked. "I think they met once at some New York soirée, and now she follows Miss Kakutani on Twitter."

I rolled my eyes.

"Rashidah's a good woman who's unfortunately stricken with low self-esteem," he said. It took me half a beat to realize he was talking about DeeDee.

DeeDee was prattling on. "But of course, I can't go further without acknowledging the hospitality of our host, who not only allows me to throw such book appreciation parties and whatever fanciful fete my little heart desires, but is also generous enough to let me stay at his sumptuous summer residence for the months in which I must serve out my time as tax resident on this island"—a twitter of mirth from the audience, many of whom were no doubt doing the same—"until I return to New York, where, of course, the action is, as we all know."

"Wow, what a sweet arrangement! I'll bet she's banging the brains out of that old fart," I whispered.

"She does seem like the type to take advantage of a hapless

man," Eric agreed, grinning. "Although I'm curious to know what makes you automatically assume that he is older, and not younger, than DeeDee, and more pertinently, what makes you think she's his type at all?"

"—but enough moaning about the paltry art scene here. I've hardly been suffering in this gorgeous place in the company of such gracious folk, and none more gracious than my host and my old friend, the generous, inimitable, the one and only—Mister Eric Deng!"

I could feel the blood draining from my face as I swiveled once more to look at Eric, who was smiling down at me now as he stood and waved to acknowledge the cheering audience. As the applause died down he sat back down and whispered, "We should definitely have lunch together if I'm not too old for your tastes, what say you, Andrea?"

11:20 a.m. A barrage of texts from Valerie, which helpfully, in lurid detail, chronicled everything that had transpired last night.

Eric Deng! she marveled.

Eric Deng, Indonesian luxe hotelier and real estate tycoon. You snagged yourself a *tycoon*

The way she described it, we were on our way to buying a ranch together and making a flock of little Erics and Andreas, instead of staying back exchanging maybe two hours of casual chitchat after discussing the finer points of *A Little Life* while I vacuumed the rest of the Fine de Claire oysters into my mouth, which I reasoned would have died for naught if left to expire, uneaten and unappreciated, in some dump. We'd done a little drinking (Valerie and I also stayed to help finish the champagne with DeeDee and Ralph Kang, one of Eric's friends, while Eric drank water—he was cutting down his alcohol intake on orders from his physician, on account of Eric's gout), and a little flirting. Ralph is gaga for Valerie, although she's doing her best to ignore it. She met him while I was hanging out in the garden with Eric, who was leaving the next day to spend some time in Vietnam for the launch of his newest hotel. There was this slightly awkward moment when we were saying our goodbyes and Eric had leaned over to air-kiss me (I think), but I was so startled that I jumped three feet back into a wall, which of course killed any hint of sexual tension. We ended up giving each other handshakes. Handshakes are what you give accountants and aunts you don't like very much—you know, the ones that give you five-dollar *ang paos* during Chinese New Year and ask you how long you intend to be alone and/or barren, before driving off at the end of the night in their latest Mercedes.

Valerie also provided me with a one-liner bio for Ralph Kang, which wasn't much (somehow, I don't think he had always been named "Ralph Kang"). He was a cousin of her original target, the white suit she had mistaken for Wilson Lam, a famous Hong Kong actor. Apparently, Ralph was some hotshot tech multimillionaire in his mid-fifties, but Valerie is not impressed by money. She's way more superficial than that: she is impressed by good looks and class.

Yet somehow Ralph had cornered her into agreeing to have dinner once he got back from San Francisco, where he's got a couple of start-ups he's mentoring.

"Please come out with us the next time he's back in town," she pleaded. "I don't want to say no to Ralph and I don't want to hang out alone with him. I need a wing person and I can't ask Lin— I mean, you and I had a blast together, didn't we, and I introduced you to Eric and now you're going to see him again, aren't you? By the way, you owe me one hundred and fifteen bucks for your half of the two Grab rides, and what did you think about that house?"

"Wha—?" I said, lost in the slipstream. Then, "One hundred and fifteen?" in shock.

"Yes, because of surge pricing and premium charges. Now stop trying to change the subject," Valerie said, blithely changing the subject. She grabbed my wrist. "And just tell me if you would be up for having dinner together. Eric is Ralph's friend and investor, isn't that a lovely coincidence? Say you'll do it," she rasped, digging her manicured fingernails into my wrist.

I said I would. This way I would have a plan B to meet Eric again, since I realized once Val and I left that he'd never actually gotten my number after asking me out in front of everyone. He struck me as a man of his word; still, it was always good to have a backup plan, just in case.

2:35 p.m. Have spent a pleasant lunch hour looking up, OK, stalking, Eric Deng. There is very little information about him online, and almost zero social media footprint. His LinkedIn profile has a decent headshot from some annual report, basically says he's an "investor," and shows that he has less than fifty connections. The lack of freely available information, even if it's curated to death like the best of whatever is available online these days about someone, is very worrying. How will I know what type of music he enjoys, if he thinks Pollock is art (yuck), if he is a cappuccino or flat white or espresso kind of guy? What are his political views? His religious views? And, more important, is his mother still alive?

I guess I'll never know.

2:38 p.m. Of course, I could ask him. But where's the fun in that.

Wednesday 9 March

7:45 a.m. Got a text from Orson asking me out to dinner tomorrow. Am tempted to say yes, even though I know he's too young for me.

8:15 a.m. Dilemma. Called Linda for advice. She got mad and told me to save myself for the wonderful age-appropriate men she'd vetted from the Tinder slush pile that she'd been painstakingly chatting to for the past three weeks, or else. Honestly, Diary, she's starting to sound a lot like my mom (but maybe I'll wait till I have access to my Facebook and Tinder accounts first before I tell her that).

9:25 a.m. Texted Orson and agreed to a dinner date, just not tomorrow as I have to set aside sufficient time to exercise feverishly over the next few days in preparation for potential shag. Have instead proposed dinner next Thursday.

Orson agreed to the date and suggested we meet at some swish new cocktail-and-tapas bar that has just opened at the revamped National Gallery.

Decided not to tell Linda about the date in case she talks me out of it.

8:45 p.m. Met Linda for dinner at Lau Pa Sat for Tinder handover. It'd been another long day at work, but I did not succumb to the usual temptation to eat a large portion of greasy *char kway teow*; instead I downgraded to a small serving of *char kway teow*, shared with an unusually focused, silent Linda, who was texting feverishly with what I assumed were my Tinder matches.

"Can I ask you something?" she said, after she came up for air. Without waiting for a reply, she continued. "Would you date a married man if he was separated from his wife?"

"Err . . . ," I said, jolted out of my own reverie by her question. "I don't know. I think I would need more details."

"Let's say they are in the midst of a divorce."

"Always a convenient lie to fall back on," I sneered. "Beloved by cheating scum all over the world."

"They live apart."

"So? That doesn't mean anything. Lots of husbands live apart from their wives temporarily, especially if they're posted abroad."

"They are both Singaporean, and they've been living apart for a year," she said. "Anyway, whatever. It's not important."

I made a halfhearted attempt at prying more information out of her but got nothing. Not that I was terribly interested, to be honest. I wanted to daydream about Orson.

She sighed. "Anyway, just as I promised, I've distilled your options down to the four worthiest candidates. Your log-in details for your Facebook and Tinder profiles are posted on our private chat. Enjoy!"

I opened WhatsApp and saw that she had set both passwords as *Iwannawang*.

10:35 p.m. Settled down on my couch with a glass of wine and launched Tinder. Looked at my four matches and read the chat histories. Linda mimicked me so well I was a little worried. Am I that predictable?

Some of the opening gambits from the four men were quite novel. The first match asked if a beer and a whisky drinker could ever truly mix and that he was "hop-ping" to find out. Another couldn't believe that I checked so many boxes on his perfect mate list so he was hoping to take me out and see if I were a genetically modified being from the future sent back in time from his desperate mother in an effort to lure him away from his work as a senior investment banker (show-off, but quirky). Then there was the opener from the third, which went, "I'm sick of being a sexy, intelligent third wheel. Help me end this nightmare now!" The fourth one said I seemed like someone that even a hardened serial killer would spare for the sake of humanity, and he was looking forward to sparing my life in person (I liked this one best). They all had nice, witty, or cute profiles, were decent-looking and age-appropriate, and responded well to Linda's version of my oddball humor, which boded well for our dates if they happened at all. There was potential here. It made me wonder if I really was missing out. I'll just take this app for a trial run, see if there are other contenders that Linda might have missed.

11:55 a.m. Oh, hey, Filipino Jason's on Tinder. Maybe he's straight? Or looking for a platonic friendship? Or beard-hunting? His family is pretty Catholic. I'll swipe right just for fun.

12:05 a.m. Ha, we matched. Sent him an eggplant emoji as a joke. Wrote:

> Isn't it way past your bedtime?

12:17 a.m. He wrote:

> I do my best paralegal work at night *stalk stalk*

Jason had a sense of humor. Who knew.

Maybe I'll swipe right on a few other profiles, just to see what happens.

12:35 a.m. Yikes. So many dick pics. So many *unimpressive* dick pics.

12:40 a.m. Complained about Twitter wasteland to Suresh, the only person I knew who would be awake at this hour, because work. Somehow, since our last after-work drink, we'd become friendly, if not friends.

He replied:

> It's 12:40 a.m.—what were you expecting? And call me old-fashioned, but I'd prefer a good setup by friends or a work romance to online dating.

Well, he can talk; he's got someone waiting for him at home, even if it's across the globe!

12:45 a.m. Interesting that he mentioned work romance. I would never go there, but that's because I have principles. And common sense.

Thursday 10 March

8:02 a.m. Woke up with a start and saw what time it was. Farrrrrrrrrrrrrk!

8:05 a.m. Must have slept through alarm because was up so late scrolling through dick pics and telling off sick senders of dick pics!!!

8:45 a.m. So I realize that I might have a *slight* problem with impulse control. Especially with technology.

9:10 a.m. Arrived at work really late and panicky, as I have to walk past Mong's office to get to mine, before I realized that Mong was still incapacitated by dengue. Rejoice!

9:13 a.m. I mean, not rejoicing because he's deathly ill, but you know.

9:45 a.m. Mong was in our, I mean, *my* office, chatting with Suresh, when I burst in. I gasped when I saw him, and my mind went blank. Out of the corner of my eye I saw Suresh smile beatifically. Urgh, great, Suresh was winning in front of the boss.

Mong gave me a look of disappointment. "You're late," he said, wheezing.

"I, ah, you see, my phone—"

"How was your client meeting?" Suresh piped up.

"Very, um, full of . . . potential," I managed to say, confused, before I realized he was trying to help me out.

Mong's eyes focused on me, laser-sharp. "With?" he asked suspiciously. He always wanted details of meetings.

I straightened up and mentally composed myself. A flash of inspiration struck. "I've, ah, developed a lead with, ah, the Dulit Group. With Eric Deng."

Mong's eyes flew open, which was always startling since they were shot through with broken capillaries, now more so than usual. "That's great news, Andrea," he said warmly.

"Er, are you still supposed to be at home resting? After dengue?" I said, desperate to change the subject.

"I missed the office."

Of course.

He ambled off with difficulty and I breathed a sigh of relief. Grudgingly I thanked Suresh for helping me out.

He grinned and said, somewhat playfully, "Did I really, though? Or did I allow you to entrap yourself in a lie you now have to extricate yourself from?"

My God, he was an evil genius!

Saturday 12 March

11:30 a.m. Success! Woke up today completely fine, not hungover at all. A miracle, considering all that had happened yesterday.

Went out for the usual post-work Friday shenanigans with the usual crew (plus two junior colleagues of mine, both female and married) to a swish whiskey bar. We were supposed to meet at 8:00 p.m., but somehow everyone except Linda was there by 7:00 p.m., even me. (Suresh and I now have an unspoken Office

Face-Time Battle truce on Fridays, where we both leave at about the same time from work; while I usually have no idea what he does after work, today I got a glimpse: I overheard someone on speaker asking him to make up the numbers for something called Kah-Tan, which is probably code for "swingers' party where people dress as MMA fighters.")

When Linda continued to be a no-show at 9:30 p.m., Jason started to get concerned since Ben had told us on group chat that he was buying (celebrating his bonus, a real whopper) and money was "no object" and Linda, who's still Chinese enough at heart, would usually take advantage of such an offer (not that she isn't generous when it comes to her own cash; she's cool like that).

"She's not replying to my texts, and I know she can't be working. Linda would never prioritize work over drinks, plus she's known as the queen of delegation at her law firm. And her WhatsApp time stamp says that she's not looked at her phone since seven-oh-eight. That's unusual."

I shrugged. "She's an adult."

Oh, yeah, the reason I was restraining myself drinks-wise—at 9:00 p.m. or so I was meeting up with one of the Tinder matches, Alex the beer pun guy (he had the most attractive profile pic), at the whiskey bar for a quick drink. Meeting IRL was fun and he got along well with Val, Jason, and Ben, but my heart wasn't really in it and I didn't feel a strong physical pull toward him, so much so that when he proposed a second date I immediately rejected him, after which he showed his true colors: he switched targets and started hitting on one of my colleagues, the sole teetotaler of the group, who's in her early thirties and the mother of twins. I was surprised when I saw them leave the bar together around 1:00 a.m., his hand unmistakably on her ass and her lips fastened to his. I thought she was happily married and a staunch Muslim—at least that's what her Facebook profile told me.

She did however text me this morning and told me not to let slip to anyone that Alex had "given her a lift home, that was all."

Right. I suppose he was also just giving her CPR.

After Alex had left, I hung around with Jason to keep an eye on Ben, who was past wasted, since Val was AWOL (she probably went home early without our noticing; she and Jason are hardly ever drunk—they "don't believe in binge-drinking," whatever that means); I myself was too disillusioned by what I had witnessed tonight to drink. So much for Tinder romances—I'm glad I have Orson to look forward to!

15

Thursday 17 March

8:30 a.m. D-day! Went to work today wearing my date outfit, since I probably wouldn't have enough time to dash home for an outfit change. After hours of agonizing, I settled on a bespoke three-quarter-sleeved kelly green DVF-style wrap dress in a flattering silk jersey fabric, with a skirt short enough to reveal my kneecaps, which were still pretty despite being the approximate hue of moonlit mole rats. I completed my look with a black Chanel Boy Bag and sexy black pair of Erdem kitten heels.

"Wow, you look so pretty," Kai exclaimed when she saw me. I wish she hadn't sounded quite so surprised, but I guess when you're in your mid-twenties and a Pilates fanatic, the bar is set pretty high.

"Thanks," I said, blushing a little as a few other colleagues crowded around and chimed in with their own compliments (except a skulking Genevieve). "I have this, erm, networking thing later."

"You have such a nice figure; you should show it off more often," Kai said, totally unaware that my hourglass figure was the result of squeezing myself into Spanx underwear that was, as she was speaking, constricting the blood supply to my limbs and brain. She winked. "We single women should look great all the time, in case Mr. Right is lurking around the corner."

I shuddered internally. What a terrifying reality to contemplate: to have to dress like this every day, when my default work outfit, sensible light wool trousers with long-sleeved silk tops, allowed a woman in her thirties to comfortably scarf down a cream cheese bagel and two cupcakes for lunch, after which she could discreetly undo the fastening of said trousers so that the belly, thus satiated, could spread out in post-digestion bliss.

The thing about dressing for a date when you're almost in your mid-thirties and not a yoga or fitness instructor is that you are no longer primping but literally remodeling. Gone are the days when you could throw on a cute sleeveless dress, spritz on some cologne, and waltz your way out of the house, sauntering under whatever fluorescent light you come across instead of shrinking back with the hiss of a vampire meeting a beam of UV light. Instead, time is spent massaging bolts of cellulite cloth called your skin, tweezing hairs that have suddenly taken root in odd spots on your face while slathering on the contents of jars of whatever low-grade toxin is now fashionable to battle the onset of laugh lines. Then you agonizingly pour yourself into a modern-day corset just to be able to wear that vaguely figure-skimming dress, hoping to the Good Lord above that your date doesn't suggest dessert.

I hope I've made it clear that I'm totally looking forward to my date, by the way.

5:00 p.m. Spent the day trying to focus on work but failed miserably. Hopped on one fantasy train after another. Recalled that one of the local celebrity TV news anchors, who like me was in her mid-thirties, was also dating a much younger man, but couldn't for the life of me remember his name. Will just google her now.

5:05 p.m. Yikes. They've broken up. Anyway, I should take this one step at a time and not start thinking of wedding hashtags. That is lame, even though #AndySonWeds is totally cool or sick or whatever slang word is used these days to denote trendiness.

6:05 p.m. I got up to go. Waved goodbye at a bemused Suresh, with whom I am still locked in a spiraling Office Face-Time Battle.

"Good luck," Kai said slyly, after I had given her my out-of-office instructions should anyone call, which was not unlikely—clients are like Dementors: as soon as they sense a surge of youthful optimism when you should be low on morale and slaving over their files as you bemoan your life choices, they come a-calling and emailing, the soul suckers.

I exited the building, took a cab to the National Gallery, and began walking with a spring in my step toward the cocktail bar. I had timed it perfectly: the sun was dipping toward the horizon and the light was warm and flattering, perfect for an al fresco dining date. Orson was already there when I arrived, dressed in tailored slacks and a crisp white shirt with an orange Hermès tie showcasing a pattern of tilted kayaks. He greeted me by pressing his right cheek against mine.

"You look so lovely," he murmured as we sat down. "I hope you don't mind, but I ordered champagne and a dozen oysters to start."

By champagne he meant a bottle of Dom Pérignon vintage rosé. I sipped the bubbly, opened the menu that the waiter handed me, and nearly passed out at the price of the champagne he had ordered—it cost what I'd imagine a black-market liver would fetch in America.

Seriously, where was this kid getting his money from?

We proceeded to have a tapas degustation menu with wine pairing. The conversation flowed easily, especially as I got drunker by the hour.

Dinner ended around 11:00 p.m. Orson insisted on paying for us both, *in cash*. As in he peeled out a wad of cash from his wallet like a magician pulling flowers from a hat. I saw the bill and realized, with some shock, that it was almost a third of my monthly mortgage installment, which meant that Orson had to have family wealth or other sources of income aside from his job; but best not to look a gift horse in the mouth right then, especially if you wanted to kiss that mouth later.

And then we were just a couple of kids on the sidewalk making out in the full glare of disapproving, sex-starved Singaporeans.

"Where we going next?" he asked, his tongue in my ear.

"My place? Or yours?" I said, my tongue in his.

"I vote in favor of your place. What's your address?"

Soon things were getting hot and heavy in the Grab. The driver was mercifully oblivious to the groping or was more focused on getting a five-star rating at the end of the ride; whatever the motivation, he kept his eyes on the road despite the kissing noises.

And then we got to my apartment in Cairnhill locked in a messy, hot embrace. I opened the door and led him in. In the silence my heart was thudding so hard that I was almost afraid it would wake the neighbors. "Nice place," was all Orson had time to say before I led him into my room. And then—murder on the dance floor! Just kidding. I'm such a dork.

4:00 a.m. Orson is gone. I think he tried to leave without waking me up, but I am a light sleeper and the merest twitch in my bedsprings shot me out of dreamland like a cannon. He smiled sheepishly, his clothes in his hands and looking remarkably illegal with his tousled Harry Styles hair and white boxer briefs. "Sorry, I didn't mean to wake you. You look so peaceful."

I grinned wickedly. "I think you had a lot to do with that. So why don't you stay the night? I'll even risk being late just for you . . ." I walked my fingers up his right thigh.

"Oh, um, that's really not necessary," he said, looking embarrassed. "Um, you know, I snore, and uh, I have this presentation tomorrow and everything I need is back home."

"Sure, go," I said, a little disappointed. "We all have to do what we have to do, right?"

"Right," he said. He bent down and gave me an awkward kiss on the forehead. "Listen, I'll call you, OK? We'll catch up soon. I'll text you later."

"All right," I said languidly. As soon as I heard the door shut and lock automatically behind Orson, I closed my eyes and slid blissfully back into a champagne-tinted, endorphin-laced dream. Life was beautiful. And I totally crushed Sponk.

Wait till I tell Linda.

16

Friday 18 March

7:20 a.m. Woke up with a goofy grin on my face. Don't remember the last time I had sex B.O. (Before Orson, clearly). Feels like this is the beginning of a magnificent chapter of life, one in which the cure for cancer will be found and democratized, politicians will work for the people, looted antiquities will be returned to their homelands, etc.

8:15 a.m. Have decided that I won't tell Linda or Melissa or anyone else I know above the age of twenty-six about my shag session, much less date, with Orson. They would never understand.

8:30 a.m. Greeted everyone I saw in the office with a big, loved-up smile, which of course made no difference since most of my fellow lawyers are dead inside or too busy to notice a change, but my walk of triumph did not go unnoticed by Kai, who gave me an actual thumbs-up when she saw me.

Am happy for you that the "networking" session went super well *wink emoji*, she messaged me a few minutes later.

I smiled fondly at my screen. Kai was a dear. I called her and we had a giggly five-minute call where I told her the redacted, sanitized story. I didn't care that Suresh was in the room; I had to tell someone about my date.

Suresh was moody after that call. Instead of congratulating me, he seemed decidedly displeased. "I don't even need to hear all the details to know you've already made a mistake with that boy," he said in this condescending tone. He'd obviously been eavesdropping on my coded conversations with Kai.

"What's it to you?" I said defensively.

His expression was unreadable. "I'm just looking out for you, that's all."

"Right." I raised an eyebrow. "I think maybe it's inappropriate for you to comment on my private affairs. Time to establish some boundaries."

He got up and left the room abruptly.

Men! You share an office with them and they think they have a right to stick their nose in your business.

8:50 p.m. Had dinner with Suresh at an expensive sushi bar in Fullerton Hotel (his treat); he'd apologized earlier in the afternoon and wanted to make it up to me. He was rather quiet. Over California rolls, sashimi, and a bottle of sake, he mentioned casually that things with Anousha were going south over the proposed move to Singapore. "She's just been offered a promotion and thinks it's a bad time to move."

He hasn't seen Anousha in over two months. Hmmm.

9:45 p.m. No text from Orson still. Hmm.

11:05 p.m. Was flicking through Tinder profiles to pass time (Candy Crush what?) and came across one that was particularly interesting for all the wrong reasons: Jonathan Beh, Genevieve's husband, *was on Tinder!* #shockhorrorgasp

Very cunningly he was using only side profile shots of himself (taken at least a decade ago), sporting large designer sunnies on those where he faced the cam shirtless, with artistic filters thrown in for good measure. I had only seen Jonathan twice, but I knew it had to be him. What gave him away was the last picture he took where he was draped casually across the hood of a massive sports car. I'd recognize this car anywhere, not least because: (a) it was a customized yellow Lamborghini with black racing stripes that Genevieve had driven to the office quite a few times, and (b) it had vanity plates reading "BIGGBEHH" that he'd stupidly forgotten to blank out.

His bio claimed that he was a carefree dreamer and philanthropist, instead of the adulterer he aspired to be. "I'll treat you like a princess . . . because you deserve it, and I can certainly afford it," boasted his profile. "Ladies always tell me that my heart isn't the biggest thing about me *wink emoji*—I meant my wallet, of course!"

I threw up in my mouth a little before taking a screenshot of this gift from God and keeping it in my Google Drive. Just in case.

11:45 p.m. No text from Orson yet. Very strange. For the last week or so we've been communicating every day.

11:48 p.m. I should chill. It's only been a day.

Saturday 19 March

5:35 p.m. Hmm. Nothing. Maybe he's traveling and doesn't have good cell phone coverage.

8:20 p.m. There's still Wi-Fi though. He should have texted or called by now.

10:40 p.m. I have got to stop checking my texts.

Sunday 20 March

11:55 p.m. OK, something is definitely up.

17

Monday 21 March

3:10 a.m. Woke up from a nightmare where I had to pee during a biology exam, but couldn't find a washroom anywhere. Tried to fall asleep but a vague, lingering unease from the nightmare kept me awake (that, and the intermittent glancing at the smartphone screen checking for a weather update and you know, Orson's texts, but not in an obsessive way, of course).

3:25 a.m. Decided to watch an episode of *Orange Is the New Black*.

3:50 a.m. Will have a wee tipple of wine.

5:00 a.m. No text from Orson. It's fine. Technically it's only been seventy-five hours or so since he left. Is it normal that I've needed to pee twice in the last hour?

7:13 a.m. Decided to stop drinking wine.

7:25 a.m. Shit, realized midway during the fifth episode of *Orange Is the New Black* that I have to be at work in thirty-five minutes. Shit!

8:25 a.m. Slunk into the office and hoped no one would notice me, but of course, Genevieve called me out in front of everyone as soon as she saw me. Bitch!

9:45 a.m. My bladder and kidneys are working a little *too* efficiently today. Hmm. But need coffee. Nearly fell asleep while peeing.

12:05 p.m. No text from Orson, still. Decided to send him a flirty little text, since it's been more than eighty hours and I won't seem desperate, saying:

> What's up, stranger? Did you lose your phone on the way home or get hit by a car? *angel emoji*

12:30 p.m. Texted Orson again:

> Haha I'm just kidding. I hope you're fine, though. Miss you, LOL.

As soon as I sent it I regretted it. Only desperate or unfunny people use LOL in their texts.

6:00 p.m. No text reply from Orson. But maybe he's busy with his work. Creative types and all. I then realized that I didn't really know where he worked. I pulled up his LinkedIn profile, which I had consulted in passing. It only contained a brief profile describing him as a creative designer and no mention of the company. Hmm.

8:30 p.m. Eating cold soup alone in my office, surfing pictures of kittens and baby otters while attempting to work on a file. I'm officially worried. Have not heard from Orson for three and a half days.

10:00 p.m. Total number of toilet visits since I awoke this morning: fourteen. Something is off.

11:50 p.m. Still no text from Orson. I must accept the truth: he is dead.

11:58 p.m. Who am I kidding? It's worse—I've been jilted.

Tuesday 22 March

3:45 a.m. Wide awake in bed. Oh God. Something is burning up down there. WTF.

5:30 a.m. Fifth time peeing in less than two hours. Each time feels like an exorcism, all sulfur and pain. I tried not to panic, but all my hypochondriac tendencies are in overdrive. Forced myself to lie in bed and not WebMD myself.

5:45 a.m. Tried not to think about peeing. Made myself lie still, like a corpse.

6:05 a.m. But to no avail. Feel completely parched yet every sip of water I take makes me sprint to the toilet.

6:20 a.m. Frantically typed in my symptoms after my fifth panic pee in three hours. One of the sites told me that I most likely have a urinary tract infection, or UTI, which sounds scary enough, but then WebMD told me I may also have:

Urethritis

Appendicitis

Diverticular Disease

Herpes Simplex Virus

Sexually Transmitted Diseases (Shit. Shit. Shit.)

Menopause (!)

Spent a half hour scrolling through pictures and descriptions of different STDs, which amplified my hypochondria. #FML

7:03 a.m. It's probably syphilis, though. With my luck. And could one contract leprosy from sex? Has that skin tag on my chin always been there? *Has it?*

8:50 a.m. "You are not going to die from leprosy," the doctor at the twenty-four-hour clinic said snidely. He was drawing blood from me for the STD screening, looking peeved at my barrage of hysterical questions. "It looks like you have a urinary tract infection, nothing more."

"How can you be a hundred percent sure?" I said, eyes bulging. "How can you be so sure about what I haven't contracted? I mean, I used a condom, but still, this is a boy, I mean, *man*, whose sexual history I know nothing of. So there is indeed a chance that he has passed me leprosy, syphilis, HIV. These diseases and UTIs aren't mutually exclusive, you know!"

Even in my hypochondria, I was lawyering him. No wonder our kind is so beloved.

"Well, it's true that I can't say for sure at this point of time," the doctor conceded without bothering to suppress an eye roll. "You could indeed be that very unlucky person that has contracted every STD known to mankind from one single encounter, along with leprosy, which isn't transmittable through sexual contact."

"Thank you," I said, gratified. "And it wasn't one single encounter. There were *several* encounters, albeit in the course of a night."

The doctor looked like he was suffering intense regret over his career choice, so I shut up.

"Miss Tang, I would advise you to stop speculating on how your life will end. Take your mind off things by spending time with your family and friends. We'll know more in three to five working days' time when we get your STD test results back. In the meantime, please finish your course of antibiotics and drink lots of fresh cranberry juice."

I cabbed home with my medicine and two liters of cranberry juice concentrate. Felt extremely sorry for myself, and was not at all assuaged by the doctor's empty assurances that it was most likely "only" a UTI—I could see the judgmental light in his eyes as he shook my hand goodbye. It didn't matter that Orson was the first man I'd slept with in close to a year, that in all my three decades plus of life I'd only been with four men, all in monogamous relationships. If I had been a man, the doctor would have looked at me with commiseration.

9:15 a.m. Called Kai to tell her I was not coming in. I think she fell off her chair. I have taken less than three days of sick leave in the five years I've worked for my law firm.

"How sick are you?" she whispered in fear.

"Heartsick," I mumbled, before hanging up. She didn't have to know that I might be dead soon, from leprosy. That's not her burden to carry.

9:55 a.m. I was feeling so sorry for myself that I decided to call the one person who had seen me through all the shameful events in my life: my sister, Melissa.

As soon as she picked up the phone, I started to blubber. "Orson hasn't texted me *at all* since we had sex and I think I've been d-dumped and I hurt when I pee and I-I think I'm going to die!" I wailed.

"Ghosted," she corrected me.

"What?"

"The correct term here is 'ghosted.' It's when . . . ah, never mind. Go on."

She listened to my tale of woe without interruption and didn't even try to make me feel stupid for being a hypochondriac. She accepted my quirks. "Look, sis, you need to give yourself a break. You made a mistake but worrying about it won't change what happened. Go fix yourself a glass of warm milk and go to bed. You sound completely ragged."

"I am," I sniffed.

"Take another day off and take your meds," she reminded me before we said our goodbyes.

I did as I was told and fell into an uneasy slumber.

Wednesday 23 March

3:40 a.m. Woke up from a troubled sleep feeling like the back of my eyes were sandpaper. It doesn't seem to be burning down there anymore, but my pee was the color of irradiated lemons.

7:00 a.m. Stumbled out of bed, dazed, my face the size of a watermelon from water retention, possibly due to the meds or the tubs of salted caramel ice cream I had been eating. Tried to take my mind off things by scalding myself in the shower, which achieved nothing except making me look like a real-life Freddy Krueger. Got depressed thinking that no one Orson's age who accidentally finds this diary and reads it would understand the reference unless they googled it. Stupid brain.

I tried to get myself out of the funk by repeating inspirational sayings from my collection of quotable quotes scribbled around my desk, but this exercise only served to hammer home how uninspired I was that I had to read other people's stupid quotes to solve a problem I should have seen coming. Instead I should be writing my own guide to life. My first piece of advice to pre-millennials in my position is this: don't date anyone who does not remember VHS. Don't even look in the vicinity of anyone who has mouthed the lyrics from anything by One Direction. Because if you do, if you are lured in by their flat bellies and full hairlines, you will live to regret it.

Just tried to find my rose gold Cartier Ballon Bleu watch among my collection of watches and can't find it. It was a present from my parents for graduating from university, engraved with a sweet message; it was one of the few times I'd seen them collaborate on something. Hmm. Maybe I left it somewhere. Will look for it in my gym bag at work.

8:35 a.m. Have unearthed a rank-smelling pair of socks that caused Suresh to dash from the room, choking, but no watch. Maybe it's with Linda. She has the keys to my place and often helps herself to my clothes and accessories, which is a little unfair because she's a size smaller than me, which means I cannot borrow her clothes, although she does have a divine collection of Hermès, Delvaux, and Chanel bags. Speaking of bags, the watch could be in one of mine. Will have to go through all of them when I'm home.

Texted Linda to confirm our lunch at noon, since it's been weeks since we last met. She's supposed to be checking on my/our Tinder progress. I made sure to ask her if she had my watch.

9:40 a.m. Genevieve cornered me in the cafeteria with a Cheshire grin. "It seems that a little birdie saw you with a certain juicy young thing at Quinn's the other day. Is it so thin on the ground that you have to date teenagers now?"

"Who served you that dish of bullcrap?" I said, frowning. I was never very polite when challenged.

"My own two eyes!" she crowed. Then she wrinkled her nose. "Well, you know what I mean. You cradle snatcher."

The truth was too humiliating, so I slunk away with my tail between my legs, no witty comeback for the Human Sandworm. The only thing I can rely on is my friends. That's why I'm going to have lunch with Linda—she's such a strong woman and doesn't need a man in her life. I must be like her.

1:10 p.m. Waited forty minutes for Linda in the lobby before I slunk back to my desk, trying desperately to focus on my work when she finally texted me with this flimsy excuse:

> **Have something work-related that cannot be rescheduled. So sorry.**

Which is fine, of course, because friendship, like romance, is flawed, and more often than not people end up stomping all over your dreams after dangling a goddamn carrot before you like . . . like . . .

"What is wrong with you?" Suresh said, jerking back from his screen with alarm. "Why are you crying?"

"Leave me alone," I blubbered. Not wanting to tell him the truth, I lied, "I-I just lost a fortune at online crabs!"

"What?" His eye was twitching.

"You know, the game of crabs, you roll a die and then you place a bet . . ." I trailed off, realizing I had no idea how to play crabs.

"Let's go out for some air," Suresh said quickly, unable to meet my eye.

We ended up having sandwiches at the new Japanese fusion sandwich bar in Raffles Place, where we did not speak for thirty-five magical minutes before heading back to the office for hard-core typing. He even patted my back and gave me an awkward no-contact-between-genitals hug when we entered the office. Someday, when Anousha finally moves to Singapore, Suresh is going to make her very happy.

8:30 p.m. Went home early today (yes, this is early for a mid-career lawyer hoping to make partner in Singapore). Made assam laksa Maggi Mee with an egg and ate it while binge-watching episodes of *Unbreakable Kimmy Schmidt*, which is the brainchild of Tina Fey, who is my hero.

11:00 p.m. Is it reflective of my own truly sad state of affairs that the thought of being imprisoned in an underground bunker with an improbably good-looking Jon Hamm alongside three other harpies is not immediately rejected by my brain as anything other than unbearable?

1:20 a.m. Oh crap! My watch! Texted Linda again to see if she had my watch.

1:35 a.m. Text from Linda:

> **I don't have your watch. When was the last time you wore it? The last place you saw it?**

The burning feeling is definitely back—but in my stomach. I remember exactly when I last wore it: on my date with Orson. And the very last place I saw it? On my nightstand, falling asleep as Orson and I cuddled.

18

Thursday 24 March

12:50 p.m. Had early lunch with Linda, who brought me to Black Swan to make up for standing me up yesterday.

We both ordered salads since we were in a rush, but when the food came, she picked at it listlessly while I finished mine in under ten minutes and ordered a flat white. She seemed distracted, and when I asked her what was up, she hesitated before cooking up a big Crock-Pot of BS and serving it to me. "It's work." She sighed dramatically. "There's so much work and I haven't seen my home in, like, days."

I gave her a careful once-over. It was true that she looked less polished and stunning than usual, her pale blue silk shirt sporting faint creases and smudges of her foundation; her hair was twisted in a messy bun and she had dark under-eye circles that showed even beneath the careful application of concealer. Linda had never let a late night out or no sleep get in the way of looking hot for work. Which meant she had not spent the night at her place. Interesting.

"Really," I said, keeping my tone neutral.

"Massimo has been keeping me so busy," she continued. "Massimo's my new client. A real super guy but totally obsessed with work. A lot of calls. Yeah." She was shredding her paper napkin in a totally not-nonchalant fashion while avoiding eye contact with me.

Alarm bells were clanging away in my head. Massimo? Who

the fuck was Massimo? Linda never called her clients by anything other than their last names, or if she really hated them, their nicknames. Something was definitely up. But it was no use asking Linda—she was never going to give me any details until she was ready to do so.

"How's the Tinder search for love going?" she asked suddenly.

I flushed guiltily. I had been so focused on Orson that I had barely replied to the Tinder messages from my remaining three matches (I unmatched with Alex, obviously), even though serial killer opener guy, Sean, was still intermittently texting me. The entire thing had more or less fizzled out and Linda's efforts were all for naught.

"I haven't really made myself available," I admitted. "After I saw Jonathan Beh on Tinder it really killed my whole desire to try online dating." I spilled about Alex and how he had hooked up with one of my colleagues, but it turns out Val had already given her all the salacious details over WhatsApp that very weekend. Thanks, Val.

Linda sighed. "There goes weeks of texting and my trusty algorithm. Well, can't say I didn't try to make Tinder magic happen." She took a bite of food. "Anyway, I heard from a birdie that you had a dinner date with Orson? Care to share?"

Urgh. Val. I held my hands up in mock surrender: I, too, had been hiding things from my best friend. "Yup, we did, but, uh, we're, uh, on a break now."

Linda lifted an eyebrow but wisely refrained from saying anything cutting. For now. "By the way, isn't your mom coming in, like, three weeks or something? I remember you moaning about it last month."

She was right: I had totally forgotten that my mother was scheduled to make a pit stop in Singapore soon. Shit.

6:50 p.m. Went home early so I could overturn the house to search for my watch.

8:20 p.m. This is bad. The watch is the last thing my parents, well, my father, gave to me, before he passed. On top of everything that had happened that week, this is the worst.

9:10 p.m. Googled anything and everything I could find about Orson aside from that basic LinkedIn page. Nothing. I've always been an awesome Google stalker, but for Orson I had curtailed my baser instincts and hadn't gone full bloodhound. Now here I was, and yet I couldn't find anything. Zilch. Nada. No Facebook, Instagram, Twitter, Pinterest, Snapchat, Foursquare, OpenRice, TripAdvisor reviews, nothing. Orson was, for all intents and purposes, a millennial ghost. It was also pretty certain that Orson wasn't even his real name, as I only found two or three pictures of him, the ones used on his "official" LinkedIn page.

I'd been played by a fucking hipster Sponk swindler.

Saturday 26 March

10:30 a.m. Finally received the results of my super expensive STD test in the post: am in the clear.

10:35 a.m. Still got conned, though. Worse still: Orson had manipulated me using evergreen techniques known to mankind since the first caveman lied to the first cavewoman and said he'd kill a herd of woolly mammoths for her if she would be his. It's as though I fell for the Nigerian prince scam in this day and age; it's that bad.

5:10 p.m. Asked Linda out for dinner but had no response. No one else in the group chat was available.

5:35 p.m. I have no friends.

1:15 a.m. Just back from an unusual group hang, with Suresh (!) and his friends.

We were just texting about work (yes, Saturdays belong to our dark overlords, too) when he told me he was going out with some friends and asked me to join them. I was still down about the general situation and I didn't know he had friends outside of work. I always thought he finished work, went home, cried himself to sleep, etc., in a spin cycle of sad adulting (I may have been projecting a little, of course).

Turns out Suresh had a whole life outside of work that involved other humans. His friends, Tu'An, Chandran, and Faisal, were buddies from law school in London, and they were all big fans of board games, in particular Settlers of Catan. So that's what Catan actually involves: instead of some swingers' club where they dress up as MMA fighters, they just sit there, eating sunflower seeds and talking about grain. And not the futures kind or the food kind—the kind printed on a deck of cards.

At first I thought it was super sad that a bunch of lawyers in their thirties (except for Chandran, who was now a "professional gamer") would be spending valuable time off work playing board games, but once I found out that Chandran, who is apparently highly ranked and had even placed in the top ten of some regional Catan championship, had made close to eight thousand American dollars winning at Catan competitions and had his own following, I changed my mind. Any hobby that (a) is moneymaking and (b) involves leader boards and national rankings was a legit pursuit in my book.

Also Catan is quite fun, as a spectator sport. As in, I watched Suresh play and screamed obscenities at his opponents from time to time.

We spent close to five hours playing Settlers of Catan and drinking happy hour beer in a gamers' café. I didn't even look at my work phone once (especially after Suresh stashed it away).

We called it a night around 1:00 a.m., after which Suresh got in a cab with me—he didn't have much choice since I had by then lost most of my motor skills. He half-carried me to my apartment and laid me down on my bed, brought me a glass of water and made me drink it, placed the covers over me, and was about to leave like a proper gentleman, when I spoke up. "Thank you for your help," I said.

He came back to the bed and perched on it. "You're welcome. Would you like to tell me what happened to you? You look miserable."

I couldn't admit to him that I'd been swindled. It was just too humiliating, and we were still just colleagues. Instead, I told him a partial lie. "We broke up by mutual agreement," I croaked. "I'm just being the appropriate amount of annoyed, that's all."

I could tell he didn't believe me, but he still didn't push it. I decided to change the subject. "By the way, about your superhero strip . . . if you don't mind, I have some suggestions."

"Oh, you follow *TLTS*?" He seemed very pleased by this revelation.

"Yes. You should consider giving Water a nemesis, or some kind of bigger purpose, not just stick to mini stories. That would give the strip the narrative tension it lacks and make it more compelling."

"Wow," he said, stunned. For a moment I was worried I had pissed him off, but then he smiled and snapped his fingers. "How could I not have seen this? You're right, he needs a larger purpose. I should give this more thought." He looked at me. "You might have just unlocked the growth phase for *TLTS*! The strip was stagnating, Andrea, and you've given me much-needed inspiration."

"You're welcome," I said. "Thank you for tonight." On impulse, I reached out and hugged him.

"I really enjoyed hanging out with you," he said in a low voice.

"Me, too," I said in the same voice.

We were still holding onto each other after the "friend-zone" three-second-hug rule, unwilling or unable to let go. I was aware that his hair smelled like coconut, and I nuzzled into it. Very subtly, the chemistry in the air had changed, and his arms had definitely acquired what can only be categorized as "narrative tension."

Oh God, what was happening? Did I . . . were we? And did I?

He lowered me gently onto the bed. I looked up, licked my lips subtly, and discreetly sucked in my belly so my boobs looked—

"Good night," he said, pushing himself off me as though I was an anti-vaxxer and he was a pharmaceutical rep. Then, quick as a punch, he was gone. I heard a door slam on his way out.

Now am not sure what to think. On the one hand, I like that he is a gentleman. On the other hand, am I not attractive enough that he would at least try to cop a feel? I mean, a borderline dodgy butt cup that could also be a reassuring, stabilizing move as he hoisted me onto the bed? Nothing?

Cupped my own butt. On the scale of tofu to steel, it rates "ten-year-old soft toy washed too many times in cheap detergent."

I wonder what kind of butt Anousha has.

1:45 a.m. Puked. Felt sorry for myself. Can't help thinking that aside from Ivan, my choices in men—i.e., Orson, Alex—have been disappointing. Maybe my taste in men reflects an underlying deficiency in my decision-making skills, off Ma's grid.

A terrifying, disturbing thought.

Thursday 31 March

7:10 a.m. I have learned my lesson, dear Diary. I must never take foolish chances and go off-piste dating again, lest I end up with another Orson. If I had stuck to the plan, I'd be with someone like Ivan instead of in this sad state.

7:13 a.m. Why had I broken it off with Ivan again?

7:14 a.m. Oh yeah. I remember now.

7:16 a.m. What kind of goddamn name is Orson anyway? I must have been high the night I met him.

Anyway, must concentrate on responsible adulting, i.e., dating suitable men and getting ahead in my career.

8:20 a.m. Texted my mom and told her grudgingly I would accept her help in arranging *one* blind date with rando's son. Baby steps, baby steps.

8:25 a.m. She texted me one word: DONE.

9:35 a.m. Valerie texted me to ask me, and I quote verbatim, "for a private audience tomorrow at Crystal Jade @Paragon to discuss an important issue concerning La Linda."

This will be our first lunch together, Together Alone. The

thought stresses me out: what if we have nothing to say to each other and I have to stare at that face for an entire lunch? Or worse: what if I couldn't enjoy my food because of it?

12:20 p.m. *TLTS* dropped a new strip, in which Water, when executing the CEO of a credit ratings agency that gave triple-A ratings to toxic mortgage-backed securities in a dark alley, meets a mysterious woman called Rhean, with similar powers as him. She looks very familiar and he can't shake the notion that he knows her from before.

This is an intriguing, and welcome, turn of events for the comic strip.

Hmm. Let me see: so the woman's name is Rhean, which is practically derived from "Andrea"; she's tall, svelte, and a redhead, the total opposite of me. Which means she's totally based on me. I'm flattered. I've never had someone literally make me a character in a comic strip before. It's almost—sweet, to be respected so much by a competitor.

Friday 1 April

Wow. This has been an intense day, and it's barely 3:00 p.m. The good news is that I survived (a) eating alone with Valerie for two hours (!) without too many awkward pauses (she's surprisingly quite funny), and (b) staring that whole time at Valerie's strange Bride of Chucky face and managing to finish my meal. The bad news is that I now know that Linda is sledding straight into a hillock of disaster-flavored turds, full speed, because I've heard some very disconcerting news.

Apparently, Valerie, who had been speaking at a private investment seminar at Fullerton Hotel (art investment for newly minted millionaires with too much money and no clue about art), had stepped out of the room to take a call when who else did her beady eyes spy but Linda, her arms around the waist of a man as they stepped into a lift heading up to the rooms. A man, she claimed, who was wearing a gold band on the fourth finger of his left hand: a married man.

"*What?* Are you sure it was Linda? This is not some elaborate April Fool's Day prank, right?"

"Positive. I was five feet away, hidden by a potted plant, but there's no mistaking Linda. She's pretty unmistakable, especially with that Fran Drescher laugh."

She was right; you could hear it from a mile away.

Valerie leaned forward, her eyes deadly serious, and whispered, "The most shocking thing was she was kissing him, *butterfly-style, all over his face* the *entire time! In broad daylight!*"

We both gagged simultaneously. Who was this imposter and what had she done to our Linda?

"Who's the Romeo?" I demanded once I'd recovered, feeling more hurt than shocked. I couldn't believe she had not confided in me, which told me that this man was special. Linda usually gave me every dirty detail of her dating life. It was part of her charm as a friend, since I could live vicariously through her sexploits, which were manifold and casual.

Valerie shrugged, her expression frozen in place. "He looked vaguely familiar, but I couldn't identify him. The guy was wearing Ah Beng* aviators. *Indoors.*" Valerie loved her italics.

We rolled our eyes in sync and shuddered. Both of us shared a dislike for people who wore sunglasses indoors when they were not visually challenged.

---

* A derogatory Singlish term for a Chinese man in Singapore or Malaysia, denoting a stereotype of having little education or sophistication in his dressing, mannerisms, speech, etc.

"And you're sure that he's married?" Linda has one rule when she dates: no married men. She'd experienced firsthand the repercussions of her parents' infidelities. "Maybe his ring is just for bling?" I offered weakly. It was dawning on me that Linda had been hinting at this in our conversation a few weeks ago, though at the time I'd assumed she was talking about one of my Tinder prospects.

Valerie snorted, which in itself is a feat because it meant she could still contort the muscles around her nose.

"Child," Valerie said in the same voice one uses to talk to, well, a child. "No man will scare off pussy by wearing a band on his fourth finger, even if it's 'just for bling.' We must face the fact that our best friend"—*mine*, I thought—"is screwing a married man, something she crucifies others for doing. I am sure he's Singaporean, at least he sounded like one, and he definitely has money: he had a Ferrari key fob dangling from his trouser pocket and a to-die-for pair of croc skin loafers, and the air of someone who's used to being listened and deferred to. His lack of discretion is a sure sign he's bad news: he was not even trying to hide the fact that he's married and cheating on his wife, which tells me that he must be a very powerful or very stupid man indeed, and God forbid he is both."

I chewed on this as I hurried back to work. Linda was not the most level-headed person when she wanted someone, but this guy sounded like bad news. I added this to the list of things I needed to resolve on an already staggering to-do list.

8:45 p.m. My nervous, staccato bursts of typing drew Suresh's ire.

"Could you please type normally," he said, irritated. "I have an angry client and an even angrier fiancée."

"Oh," I said. I glanced over and saw him staring blankly at the screen with an expression I knew well. It was what I called the Monday Horror Show™ face, a combo of constipation, existential horror, and resignation. With some hesitation, I got up, went over, and gave him the chastest, most scholarly of shoulder pats. Suresh's shoulders were dangerous territory: they were taut with muscles that invited lingering caresses. I quickly brought up mental images of hairy men in tight polka-dotted Speedos to quell any unruly carnal urges. "Do you want to talk about it?" I asked in my most professional school counselor's voice.

He sighed and leaned back in his chair. "Yes, but are you sure you really want to hear about it?"

"Sure!" I said, widening my eyes. "Isn't that what colleagues are for?" *Yes*, I thought, mentally channeling Mr. Burns, *tell me your deepest darkest secret, which I will never use against you, pinky swear, muahahaha*.

"Not really." A small smile creased his face. "But it's what friends are for. And we're friends, I'd like to think."

"Well, friendly rivals, anyway," I said, trying to keep my gaze from straying off the planes of his face toward those insanely sculpted shoulders.

"We've had a fight," he said. "Noush and I . . . we've had a massive row about Singapore. She doesn't want to move here, and I don't want to move back to London. I get it. I mean, I loved London as a child and a student. But Singapore is my home now. I want to be with my parents."

I shrugged. "I'm not saying I'm on her side, but for the sake of argument, if one of you has to move, why can't it be you?"

He got up from his chair and began pacing. "Look, it's much easier for her to find a job here, with her excellent credentials and experience—she even has a standing job offer from one of her former professors who's working in a private hospital here as the head of his department! Besides, being a working lawyer in London at a law firm like ours is not great. I barely slept five hours a night and I was working myself to the bone—I mean, even more so than here. I hated working and commuting in London—all that smog and cold weather and long commutes in the Tube where it gets so crowded that someone's nose is always wedged in your armpit."

"Right," I said. The idea of pressing my nose against Suresh's suit in a crowded train was oddly more appealing than it ought to have been.

"I just want her to be here, you know? Anousha's my fiancée. We should be in the same city, don't you think? If you were my fiancée, wouldn't you want to live with me instead of living across a fucking continent and being a couple only on paper? Does she even love me?"

I kept quiet. I knew the answer to that question, and it wasn't something I think he would have wanted to hear right then. Instead, I said, "Maybe you should go to her. Go to London. Take some time off to, urm"—I made my voice soft, like my unflexed butt—"*rekindle the romance.*"

He rolled his eyes. "Nice try, woman. You're not out-billing me. In fact, maybe it's better this way so I can, y'know, *focus on my work.*"

I narrowed my eyes. Looks like we were in for a long Office Face-Time Battle tonight. Unluckily for him, I had forgotten to wear deodorant and I'd just had a three-bean chili from the new Mexicana place down the street with dangerously empty seating. Game on.

Saturday 2 April

4:05 p.m. Went to the office to work on the contract that I should have been working on during the week. Was not surprised to see Suresh there, looking a little rumpled and bleary-eyed, like he'd not gotten a lot of sleep. We greeted each other by grunting, then lapsed into companionable silence, broken only by furious typing and the occasional call. We've developed this unspoken routine where we take turns making his famous chai. Sometimes sharing an office with him isn't so bad.

8:15 p.m. Found a lull in work and exploited it to send a text to Linda asking her out for lunch next week. Haven't seen her in a while.

8:30 p.m. Linda texted me back to tell me she was in the Cayman Islands with "a client." Hmmm.

9:10 p.m. Speaking of bad news, my mother's friend's son just texted me to introduce himself and ask me out for dinner next Friday at a swanky meat place called Ho Sek.

I googled him and almost fell out of my chair.

Someone Up There was having a laugh, a very dark one, at my expense.

Monday 4 April

It's my mother's birthday today. Dialed her number and let it ring twice before hanging up like a coward. Decided to send her a WhatsApp message instead, then promptly muted all notifications on the chat in case she replied. Have already sent her a birthday card over the weekend and sent it via international priority mail to her place in Kuala Lumpur. The art featured a cute, harmless penguin holding a bunch of flowers. I drew a cross on its chest and wrote "Have a blessed birthday, Mom! Jesus loves you!" in perfectly spaced capital letters and black ink. She should not be able to find any fault with this year's card. I hope.

Tuesday 5 April

7:15 a.m. This just came in from my mom:

> **I know Jesus loves me, but do you? You know what I want for my birthday. *emoji of a wedding dress* *emoji of a couple* *emoji of a three-person family unit***

Her emoji game is on point.

She followed up with another text:

> **Good luck with your date this Fri. Remember, God is watching.**

Gotta give her credit for being consistently annoying. And omniscient.

1:15 p.m. Called Linda, who was back from the Caymans, and told her my mother had strong-armed me into accepting a blind date.

"What's his name? Age? Occupation?" Linda said, presumably already in Google stalk mode.

"Chuck Tan Ka Seng. Forty-seven. MD."

"Dear God."

"I know."

"He chose—?"

"Yup. I'm pretty sure he chose the name 'Chuck.' As in Chuck Norris, not Chuck Bass."

I heard frantic tapping and a gasp. I knew exactly what she had found because I had had the very same reaction.

"It's going to be fine," Linda said, with barely suppressed laughter.

"Is it, though? Is it? How will I ever look at him with a straight face?"

"Diazepam," she said immediately.

"Thanks, but I prefer to keep my stash for when my mother turns up."

"Speaking of names, I almost wish I were back in Hong Kong," Linda said. "At least people there were creative. I mean, I'd give an actual kidney to meet a Pegasus or an Aristotle again. Or even just a boring old Handsome. At least I can abide by 'Handsome.' It shows a certain confidence, an assuredness of being." Slurping noises. "I envy you, Andrea. I really do. Blind dates and fertility deadlines sound so fun."

"Shaddup," I said. Linda was lucky: her parents, who were in the timber and mining business, were usually busy arranging for "accidental" land clearings instead of blind dates. Anyway, she didn't have the same, or any, external reproductive pressures. Although she's an only child, her father has what she euphemistically calls "backup children." Several, in fact. Furthermore, at the rate he was accumulating wealth, there was no issue about her marrying "up" to help the family. If Linda were to marry one day, she would, quite likely, be doing it for the right reason: fear of dying alone.

Wednesday 6 April

10:15 a.m. Ooh! Flowers! A massive bouquet of showstopping rich purplish-maroon peonies was delivered this morning, and they were not for Kai but me!

10:30 a.m. They were from Eric Deng, actually. He sent them with a card saying, "I'll be back in town. Will see you soon." I knew he would know how to find me. Which sounds creepy but is really not.

When I brought the flowers into the room Suresh promptly started sneezing. Turns out he is allergic to beauty. Anyway, have left the flowers outside with Kai on her desk, so that I can see them.

Val, who's an expert in beautiful things, told me that these are Black Beauty peonies, upon my sending a pic of the flowers to her. So there's another layer to the flowers, since I told Eric that *Black Beauty* was the first book that moved me to tears.

Thursday 7 April

11:35 a.m. Got a text from my blind date, Chuck, that literally said he was reminding me that we were meeting tomorrow. Not a "Can't wait to see you!" type of message, just a reminder to show up. What a total contrast to Eric's flowers. Anyway, Chuck's text came at a good time since I had totally forgotten about the date. Am tempted to cancel as I'm handling a difficult closing, deadline today. Consulted the group chat. Everyone told me to stick with it. Linda posited that since I haven't been on too many dates in a while I should take this, just to stay sharp. Val concurred that I needed all the help I could get (thanks). Ben and Jason, probably eager for the entertainment value they will surely derive from this, begged me to go ahead. Begged.

Am a little nervous about Friday. What do people say on dates these days? Do they even talk anymore or just scroll through their smartphones in companionable silence, waiting till they stumble upon a suitably benign news story or Instagram feed to share with their date? Will have to read up on what's trending and hope that he's equally ignorant on what makes young people ill these days.

On the off-chance that my mother's blind date might turn out to be the love of my life, I went and got an emergency cellulite massage and wax session at my favorite Vietnamese place. Which, by the way, is run by the same family that runs the deli downstairs.

Friday 8 April

6:45 p.m. Left the office muttering about a networking event I had to attend, to which Suresh gave a grunt of acknowledgment. Felt guilty since I have some follow-up from the closing to do, but as Linda reminded me, I've given enough of my youth in the service of faceless corporations to justify leaving so early.

I went to the date with the enthusiasm of a carnivore to a PETA conference, even though the restaurant, Ho Sek, was a well-regarded fixture in the local gastronomic scene, specializing in roast meats done in a variety of ambitious styles.

Chuck was already seated at the table, his back facing me as I walked slowly toward him. He was dressed in a light blue denim shirt, beige trousers, and tan moccasins. Since there was an off-chance that he could one day use my (legal) services, I had put on one of my LBDs (Lawyerly Black Dresses*) and black ballet flats.

Both of us were making as much polite effort as possible to not dress to impress.

* A whisper of cleavage, some knee, sleeves, body-skimming.

I circled the table and said hi, just as he pulled his chair back and extended his hand in a handshake. We shook hands, which never bodes well for romance. I made a mental note to sanitize my hands under the table even as I gave him a quick once-over. He was a firm 6.5 in looks, but given his professional choices, I could only raise his overall score to 4.

"Thanks for coming out tonight, Andrea," he said, in perfect accentless English. I raised his score to 4.5. Still, too little, too late. There was, on my side at least, no chance I would ever want to exchange any kind of fluids with him. I suspected he thought the same, as he was not doing the eye dip that most men unconsciously perform when confronted with cleavage, even inordinately modest ones.

We exchanged some pleasantries and quickly moved on to the Dating Small Talk. He was a skilled, easy conversationalist, but we both knew we would have to discuss our professions sooner or later. I for one was dying to ask him many, many questions, but I knew he had to broach the topic first. I prayed that I could hold it together when the time came: we needed to get through dinner so we could report to our parents about a suitably grave physical/mental flaw discovered during the course of the date that would imperil the bloodlines.

"So, Andrea," he said, at last, after we were done with our main course (mine a lovely barramundi swimming in browned butter, served with broccolini and roasted leeks, his a pork tenderloin paired with new potatoes and some kind of salsa), and we had to make a decision whether or not to ask for the bill or order dessert. "Why did you decide to be a lawyer?"

"Ally McBeal," I said. "I mean, justice, pencil suits, courtroom drama, and all that, yadda yadda yadda, but enough about me—what about you?" The entire sentence was said in one breath.

"I like big butts and I cannot lie," he did not say. Instead, he launched into a long story about some poor uncle dying of colorectal cancer while he was in medical school. I deflated. Dear Diary, I realize that I am a juvenile individual with a puerile sense of humor. But God, a proctologist? Of all the specializations in the world?

I am certain that proctology is the only medical specialty that a Chinese parent would prefer not to brag about but to keep in the dark. And the poor proctologist can come from Harvard Medical School, but he'd still be the butt of jokes.

Haha. Butt.

"Andrea," Chuck said, just as I had begun composing an amusing limerick about butts.

"Yes?" Had I been speaking aloud without realizing again?

"I'm sorry, but I have to go."

"What?" I said. "Already?"

"I have a surgery," he said, looking apologetic. "Tonight. At SGH.* It's for a state minister, so, you know, I have to run."

He had agreed to a date on a night he'd already scheduled a surgery? What a douche. That state minister had better be on his deathbed.

Still—he hadn't even thought I was worth it enough to meet me on a night off?

We split the bill in silence, dispensing with the check dance.

It was 9:05 p.m. when I called Linda for commiseration from home. The first thing she said was, "You know he could have been lying, right? Why so many details?"

"That did come to mind, but I had to reject it as a possibility since my self-esteem would not take it otherwise."

She said it was OK. She said knowing me, there was no way he would have been worth it. "I mean, you could never talk about work with him, and once the romance is gone, and you've already figured out each other's political and religious beliefs, finances, and sexual history, what else is there to talk about?" Loud mastication

* Singapore General Hospital

of something small, with fragile bones. "Just think about it, him telling you how a colonoscopy went. Or how best to beat hemorrhoids."

I sighed. She was right, of course, but still, the idea of him pulling an imaginary surgery out of his ass just to get out of a date with me still felt like a shitty move on his part.

OK, Diary, I'll stop now.

10:25 p.m. Told my mother that Chuck told me he had failed a year of med school, even after getting a tutor assigned to him. Worse, he had graduated bottom of his class. She will never bring him up again.

11:15 p.m. Still . . . another one bites the dust. Dating is *tough*.

21

Monday 11 April

8:35 a.m. Came to work this morning to find Mong at my desk, looking like he had just downed three Red Bulls in one go, which incidentally I had seen him do before.

"*Eric Deng* is down the hall in conference room Integrity," he said urgently. "And he's asking to meet *you*."

Sorry to go off topic, but seriously, why do people *name* conference rooms? It's bad enough that we have to have meetings in them. Honestly, it would be like naming washrooms. Also, if we're going to name them, can we at least use names closer to the truth, like Endless Boredom, Pointless PowerPoint Presentations, and Room Not to Have Sex In, Ever, It's Not a Good Idea, Especially with Your Boss? You know, go wild, be creative.

Anyway. Back to the matter at hand.

"Let me grab a fresh legal pad," I said, slapping on my "I'm on It" smile even as my palms began to sweat. Oh, Diary, why can't I be an elegant, dry-palmed woman around men, like Linda? Is it because she went to Cheltenham and I went to a Malaysian high school run by nuns who used to warn us about men and the multitude of diseases they carried in their pants? ("Germ baskets" and "virus cradles" were the exact words used, I believe.)

"Don't just stare at the wall, go now! And start the clock!"* Mong said. His voice brimmed with emotion. "I'm so proud of

* Start billing. Duh.

you, Andrea. Landing Eric Deng is exactly the kind of win that would boost your chances of making partner this year ahead of the others, I'm sure of it."

Then he shoved me out of the office.

I half-ran, half-hopped as fast as I could to the conference room, slowing down to a careful sashay a few doors away. I saw him before he saw me, since the walls of the conference room were all frosted-glass panes and diffused lighting. I took a deep breath, wiped my palms down the sides of my skirt, and opened the door a little harder than I had intended. The door handle smacked the interior wall with glass-shattering potential. We both cringed, then heaved identical sighs of relief when nothing broke.

Unlike the last time we met, Eric was wearing Full Bosswear: an elegant gray three-piece suit and a bow tie in Hermès orange, his shock of graying hair combed, the same pair of twinkly light brown eyes with their laugh lines now showing a hint of steel in the harsh daylight. Although he had what could only be termed a "dad bod," he was tall and broad-shouldered, he had great posture, and his skin was tanned and healthy-looking; he could have easily passed as someone a decade younger, and not in a Valerie Gomez I-like-standing-only-in-dim-nooks kinda way.

He looked good.

He came up to me, palms outstretched for mine, and did the European cheek press, lingering longer than was strictly necessary on each cheek. "Hello, Andrea," he said in his gravelly voice.

"Hello," I said, playing it cool, since he could either be here for business or a date. We sat down. I fiddled with my notebook and uncapped my fountain pen to look more professional. "What can I help you with, Mr. Deng?" I said, primly.

"Oh, I was hoping we were on a first-name basis now, you know, since you've already called me an immoral old fart," he said, poker-faced.

I grinned and took a risk. "I'm sorry, Eric, you're clearly not old. As for immoral . . ."

He laughed. "You're forgiven," he said, smiling. "I'll cut to the chase, since I'm aware that your boss probably thinks that I'm here to give your firm some business—I'm not. Tan, Victor & Partners have taken care of my best interests for close to twelve years, and I don't believe in mixing business with pleasure. I'm here for personal reasons."

"Oh," I said, pleased and disappointed at the same time. It would have been a lie to say I wasn't disappointed at all. I'm still a fee-earner-on-partner-track at heart. "Does Tan, Victor & Partners have a great M&A practice like ours?" I said gamely. "I mean, Mong is the best." And I'm his number two, I wanted to add.

"It definitely doesn't," he said, looking thoughtful. "But maybe one day. I do have a couple of parallel funds that are invested in Ralph Kang's businesses, and he's mentioned to me that he's a client of your firm's, so maybe one day?" His eyes were twinkling. "I'm here to ask you for your number, formally, and to arrange a date with you."

Oh my. Could this man get any more romantic? (Not being sarcastic, I've literally always wanted to be asked out by a client, à la *Pretty Woman*, but with less prostitution—let's face it, lawyers are paid by the hour, so . . .)

I smiled at Eric and said, only half-joking, "Only if you put me as the lawyer in charge of your next corporate raid."

He grinned and shook my hand, firmly. "It's a deal."

We discussed our schedules (well, his) and I penciled him in for a lunch date on 30 April. He had a hotel to open in Dubai and would be quite busy for the next two weeks.

"Oh, and it might be a bit cheeky to throw this at you after you've just accepted a date with me, since it's like getting a two-for-one after a deal's already been made, but please do join me and

Ralph for a dinner next Saturday. I think he would like to see your friend again, Val, but he's not good with women, especially those he considers out of his league. So I thought we could double date."

"Of course, and I'll ask Val right away if she can make it." I didn't tell him we'd already made a plan for me to join her, in case Ralph asked.

After he left, I immediately texted Val, and she agreed to be there. It was going to be an interesting night indeed.

Wednesday 13 April

1:50 p.m. Apparently, when you try to do a good turn unto one friend, the universe punishes you brutally.

We were having lunch, Linda and I, after not having seen each other for weeks. Sure, I'd been busy and so had she, but she'd never been a hard one to pin down for a quick catch-up, and lately it seemed like she would always have an excuse not to see me.

Linda was twenty minutes late, so I had little time for small talk. We ordered a bottle of sparkling water and two spag bogs, and I launched my inquisition without further ado. "People have been seeing you around town with some mystery man, and I for one am sick of being the last person to know, so, you know, spill!"

Linda's jaw dropped and she took a moment to compose herself. "Oh dear, I guess we're not being too subtle, are we." She giggled nervously. "Look, I'm so sorry I couldn't tell you, trust me I'd been dying to, but I couldn't. My partner is a very well-known person in Singapore, and he's separated from his wife right now so we've been keeping this whole thing under wraps."

"Valerie saw you at the Fullerton."

"Ah, crap. I knew we should have gone to my place instead.

Anyway, there's really not much to tell. We're still figuring things out. Maybe once his divorce is finalized . . ."

I folded my arms and glared at her.

"All right, all right, I'm going to show you a photo, but you have to promise me, if you recognize him you have to keep his identity to yourself."

I was intrigued. "Is it a movie star?" I guessed. "The one that owns a Macau casino, what's his name, Darryl—"

She reached over and grabbed my right hand before I could move away, squeezing with anaconda-like strength. She narrowed her eyes at me. "*Promise me* you'll keep his identity a secret," she hissed.

"OK!" I yelped. "I promise!"

She relaxed her grip. "Good. I don't want to have to hurt you, but I will." She took out a smartphone, scrolled through some images before handing the phone to me with manga-shiny eyes.

"OMG," I said, staring in disbelief at the image on Linda's phone.

"Isn't he amazing?" she cooed.

From the smartphone screen, a sharply suited, bow-tied man of average height and build stared cockily up at me with a pugnacious leer. To be brutally honest, he was unattractive. He was so unattractive that he was in the negative interest rate attractiveness territory. Linda's man had the bone structure of the default Twitter egg avatar, was balding, and had a champagne gut. Then I realized that I knew the man and I started putting all the pieces together. Her lover and client was Massimo Poon, one of the richest men in Asia (or rather, the only grandson of one of the richest men in Asia), noted playboy, philanderer, and little else. Despite only being in his mid-fifties he was already knee-deep in the quicksand of his third, apparently failing, marriage. How could this be the man who had finally succeeded in sweeping my best friend and dearest cousin off her feet?

There was no other explanation for it—it was black magic.

I took a deep breath. "OK, Linda, you're not desperate for money, *that* I know for sure." Linda's paternal family tree was an off-brand Marcos (or so it was rumored); the family had substantial interests in several mining and timber companies, with land to burn in Borneo. Literally. "So please tell me what you see in this man, because I'll be honest, based on this very unfortunate high-def selfie, I have a real hard time understanding the attraction." And before I could stop myself, I added, "Plus he's not just old money, Linda—he's *old*!"

Linda glared at me. "Could you be more shallow? I'll have you know that Massimo is a darling. I'll bet you didn't even know he's one of the biggest patrons of the Singapore Red Cross and that his foundation sponsors dozens of children in Cambodia. He's smart, fearless, and exuberant. We get along so well, and we connect on so many levels." Her eyes had a faraway look. "I haven't met anyone with whom I can discuss politics, conspiracy theories, religion, mid-century modern architecture, and *super yachts*. Ever."

"He sounds perfect," I said snidely. "For an adulterer."

Linda sniffed. "Well, judge all you want, but I'm not breaking up with him. He's going to divorce his wife, and then we'll really be able to take our relationship public." Her voice grew dreamy. "Did you know I'm the *first* woman he's dated who's in her thirties?" She giggled. "You know, since he turned fifty."

I felt myself getting annoyed. "You say that like it's a good thing!"

"Why are you so prejudiced? Poots is real with me, and I am with him. He may have made mistakes in the past—"

"Yeah, like three wives and several high-profile mistresses."

"That's the past. He didn't know what he wanted back then."

"I'm sure he absolutely knows what he wants now—fresh meat."

"Why are you being so reductive about this? You don't even

know him and you're dismissing him." Her voice was strained. "He's the first man I've dated who doesn't care that I don't want children."

"That's because he probably doesn't want any with— That's because he probably has too many illegitimate ones of his own! I mean, have you done your homework on this guy? Do you remember the tabloid stories of him and every single TVB starlet worth a damn in the noughties?"

"He's changed!"

"No, he hasn't!"

"Yes, he has!"

"No, he hasn't!"

This brilliant exchange went on for quite some time. Our voices were so loud that the tables around us fell silent, but we were beyond caring. I was mad, fueled by my own desire to protect her from a man I thought was using her just like Orson used *me*. How could she be so blind? When Massimo was done with her she'd just be another notch in his bedpost, nothing more.

I changed tactics. "He's still old enough to be your father."

"And?" She crossed her arms. "You always told me that I had *daddy issues*." Linda's father had been a classic absentee parent, a "special-occasions dad" who she only saw whenever she was celebrating a milestone. "Maybe I like that he is old enough to be my dad! Maybe he even *looks* like my dad." She gave her trademark barking laugh. "How's that for your desktop psychoanalysis!"

A silence fell, thick and unpleasant, between us. I had never been so riled up in a conversation with Linda—we usually resolved our quarrels swiftly, over alcohol. When I spoke again, I tried to keep my voice down in order to get through to her. "Do you really think it will last? He's a known womanizer. Come on, Linda, open your eyes. A tiger can't change its stripes. It's what you tell me all the time."

"Maybe I was wrong. Maybe he is the exception to the rule." Her voice was bitter. "But you're just like the rest: you judge him before knowing him."

"You're not thinking straight," I insisted, raising my voice. "Massimo is clearly a bad choice."

"At least I'm true to myself and I go for what I feel is right for me. I know that's a concept you are *so* familiar with." Her voice dripped with sarcasm. "What I don't get is why you're suddenly interested in policing my love life, when you used to gawp from the sidelines, taking notes."

That hit me with the force of a knee to the groin. "Maybe because you've never been serious about a man before," I almost shouted.

Her jaw dropped. "Great, now you're slut-shaming me."

"I'm not!"

She narrowed her eyes. "You know what I think? I think you're afraid that I'll find love, and you'll be left behind in a job you don't even like, with your average expectations out of your average life."

"I don't think there's any danger in you finding lasting love here," I said acidly.

She pushed her chair back with a loud clatter, threw two fifty-dollar bills onto the table, and strode out of the room without a backward glance.

As I picked up the cash, I was trembling with suppressed fury, trying to put on a nonchalant face in front of the other diners to minimize the burning humiliation I felt. But it was hard. She'd just accused me of being passive and basic. Sleepwalking through my own life. Just because I'm a little risk averse and I have parents who cared enough about me to take an active role in my day-to-day affairs.

1:30 a.m. Can't sleep.

1:50 a.m. Still can't sleep.

2:15 a.m. What she said about me isn't true, is it?

2:35 a.m. I'll just have one glass of wine to help me sleep.

2:55 a.m. And a whisky. Or two.

3:40 a.m. Whos needs Linda. I l finf new fiends she'll see1!

Thursday 14 April

6:55 a.m. Urggh. My head. Is it time for work already??

8:10 a.m. Suresh took one look at me and ran for coffee and a glass of orange juice.

9:25 a.m. Dying. Went to the toilet, found a clean stall, put the lid down, and sat with eyes closed, just for a bit.

10:10 a.m. Woke up when phone vibrated. Nearly dropped phone. Have a client's call due in about twenty minutes. Crap. Ran out of toilet. Went back to office and told Suresh casually I had been on super long conference call with a client. Suresh's deliberately expressionless expression told me everything I needed to know: he knew.

10:25 a.m. Client emailed to cancel conference call. *Thank God.*

10:27 a.m. Snuck a peek at mirror when Suresh left the room and realized *how* he knew: long line of crusted drool on chin. I am the epitome of a successful, well-adjusted woman.

11:30 p.m. I will never drink again.

2:07 p.m. I will not drink again—this week. Am feeling slightly better after lunch.

4:00 p.m. Two coffees, five glasses of orange juice, and four paracetamols later: hallelujah, I am healed!

5:15 p.m. Is there a platform for people looking for friends, like Tinder or Sponk, only platonic and not filled with dicks?

Tried asking Suresh without giving away fight with Linda. He shrugged and suggested I build one. Then he invited me to hang out with his Catan group again, to which I declined. It's one thing to have no life, another to spend it playing board games with no intention or ambition of going pro one day.

5:33 p.m. I have friends. I have Val and Jason and Ben.

5:40 p.m. Wait, these guys were all Linda's friends first. Would they want to hang out with me if they had to choose between the more glamorous, moneyed, interesting, and beautiful Linda and me?

5:55 p.m. How did it get to this? I thought I'd have more friends at this stage of my life, even if you take away those who'd gone off to have families, because how can I compete with Montessori enrichment classes, PTA, and Club Med?

It's quite shocking. Maybe I should build that platform. One day.

6:10 p.m. Googled "how to build an app." Seems easy enough. Just need to learn how to code. How hard can it be?

6:30 p.m. Tried to teach myself some code, surreptitiously, via an online course, but very nearly stabbed myself with a pair of scissors in desperation. Was too diffic— I mean, it's very, erm, not my cup of tea. Thank God my mother never knew that programmers would be the next big thing, otherwise this would have been my life.

6:33 p.m. Could still hire people to build the platform though.

6:40 p.m. Shook myself out of a daydream where I had built the next unicorn platform, something something techy, and was now a sexy billionaire with a direct line to designers Roland Mouret and Joseph Altuzarra.

6:45 p.m. Mmm. Joseph Altuzarra.

6:48 p.m. Shit!! Realized I've sent an email to a client literally with words "Mmm. Joseph Altuzarra."

6:50 p.m. It's OK. Have recalled the message.

6:56 p.m. Shit, Joseph Altuzarra is gay. Not that there had been any chance of us getting together in the first place. Still, a girl can dream.

6:59 p.m. Mmm. Joseph Altuzarra.

I came home and found the door unlocked. Now I live in a pretty safe area, with security and key card. It was unlikely that someone could have gotten past the security unless they lived on my floor itself. Yet there was my door, ajar.

"Hello?" I said, my voice shaking. When I heard nothing, I plucked up my courage and walked in, holding my keys in my hand as a weapon. The living room was dark except for a sliver of light from the guest room (*where I keep all my designer bags, the smart fucker!*). I tiptoed in, grabbing blindly in the darkness for my umbrella. I planned to jab the housebreaking sucker in the eyes, and when the guy was on his knees screaming as he contemplated his costly mistake, I would stand over him and laugh in his face, and—

"Hey!" a voice said behind me. I screamed and jumped three feet in the air.

"It's me, you silly billy." It was my mother, slithering out of the shadows to join the living in jeans and a white kurta top, her unnaturally black hair in a severe bob.

"What," I gasped, gripping the edge of the bar counter for support, "the effing *eff* are you doing here *today*? Could you not have made a sign . . . for that matter, have you not heard of the courtesy call? The call you make to your daughter to warn her that you're coming a few days ahead of schedule so she doesn't scare herself shitless?"

Ma tooted and wagged her finger at me. "Language, darling. Do you think you will trap a bee with vinegar, as the French say?" She did a volte-face and walked toward the kitchen, motioning me to follow her. "Besides, if I warned you, do you think I would be seeing you in your natural habitat?"

"And miss an opportunity to criticize your own daughter?" I muttered.

"Drink this, your breath stinks," she said, thrusting a glass of cold orange juice in my face. "You have an obvious vitamin deficiency, among other things, judging by the crepey texture of your facial skin." My mother, ever the encouraging soul.

I downed it and made a face. "Is this juice expired? It tastes like a rat drowned in it."

"You're probably not used to drinking something nonalcoholic." She waved her arms at the kitchen countertop, where nine empty wine bottles stood. "Looks like someone's been celebrating or stressing a little too often lately."

"That's my recycling stash," I said. (It was not.) "Urgh, why the heck am I defending myself? I'm a godda— freaking adult, for fu— cripes' sake!" I reached around her to open the fridge door and grabbed for the half-empty bottle of rosé I had stuck into the juice compartment two days ago—only to find it stocked with innocent boxes of cold-pressed juice.

"I got rid of all the liquid poison," my mother said nonchalantly as I swore.

"It's OK, Ma." I opened the freezer compartment, rooted around under the bags of frozen peas and whatnots, and reached my emergency stock of miniature vodka bottles. I grabbed a mug and sloshed a generous helping of vodka, neat, before gulping it down, much to my mother's disgust.

"Hah!" I said between gulps of burning vodka. "Hah!" I felt like the most childish thirty-three-year-old on the face of Earth. Who got one up on their mother now? Alcoholic Andrea, that's who!

She said, with perfect nonchalance, "By the way, I just dewormed you. You might want to slow down on the alcohol."

I spat out my vodka.

"Silly billy. Not in your vodka. In your juice!"

The earth tilted beneath my feet. "What . . . what did you put in me?"

She gave a "What, me?" shrug of innocence. "Oh, just an eensy weensy tab of Zentel."*

"Oh God," I whispered. The woman was crazy. It was lucky that she was well into her sixties and a woman with little patience for pharmaceuticals; I could picture her as a predatory millennial hipster with a stash of roofies, meth, and Mexican Viagra. She would have been a very successful drug dealer.

She smiled slyly at me. "You know it was my birthday last week, right?"

I gathered myself. "Yes, Ma, I sent you that card and those messages."

* A popular brand of deworming medicine.

"Yes, that cheap Hallmark card. How lovely. But I don't care that my children are too cheap or too heartless to buy me gifts anymore. I don't care about the material things. Sadly, the one thing I really want, that is, to be a grandmother . . ."

"Oh my God!" I exclaimed. "I've only been home for *ten fucking minutes. Ten!*"

"All my friends' daughters are married with good prospects, with kids. And me? When will it be my turn? Both my daughters have *no interest* in doing the same. *Zero.*" She pointed a finger accusingly at me. "How come even an unattractive older woman like Helen can find a *gweilo** to marry, but you can't?"

I grabbed my hair; there was a soft thrumming sound in my left ear. My vision swam and my face throbbed.

"All right, all right. I can see you're going to make a big deal out of nothing. I'll stop." She sighed. "It doesn't make a difference anyway. My children don't listen to me. I might as well not exist."

Don't lash out. Don't lash out. Take deep breaths and think happy thoughts.

I imagined myself strangling my mother. "I'm going to my room," I said, when I could finally feel my face again. "I'm going to change into shorts, so if you feel like moving on to physical abuse, it'll show better."

"You're being overdramatic," said the woman who had just drugged me.

I opened the door to my room to change out of my work clothes and received the second shock of my life when I opened my drawer.

I screamed. I thought I would never stop screaming. I was sure I would die from a brain aneurysm mid-scream.

Drawn by my pain, my mother clattered into the room.

---

* A once-derogatory Cantonese term that Cantonese-speaking folks use to refer to people of white European ancestry, meaning "ghost devil man" in Cantonese. I know, I know, the Chinese can be *so* tactful. (pro-tip: If you hear *sei*, which means "dead," prefixed to it, as in *sei gweilo*, it's meant to be rude.)

"What. The. Fuck. Is. The. Meaning. Of. This?" I said in a deadly calm voice, pointing to my empty underwear drawer. Empty, except for my gym underwear, i.e., stretched-out gray cotton undies.

She couldn't have stopped there; I walked to my bedside and yanked open my nightstand drawer. All the condoms were gone.

"Where. Are. The. Condoms?" I said, in the same voice.

"In the bin with your black lace panties, where they belong," my mother said matter-of-factly. She gave me a look of disapproval. "By the way, you really should lose some weight. I noticed you have gone up two sizes. Who's going to want you if you're fat?"

It took all the willpower I had to stay planted on the same spot. "Please leave. Now. Before I explode."

"Don't be silly. I can't leave now. I'll leave tomorrow, when I can travel safely in a cab and not get raped." She clapped her hands. "Besides, I made dinner for the two of us. So come, eat with me. I made you your favorite drunken mushroom chicken with garlic bok choy."

My stomach rumbled; I hadn't eaten since lunch, and I was so hungry. But my principles . . .

In the end, my stomach made the decision for me. I would deal with my mother next time, like when she was old and immobile. Let's see how she would like staying in the local Methodist-run nursing home.

After we had eaten, I tried to uncover the reason why she was in town a week early.

"Can't I visit my favorite daughter without reason?" she said.

I narrowed my eyes. "I know you. You never visit without reason. Spill, Mom."

She hesitated. "Well, if you must know, I got a text from your sister. She wanted me to know that Kamarul proposed. And she accepted."

I whooped. At long last! I couldn't believe that Melissa and Kamarul were finally getting hitched—they had been waiting for so long for the right time (i.e., my mother's blessing), but clearly they'd had an epiphany and decided to stop waiting and go for it. I couldn't be prouder of them.

"Well. They can go ahead and get married without me, because I may not be stopping it, but I'm certainly not going to the wedding. I need you to tell her that because I'm still not speaking to her," my mother said.

"Why not?" I demanded. "Aren't you tired of this foolishness by now?"

"You don't understand where I'm coming from, but trust me, I know better," she said angrily. "Melissa is going to regret this. She's going to give up everything for a man—her culture, her potential inheritance from Auntie Wei Wei—everything. It's a stupid move."

I piled more of the food on my plate and stood up. "I'm going to bed, and you can tell her yourself," I said curtly.

"I'm not talking to her until she breaks up with him!" my mother called to my retreating back.

I slammed the door behind me to give vent to my feelings. My mother was so stubborn and narrow-minded. It's a good thing I'm nothing like her.

Friday 15 April

7:40 a.m. Ushered my mom into a cab. She looked contrite, but I wasn't falling for it. She can bitch about her children with Auntie Zhang, another Singapore-based sibling of hers; two of the latter's children were struggling actors and the youngest was a "social media influencer" with less than one thousand followers. The two of them could happily debate which of their children had disappointed them most.

12:30 p.m. Had a lovely video chat with my sister and Kamarul, who are in Bukit Larut on some hipster rustic treehouse retreat to celebrate their engagement. Was a little miffed that Melissa didn't call me to tell me immediately (it had happened last Friday), but she said it's because she was worried that if she told me, I'd blab all over town before she gathered the nerve to tell our mother. As if!

When she asked me if our mother was attending, I said, "At the moment, it seems like she's undecided, but let's see."

Silence.

"All right," she said softly.

"Tell me about the proposal!" I almost shouted to compensate for the downward turn in mood.

He had asked her one night after dinner, in their home on one knee, after presenting her with a cake he had baked himself (a terrible fail, but she was touched by the effort even though the whole house now smelled like burned caramel, hence the retreat). She did confide in me, when Kamarul excused himself to give us some space to dissect the proposal (and the ring, duh—around one carat Asscher-cut, platinum band), that she was struggling with having to convert to Islam in order to marry Kamarul under Malaysian law.

"You don't want to?"

"Well, there's no other way," she said. "Not if we want to get married in Malaysia. In any case, we can't go on living in this limbo. Even if a choice was possible, if I don't convert, his family will be very disappointed. His parents won't cut him off, but his community will. It's a lot of societal pressure."

Families—wherever you stood, there they were, poison-dipped pitchforks to your back.

"Would you ever consider leaving?"

"Malaysia?" A sigh. "No. No matter what, it's still home. And then there's Ma . . ."

We both fell silent.

"Look, wherever you are in the world, you can still send me Ma's allowance and I'll remit it to her from my account, as per usual." For some time now, Melissa had been sending me money for our mother's living expenses, and I would wire that sum, along with my contribution, to our mother every month. It's a token sum, of course, as our mother had a small but decent income from two rental properties in Kuala Lumpur, but it's the way many of us Chinese kids repay the debt that we owe our parents for them sacrificing the best years of their lives by working so hard to send us to the best schools, etc. Told you: we're the best pension plan.

"That's not it," she said heavily.

"She'll come around," I said, with as much conviction as I could fake.

In any case, we ended the conversation on a positive note: I will not be required to wear any Grecian-inspired maid-of-honor gowns. There will be sleeves, yards and yards of them. Thank God.

Sunday 17 April

Linda and her mystery man have finally been outed by the press. They'd been photographed on a yacht with their naughty bits hanging in the breeze in Cannes at some after-party. Well, actually they were in the periphery of a picture with someone from One Direction or similar, and that naturally caught the attention of the news-starved Singaporean press. "Billionaire Playboy Brings Mystery Woman Onboard Tech Superstar's Mega Yacht!"

There, in the blurry enlarged pic, was Linda in the world's smallest white string bikini, one that a toddler could have crushed in its fist. Barefoot, she stood almost half a head taller than Massimo.

"She's *really* with him?" Valerie said disapprovingly when we met up for a drink session that evening with Jason and Ben at a new Mexican fusion cocktail-and-tapas bar. Valerie knew about Massimo's unsavory reputation.

"Unfortunately, yes." I noticed that Jason was also in some kind of funk, staring stonily at a spot behind my head and downing beers. He'd been acting weird in the last group hangs. Then again, the chemistry of the group hang had been off without Linda. Clearly, she found "Poots" a much more fascinating specimen to spend her time with. My spies in her office told me that she was billing the bare minimum to get by and was always out for three-hour-long "lunches." But now that she and Massimo were having all kinds of unnatural nocturnal dealings on top of his being her client, the bosses were never going to fire her—they needed her to keep the law firm's Ponzi-like billing model going.

If only they knew the means she was using to hook him, I thought sourly. Then I thought of all the cleavage-baring client-relationship managers I knew in private banking, and I sighed. Singapore, though conservative, understands that sex sells (even if they weren't necessarily having it themselves). Linda's bosses might have stiff upper lips, but even they weren't going to thumb their noses at Linda's questionable merger-and-acquisition tactics.

Urgh. Linda always came out on top.

"She'll come around," Ben said. "She'll find herself a winner." He meant himself, clearly.

"I don't know about that. She likes her men vapid and rich, preferably with a few STDs," I said cattily.

"Excuse me," Jason said, pushing his chair back loudly and walking away.

"What's wrong with Jason?" Valerie asked, uncharacteristically observant.

"Bad nachos?" I said.

I gave Jason a quick once-over when he returned. He was definitely not taking any drugs in the toilet because he looked even more dejected than he had before. Dude was so miserable he ordered three rounds of drinks for everyone. What is going on with my friends?

Saturday 23 April

Spent the evening with Ralph Kang, Valerie, and Eric Deng at one of the old-school fine-dining Shanghainese restaurants I can never remember the name of.

Even though she was less than thrilled about seeing Ralph,

who she found lackluster and coarse in appearance, it didn't stop Valerie from dolling up. She wore a triple-strand Mikimoto pearl necklace and a delicate, long-sleeved, body-hugging black velvet-and-lace dress, paired with spectacular black Charlotte Olympia Paloma heels and an Alexander McQueen Small De Manta clutch of mine (well, Linda's). As for me, I played it low-key and wore one of my wrap dresses in navy blue and low kitten heels. I was nervous about the double date. I hadn't seen Ralph since the fateful Sexless Book Club or Eric since he ambushed me at work, so I was a little nervous about how the chemistry between the four of us would turn out. Plus if things didn't go well tonight, Eric and I would have awkwardness to smooth over when we went on our date next weekend.

Dinner did not start well. When Valerie and I arrived, the two men were deep in heated conversation and Ralph was red with displeasure. He acknowledged us with a curt greeting before storming off.

Eric leaned over and whispered, "Sorry, we just saw his ex-wife a few tables away. She's here with her Chilean salsa instructor, who apparently was the one she was cheating on Ralph with, hence the stroppy mood."

Ah. The ex. Eric told us that Ralph had left to see his friend, the chef, about kicking them out of the restaurant.

"I should go with him, just in case he tries to create a scene with her. He's not one to shy away from confrontation, and I know he's been dying to beat up Vicente." Eric excused himself and hurried after Ralph.

Val's eyes were huge with respect and desire. "He is so *manly*," she whispered to me.

There was a brief commotion and the ex-wife and Vicente were unceremoniously booted out of the establishment, but Ralph's mood did not improve. New bottles of wine appeared and things went downhill from there. Ralph was a belligerent drunk, and the more he drank, the more silent, and redder, he got. At one point he just stopped talking entirely. Eric, bless him, tried hard to get a conversation going, but to no avail. After an hour or so, I had had enough. I told the group I had a closing and that I had to leave, at which point Ralph snapped out of his fugue state and called for the bill. When the waitress arrived with the check, Ralph took out his credit card (a flashy JP Morgan Reserve) and loudly insisted he pay for the table (not even looking to see if the amount was correct), but when she was about to leave, I got up and stuck my grotty credit card into the check presenter in her hand, asking to split the bill in half for me and Val (I would claw back the money from her later)—no way was I going to let some rich guy buy us off to feel better about how badly he had behaved the whole evening. Ralph was upset and the discussion got heated between us while the poor waitress stood there, pale, until Eric intervened, taking both cards out of the waitress's hand and replacing them with his, a gold-edged black one I didn't recognize. "Dinner's on me," he said, waving her away in his easygoing manner, even though his voice was an order.

Once we were out of the restaurant, Ralph having stayed back to speak with the chef while Valerie reapplied her face in the ladies', I pulled Eric aside to unleash my frustration. "Your friend was a jerk today."

"Excuse me?"

"You saw how he was in there. Loud, rude to Valerie and me, drunk!"

He pulled out a cigarette and stuck it, unlit, between his lips. "So?"

"So!" I sputtered with indignation. "That's just not the way it's done, that's what. You don't act like this on a date." I was also very disconcerted with his attitude. Birds of a feather flock together, etc.

"And what do you want from me?"

"An apology. An explanation for his appalling behavior. I don't know."

He lit the cigarette and took a deep drag. "I'm going to smoke this cigarette, then I'm going to address the situation. Do you smoke?"

"No," I said sulkily. "I quit." (Although I did occasionally stress-smoke, I did not add.)

"Then please excuse me."

He then walked to the other end of the parking lot and smoked his cigarette while I gradually cooled down. By the time he was back I was much calmer.

"OK, here's my take. Ralph's being rude today, and I apologize on his behalf, but he's a curmudgeonly dog most of the time. He's a highly stressed individual, that's why he looks so bad. I'm not telling you this to excuse his behavior, more to give you some context: the man's been hurting from his divorce and he's not masking his feelings even though you're not close to him, and you'll find that in some circles that's about the most refreshing quality a man can have. Isn't that what you millennials love to harp on about? Being authentic? And Ralph is not much older."

"Why, I mean, I don't . . . well, I guess when you put it *that* way, we could all . . . you know. Well! This!" I blathered on in this fashion, flattered at being mistaken for a millennial. Then the penny dropped. "Wait—how old is Ralph Kang?"

"Ralph? He's thirty-nine."

My jaw dropped. He looked so weathered.

"And I think your friend is old enough to decide what she wants without you policing her. Did she even put you up to this tirade?"

"No," I conceded. "But I could see that she was uncomfortable with his actions."

"Maybe you were projecting. Because from where I'm standing, those two have not come out of the restaurant in the last twenty minutes or so that we've been out here. I'm pretty sure they're in the toilet getting acquainted."

I glanced at my watch and groaned.

"You need to relax, Andrea Tang," he admonished. "You're very . . . tightly wound up."

"So I've been told. It's part of my charm."

Without missing a beat, Eric said, "No, it's not. You have much more going for you than your anxiety."

I waited for him to tell me what I had going on for a few beats, even if it were irreverent or inappropriate ("—like your crazy eyes or your hefty body odor!"; "—such as your ability to tell, from one sniff of a baby's head, whether they will grow up lactose-intolerant/racist!") before realizing that he had stopped talking and was looking at me expectantly. I guess the kind of witty rejoinders I craved, that people like Linda and Suresh supplied at the drop of a hat, were not everyone's forte, and at that moment I missed Linda. "I'm glad," I said. "So tell me about your authentic self then while we wait for those knuckleheads."

He chuckled. "You mean you haven't Google stalked every last bit of available information?"

"There, um, isn't much about you dating back more than twelve years." He was an older man, and having a scant digital (especially social media) trail was pretty common with men his age, was what I wanted to say. Although it did not explain why Valerie couldn't find much on Ralph on the internet. "And not a lot on Ralph, either."

"Ah, my skimpy Facebook and LinkedIn profiles." He grinned. "What can I say, I like being mysterious. And Ralph, like me, is just about as discreet as you can get, for his level of wealth. I respect that."

"Sorry, but I don't do mystery; in fact I got badly bit just a few weeks ago by mystery."

"Oh, how so?"

"Someone I met online stole something from me."

"I'm sorry to hear that. Maybe I can help."

"It's a dead end. Never mind." I was sorry I'd brought up Orson and tried to change the subject. "So tell me, what's not on the WWW? Who are you?"

"Well, it looks like those two are still in there, so clearly we've got time. But first things first: do you smoke cigars?" He had magicked one out of his jacket pocket.

I nodded. He lit the cigar and passed it to me. I puffed on it a little self-consciously, coughed, and passed the cigar back.

He cocked his head and listened to the faint music from the restaurant. "They are playing my favorite song, by Teresa Teng. That's a good sign. Would you do me the honor?"

He held out his hand and made a gesture for me to step into his arms. I did so after a slight hesitation. It seemed no more unusual than our previous interactions had been. Why stop now?

We started to slow dance in the parking lot, him puffing vigorously on his cigar over my head while I listened to the beating of his heart.

"Here's the deal, Andrea Tang. I know you think I'm a wild card because you can't google my life story, but I'm going to change that: I'm going to lay all my cards in front of you. I'll do that because I trust you." A pause as he puffed on his cigar and whirled me around before dipping me. "I am fifty-two. I've never been married, but I have a six-year-old daughter who is deaf and whose mom was someone I had a one-night stand with. For the past six years, I've been supporting them both. The mother has a strict confidentiality agreement with me. The child lives with me every other week, and I pay her mother a decent allowance to ensure they are both comfortable and the mother can further her studies at a local university. Was that too much of an information dump for your due diligence? Are you scared off?"

I thought about it. His honesty had been so striking, his tone so matter-of-fact, that I was underwhelmed. A masterful performance. "I don't scare easily." Then I recalled something that had been bothering me. "There is one little thing . . . ," I said hesitantly.

"Oh?" His voice had a velvety texture to it.

"Who's DeeDee Halim to you? Why are you living together?"

He laughed. "Rashidah? DeeDee is a good friend, nothing more. Our parents are close. Trust me."

Trust me. We continued to sway in the empty parking lot. With anyone else it would have been ludicrous. "Most women would not be so forgiving of my past—I must say that one or two women I've tried to start a relationship with couldn't look past my daughter's existence. But I've never regretted having her in my life, not for one minute. She's the best thing that's ever happened to me."

"Why don't you marry the mother? You obviously care for your daughter."

"I've considered it, but it feels a little too convenient. Marriage is a beautiful institution, and I don't want to cheapen it by entering into it just because I got someone pregnant. It would have been different if the mother and I had an existing relationship, and my daughter resulted from that. I've tried to do right by both of them, all the same."

I played devil's advocate. "You could have just ignored her claim."

He raised his eyebrow. "No. My parents taught me that whatever I do in life, I must be ready to shoulder the responsibility of the consequences."

A dutiful man. "Where are your parents now?"

"My mom passed away more than twenty years ago, and my father lives in Hong Kong now. I see him as often as I can."

"He doesn't live with you?" I heard the judgment in my voice.

"No, but that's because he's remarried and I would think his second wife, my stepsister, and half brothers would prefer I don't see him so often. Anyway, he's got Alzheimer's, so I don't think he even recognizes me anymore." He stopped moving, gave me a rueful smile. "I'm no spring chicken, Andrea. The day approaches when I won't have my parents with me, and it is sad."

He's filial, my mother's voice screeched excitedly in my head. "Shut up," I muttered.

"I'm sorry?"

"Er, nothing." I blushed.

We had just been standing there with his arms around me. He let go of me gently. We smiled at each other.

"I don't think those two are coming out anytime soon," I marveled, a little surprised that I had forgotten about Valerie and Ralph.

"We should have dinner next week, instead of lunch," he said.

After the emotional wringer I put him through, there was no way I could say no. Dinner it was.

1:05 a.m. New strip from *TLTS*. Water sends out a coded message via the local paper's Lonely Hearts column, asking for Rhean to meet him at a local bar, time and date given. He waits for her to turn up, with no idea if she's seen the ad.

It's a long wait, with only beer to keep him warm. Water gives up. But just before he leaves, she appears. Water is struck by her face. It is not a classically beautiful one by any measure, too hard. Only the eyes are soft, like gray stars. Her hair curling masses around that face in flames of red. Trembling, he asks her who she is.

"Don't you recognize me?" she asks.

"No . . . I'm afraid not."

"Ron, it's Louise." She smiles, sadly. "But you can call me Rhean now, I suppose."

Turns out Water's wife did not die in the freak accident at their lab but was spirited away by the bosses at the lab and experimented on. When she escaped, she went looking for him and caught him in the act of gutting a well-known hate preacher. Instead of being horrified, she was overjoyed to see him again and wanted to reach out to him so that they could meet, but only in a public space. Just in case.

Water stares at her, thunderstruck, as memories from his past resurface. He walks toward her to embrace her, when they realize, for some reason, this is a physical impossibility—they are repelling each other.

"Like repels like," he says, comprehension dawning on him.

They stare at each other with horror.

OMG! Just let them have that moment, Suresh, you monster!

Sunday 24 April

Have not seen Linda for so long. Hate to admit it but miss her. Can't even remember why we were in a fight.

Oh yeah, she's a rude harpy.

But she's *my* harpy. And didn't we all, like Monsieur Ralph, have our bad days? Don't we all hurt each other from time to time?

Decided to text her to see how she was doing.

You alive? X

She replied immediately.

Yeah *tree emoji*

Heartened, I typed:

So guess what, went out with Val and these two guys I met with her, Eric and Ralph at a book club.

So I've heard. Val couldn't keep her mouth shut. So how was your date with Musty and Fusty?

I giggled. **Which is which?**

Can't tell them apart? Linda texted.

Eric thinks I'm a millennial! *grin emoji*

You look so young, so I'm not surprised, Linda admitted generously. The ice, it seemed, was beginning to thaw.

"But you *are* a millennial," Jason told me, later, in my apartment. He had come over to hang out with me after I sent out an SOS on the group chat for a "drinks-free evening." "You're what? Thirty? Thirty-one?"

What a darling! Someone should marry Jason right away. "Thirty-three. Ish."

He did the math and started googling the birth year guidelines for millennials. "So you were born in the mid-eighties. That means you're officially one of us, according to Pew Research and the US Census, which puts the cutoff point at 1981."

Felt the existential crisis of being a millennial hit me in the gut. Dear Diary, I am not good with social media. Facebook is already a minefield, and I use Instagram and Twitter purely as stalking/fact-finding tools. And look at how my attempt at online dating went.

"It's OK," Jason said, soothingly. "You don't have to be number one at everything."

11:55 a.m. Wrong, Jason, wrong. Thy challenge is accepted. Have just ordered bestselling e-books written by fellow peers more zeitgeisty than me: *Instagram for New Influencers*, *Reddit-Ready!: Forums for Success*, *How to Break the Internet with Your Latest Selfie*, and *Tweeting for the Modern Jezebel* and will finish these e-books tonight. I must not let my generation down.

Monday 25 April

1:45 a.m. Will just have to let the entire generation down. These e-books are barely readable. Nobody can spell anymore. We are all doomed.

7:05 a.m. Ooh, text!

> **Andrea, I can't wait to see you when I'm back from Dubai. Would you please do me the honor of having dinner with me this Saturday at Les Deux?**

Not a hashtag, acronym, emoji, slang word, abbreviation, contraction, typo, or bad punctuation or grammar in sight. What a man.

9:15 a.m. Just got an earful from a client because I, or rather one of my minions, forgot to capitalize one letter of a company's name on a board resolution, which was still in draft form, by the way.

Well, just wait till the lawyers of the Gen Z cohort are unleased upon the world. Forgetting to capitalize will be the least of anyone's concerns.

Tuesday 26 April

One of those weeks at work that makes me wish the zombie apocalypse would come already.

Thursday 28 April

Put out one fire only to have another one pop up on another file. According to a carefully worded report from the Luxembourg law firm working on the same deal, there was a slight hiccup with one of the proposed acquisitions by our client, a Singaporean private equity firm called Sungguh Capital. But in the hierarchy of clients, the one whose closing I'm working on has bigger money balls, and the deadline for the closing is tomorrow, so I red-flagged it in my inbox.

Out of (morbid) curiosity I opened the Flagged folder, just to see what items I had pending.

OMG.

Friday 29 April

7:15 p.m. Done. Going to a seedy karaoke dive bar in Katong with Suresh, who was involved in a separate, equally hellish closing that was done the evening before. Dive bar was Suresh's suggestion. The two of us look like extras from an undead movie because of our respective closings, but it's OK because the dive bar will be populated by older men and it's very dark, making me look fresh and vigorous in comparison. He gets me.

1:10 a.m. Got hit on left and right and bought zero drinks the entire night, although I've been very careful not to binge-drink as I have a date in less than twenty-four hours and don't want to balloon. Am living the dream. A dream where the bar is set very, very low.

Saturday 30 April

10:04 a.m. Up early. Strange. I didn't even think I was that excited about going on a date with Eric Deng. Who knew.

10:35 a.m. HAVE NOTHING TO WEAR.

11:07 a.m. Going shopping, as have nothing to wear.

11:15 a.m. Texted Valerie to come with, but when I checked her Last Seen time stamp, it seems she's not looked at WhatsApp for the past thirty hours. Wonderful.

1:20 p.m. Bought a dress. Fine, three dresses. And LV bag. Must accessorize to impress. Plus the bag can be used in my professional life, thus is multifunctional and will pay for itself over time.

6:45 p.m. Showered, exfoliated, depilated. Staring at the slinky, backless or cleavage-revealing clothes I bought. All are terrible choices, too date-clothesy when really the image I want to project is: yes, I am attractive, but would you and I be better off if I were to become your lawyer?

7:05 p.m. Doorbell! Shit! Must find some item of clothing that is black and body-hugging but has a lawyerly hem!

11:55 p.m. Back from Les Deux. Interesting evening. The whole thing about conducting myself properly with Eric Deng, him being a possible client and all, gave the date an electric charge of the forbidden, i.e., sexual. Also maybe because lots of Montrachet wine, haha. The second bottle was all that was needed for me to shift gears. Suddenly the age gap is not that big a deal. We both like oysters, for example, and democracy (Eric's family fled China in the '60s). Surely that is a good enough basis on which to start a relationship.

We talked about many things: his family history (well-connected, powerful and rich, but lost everything when they fled, although they quickly rebuilt their fortunes in Indonesia) and mine (migrant laborers on both sides, clawed their way into middle class); our common interests (politics, human rights, and poetry); favorite food and drink (Sichuanese and Malaysian food for both of us (!)), pet peeves (him: people who go barefoot on commercial planes—well, on the rare occasions when Eric has to fly commercial business; mine: kept wisely silent, as there were too many to list without seeming unstable).

At one point during the dinner, he put down his fork and said, "You know, I've got a confession to make."

"What is it?" I said, immediately wary. Can't say I hadn't been waiting for this. It had been too easy, the last info dump.

"I admire what you do, a lot. It seems so exciting."

"Really," I said in a neutral voice.

"Well, when I was at university—"

"Which one?" I asked eagerly.

"Oxford."

"Nice, very nice. Good one, that."

"Thanks. May I continue?"

"Sorry, yes, please."

"I had read law and wanted to go whole hog, become a barrister, but my father stepped in and asked me to come home."

"Why?"

"He wanted me to stay in the family business of hospitality and real estate, not waste time as a barrister. So I did. I came home. I resented him for it at first, but have made peace with it now."

The idea that being a lawyer is "not good enough" to a Chinese family—well, that just shows you the difference in status between his family and mine.

"It's not that fun," I assured him. "Ruling an empire sounds way more interesting."

Eric smiled ruefully. "When I first took over it wasn't great for me. I felt like a cake topper. The company already had a very established growth plan and an excellent management team, and my father was always peering over my shoulder as the chairman. It's only in the last decade, after his Alzheimer's, that . . . I could spread my wings, make my mark. The green hotel brand, Lana, is my other child, really. And I guess in hindsight, it was the right choice."

Hmm. I suppose in a way our paths had some similarities, although he was persuaded to run a multibillion-dollar empire, but there you go.

Food was very good, so good that if he had made his move after the second bottle of Montrachet I might have let him kiss me. But he didn't. He played it very coy and proper, gentlemanly. We made plans to see each other when he gets back from Chengdu. Will just wait and see. At least I'm dating someone who won't filch my jewelry—the watch he was wearing, a beautiful A. Lange & Söhne chronograph, cost more than the down payment for my two-bed apartment—if anything, he should be worried about me filching *his* things.

The conclusion at the end of the evening is: I'd definitely prefer to date him than do business with him. And that's saying something. The wheel of my dating fortune was, it seemed, finally spinning me upward; my luck was turning at last.

Monday 2 May

Valerie and Ralph finally resurfaced on my radar. By Monday morning, she had proclaimed her love for a "mystery man but shh!" on social media, to wit the whole world, because she had 17,300-plus followers on Instagram (How? Who? Why?) *and* more than two thousand friends on Facebook, *including Ralph Kang.*

I missed Linda terribly—she would never have done anything sappy or publicly embarrassing like this. She also didn't fall in love as quickly as dropping money into a collection box. Her personal motto was "It's only love if you would give him your liver"—inspired by what Singaporean heartthrob and actor Pierre Png did for his then-fiancée/now-wife, actress Andrea De Cruz, in 2002, a courageous and loving feat so chivalrous that it exploded the ovaries of every single girl and woman who heard of it, even us young adults across the Causeway in faraway Kuala Lumpur. It's been almost a month since I last saw her. A month since she last called me a dingus bat. A month since she had last pinched me for pronouncing a word in American instead of British (the Queen's?) English.

I missed her.

"Ahem," Suresh said over my shoulder. I let out a shriek and dropped the photo frame on the floor. "Should I leave you two alone?" he said, in reference to the very unglamorous headshot I was mooning over, a framed photo of Linda as a teenager. It was comforting to see her as she once was, frizzy-haired with braces and tadpole eyebrows, the Vicky Adams before Spice Girls and David Beckham.

"Buzz off, buzzkill," I said, wheeling around in my swivel chair to glare up at him, instead of maintaining an otherwise indecent eyeline. "Don't you have your own woman troubles?" He and Anousha were still arguing over a free house. Goddamn spoiled rich people.

Suresh grinned. "Touché. By the way, bad news. I just ran into Mong in the pantry."

"What did he want?"

"Apparently the both of us have to be in Luxembourg tomorrow on his behalf. Remember that due diligence report that Loesch sent to you last week, the one that made you stress-eat a pack of gummy bears?"

"Hmm," I said. I eat a lot of gummy bears, sometimes even when I'm not stressed.

"Sungguh Capital wants us to check up on an issue that the Luxembourg lawyers have identified in their due diligence report on VizWare's Luxembourg holdco." Sungguh was coinvesting in some newfangled drone technology used in Spanish and Portuguese farms called VizWare, and the Luxembourg holding company (or "holdco," in lawyer-speak) was, erm, holding everything in a very sexy (if your fetish was tax efficiency), totally legal tax optimization structure. It was a big acquisition and Suresh was also working on the file, although I, haha, was lead senior associate. Hahaha.

"Why can't Mong ever come to us to just tell us a charming factoid or a knock-knock joke?" I muttered.

"He wouldn't be the Mong we know and love if he did."

I sighed. "Don't I know it. But why do we have to personally fly up? It's just a delayed filing of some accounts. It seems like something we can sort out over the phone."

Suresh shrugged. "The investment committee prefers that we

fly over to speak to the Luxembourg lawyers, do our own informal due diligence. Also the Singapore desk rep from our London office, Tristan Langford-Bauer, will be on hand to give his input on the acquisition. He's very familiar with Luxembourg holding structures and is a tax expert, and since he is attending the ALFI conference anyway, he thought he'd lend a hand. So we're going to Luxembourg!"

"Urgh. But it's so far."

"Yes, but the client has promised to put us up in a fancy place and fly us business. We leave tonight."

I pumped the air with my fist. "We're going to Luxembourg!"

Suresh patted my back. "Don't worry, it won't be all fun and games. We'll also have to attend the same showcase and the gala dinner because Langford-Bauer thinks it's important for the Singapore office to be there, mingle, blah blah, rich people, blah blah."

I rolled my eyes. "That sounds exciting."

"I look forward to traveling with you and finding out all your weaknesses that I will later exploit," Suresh said, poker-faced.

"Ditto," I said, puffing out my chest to appear larger to my opponent. In a purely nonsexual way.

Anyway, Luxembourg. Land of hills and medieval cobblestones, asset management firms and farmers, Pinot Gris and good pork. So Suresh was coming along, but how bad could it be?

26

Tuesday 3 May

12:16 a.m. Very bad start to our trip. Left home later than planned because I had to put on makeup before meeting Suresh at the airport at this ungodly hour.

Speaking of which, why do people use the expression "ungodly hour"? All hours are godly. It just depends on who your god is.

Made it to the airport with only minutes to spare before they closed check-in, but looking fabulous (for myself, obviously, not because I was flying with Suresh). Made it through security checks and frantically texted Suresh, pretending that I had been there for the past hour. No luck. Apparently the freak had been there for *two hours*, pottering around duty-free, thoughtfully buying boxes of pineapple tarts and TWG tea to cart all the way to Luxembourg.

As if clients, the Sauron-worshipping tapeworms that they are, can be appeased by pineapple tarts.

The only thing that tapeworms understand is, erm . . . hmm. I don't think tapeworms actually have the capacity to understand. Well, then the only thing tapeworms are driven by is . . .

What *are* they driven by?

12:25 a.m. I now know all the types of intestinal worms you can get and how to get them.

Suresh was engaged. And from what I knew about Anousha, she seemed like the kind of woman who would practice her own version of sati and throw a rival onto a burning funeral pyre.

11:55 a.m. Was reading news (fine, tabloids) when I came across a feature of Helen and Magnus's engagement party in *Tatler.* The bitch had not invited me!

Saturday 14 May

A knock on the door. Waited for Linda to open it since she has colonized the living room, even though there is a perfectly functional second bedroom with a proper double bed. Maybe she is now allergic to the sight of double beds.

Waited for a full two minutes before I realized that Linda was not budging. Walked out and saw that Linda was sleeping, naked as a daisy, on the couch surrounded by an empty bottle of vodka, a bottle of Chinon red, half a bottle of Patrón, a small bottle of Evian, and several bottles of Tiger beer. Maybe she wasn't even sleeping; maybe she was dead.

I opened the door. It was Eric Deng, standing in the hallway in a pale lemon polo shirt and khakis.

"Are you going to gawk at me or invite me in?" he said, after a few seconds of stunned silence had passed from my end.

I collected my dignity (I was in a god-awful Ramones T-shirt and a pair of graying cotton shorts) and said, "My friend Linda's naked in my living room. You can't enter."

"Well, get dressed. I'm taking you out to champagne brunch."

I pretended to hesitate; he had me at "champagne."

"I'll wait in the car," he said, a small smile curving his lips. "Take your time."

We arrived at the St. Regis twenty-five minutes later (I had taken ten minutes to complete my toiletries, apply makeup, and throw on a respectable flowered sundress). It was only while I was in his car that I realized that my pretty peep-toe sandals were exposing, in all their glory, the remnants of a month-old pedicure. I tried to angle my feet away from his sightline, but I was sure he had seen them: Eric Deng was not a man who missed such details. I'd felt like a fraud in his gleaming, immaculate car, even though he himself was delightfully, gently rumpled, in hair and clothing.

"I got you a gift," he said after we'd ordered. He pressed a small, brown paper–wrapped parcel in my hands. He raised his eyebrow. "I'm not sure it's as good as flowers, but I think it'll last longer."

"Oh!" I said, my manners forgotten. I felt a bolt of excitement in my stomach. "What's . . . what's it for?"

"For being such a lovely companion," he said. "Companion." What an odd choice of words. We could have been knitting buddies.

"Open it," he urged. I tore through the wrapping like a kid, thinking it was a Moleskine or something practical.

"Oh!" I said in a tiny voice when I saw the cover. Then I opened it, trembling. It was a first edition, signed hardcover of *It Catches My Heart in Its Hands*, my favorite book of Charles Bukowski's poems. A poet I had once mentioned in passing, over two months ago, at the Sexless Book Club. He'd remembered.

The inscription in his elegant cursive read:

Andrea,
Here's to the beginning of new, poetic exchanges.
Eric

"Eric, this is too much," I murmured, embarrassed, pushing it across the table to him. "I can't accept this."

"You must. It's got your name on it." He pushed the book back. "I can't return this, you know."

During the champagne brunch he regaled me with stories of his recent business trip throughout Mongolia and China, meeting with potential codevelopers for his passion project, the Dulit

Group's Lana brand of luxury eco-hotels. His passion for the project, and his fascinating anecdotes on his travels and his business, made the hours pass quickly. By the time we'd finished around three o'clock, he had to go for a coffee with a colleague and I was reluctant to leave his side. He was just so easy and nice to be with. I had the sense that when it came to him, I was struggling upstream when I could be cruising with the current to him, the inevitable conclusion to the tale of the woman I wanted to be, if I would just let him be that to me.

And—I cast a sidelong glance to him, my heart beating faster when I caught him looking at me in his frank, admiring way—why not? The attraction was there.

He walked me to my door like a gentleman, waited to see if I could find my keys, opened the door for me after several fumbles at the doorknob, and once the door was ajar, bid me goodbye with a soft peck on my right cheek.

"Wait," I slurred, grabbing his sleeve and pulling him close, even as I was unsure of what I wanted to achieve as I did so. But he put his free hand on my shoulder and held me at arm's length.

"You're drunk," he said.

"I'm sober," I said, trying again.

"Don't make this . . . it's . . ." He swore in bahasa Indonesia. "Look, I've got to go. I'll see you soon," he said. Then he turned on his heel and left. I watched him go, let myself in, locked the door before I stumbled into the living room, humiliated and definitely less sober than I had initially thought myself to be.

"Look what the cat dragged in," Linda said snidely, in the exact same spot on the couch. She had barely budged, except her entourage of bottles now included three new empties of white wine and two bags of Kettle chips.

I walked over, dropped my tote bag (and the book, secure in its wrapping again) on the floor, sank into a bean bag, and slept.

Sunday 15 May

I went to the office today, thinking I could work through the swirl of confusion that seems to be my thoughts these days (and also to escape La Linda, truth be told). The book of poems I had stashed in the drawer of my nightstand, untouched. I felt like if I opened it, there would be no turning back.

I was looking forward to billing some long, hard hours while ordering in brunch. In the absence of a suitable companion with whom I could have said brunch, the twisted adrenaline I get from milking some faceless corporation dry, fees-wise, would have to do.

The office was a picture of Sunday industry: smart casual threads, Nespresso coffee, and the acrid base notes of yesterday's hangover mixed with ambition. As usual, several gung-ho juniors, a.k.a. minions, including Suresh's and mine (Josiah and Xi Lin), were milling about, putting in face time and billable hours that we would have to slash later, but still; this being a week when several closings were at hand, one could also see a few senior associates, and even the occasional partner, hard at work, slave-driving their juniors. Then there were those partners who, despite not having any real need to be in the office, chose to come in that Sunday to seek refuge from their progenies/marriages. I took it all in and felt my anxiety ebb away. This was my safe place, my second home.

Until I entered my office and saw Suresh.

The thing is, it's been weird between Suresh and me since Luxembourg. We would oscillate between laughing chummily over some shared joke and stone-facing each other for extended periods of time in a day; we avoided being alone in our shared office for long (I even started smoking again just to have an excuse to duck out of the office). Even Kai commented on it when she cornered me privately in the washroom. "There's a weird tension in the air. What's wrong?" I told her it was because we were both fighting for the same promotion, but my private impression was it was because we couldn't decide if we wanted to string each other's intestines like fairy lights over the walls or smush our genitals together.

Now, happening upon him working in a slim-fit chambray shirt and dark jeans, I knew it was definitely the latter, on my part at least. I wanted to lock us together in some isolated padded cell, throw away the keys, and smush genitals all day long. My stupid treacherous libido.

I took my seat after grunting a hello at him, careful not to look at his chiseled face.

"Hey there," he said in a neutral tone. "Didn't know you'd be coming in today."

"Is there a problem? It's my office, too," I said testily. It was my office *first*, I corrected myself mentally.

"No problem," he said. "Just thought I'd be alone today. Get some real work done."

"Does my presence bother you?" I countered.

"That's not what I meant, I just meant—well, you've been busy."

"Yeah, I've been busy with someone," I said.

"Really," he said evenly. "With who?"

"Remember Eric Deng? Big-shot tycoon? Yeah, we've been seeing each other."

We lapsed into loud, passive-aggressive typing for the next few minutes. It was like being in a firing range. My fingers and wrists began to hurt.

"Hey," he tried again.

"What?" I said, still typing loudly.

"This is very juvenile," he said.

"What is?" I asked, typing louder.

He got up and came over to my side of the table. "Will you just *stop* typing for one second and have a real conversation with me? Look at me."

I stopped typing and looked at his Adam's apple, the least sexy part of his anatomy. Aren't Adam's apples just the weirdest? Find one and really study it, just take it in. Really eyeball it. What does it remind you of?

He reached out a hand and pushed the hair out of my face. "Why can't you look me in the eye?"

I forced myself to do so, even though I was trembling. "You know why. Because I'm trying to keep this relationship a platonic one for both our sakes and you're being really unfair."

"How so?" He was bent over me now and exercising some kind of cobra stare on me.

"You're being deliberately provocative when you shouldn't be."

He stroked my face. "Like this?"

"Don't touch me," I whispered, my arms snaking around his waist. He lifted me out of my seat and—

A loud rapping on the door jolted both of us apart. He fled to his side of the room just as the door flew open to reveal Kai, who was red with excitement.

"Oh, great, you're here, Suresh!" Kai said, sauntering into the room wearing a hobo's singlet and what looked like the shredded remains of a leper's jeans. She called out over her shoulder, "Come on in. Your hunch was right!"

"What are you doing here?" we chorused at the same time in high, guilty voices. I was subtly hyperventilating.

"Someone special roped me in for a sweet surprise. You are going to be so thrilled," Kai said.

That was when I saw that she had someone with her; a woman was standing behind Kai, her face partially obscured.

"Voilà, lover boy!" Kai said, stepping aside with a flourish. My jaw dropped: there was no need for introductions—I knew who she was. I'd seen photos of her on Suresh's phone. But there was something else about her face that was familiar. What was it?

She glided into the room in a powder blue sari that was embroidered with silver thread and the tears of little Indian boys. Our eyes met briefly, her kohl-rimmed light brown ones narrowing as she assessed me. I could tell she thought of me as a threat. Kai, ever the perceptive one, sensed the crackling tension in the air and decided it was time to leave. Then it was just the three of us.

I sneaked a peek at Suresh, who was staring at her with his mouth ajar, an understandable reaction considering he'd not seen her in ages.

"Darling, I missed you," she said to him in a throaty, intimate voice, as though I was just a coat rack with eyes and they were alone in the room. She tilted forward to kiss him even as he slid a panicked glance in my direction; but what could I do? Anousha was now in town.

Part III

SALTY WITH AGE

Monday 16 May

Called the office and took a week off. Kai was worried, but I assured her once again I was not close to death's door but had to deal with "an urgent family matter."

Mong was not so understanding in his email. "What family? The whole reason I hired you was because you have no family in Singapore! And you said you were single!" I had to tell him I had contracted viral fever and was close to death's door, upon which he stopped emailing.

Anyway, am on my way to the airport now with a disheveled Linda in a limo cab. We're flying to the Maldives in two and a half hours! Linda's dad's friend's business partner owns a swanky six-star resort there, and since it's the start of the monsoon season he's been pretty generous in giving us free accommodation in one of his two-bedder villas: the only thing we'll have to pay for is any F&B (code for "alcohol") consumed throughout our stay. Smart move, Linda's dad's friend's business partner. Smart move.

Linda was, understandably, quite furious that she had been kept in the dark about Luxembourg and the whole lead-up to yesterday's shenanigans until today. She revived from her fugue state of Massimo-less depression to give me an earful when I confessed why I needed to get away from Singapore; even though she liked Suresh, who she'd met several times at various lawyerly events, she was worried about his baggage (I know, I know, this coming from the lady who had been dating a married man).

"Not only were you pooping where you eat, you had to go for the pretty toilet magazine, didn't you?" she said, pulling another nonsensical metaphor out of thin air. "I always said to you, Andrea, stay away from the pretty boys, they're poison, but did you? Did you listen to La Linda?"

"You said stay away from the boy toys, not pretty boys."

"Stay away from the kiddos *and* the pretties. Pretty boys are to be avoided like the plague. They are so prized, their sense of entitlement is beyond that of pretty girls. They've never had to work hard in bed, ever. I won't be surprised if Suresh turns out to be a bad kisser and a stinker in bed—the boy looks like that K-pop star you're always mooning over—what's his name, Won Won? Bon Bin? Bing Bong?"

"Won . . . Bin . . . ," I said through gritted teeth. "He's an *actor.*"

"Actor, pop star, whatever, I say 'same-same in Korea,'" said Linda dismissively.

"*Those are two separate professions—two!* And how can you even confuse Won Bin with Bing Bong? Bing Bong is a character from *Inside Out*, a beautiful animated film that we've watched together, *twice*!" I hissed. "Did you even bother reading the Henry Chong brief I made for you in preparation for Chinese New Year?"

"Why are we arguing about ancient history? Especially since you've only got yourself to blame for being such a crap liar that no one bothered to ask for a photo of Henry," was my best friend's cavalier reply before she pulled out a hip flask that smelled suspiciously of rum.

Too late to back out of Maldives trip now. I'll have to charge all bar drinks to her credit card.

5:10 p.m. Maldives is amazing—clear skies, cotton-candy puffs of clouds, lush vegetation. We flew in a sea plane to arrive at the super exclusive eco-resort. The resort is insane, wooden villas on stilts perched over crazy aquamarine water and undead coral beds everywhere. And since it's super low season, the management is offering us a villa each! This trip is going to be off the charts. I feel sorry for all the suckers missing out on the low-season rate.

Linda, my pet, has pulled out her AmEx Centurion and passed it to the hotel, quibbling not. We're going to be drinking till we turn as blue as the water.

6:05 p.m. Urgh. It's started to drizzle.

6:08 p.m. Shit, the 4G is down. No internet!

6:20 p.m. Total downpour.

6:25 p.m. Wi-Fi dead!

6:33 p.m. Still dead!

6:58 p.m. STILL DEAD!

7:15 p.m. Decided to go hang out at the bar, since there was nothing else to do in the villa. Thought of dashing through the drizzle but found that rain had turned into a storm with mad buffeting winds. Called the butler. He came with a huge umbrella, which was useless as the rain was falling *diagonally* (?). My long peasant skirt was drenched by the time I arrived at the main restaurant, where Linda was waiting, somehow dry and unscathed.

9:00 p.m. Excellent nosh, wine. Who cares if rain? Who cares about Anousha and Suresh? More wine!

10:45 p.m. In villa. Discovered that I could get 4G if I stood very still two feet by the open window in my bathroom, on top of the toilet lid, which is surprisingly solid. By turning work phone, which had sporadic 4G connection, into a hotspot, I was able to use my personal phone. Launched Sponk just for shits and giggles and was amused to see the bar manager on it. Who was he hoping to match with, the guests? There's like thirty-five of us, max; low season it being. Hmm. Oh well, he is rather attractive. Maybe—

10:47 p.m. Linda walked into the villa, found me in the washroom and confiscated my phones. All three of them. Says she will only return the office phone to me on Wednesday—if I'm good.

11:05 p.m. There is no twenty-four-hour computer room. What kind of six-star resort is this?! And apparently, according to the receptionist, because we were "in the middle of nowhere," the Wi-Fi will not be fixed till Friday. *Friday.*

Tuesday 17 May

Has not stopped raining, and I have not stopped drinking with Linda, since this morning; absence of phones (thus, work) is causing anxiety that can only be soothed by copious amounts of wine.

Hit on the bar manager IRL during the Tuesday Tequila Sunset Hour and was rejected like an expired credit card. No wonder no one tries in real life anymore. Don't even know what I was trying to achieve. It's almost as though I'm self-sabotaging.

Wednesday 18 May

Raining again, surprise, surprise.

No office phone from Linda. It's fine. Let Suresh handle all my work crap.

Did nothing but eat and drink. Reread somebody's copy of *Kane and Abel.* I don't know what it is, but I've been to resorts all around the world and there is always, always a novel by Jeffrey Archer, Judith McNaught, and/or Michael Crichton in each "community library." I wonder what books will be in a doomsday bunker.

Mojito Magic Hour at the hotel's pool bar. Snagged myself a spot at infinity pool bar and waited for Linda to arrive, but she never did. Drank alone. Linda and the bar manager emerge from her room, both looking distinctly worse for wear.

When Linda saw me her face blanched and she cried out after his retreating back, "Shafiq, remember to unclog the tub, too. It's very, ah, clogged. Thank you for your good work on the air-conditioning."

Dear Diary, his name wasn't even Shafiq—it was Abdul. For Linda to voluntarily screw the help, there must have been a paradigm shift in how she approached dating; usually she only goes for those with power and/or status. Maybe this whole Poots incident has caused her to reevaluate her beliefs.

Thursday 19 May

Phoneless in Maldives

Net Sematary

(No) Avatar

Good Lord, what did people do before the internet?

Friday 20 May

8:15 p.m. Sun out today so decided to go swimming in the sea for the first time since landing. It was fun until something stung me and I nearly exploded in pain. Had to get treated by the nurse, who told me that it looked like a "common jellyfish sting" and I did not need to be emergency evacuated as I was, she insisted, "not going to die" and that she was sure despite "only being a resort nurse." She shunted me off to the recovery room, which was basically a room with a massage table and a small medical cabinet, hardly reassuring at all.

Had time to reflect, sober, in the recovery room. Maybe I'm truly self-sabotaging, since am allowing myself to be seduced by unavailable Suresh rather than wholeheartedly giving Eric Deng a shot. It's time to grow up and *stop* being like Linda in this respect. She was not a good role model in the romance department.

Saturday 21 May

Rained all day. My plan to access internet through PC in "reading room" was foiled as apparently "the torrential rain and thunderstorm prevented the technician from flying." Wished I was back home in Singapore, where I have phones and a computer and Netflix. Nature is cool, but there's only so much one can take of it, sans filter.

Then, miraculously, and rather cruelly, the rain stopped an hour before sunset.

Since it was our last night anyway and we must drink, we went to one of the pool bars to watch the sunset. Linda popped a bottle of vintage Krug champagne. "It was a good vacation, wasn't it?" she said, after drinking straight from the bottle. "No phones, no men."

I chugged the champagne before passing it back to her. I watched the sun melt into the ocean like something out of Candy Crush. "It's so good to be off-grid," I said, lying.

"Great, then I'll pass you the phones tomorrow."

"Yeah, whatever." I could take another twenty-four hours, no problem.

Linda smiled into the middle distance; I recognized her impression of Scarlett O'Hara in *Gone with the Wind*. "You know what? I think I'm going to be fine," she said. "Thanks for hosting me at your place for so long. I'll be out of your hair by the first week of June."

Hallelujah!

Sunday 22 May

9:30 a.m. Sky is an untroubled blue. Not a cloud for miles around. WTF.

8:45 p.m. Landed. All three phones restored to my possession. It's good to be home.

9:35 p.m. Not good to be home. Mounting panic scrolling through ominously titled email chains dated from Friday. Apparently the coinvestor, Chapel Town, is now pulling out of the deal, and although the reasons and details are not clear, it is very bad, since that would leave Sungguh Capital waving their dick in the wind. And private equity firms generally don't tolerate being made to look foolish. Someone was going to pay. Just hope it's not me.

Monday 23 May

8:15 a.m. Back in the office. Saw Suresh. Promptly ducked out of office. Went to the library with my laptop to work, pretending to be very busy with a stack of random statutes on my table. Was actually doodling on my legal pad and being totally unproductive, as I was not even sure there was any active file under which I could bill this time thus spent as "research."

How the mighty had fallen.

Suresh sent me a bunch of texts and emails trying to get me to discuss what he calls "VizWare-geddon." I closed them without bothering to read past the first line, just in case it was an excuse to get me to talk about us. The idea of being in the same room or file with Suresh made me want to run back to Maldives and spend the monsoon without Wi-Fi. There was also something else acting upon me, a foreign emotion: indifference. The strange thing is, even though I had originally been upset about VizWare potentially not being acquired after all my hard work, I couldn't find the strength to get a move on fixing it. I could be making some calls, writing some emails to find out what was the underlying issue—*but I just didn't want to*. Maybe, after my first week off in five years, I just needed time to get back into the swing of things and to care about my work again. You know, the way most people feel on Mondays—times a thousand, I suppose.

It's just . . . the idea of working so hard for clients like VizWare, for guys who'd rip into me like I was beneath them, just made me, well, less than enthused.

I tried to psych myself up about putting in the hours by thinking about the financial freedom I would have once I was top of the pyramid of rats. It helped, somewhat. I needed to regain my Winner Mentality.

Then I went to Mong to talk about the VizWare acquisition,

preparing to shoulder the fault of the stalled transaction with the equanimity of a eunuch confronted with the threat of a kick to the groin.

Mong looked up at me and said, "We don't know why Chapel Town pulled out. It's probably not even your fault. And if this is the way you're going to act after taking a week off, you might as well resign right now. I didn't raise you to be a quitter."

I was emotional. "Sim Mong, thank you for believing in me."

"Sure." He paused for a second before saying, eyes not quite meeting mine, "Also you should know that you're no longer the lead senior associate on the file as the other partners have requested a change."

"What? But . . . but am I still on the file?"

"Ah, that. Well, actually, you're off the file completely. I'm really sorry, but don't worry, you're doing really well otherwise."

"But Sungguh Capital is one of my biggest and oldest files."

"There'll be others."

I held it together as best as I could as I exited his office. Then I lunged into the Integrity conference room and let out a scream of anger.

7:25 p.m. Found out via text from Kai that Mong is no longer the partner on the file (it was now Yasmine Sidek's file; Yasmine was Genevieve's supervising partner and the latter's PA, Jill, had blabbed to Kai), but the client had requested that Suresh stay on as the lead since he had performed well in Luxembourg. Was that why Suresh wanted to talk? Had his whole nice-guy act in Luxembourg been just that—an act?

It had to be. I was a fool to trust him.

Stormed back to the office to confront him. But he had already gone home, not even bothering to Office Face-Time Battle. Coward.

11:20 p.m. New strip from *TLTS*: since Water and Rhean can't be together, physically, they've decided to do the one thing they can do, and do well, together—they kill.

Hmph. No parallels with Suresh's and my real-life situation, of course.

I whipped out my phone.

You thief, I wrote to Suresh, but did not send. Because I hadn't just been referring to work. Sending him such a text would have been a stupid, heart-baring move, lacking in strategy—in short: not a Power Move. No matter what I felt, or what he had done, Suresh was still my colleague. I had to pretend to respect him.

Thursday 26 May

8:05 a.m. Got an email from Suresh that he had accepted a three-month secondment in Jakarta. This doesn't seem like the kind of thing one would do when one's fiancée makes a long-awaited move to Singapore, but what the hell do I know.

Also: he told me that he'd been "offered" and he had "immediately rejected" the offer to be lead senior associate on Sungguh, which would now be overseen by Genevieve. That means nothing—maybe he thinks it's a matter of time before Sungguh ditches our firm for good. I can't believe I trusted him.

His betrayal is the only reason I'm upset with him, of course. No other reason.

4:50 p.m. Oh shit. Just saw Massimo Poon and Berenice Chan featured on local news for their "lavish, retro-inspired vow renewal ceremony in Bali." Shit.

9:10 p.m. House is suspiciously quiet. Thought Linda was not home until I found her lying, passed-out drunk, behind the couch. Had to prop her up with some pillows and cover her with a blanket, because she was, once again, butt naked in my living room. But I'll deal with that another day.

Friday 27 May

1:25 p.m. It's really not been my week.

Just received news that the VizWare deal is definitely off. Apparently the founder of Chapel Town just passed away from natural causes, which in his case was old age (he was close to ninety). The general counsel of the firm wrote to us to say that nothing will move until the son has come on board and has had a chance to decide on the pending investments, but that would have to wait till they had sorted out other estate matters.

Well. There's nothing much you can say to that. It was too late for me anyway, because the founder's death hadn't absolved my part in the whole Luxembourg kerfuffle that had delayed the signing in the first place. And now Sungguh Capital was pissed at me and the firm.

Things were not looking good for my case for partnership.

I asked Mong what I could do to make up for potentially jeopardizing the Sungguh Capital relationship, since I was already billing like crazy.

He thought about it. "Bring me a huge new client the scale of Sungguh Capital or get the VizWare closing back on track."

Well, that's it, I'm doomed.

2:25 p.m. Got tired of playing out worst-case scenarios in my head and called Eric to ask him out; he said yes. We're going to watch a community (!) musical tonight.

10:25 p.m. My dejection must have shown on my face, because Eric asked me what the problem was. Told him all about the Luxembourg fiasco without going into details about the parties involved, and told him about Mong's challenge to me.

He listened attentively and then said, jokingly I suppose, although he hardly ever jokes, "I guess that means I'll really have to give you some business."

I laughed. "Well, I don't know if that's appropriate. It smacks of nepotism."

He looked bemused. "Why wouldn't it be? We're not dating."

"We're—not?" I said, taken aback.

"No," he said, a smile creasing his face. "Not yet. So, I don't see any conflict of interest that prevents you from being my lawyer if I do pass your firm some work, do you?"

"Nooo," I conceded. Although I have to say, dear Diary, that I was disappointed to learn that we had really been attending that atrocious play as platonic companions. Because we could have just had a business lunch.

Also—I was starting to like him. In a not-strictly-business kind of way.

Urgh. Just my luck all over again.

Wednesday 1 June

11:28 p.m. Mong called me this morning with an excited voice. Turns out Eric had indeed given a file to my department, with the strict instructions that I would be the lead senior associate on it.

I was flushed with pleasure at the loud stream of hearty congratulations from Mong. The only thing that detracted from my pleasure was the strange feeling of guilt and shame I felt. But surely this was not nepotism—he said it himself: we were just casual friends!

Speaking of which, we're going out again tonight, for a dining-in-the-dark experience. As friends, of course.

Thursday 2 June

Went with Eric to Karma to watch stand-up comedy, of the open-mic, anyone-can-do-it variety. I've always enjoyed the thrill of unearthing new talent at open-mics.

Not tonight, though. Heard so many bad jokes about porn and masturbation that at the end of the evening I couldn't look Eric in the eye for suggesting that as a fun night out.

Friday 3 June

Tonight we're watching an arthouse film, German, Cold War, subtitles only. The potential for amorous overtures at a film such as this is just—endless.

At the rate we are going, I'm beginning to think he's friend-zoning me.

Saturday 4 June

11:25 a.m. In a foul mood. Just woke up and found Linda doing something completely inappropriate on my living room couch. When we came back from Maldives, she'd promised that she would move out; she's still parked in my living room, moping and bingeing rom-coms when she's not at work. All because of Massimo Egghead. My beautiful leather couch is no longer cream-colored but gray, and there is a permanent smell of vodka in the air. I may never get rid of her.

I *need* to get rid of her.

2:10 p.m. Back from solo lunch. Could have had lunch with Eric, who asked yesterday, but decided not to. I'm very confused: is he really trying to be my friend? Can straight women and men, where at least one of them finds the other attractive, ever just be friends without it getting complicated?

In contrast, Valerie and Ralph Kang were regularly smushing uglies in all manner of dwellings and non-dwellings around the city-state. Mr. Kang, it would seem, delighted in having outdoor sex, especially in seedy back alleys where the possibility of contracting dengue along with jail time for public indecency and internet infamy got him hot and bothered.

"Younger men are just so . . . vigorous," Valerie gushed, while I barfed a little into my mouth. Not wanting the sex gravy train to stop, she was even contemplating getting butt implants at his suggestion. I told her it was a bad idea and sent her loads of "surgery gone wrong" listicles, but she was too far gone, even if she didn't care to admit it. What was a butt implant in the grand scheme of things if you're already mostly flammable?

"I've got some referrals for a good plastic surgeon in Bangkok," she told me. (*Really?* I thought. *What happened to your* current *surgeon(s)?*)

"Why have elective plastic surgery if you've, er, never had any before?"

"Ralph might be my last chance at the One. I'm already forty-s— Never mind," she said, flustered.

"You don't look a day over twenty-eight," I lied automatically. She appreciated it, though. Sometimes that's what we need from our friends: sweet, sweet lies. "Ralph looks *so* much older compared to you."

Valerie perked up. "He does, doesn't he? He could use a good maintenance regime consisting of a monthly chemical peel, IPL photofacial, and maybe either a vampire facial or a Venus Freeze to hold everything together."

"Right, right," I said, making mental notes of everything so I could google later.

Linda, though, was a whole big pile of cow poo that needed more than the glue of lies to hold her all together. For some reason the news about Twitter Avatar Man and his third wife had really gotten under her skin. Nothing I said or did made any difference to her fugue state when she was not at work: not bribery, not threats, not even flattery. She didn't want to engage or talk, even about herself; she was increasingly lax about personal hygiene and upkeep; she wouldn't even eat, she, a woman who once cry-ate her way through different body parts of a suckling pig in front of me when she had a bad breakup at uni. It was like living with a teenager again, except this teenager was a functioning alcoholic with bottomless funds to cushion her downward spiral.

The situation needed to stop—I needed help. More specifically, I needed outside intervention.

Sunday 5 June

Spent today in the office. Opened the door and half-expected to see Suresh, placidly typing, before I remembered that he was a slimy file-stealing worm that had a fiancée.

Had a foursome with Eric Deng and two strangers—in a board games café (tsk-tsk, gutterbrain much?). Over three hours of intensive Monopoly, which is one of my favorite board games, although midway I flashed back to Catan with Suresh and had to dig my fingernails into my palms to stop myself from comparing that night with this. Didn't help that it was in the exact same board games café we were last in.

Midway during a particularly intense round of gameplay, Eric got up to get me a beer from the counter—and I totally slow-checked his butt. And then I looked up and caught him clocking me doing just that. The old, passive me would have frozen and ducked my head or pretended he had something on the seat of his pants, but the new me, the I've-seen-things me, met his gaze full-on. A challenge was issued. Ball's in your court now, Eric. I'm not friend-zoning you at all.

Monday 6 June

Nearly tripped over Linda's prone figure on the way to work. When asked, she said she had permission to work from home that day.

And then I found out the extent of Massimo's depravity. Kai had heard on the PA grapevine that Massimo was still a client at Linda's law firm—what's more, he'd specifically asked for her to be the partner in charge for his files, so that even while she was dodging his calls (she is made of very stern stuff, in her own way), she couldn't dodge him at work if he chose to show up. That's why the firm is being so lenient with her—because she's still one of the top billing partners. And that's why she's choosing not to show up at work on certain days.

Scary how much your PAs know about you. That's why, in our world, we have a saying: keep your PAs close; keep your enemy's PA on retainer.

Saturday 11 June

I've decided to bring Jason into the mix. If there's one aspect of Linda's personality I can count on, it's her vanity. Having a young, attractive male in the house would be just the thing she needed to jolt her back to her normal self.

It's a sign of how Singaporean I'm becoming: relying on Foreign Talent to work on jobs I don't want to do myself. Go me!

Anyway. I invited Jason to have brunch at my place today, but not before letting it be known to Linda in an off-hand way that Jason was coming, and in less than thirty minutes she had showered; washed and deep-conditioned the rat's nest that had sat on top of her oily face for two weeks; scrubbed, toned, and moisturized; sheared off her armpit and leg hair; and poured her skinny frame into denim shorts and an airy boho-chic white top she had "borrowed" from my closet, looking fresh-faced and beautiful without makeup. She'd even brushed her teeth and gargled. My plan had worked like a charm.

"Hi, Jason," she said primly, sipping on a glass of iced tea (iced vodka with a smidge of tea) when Jason sauntered into the living room carrying cupcakes and looking like he had walked out of a Gap commercial.

"Hey," he said cautiously; I guess he wasn't used to being the center of her attention. Linda put on her best wide-brimmed smile and gestured for Jason to sit beside her at the round dining table. I rolled my eyes as I watched him approach, without guile. It was like watching Bambi circle a panther, thinking the latter wanted to be his friend. He should be afraid—she hadn't eaten a man in weeks.

Nonetheless, brunch went better than I could have envisaged. We talked about everything light and airy, nothing serious (that had been the brief to Jason), and Linda lost a bit of that old dishrag look in her eyes. Brunch became drunken dinner became drunken movie marathon, and everyone was having a whale of a good time, not least because I had appointed myself Linda's new chastity belt, having wedged myself between Jason and Linda for maximum Rebound Romance Inhibiting Efficacy (it's not an easy task for any man to resist Linda once the old girl started turning on her charm). For this visit, Jason's purpose was to act as much-needed eye candy and trigger Linda's dormant hormones; now that the purpose had been served, I had to keep her from consuming him—it was early days, and he was becoming dear to me. Having Jason and Linda around made me realize how much I had missed my friends, even flighty Valerie, who had now replaced me with Ralph. I was not going to let Linda's raging libido and loose morals endanger the delicate pH of our raggedy band, at least not yet.

Later, when Linda had drunk herself into a dark, mumbly sleep on the living room floor, Jason and I hung out in the living room, watching episode after episode of *Keeping Up with the Kardashians*, with Jason giving me a blow-by-blow to catch up on the backstory I had missed by not following them from the beginning; he definitely had an unhealthy knowledge of the Kardashian/Jenner family trees.

We were discussing which Kardashian/Jenner each one of us was most like (I was allegedly a Kendall, for being low-key) when Jason piped up, "You know, it's funny that you guys are so close. You seem like polar opposites. I know you're related, but how did you become friends?"

The Linda and Andrea origin story was not complicated, I told him. We more or less ran in the family circles, having grown up together in Malaysia before Linda emigrated with her parents to the Philippines when she was ten. But we didn't grow close until we bumped into each other at the law faculty in the same university in London. Then we started spending time with each other—her dependency on my meticulous notes probably the main driver at first—and became close over time. We had had some good times in London before I had to come back to Asia. I'd like to think I was one of the reasons she chose to relocate to Singapore over Shanghai when she was given the opportunity to grow her law firm's presence in Asia—that, and the local hawker food scene. I liked her fierce devotion to her tribe (well, except for her recent flakiness, that is), and I envied her untidy, adventure-filled lifestyle, where anything could happen and did. I don't want to be her, but I'm a little in awe of her.

OK, maybe I want to be like her, just a tiny bit.

"She's always challenging me to step out of my comfort zone," I said.

"That's exactly what I like about her," Jason said, blushing.

And then the veil was lifted from my eyes: Jason had always been into Linda!

A bolt of lightning hit me, a kill-two-birds-with-one-stone kind of lightning. A sly idea formed in my head.

"Hey, I've got a brilliant idea," I said. "Why don't you move in? I have an empty room and you have a crazy housemate. I'll charge you minimal rent, and I can finally evict Linda." *And that way, you can always be around me and Linda.*

"You're a little afraid of her, aren't you," Jason observed.

"Yep." I admitted this a little shamefacedly.

"It's a good thing I'm not. I've dealt with women like her in my family, and I know exactly how to handle her. So yes, I'll be your fall guy."

We shook on it and continued watching TV until we fell asleep around dawn. So it's settled, Diary—Jason moves in with me in a little over two weeks. He has no official lease in his old place anyway and is practically squatting in the broom closet he calls a room.

I also now have an excuse to evict Linda. I am very happy. I can't wait to tell her when she wakes up, if she ever does.

Wednesday 15 June

Linda has been giving me the silent, wounded treatment since Saturday, but my eviction notice seems to have kick-started a getting-her-shit-together movement. Interestingly, she has moved into the spare room. The living room is bottle-free and the floors swept and mopped; even the couch has been buffed with some kind of cleaning product and looks almost presentable. My fridge has been restocked, or, rather, stocked for the first time, with fresh fruits and gourmet food like French and Spanish cheeses and healthful artisanal dips. Even the alcohol has been replenished. Best of all, Linda has started showering regularly again. She's even keeping regular, respectable working hours.

I should have threatened her with eviction weeks ago.

9:55 p.m. I came home today to find Linda and dinner waiting for me. Linda made spag bog from scratch. She motioned for me to join her at the dining table. I'll admit that I was hesitant—she hasn't drunk since Sunday, as far as I know, and she was unpredictable when sober. She also had abandonment issues, an explosive temper, and was very, very dexterous. I sat down at the farthest end of the spotless table from her.

She served me the pasta and we ate in silence. The spag bog, with its blend of beef and lamb mince, was delicious, but I couldn't enjoy my food. Linda wanted something from me, and I was afraid I knew what it was.

"Please don't kick me out," she finally said, mid-meal.

I sighed. "Jason's all packed and ready to move in," I reminded her. "And you have your own place. You've been squa— living in my living room for over a month. I'm sorry, babe, but you can't stay here forever."

"I'll pay rent," Linda pleaded. "I'll pay triple what Jason can offer you!"

"You know I didn't ask Jason to move in because I need the money," I reminded her gently. "Now, what's really going on?"

Her lips trembled. "I don't want to be alone in that apartment, after what happened. I-I don't feel safe."

Oh, jeez, I had no idea that she felt unsafe. I got up and gave her a tight hug. "Listen, that jerk does not deserve your tears and we are going to clear the shit out of your house when I get there. Plus, Berenice's visit was just a one-off incident and we're going to make sure nothing like that ever happens again, I promise. Tell you what, this weekend I'm free, so I'll get a contractor to come over to yours and we will install the most badass security system we can find. No one's going to be able to break into your home ever again."

She sniffled and nodded, clinging on to me like I was the only buoy in a turbulent sea. There was something touching about seeing Linda so vulnerable. It almost made me feel sorry for her, until I remembered that she liked to sleep naked, and that, among other unspeakable reasons, was why I was going to have to reupholster my couch, if not burn it altogether.

Friday 17 June

2:35 a.m. Went to the kitchen to get a glass of water and found Linda doing the unspeakable on my couch again. She moves out TOMORROW.

You know, this whole Poots saga has reminded me that we have to make sage dating choices. Obviously, one cannot be ruled by libido and have zero quality control (Linda).

I thought fondly of Eric. The other night, after Monopoly, he had given me a hug that had lasted longer than three seconds. We were definitely getting somewhere. In the fullness of time.

Saturday 18 June

3:15 p.m. Just came back from Linda's, where a state-of-the-art security system has now been installed by two men who looked like they had, at one point or another, broken out of a maximum-security prison. The security system incorporates biometric readers, security cameras, light and motion sensors, and other nifty extras, including a monthly subscription to the security firm's surveillance services. Linda's father is going to find a very interesting surprise on his Centurion supplementary credit card bill this month.

8:05 p.m. Linda sent me a short WhatsApp video of her lounging in the living room watching a Will Ferrell movie, a glass of white wine in one hand. She gave me a thumbs-up. All seems well.

11:40 p.m. Heading to Linda's. She said it's an emergency.

1:45 a.m. Back at mine *with* Linda. She refused to let me leave without her. She's unpacked and installed herself back in my living room again to my great chagrin, claiming that my spare room is "really a closet."

2:20 a.m. I have *got* to stand up to the women in my life, otherwise I'm never going to be rid of them. At the rate Linda was going, I won't even have space to accumulate cats, much less a worthy partner!

33

Saturday 25 June

4:15 p.m. Hurrah! I'm finally free of La Linda.

With Jason scheduled to move in with me in a few days, things were coming to a head. Linda's refusal to budge was becoming tiresome, but as I was still unable to directly confront her, I decided to outsource the dirty work to Jason again.

He came over this afternoon when Linda was at her worst: belligerent, drinking, and watching *Saw IV* (see why I had to get rid of her?). I opened the door and nodded grimly at him, because he was about to face the beast when she was not wearing her civilized mask. But Jason was happily made of sterner stuff. He strode over to the TV and turned it off, before snatching the bottle of wine she'd been necking from her. And placing it in front of his crotch. Smart move.

She barked some obscenity at him.

"Pull yourself together, Linda," he said. "Is this appropriate behavior for someone your age? What are you, too chicken to deal with the reality of living alone and so weak that you have to get drunk in order to get over a flaccid lump of a man?"

Linda got to her feet and gave him a hard slap. Which, to his credit, he took without shrinking (she's a tall woman and a boot-camp workout fanatic).

"Asshole," she said, before she launched herself at him.

And then they were making the most hideous sounds in my spare room for, like, four hours. I know because I left the house to seek refuge in a café and came back to a cacophony of noises I would expect from a gorilla enclosure at the zoo.

And now it was raining elephants outside on a dead-end Sunday. But not enough to drown them out. I speed-dialed Eric.

I quickly filled him in on my desperate situation. "Please, there are a bunch of animals in my house doing bad things to each other and I need to get out of here pronto. Take me to your next activity. I'll indoor ski, learn how to make pasta from scratch, watch a documentary on Christian Scientists, whatever. Just please get me out of here!"

"I've got a better idea."

He came over and picked me up. I was surprised when we drove up in front of his house on Jervois Hill, which I hadn't been to since we first met at the Sexless Book Club. For some reason my heart was pounding and my palms were sweaty, not least because there was a very real chance that he was going to suggest we go bowling in his very own home bowling alley, which I suspect he has tucked away somewhere in that mansion of his. I mean, we had done just about everything else.

He dropped me at the front door and I waited for him to park in the underground garage, sweating. He opened the front door, I entered, and we stood awkwardly in the hallway, unsure of where to go next. Especially me. Because you know, his house had *wings*.

He cleared his throat. "I have this really nice collection of Japanese whisky, so we can spend the evening whisky-tasting," he said. "Don't worry. I won't make you watch any documentaries."

"Great," I said, flushing. Here's the thing about Eric: he wasn't joking when he said that. He really was *just* explaining.

"Oh, and Rashidah's away, so . . ." He shrugged, looking a little flustered. "We don't need to, ah, worry about being sociable, you know."

"Well," I said. "I think I might need a break from drinking . . . and I really just want to be with you, alone," I added with meaning before he could suggest bowling, chess, foosball, or worse, Catan.

"Follow me," he said in a low voice.

"Oh, I'll definitely need to, or I might get lost," I replied, trying to be flippant even though I was perspiring in anticipation, my standard move.

He led me up a stairwell and into his bedroom.

3:10 a.m. Dear God. The man has *stamina*.

Monday 27 June

So yesterday Eric and I *grin emoji* were just lounging around in his home bowling alley (I know), having gone through just about every position known to man, when he turned his sexy dad bod to me, kissed me on my nose, and said, softly, "I really like you, Andrea."

"Oh," I said, pretending to pull on my clothes. "I assumed that was how you treat all your mortal enemies. I'll go now."

He did not laugh. "Wait, what?" he said. Honestly, sometimes it was disconcerting how little he got my sense of humor.

"I'm kidding."

"Oh." He still looked perplexed.

"You were saying, about how likable I am?" I prompted, trying to re-create that moment of intimacy.

"Yes, and what do you think about me?"

"You're acceptable."

He smacked my bum. The plush, special acoustic panels absorbed the sound. Ah, to be so rich.

"No, really," I cleared my throat and avoided meeting his eyes. "I think I like you, too."

"Good," he said, looking relieved. "I thought you would start laughing in my face. You're so wonderful."

"What?!" I blurted, before bursting into laughter. "Stop yanking my chain!"

"I'm sorry?" The same perplexed look.

"I mean, stop joking."

"But you are, and the crazy thing is, you're so hard on yourself. Don't you know how beautiful and smart and exuberant and put-together and—"

"Shuuddddup," I said, getting embarrassed.

"You're amazing," he said, leaning over to kiss me. And something else extremely naughty. Yum.

"I've never had a guy compliment me so much after sex. Usually they just escape," I deadpanned. "The perks of going out with an older guy, eh?"

He did not laugh. "So it's official then, we're going out together?" Eric asked, looking strangely vulnerable.

"Er, yes? I mean, yes!"

He gave me a long, searching kiss. "Then I'm glad."

Thursday 30 June

7:35 a.m. Eric left this morning to go on another weeklong business trip to Beijing, after we had spent the last few nights together. (He would pick me up after work and bring me back straight to his place, skipping dinner entirely. *ahem*)

I have to say, I'm *so* glad to be done with dating in general. And not just by hooking up with any average Joe: I was dating Eric Deng, the ultimate trophy man, the Birkin of Boyfriends, the kind of man the Chairman page of annual reports for a Fortune 500 was designed for! And I wouldn't even be his second wife! I mean, if he decides to put a ring on it one day, I would be his starter spouse! An older, but still much younger (than him) starter spouse! I was *finally* winning in the Game of Life. Not only was my career (semi) back on track, but I had landed a man who was every Asian Tiger Mom's wet dream for a son-in-law.

8:02 a.m. Yuck, the words "wet dream" and "son-in-law" should never, *ever* be uttered in the same sentence.

11:15 a.m. Idly, I flicked open *TLTS* to see what Suresh— I mean, to see what Water was up to. Things were coming to a head with Water and Rhean. Their energy as a vigilante couple was explosive, and things were getting out of hand. A lot of collateral damage was happening in their kills. They weren't trying to contain themselves. It was as though their pent-up desire for each other was making them act recklessly in other areas of their lives.

I checked out *TLTS*'s follower count and was staggered to see it was now hovering at close to 150K.

Friday 1 July

Jason came over to survey the apartment before moving in; he wanted to see if he could get rid of any of his stuff if needed.

I asked him how much space he would need as Linda's belongings still littered half of the living room.

"I have a desk, a chair, a small box of kitchen utensils, and maybe two large suitcases and a carryall. That's it."

I begged him to simplify my life. He handed me a book from his backpack. "Read this. I was going to bring it over to Linda's the next time I see her, but you can have it first."

"*The Life-Changing Magic of Tidying Up*," I read, in a voice laced with skepticism. "By Marie Kondo. What, I can't just chuck stuff in a drawer? Dude, this looks hard."

"Hey, there are no shortcuts to enlightenment. Face it: everything in life involves work."

I fought the urge to kick him in the shins.

We celebrated by having a boozeless dinner à deux (takeaway

pizzas from a nearby pizzeria). After we were done, he cleared the table and shooed me away when I offered to help with the washing up. Then he made us both rooibos tea and we watched a Steven Seagal movie. It was all very civil and pleasant, until I heard the door open.

"Hello, chickadees, guess who?" a familiar voice crowed. My heart sank. It was Linda. I had almost forgotten she still had the spare key to my apartment. She walked over and plopped herself down on the couch between me and Jason.

"What are you doing here?" I protested. "I *just* got rid of you."

She shrugged with a "Who, me?" expression. "I needed to get the rest of my things, didn't you say?"

"Yes, but I *said* I'd call you and arrange a time."

"No time better than the present." She gave Jason a long kiss. "Did my little kitty miss me?" she mock-growled.

"I sure did," he said. He was stroking her face. "God, you have such good skin."

I sighed. "Please go to her place. I have thin walls."

They ignored me.

I went to the office. It was safer that way. I was already regretting asking him to move in.

Saturday 2 July

9:45 a.m. Turns out I didn't really have to regret for long.

I woke up to a loud banging on the door.

Opened it to find Linda, who had, it turns out, accidentally left her key at my place yesterday. She was wearing a white strapless sundress, a straw fedora, and slip-on Avarcas, an ensemble that only looked good on girls or women built like her. It is very annoying. Especially when she was up so early on a weekend and forcing me to join her on the bright side.

"Guess what?" she sang, dancing past me into my apartment.

"What?" I muttered, slamming the door and plodding in after her.

"Jason agreed to move in with me!" she chirped.

"What?" I said again, flabbergasted. Didn't he *just* agree to move in—with me? Or had I just dreamed that it happened? "Why?"

"Why not?" she asked. "We already spend all our waking hours together at mine or at yours anyway."

"Right. For all of one week since you started shagging. Solid decision to move in together immediately, of course, but who cares what I think. So when is he moving out, if he hasn't already?"

"In three days' time."

Efficiency, thy name is Linda's Vagina.

"And this way, I cancel the security subscription that I signed up for, and Daddy can restore my Centurion card."

Ah, two birds with one stone: money-saving Chinese-lady logic. I couldn't argue with that. "Congratulations," I said in reference to the restoration of her good fortune, giving her a hug.

"Thanks," she said, grinning. Then her face grew serious. "I mean it. For everything. For Jason, especially."

"I didn't do anything in that respect," I said, with false modesty. I totally made them happen.

"You totally made it happen," she said, because she was perceptive and we'd been friends for a long time. "Jason is a sweetheart. Before Jason, I was a mess when it came to dating—I couldn't see it, I know, but I was."

"I could see it," I quipped. "You were the biggest self-sabotager I'd ever met. You had the worst taste in men. The worst."

"Shut up. *Fine*, I'll admit that I have a *slight* predilection of dating men who just didn't want me enough, men who weren't available, in some toxic way mirroring my own daddy issues, maybe."

"You said it, not me."

She made a face. "God, I hate being a cliché, but then there must be some truth in how these clichés come into existence. Anyway, that phase of my life is over. I'm so glad to be done with toxic men."

I thought about Eric Deng. "You know what? It pains me to say this, Linda, but you've inspired me to do the same."

"Eric Deng?" she said, eyebrow raised. "Well, it's official now, ain't it?"

"Yes," I said, blushing.

"Great. Then it's time he met the Don."

In case you didn't catch that reference, dear Diary, she means herself.

Monday 4 July

11:25 p.m. Celebrated Fourth of July ironically with the usual suspects (*avec* Eric!) at my place, in honor of Linda's unofficial moving out.

Since it was American Independence Day, Ben, who had dual US-British citizenship, and Linda, who I doubt has actual work and had my house key, had decided to take charge of the decorations. The house was decorated with blue, white, and red pom pom balls and crepe streamers, with a carpet of irregular-size silver balloons. My bar table was covered with bottles of bourbon, rum, whiskey, and vodka, and there were Ikea glass tumblers and an ice bucket with ugly mass-produced ice cubes. Very "Ice Bucket Challenge," not Eric Deng at all.

I was very nervous, not just because I'd been inhaling helium and still sounded like Alvin the Chipmunk. Eric was different from the people I hung out with. Eric was, how can I put it politely, well—he was much more well-adjusted than most of the so-called adults I knew. Also he was older. I was mostly worried that Linda would rip him to shreds. Linda . . . oh, Linda was a bloodhound, and she'd been fed very few scraps in terms of my love life over the past nine years or so since I'd been in Singapore. She'd never approved of Ivan, and I wasn't expecting her to like Eric either. She had such high standards for people dating everyone else but herself. I warned her to be nice, and she replied something like, "The Don will apportion grace and magnanimity as befits the supplicant."

Honestly, I really don't know how we became friends.

Linda and Ben were at my place by seven to help decorate the living room (the door to my bedroom had been safely locked up—I couldn't risk Eric wandering in and seeing the amount of stuff I had). Everyone else started arriving around eight. The alcohol, it must be said, was flowing very freely. By the time Eric was due to arrive, everyone was cheerfully wasted, except for me. I had the performance sweats: I needed my friends to like, to approve of, Eric. I don't know where this group approval system comes from—it must be some kind of evolutionary hangover from back in the day when everyone had that one cave to hide out in from mammoths or icy vortexes, and you didn't want to be the person bringing back a mate who smelled like warm fungal soup or who went around dry-humping the wood pile, so you got a few of your more discreet buddies to check them out, and if the potential mate didn't pass the test, all the buddies basically clubbed the mate to death to protect the species. Same thing.

In my mind's eye, I pictured Eric saying something about how he didn't believe in miscegenation and all of my mates jumping on him in a whirl of Looney Tunes limbs. These were the kinds of deep dark things that you unearth sometimes months, years into a relationship. Plus he didn't have a digital trail, like Ratfink Orson. Urgh. Naturally I was a mess by the time he rang the doorbell. I had to steel myself with a fortifying shot of bourbon.

"Hi, everyone, this is Eric!" I chirped, barely stopping myself from shouting "Deng!" as I led him in. Thankfully I was back to normal. Voice-wise.

He was wearing a deep blue and teal batik long-sleeved top and beige chinos. And—I did a double take—white Adidas Stan Smith trainers, with green trim. Why was he wearing Stan Smiths? He never wore anything other than suede loafers or dress shoes. It looked super incongruous.

And . . . and . . . were his chinos . . . *slim cut*?

"You like?" he stage-whispered.

"Hmm-mmm," I replied. Best to say nothing if you were still digesting the visual stimuli.

Linda breezed up to him and shook his hand. "I'm Linda," she said, before I could introduce her.

Eric smiled and shook her hand. "And I'm Eric."

"So I've been told," Linda replied breezily. "Now, I've made my famous truth serum, and you and I are going to go to a corner and you're going to divulge your deepest darkest secrets." She handed him a mug of her proprietary blend of twenty-one-year-old Yamazaki whiskey, neat, her preferred drink.

"Do I have a choice?" Eric joked, smiling as he accepted the mug, not at all freaked out when he really should have been. She had been known to bite. Literally.

"Be nice," I called anxiously to their backs as Linda hustled him away to the balcony.

"I won't," Linda shouted back. Then she slid the sliding doors closed and I saw two cigars being lit.

They came back almost an hour later while we were streaming the live coverage of the Fourth of July celebrations and drinking. I watched Eric closely for signs of trauma, but he looked fine. Linda was now in her friendly networker mode, smiling and touching his arm now and then as she chatted with him. She threw me a wink and mouthed, "He's legit." I wondered what they had discussed, and more specifically, what she had gotten Eric to disclose about me.

I was glad to see everyone, especially Linda, getting along with Eric, and vice versa, despite the difference in age (and maturity). Linda was particularly joyous, twinkling under Jason's warm attention and Ben's undeniable jealousy. Ben and Valerie left around midnight. Linda and I hung back to talk in my room while Jason and Eric chatted on the balcony and smoked more cigars. Apparently things were going well with her and Jason, and they were making plans to spend Christmas in the Philippines. (How many days of leave does this woman have??)

"Oh, and I think Eric's a solid guy. I made him run the gauntlet of questions and he didn't even flinch. He's an honest bloke and he's terribly into you." She patted my back. "I didn't get it before, but now I do. He's the unconventionally sexy kind, in a deviated septum, dad-ish way."

"Stay away from him," I said immediately, alarmed by the dad reference.

Linda chortled. "It's OK, I'm good with who I have." She said this with a soft smile on her face. "But as your oldest friend, Andrea, I'm a little surprised. I feel like you're taking the easy route."

I was scornful. "Choosing Eric is choosing the *hard* route. The man's got a young daughter and he's from another generation. But I think he's worth it."

"Yes, I understand that he is a good catch, Andrea, but let me try and put it in a way you'll understand. It's like aiming for second-class upper when you should be getting a first-class degree."

Now I was annoyed. "Eric is first class, Linda."

"OK, fine, let me use another obtuse analogy: it's like getting first class in medicine when all you wanted to be is a pharmacist."

"How dare you?" I said in richly shocked tones.

Linda shrugged. "Look, you know me. I'd rather get a third in pharmacy than medicine, so long as it's pharmacy I'd rather be *doing*." She gestured at Jason who was standing by the window in a sleeveless top, looking conventionally sexy and perfect. Honestly, if that was third class, something had to be majorly deviated under his shorts.

When it was time for Jason and Linda to leave, all of us helped to move her remaining stuff from the living room and the spare room into a rental lorry. I know this sounds strange, dear Diary, but when the last box was loaded and the lorry drove away, I felt a twinge of regret, mostly because I could no longer borrow the sweet bags that Linda had left at my apartment. But then Eric gave me what started as a shoulder massage and—yum.

Saturday 9 July

Suresh just dropped a new *TLTS* strip.

The situation is getting even darker. Whole montage of new murders, more inventive, darker, and more daring than ever, when suddenly Water and Rhean discover that, for a short window after they've killed and when they have taken the form of the people they've ended, they can physically touch each other, strangers in flesh but familiar in every other way.

At long last, standing on top of a gristly mess, Water and Rhean embrace in a super hot scene of unfamiliar limbs.

Also he is at 312K followers. Not that I checked.

Sunday 10 July

11:20 a.m. Brunch in bed that Eric made for me (toast with butter and jam, kale and banana smoothies—Eric gives his staff Sundays off). Had sex in his room and the bowling alley. The acoustics in the bowling alley are amazing.

2:15 p.m. Had sex in the home theater. The acoustics in the home theater room are amazing.

DeeDee's in Paris and staying for the Fashion Week shows. She won't be back till October.

Eric says we can do it in her room if we want to. I demurred. We've all got to draw the line somewhere.

4:20 p.m. Did it in DeeDee's bedroom (in the walk-in closet *and* the bed). Her room has mirrors everywhere and mood lighting. The acoustics are amazing.

Hey, she doesn't pay rent.

Wednesday 20 July

7:30 p.m. Eric left for Rome today. Worked listlessly via remote connection on some files, but there was nothing urgent, for once. Summer holidays and most of my clients being European meant, for the first time in a long time, I had some free time on my hands to relax, to pursue my creative impulses.

So I launched Candy Crush.

10:20 p.m. Out of boredom decided to read *The Life-Changing Magic of Tidying Up*. When I finished I went into my closet and realized that even though my worldly possessions, most bought with year-end bonuses, did not necessarily "spark joy" in the normal, Kondo sense, they certainly sparked an almost perverse pleasure as I sniffed them while reminiscing about the clients I had helped dominate their respective fields.

Thursday 21 July

10:15 a.m. Urgh. Work. Is. So. Boring. Why do humans have to work? Work is so stupid. The best things in life, like sex, are free after all. Well, mostly. But must continue billing. The qualifying round of interviews start in August, and I'm so close I can almost see the engraved name plate:

ANDREA TANG, PARTNER

Chills, I tell ya, chills, especially in the sweet font I'd chosen for this purpose.

It feels a little weird to be all alone in the office, which suddenly seems unnaturally quiet without Suresh's extravagant muscles to absorb all that noisy typing, what with him still away on secondment in Jakarta working for a major client of his. I don't know how Anousha is taking it. Why is he accepting to go away on such long secondments when his long-awaited fiancée is finally in Singapore? Makes no sense. Speaking of Anousha, Kai told me that she's working in one of the leading private hospitals in Novena as a senior consultant, which is like the equivalent of my rank, I think. Good for her. I don't care.

Saturday 23 July

Went out clubbing with Ben, who has been in mourning ever since Linda got together with Jason. I guess he was hoping that he would have been the one that would one day wear her down.

Ben wanted to go clubbing because he believed, falsely, that he could "pick a girl up," which is a pretty misogynistic thing to say. Also does anyone actually hook up in clubs anymore? This is the second time I've been out with Ben, and it's not looking good.

In the end we left at 1:30 a.m., each citing work commitments the next day, but dear Diary, I caught Ben yawning many times on the dance floor, especially when they played dubstep, which as we all know was invented by a cunning demon, someone who was definitely an up-and-comer (if not management itself).

Felt very old. But in a happy, triumphant way—I was beyond the singles club scene. I was loved.

Sunday 31 July

Opened the door to find a huge bouquet of blush pink peonies (my favorite)—carried by Eric.

"Surprise," he said, softly. He enveloped me in a lovely hug.

He'd completed a deal early and had come back from Europe to hang with me until he had to fly to Brazil on Tuesday with Diana, his daughter, for summer holidays.

"The elusive Diana, I'm almost jealous of her," I teased. "When will I get to meet her?"

"Soon," he promised, but his offhand manner suggested that I had to pass other hurdles before he would introduce me to his beloved. He was very, very protective of her.

"Anyway, with the time difference and work and family, it might be difficult to chat as often as I'd like, so I thought I'd make up for it."

"Oh really?" I said, nuzzling his neck. "How are you planning to make up for it?"

He showed me.

Tuesday 2 August

Miss him already.

Friday 5 August

Had an intimate (ahem) video chat with Eric. It was his first time, supposedly. He's very good with, erm, filters, and demonstrates an uncanny ability to choose the right words and, uh, sounds. I can't wait for him to be back.

Monday 15 August

I opened the door to the office this morning and jumped when I saw Suresh. In the excitement of my new relationship with Eric, I had somehow repressed the fact that he was due back in August, after having completed his three-month secondment to Jakarta. The first round of selection interviews for partnership would be held this Friday, so that explained why he was back.

"Hello," he said guardedly.

For a moment, we stared at each other, embarrassed, and then he stood and engulfed me in a tight, lingering bear hug that left me breathless.

"Missed my ugly mug?" he said, after I'd gingerly let go.

"Not too much," I said with a wry smile. "I've been billing tons of hours. You'll never be partner now."

"Oh yeah? I slept with Mong. Top that."

I giggled and somehow things were almost normal with us, for a few seconds at least.

"I'm not kidding. I'm gunning for partnership. You better watch your back," he said with a grin. Then he made a face. "Actually, come to think of it, that's the only way I'll be able to afford the wedding Anousha wants. She wants to hold it at Fullerton Bay Hotel, with clouds of white roses, a string quartet, a live band, and an open bar no less."

"That's going to hurt." I had *almost* forgotten they were supposed to get married next year.

"Yup. Apparently after I told her about Genevieve's *ang pao* matrix, she thinks that she can make money off our guests. Trouble is, Anousha's a coconut. She's forgotten that we Indians are skint, and half of our guests are coming from India. We're gonna end up in debt now that her parents are totally not chipping in for the wedding nor giving us any dowry since she's moved to Singapore. And my parents are not rich. Even with our combined salaries, this wedding is still going to set us back significantly."

"Then don't hold it in Fullerton. Have it somewhere less fancy."

"Noushie would never— I mean, it's been decided."

"It's your wedding, too, and you don't want to get in debt."

Suresh sighed. "You know it's not that simple. Noushie has . . . certain standards. She's connected. The wedding has to look good. If it were me, I'd just elope, but both sets of parents would kill me."

"I'd elope, too, if I had to pay for a huge wedding," I said. "Although my ideal wedding, if I didn't have to meet the expectations of my mother, would be small and intimate, on a beach."

"Mine, too," he said. "Somewhere in the Polynesian islands, where it's—"

"Far and expensive enough so the people you courtesy invite don't make the effort to actually come, unlike Bali?"

"Exactly," he exclaimed.

I shook my head, marveling at how much on the same wavelength we were. "Too bad we're not getting married to each other."

Suresh looked at me strangely. "Yeah. Too bad," he said.

"But you'll invite me to the wedding, yes?"

He shrugged. "I have no choice, since we share the same office. Otherwise you might start spitting into my chai. Especially once I'm made partner over you."

"You wish," I said. "Have you forgotten? I'm not getting married next year. You are."

"I almost wish I wasn't," he muttered. "But if I didn't, I'm not quite sure I would be able to keep my life. Much less sure I'd keep my job. My future father-in-law will see to that."

It was an odd thing to say, but I let it slide. It didn't make sense—what did his future father-in-law have to do with his job?

Anyway, not the time to dissect this. Am on my last burst of billing. Got to make those numbers pop for Friday's interviews.

Friday 19 August

First round of interviews with the Partnership Committee is done, finally! Super exhausted but am feeling positive.

Tuesday 23 August

2:35 p.m. Valerie called with great news: Ralph just proposed to her! It happened after a work lunch at Forlino's. Having been invited by one of Ralph's least favorite clients and his wife for business lunch, Ralph and Valerie quaffed two bottles of pricey Venetian red and ate some fine Italian food, and once the client and his wife had left, Ralph had proposed with champagne and tiramisu, putting it all on the client's tab. Classy.

"I'm going to be a married woman again," Valerie shrieked. "Oh Lord, I've been waiting so long for this to happen!"

I offered her my heartiest congratulations before gently hanging up on another high-pitched squeal. Opposite me, Suresh wrinkled his nose at me and asked, "Did someone win the lottery or something?"

"You could say that. Valerie is engaged," I said. I added, "To someone she really cares for."

"That's great," Suresh said. He knew Valerie, which is to say he had heard so much about her from me that they were almost real friends.

Anyway, since he's been back and we're sharing an office again, from what I can gather Suresh's relationship with Anousha seemed to be back on track. In the sense that she was leading and he was following dutifully with minimal resistance, as far as I could tell. Every phone conversation with his beloved was now completely conflict-free, now that she was working in Singapore and they had put the dark days of free Chiswick bungalows behind them. So what if the light from his eyes had faded and every time she came to get him at the end of the workday he wore the frozen smile of an unwilling child bride? That was *his* problem. Anyway, Kai told me that he had already accepted a follow-up secondment in Jakarta, so that should help the situation. And then he and Anousha would get married.

Of course, I was happy for the both of them. So happy. And in one week's time, my better half would be back from his tour of South America with his daughter, too.

Thursday 1 September

Bring out the Red Bulls: Eric's back. Yay!

Saturday 3 September

Eric and I were having breakfast in the eastern sunroom (go figure) when he invited me to fly with him to Madrid tomorrow. "It'll be fun. You've never been and I have time off between meetings. We could visit the Prado museum. It's one of my favorites in the world."

I groaned. "I'd love to, Eric, but I have work, remember? You're dating a member of the working class."

He lifted an eyebrow. "So call in sick. Why do you care? You're always complaining about work." He caressed my face. "I'll bring you to the finest restaurants, we'll go shopping . . ."

I swatted his hand away. "Stop teasing me! I really can't. If I'm going to make partner this year, I have to outdo Suresh and bill more."

He pressed his lips against my neck. "But why are you so bent on making partner? Do you even like what you do?"

"What do you mean? I *have* to make partner," I answered automatically.

Somewhere between collarbone one and two, he said, casually, "You know, if we got married . . ."

I inhaled sharply. "Married" was a trigger word for me.

"If we got married *one day*, you could just stop working, be a *tai-tai*,* do whatever you want instead, like start a charity, work in one of those development aid organizations. You'll be much happier."

I stiffened. "That's sounds so . . . *Stepford Wives*. And I'm not interested in being that."

"Not at all! I didn't say stay at home and be the perfect homemaker in heels—that's sexist. Suggesting you use your time in a more worthwhile manner by working on something you believe in. Plus I'm not making you quit a job that you love more than anything in the world. You *hate* your job. You called it 'indentured labor,' if I recall correctly. That if you weren't in debt and didn't have loans, you'd have broken free from your corporate shackles, to quote you."

He did have a point; I didn't *love* corporate law. "But I'm very good at it. And I want to be financially independent from my partner, whomever he is."

He looked amused. "A feminist slave to the system. Suit yourself, but then work in a field that you enjoy. What do you like to do?"

I fell silent. When Suresh had asked me, I'd joked about wanting to be a mermaid or a marine biologist, and I had once flirted

* Singlish for a lady of privileged means, i.e., with lots of leisure time and money, both of which are typically spent on shopping sprees in designer boutiques, eating in *atas* cafés, "rejuvenation treatments," and fitness/dance classes (and sometimes, the instructor(s) that teach those classes).

with the idea of writing as a career, but the truth is I don't know what I would do, if I had the freedom to decide. Growing up I'd never been asked that question before, because I'd never been given a choice. Since I sucked at math (meaning it didn't come easily to me; doesn't mean I didn't get straight A's all the time), my mother narrowed it down to "lawyer." And the right kind of lawyer, of course. Not ones that worked for legal advice centers or nonprofits.

I had only the vaguest notion that I wanted to protect the underdogs of the world with my sick legal skills.

"I don't know what I'd want to be," I said.

He laughed and kissed my forehead tenderly—I had spoken out loud again. "So what's wrong with being a *tai-tai*? You would be free to pursue your dreams. Start a foundation and champion a cause you care about. Be an activist. You are such a passionate person. There must be a cause you care strongly about. Gender equality? Fair trade? Cyberbullying? Anything is possible."

With your money, I said in my head. That was the unspoken part of his sentence.

"Think about it," he whispered, now nibbling at the sensitive area under my collarbone, his right hand sliding down my spine and under my top. "You could finally do what you want. You could be happy. I could help you."

I toyed with the idea of being a *tai-tai* until my focus was brought elsewhere. Mmm.

Sunday 4 September

And off he goes, again, to another business meeting in Spain.

With him gone, I had time to mull over what he'd said. If money wasn't an object, what would I be? If I didn't know, was it bad to try to find out under someone's patronage? Eric was offering to free me from being a slave to the system, but was what he was offering real freedom? And how could I consider myself a feminist if I did that? But was being a feminist as important as being free to live the life I've always aspired to have, i.e., quit a job I hate and have enough money to buy whatever I wanted? Could it even be possible without some kind of blood sacrifice and was Eric Deng actually the devil?

I chastised myself for constantly putting down Eric. He was sensitive, worldly, family-oriented, wealthy. He was a goddamn find. And if there was anything Linda taught me over the last few months, it was that love came from unexpected places, and I just needed to open my heart to let it in and not be blinded by preconceived notions incepted by Disney and De Beers, that love had to *feel* one way or another to be authentic.

Thursday 8 September

Renovations for the new floor have finally finished. Suresh will be moving out next Friday.

We decided to have a casual dinner in our office to celebrate his leaving, since it happened to be one of his rare days in town. He ordered takeaway pizza, then we grabbed some Belgian beer and a bottle of Riesling from the pantry (clients love sending their lawyers alcohol) and, for dessert, cookies from the vending machine. He didn't mention that it was his birthday, which I had remembered but had chosen to ignore, and I didn't bring it up; I did think it was strange that he had chosen to spend it with me instead of with Anousha, seeing that he had no real active files back here and could certainly afford an evening off.

Strange, but flattering.

"I'm glad you're here. I wasn't sure if you would be," Suresh said as he poured me a glass of Riesling. He cleared his throat. "How's Eric?"

"Good. And Anousha?"

"Good."

"Chiswick didn't come between you? All fences mended?"

His lips thinned. "No and yes. We're going to Langkawi for a short vacation next weekend, after she gets back from Greece from a medical conference. We really need to reconnect."

I struggled not to barf at the idea of the both of them literally doing that. "Oh, nice," I managed. "Which resort?"

"Four Seasons."

"Fancy."

"I have to step it up," he said lightly. "Isn't being fancy the reason why men like Eric Deng get women like you?"

He was joking, but for some reason it rubbed me the wrong way. I tried to laugh it off, but I recognized the barb underneath that throwaway comment. Eric's largesse was not the reason I was with him, of course. I never asked for the gifts he sprang upon me; I went out of my way to make sure that I paid for my share of the entertainment and F&B whenever Eric Deng asked me out. I didn't do the check dance—I paid. Once I nearly sliced open his palm grabbing the credit card out of his hand, so eager was I to be the one to pay for the meal.

Still, there had been other occasions when I'd just been out of my league in the face of his generosity. Those VIP opera tickets . . . that surprise staycation at Capella . . . those vintage Burgundy wines that he would always insist on having when we dined French . . . that sublime meal with the superlative sake pairing at Waku Ghin . . . I hadn't paid for those, couldn't even afford to pay for my half. Not to mention the gifts he showered me with. Who could forget that Charles Bukowski; the Van Cleef & Arpels diamond studs he insisted were "no big deal, a trinket, really"; the occasional designer bag . . .

Whatever. Suresh is one to moralize. He tried to steal my Sungguh Capital file. Can't forget that. Glad he's leaving again for Jakarta in two weeks.

Wednesday 14 September

Awkwardly said goodbye to Suresh, who now has his own office. And his own PA, Hong Lim, a young man who Kai said was not part of the PA web of gossip. Apparently Hong Lim had *principles*.

Well, he's really out of my life now. There's nothing to hold us together. We don't have to pretend to be friends anymore.

Kai dropped in after he'd left to comfort me with an Earl Grey and lavender cake. We ate it in silence, contemplating the empty space where Suresh's desk and chair had been. Can't believe I no longer have to hide my burps or farts by coughing, a move that no doubt never fooled anyone as I could never cough convincingly, being either too vigorous or too weak.

Worked a bunch till it was past dinner time and I finally decided to make a move. I looked at the half-eaten cake and thought I would put it in the pantry so that the others could partake thereof. I wondered if anyone from the team was around.

I poked my head out of the office and realized with a start that the floor was almost dark except for Mong's office, once again. The door was open, and no one was in. Where was he? He should have been at his desk as, according to our shared calendar, he had a conference call in an hour with New York and he was taking it from his office. He probably hadn't eaten yet, actually, and might appreciate some cake.

I walked to his door with a slice. "Mong?" I called, knocking out of habit before walking in to put the cake on his table.

His screen was unlocked and lit. A draft email was up.

I wasn't going to read it until I saw the subject matter of the email:

Proposed candidates for promotion from M&A

I couldn't read it, dear Diary. It would be a clear breach of privacy. And trust. I couldn't. So I did.

It was Mong's email in response to a chain of discussion regarding, among a couple of other M&A names, me and Suresh.

And it read:

Dear partners,
In terms of both candidates, Suresh and Andrea, I do think that Suresh is the better candidate

No. No fucking way.

I rubbed my eyes in case, you know, I had a tumor that was causing me to see betrayal where there wasn't. But the same email was still displayed there, with the same words.

Un-fucking-believable.

Before I knew what I was doing, I had taken out my personal mobile phone and took a picture of those painful words. Then I snatched the plate of cake off his desk and walked out of his office in high dudgeon.

So Mong didn't think I deserved the one thing I'd been working toward my whole career. Well, then—he didn't deserve artisanal cake!

I felt like someone had kneed me in the gut.

Then my heart began palpitating and I got all sweaty and gaseous.

Whenever I get destabilized by news, I tend to drink. I took out my emergency bottle of Patrón and poured myself a shot that I quickly downed. Then another. Then another. And maybe a couple more in quick succession.

And then my eyes narrowed in rage. How could Mong do this to me? I was his Padawan. He'd called me his Work Daughter and I reciprocated by referring to him as my Work Dad. And he'd always claimed to have my back.

I felt sick. And in need of affirmation. Or a shag. These were tumultuous times.

I ran to the taxi stand and hailed one. It took me to Suresh's condo in fifteen minutes (we knew each other's addresses because we're each other's backup on files).

Once dropped off at the main gate, I found Suresh's block and rang his unit, hoping that I had remembered right that Anousha was still in Greece for her medical conference and not with him.

A sleepy voice mumbled, "Hello?"

"Is Anousha in?" I barked.

"Wh-what? No," he said, befuddled.

"Then let me up."

When I got to his door it was already open. Suresh, rumpled, stood in the doorway. He was dressed in a thin T-shirt and ratty pair of cotton boxers and T-shirt and looking bleary-eyed, sleep oozing from his eyes and flecks of drool on his chin (hey, it's not like I'm writing a romance novel here).

"I need to talk to you in private," I said, marching past him into the apartment. "I've got news." I was all keyed up and no doubt looked a little crazy.

"Nice to see you, too, Andrea," Suresh said sarcastically after he'd shut the door. "I'm only dressed in my boxers and I did not invite you in."

"This won't take more than a few minutes," I said, throwing myself onto his couch.

Or maybe more. I took in the sculpted abs just visible through his T-shirt. Even in my drunken anger, I was impressed. How was this guy a comic artist? I squinted hard. Was that daubs of . . . paint on his chest?

"Can I help you?" Suresh interrupted my thoughts, his hands crossed over his chest.

"Nice apartment," I said, making conversation, trying to keep my voice even. I jumped up from the couch and started walking around, peeking in rooms without shame. Adrenaline does that to you—so does five shots of tequila.

There was a light in his study; he'd been working on something.

Distracted, I walked in and saw a beautifully rendered portrait of Water and Rhean, bodies entwined while the world burned. Suresh had painted it in A3 size with gouache. It was breathtaking.

"You approve?" Suresh said, entering the small room and standing barely two feet away from me in front of his desk. My heart was beating even faster now.

"I didn't know you can paint."

"I'm not a natural, but I took a course." He was still studying me in a wary manner. I couldn't blame him: I didn't even know exactly what I was doing there.

"I came here to tell you something."

"So you've said."

"Hey, give me a break. I'm not here to take a meter reading. What I'm about to say is . . . is difficult."

He raised his eyebrows and said nothing.

"Mong is going to put forward your name for partnership, not mine."

"What?" he said. "How . . . what . . . ?"

For a second I thought I was going to rage-jump his bones, but before I knew it, tears were pricking my eyes and the urge was gone. "I don't understand it. I don't. I bill more than you. I have seniority. It makes no sense."

"Are you sure it's not a mistake?"

"Positive," I said raggedly. "Mong is the least ambiguous writer I know. I saw the email on his screen, when he was away. I even took a screenshot for proof. I've read the damn thing a dozen times."

"Shit," he said. "I'm shocked. I really thought you were going to get it in the end."

"Apparently . . . apparently they think otherwise."

To distract myself from my desire to puke, I picked up one of the silver picture frames (heavy, Tiffany, probably Anousha's) and glanced at it with some curiosity. It was a picture of Anousha with her arms around an older man and woman with a remarkable resemblance to her—her parents, presumably. I squinted. The man looked very familiar. Where had I seen him before?

Suresh came over to me and put a hesitant arm around my shoulder. "Andrea, I'm really—"

"Who's this?" I asked, pointing at the man next to Anousha.

His eyes grew shifty. The man had no poker face, like me. "Oh, him? That's Noush's dad. You know, Mr. Singh."

Mr. Singh. Mr. Singh. Then the coin dropped. I remembered where I had seen that aristocratic face before: hanging in a gilded frame above the receptionist in the lobby!

I dropped the frame with a dramatic clatter onto the teak tabletop. "You shit," I hissed. "You lying sack of shit."

Suresh grimaced and started backing away from me. "What now?" he muttered.

I pointed at him like we were in Salem in the 1600s and he had just announced that he voted for legalizing witchcraft and women's suffrage. "Anousha is Inderjit Singh's daughter. Your fiancée is the daughter of one of the founders of Singh, Lowe & Davidson!"

"Yes, and?" replied Suresh, feigning innocence. "It's not like it's anyone's business."

A cold fury enveloped me. "Oh, but it is," I hissed. "It's a goddamn conflict of interest, that's what it is, and it should be declared, especially when you're on the partnership track."

"But I'm not," he said, the lying turd, now approaching me with a placating palm outstretched. "I mean, I was. But I . . . it's . . . it's complicated. I'll explain it all later. I want to know why you came here tonight. Tell me, please."

"Don't try to change the subject, asshole. I see everything clearly now, how you *lied* to me, manipulated me into— I mean, you were scheming to get partnership all this time . . . b-by getting into my hear— head to confuse me, you . . . you pinworm infection!"

"What? What the hell are you on about?"

"So you deny it?"

"I was not scheming, and I certainly wasn't hiding the fact—I mean, I . . . *Fuck!*" He pulled his hair in frustration. "I have *never* used my relationship with Anousha to advance my career, how can you even—"

"Fuck you," I said.

"I can ex—"

But I didn't want to listen to another lie, so I did the only thing I could still do with dignity: I ran.

9:45 p.m. WhatsApp messages and texts from Suresh. I have deleted them without reading. There's really nothing left to say. Putting the phone away.

10:05 p.m. Several missed calls from an unidentified number. What is this, amateur hour?

10:25 p.m. Voicemail from Suresh. Deleted.

11:45 p.m. Work emails, too? Too bad we're no longer working on any files together, asshole. I deleted all of them without opening a single one. Then emptied the trash folder before I could change my mind. Archived all his incoming mail to a folder titled "LYING SCUM FOREIGN TALENT (HERE TO STEAL MY JOB)."

How could I have ever liked him, maybe even more than platonically, when I have a man like Eric Deng? (Also, why was it always "Eric Deng" in my head and not just "Eric"?) How could I have put everything I have with Eric in jeopardy like that? What was it about Suresh that tripped me up like this?

1:08 a.m. Asshole cowaqrd. Wine bertter lover. Who needsa the asshol ewhen I ahv wwine . . .

39

Thursday 15 September

5:15 a.m. What's the point of trying to sleep when I have a knife in my back? Can't believe Mong wasn't going to propose me for partnership this year, just because of VizWare. After everything I worked for. As for Suresh . . . hiding the fact that his future father-in-law is Inderjit Singh.

Nest of vipers, I tell you. Nest of vipers. Thank God I no longer have to share an office with Suresh.

Well, there's still a chance I can get Mong's and everyone else's vote, if I salvage VizWare.

8:12 p.m. Suresh had dropped a new strip on *TLTS*. Water and Rhean had moved past killing for "good" but were now killing to satisfy their own needs for each other.

It's not looking good for our murderous couple.

Wednesday 21 September

8:00 p.m. Left work earlier than usual. Couldn't concentrate. What's the point?

9:15 p.m. Home. Launched Angry Birds. Opened bottle of wine and bag of off-brand Cheetos.

9:35 p.m. Opened second bag of off-brand Cheetos. Dejection apparently increases my appetite.

11:45 p.m. Put phone away. Eyes blurry. Another thing my law firm has taken away from me.

1:15 a.m. Couldn't sleep again. I decided to go to my safe place: the twenty-four-hour supermarket.

I love supermarkets. I go to supermarkets to calm down when I think of making a break from society. I enter feeling lost, but after an hour I come out calm, soothed, just a little fluorescent-light blind and drugged, but with my sense of self and worth restored. There is something so deeply meditative about walking along in the supermarket aisles: all that choice—that illusion of choice.

Let me explain. Most of the brands you see in the consumer goods section, even those fancy, seemingly independent, hippie ones, are owned by oligopolies, the same few faceless multinational corporations. So while you're boasting that you're a "made-by-Amish-virgins-in-Kentucky" kind of granola girl or in the "monk-blessed-and-French-mountain-filtered-piss" bottled water camp, you're all eating the same GMOs, absorbing the same chemicals, drinking the same microplastics.

Oh yeah, what was I talking about again? Loving supermarkets. Right.

So here I was, leaving the toilet paper aisle and about to shuffle along to the cereal aisle to grab myself the latest sugar GMO bombs when I saw something that made my blood run cold:

Ivan. In the flesh.

In a T-shirt and *cargo* shorts, walking hand-in-hand with a familiar figure wearing a long, sleeveless white cotton dress.

And they were heading my way.

I was just about to turn around and flee the supermarket when Ivan looked up and our eyes locked.

Goddammit. Why did I have to run into Ivan when I'm buying toilet paper? Not even the fancy embossed kind, just two-ply, *basic* toilet paper, dear Diary, the kind you find in second-rate communal working spaces, in an economy pack. WHY COULDN'T IT HAVE BEEN THE FANCY QUILTED FOUR-PLY BLACK TP? WHY? WHY? WHY?

AND WHY WAS I WEARING JHORTS?

He began walking toward me with the woman. I steeled myself by doing a Kegel. I looked her over as discreetly as I could: Chinese, my height (who am I kidding: she's taller), younger, longer-haired, but overall, she looked a lot like me (maybe slightly more snaggletoothed—and hunched). It was the same girl I had seen in the bar with Ivan, ages ago. The night I got entrapped by Orson.

"Hello, Andrea," Ivan said tersely.

I smiled my most professional smile. "Ivan," I said, as though we were distant relations instead of people who had once smushed uglies on his mahogany desk in his super luxe Hong Kong office one morning in plain view of office grunts in the opposite tower, if they had binoculars or time to look up.

He did a head twitch in the girl's direction. "This is, ah, my girlfriend, Nessadalyn."

I did a double take. "I'm sorry, Ness—?" I genuinely didn't catch her, erm, name.

There was a flash of anger in his face. "Nessadalyn," he repeated. He glanced pointedly at my toes, which were a little grubby, because #AllWorkNoLife. "Going somewhere?" he said, rather nastily.

I'd forgotten he could do that, cut me with a snide throwaway comment. "Yes," I said. For some reason, the lie popped into my head. "I'm going on a staycation with my boyfriend, Eric."

Hah! Game on, Ivan.

He didn't respond, but he looked like someone had run a cheese grater against his Virus Cradle. Nessadalyn, perhaps sensing that all was not well, decided to speak up. "Pleased to meet you, Andrea. I've heard many good things."

"Of course," I said, knowing that she was lying. "And what do you do for a living, Nessadalyn?" Straight to the point.

Nessadalyn smiled. "I'm—"

(A catalog model! An escort!)

"—working at a hedge fund."

"Oh," I said. "As?" (Hoping she would say PA.)

Serene smile. "Quant." She patted Ivan on his head. "I'm gonna be his sugar mama."

Ivan smirked at me. "We're going to have incredibly intelligent and cute babies."

"Oh, who said anything about babies?" Nessadalyn said with a twinkly laugh. "I'm barely twenty-seven, you old dog."

Ivan was thirty-eight.

"What about you?" she purred, clearly winning.

"I'm a senior associate in a top law firm." Said out loud in this manner I sounded so sad. I didn't ski in Val-d'Isère; I was past my peak hotness; I was just a senior associate.

"That's so impressive," Nessadalyn said, looking pointedly at my giant pack of toilet paper.

"Well," I said, confidence at an all-time low. "I should really get going to my boyfriend's. He, ah, wants me to, ah"—a flash of inspiration—"take a look at some of his firm's legal documents because he's got this huge launch of eco-hotels coming up, the first one being in Vietnam—maybe you've heard of it, I don't know, no biggie—the Dulit Group?"

Nessadalyn nodded, impressed. "Beautiful properties, superb branding. You're so lucky to be part of this deal."

"Thanks," I said, bemused. "Well, Eric, the group CEO and majority shareholder, is a lovely guy, too."

"Who?" Nessadalyn said, confused.

Ivan cleared his throat. "Nessie, do you mind if I speak in private with Andrea?"

"Not at all. You take as long as you want." Intelligent and desirable, Nessadalyn was not threatened by the likes of me.

"Really?" Ivan said, when she was gone. "Still?"

"What?" I said, gearing up for a fight that should have come a long time ago.

"I know you, Andrea. You wanted to make her feel small in the beginning, didn't you? But unluckily for you, I don't date stupid girls—or do you still think so little of me?"

"I never thought little of you," I said, stung.

"Please. You never respected me because I was part of the system and I was cool with it, and you thought you were somehow special because you wanted out 'someday.' But guess what, Andrea, you're still in it, you still measure yourself against it, and maybe you just need to swallow your pride and realize that it's too late, you're part of the Matrix, you're no better than me or Nessie. Tell me: how's your crusade to save the world going? Saved any disenfranchised people lately?"

I had nothing pithy to say.

"You either accept what you've become or reject it, then maybe you'll make peace with it and learn to be happy."

"I *am* happy," I retorted, affronted.

He laughed. "You don't have to convince me. And your new paramour—Eric, is it?—I hope he knows what he's gotten himself into: a woman in her mid-thirties who still doesn't know her own mind but thinks she does."

"At least I don't have a made-up name," was all I could come up with.

"Grow up, Andrea. Or at least get your priorities right." Then he walked away.

I spun around on my heel and headed toward the cashier. "I'll show you," I said, through gritted teeth, as the cashier eyeballed me warily while she rang up my purchases. "I'll show all of you." Ivan was wrong: I was decisive, I knew what I wanted, who I wanted, and I was going to be happy.

Thursday 22 September

Showed Eric, who'd just touched down from Indonesia, where he was scouting for the perfect island for his new boutique hotel, just how much he meant to me, several times.

When he'd caught his breath, he asked me what that was about.

"Can't I shower my boyfriend with appreciation?"

"Sure, if it involves that kind of literal back bending."

"I missed you," I said.

He kissed me. "Almost makes being away from you for so long worth it."

"You should be around more often," I said, meaning it.

"All right," he said, looking meditative, his left hand tousling my hair. "All right."

Saturday 24 September

4:15 p.m. Eric called. "I'm outside your house. Get dressed and come down."

I bristled a little at his tone. "Order much?"

"Sorry, but I'm just—well, I think today is the day you should meet Diana. I've been waiting for the right time and now that I know we're serious about one another, it's time to introduce you to her."

"What?" I panicked. "But I haven't shav— I mean, I need to iro— I mean, I need time to get dressed. I'm a lady," I said, drawing myself to my full height.

"My darling, my daughter doesn't care how you look. She only cares about meeting you. I've told her so much about this wonderful woman that I'm dating, who's quirky and adorable and intelligent and just so funny."

"Go on," I said, pleased.

"Andrea, come down. I'm going to introduce her to you. Right now."

"She's in your car, right now?" I panicked.

"No, I'm going to bring you to her mother's place. Get dressed."

He drove. That, in itself, was an anomaly that spoke of the secrecy surrounding the situation, as I knew that Eric hated to drive. My heart was in my stomach the entire ride. I was finally going to meet his daughter. It was a big, big deal for me, and for him as well.

When we arrived at the gates of the condo in Bukit Timah, I was quite frankly drenched in sweat, despite my best efforts to calm myself down by imagining myself frolicking on a beach full of golden retriever puppies. (Effective, isn't it?)

He called the apartment to let her know we had arrived, then he tapped the keycard and brought us to the penthouse. He knocked on the door and a young, slim Chinese woman answered.

"Hi, Maria," he said. "Where—"

"Hi there," I interrupted, sticking my sweaty palm out and enthusiastically shaking the hand the surprised woman proffered me. "My name is Andrea. It's so nice to meet you and your daughter at last. I—"

"This is Maria, Anne's helper."

"Oh." I blushed, releasing Maria's hand. She smiled reassuringly at me as I muttered my apologies. We followed her into the living room, which was decorated in stark, minimalist style in shades of gray and off-white.

There, seated under a painting of a pastoral Italian countryside, were the women of Eric's life: Anne and his daughter, Diana.

Anne was nothing like what I had expected. Dressed in simple black jeans and a sleeveless tank top, she was small-built, voluptuous, Indian; young and pretty, but not exceedingly so. I estimated her age to be mid-thirties. I had been expecting a tall, thin, twenty-something Chinese supermodel for some reason. I was relieved.

"This is Anne," Eric said. Anne and I nodded at each other. "And this is Diana, my daughter."

"Hello," I said, shaking both their hands. "It's very nice to meet you," I said to Anne before repeating my greeting slower to Diana, not sure how else to communicate my pleasure at finally being introduced to her.

"Let me," he said. Then he turned to his daughter and began

signing. His daughter smiled and nodded at me before signing her reply. I watched in fascination how swiftly they conversed in a language I knew nothing of. Anne watched the conversation with a pleasant smile, but I could tell she was not pleased to see me; when she caught me staring at her, she met my gaze squarely, with icy displeasure evident in her eyes.

"She says she's glad to meet you and she's doing great, now that she's met Papa's future wife," Eric told me with a grin. I glanced quickly at Anne and saw her flinch.

"Girlfriend, just girlfriend," I blurted. Eric's lips thinned.

Anne stood up. "I'm going to give you all some space," she said. "I'll be back in an hour."

"All right," Eric replied. Anne kissed Diana and then gave Eric a very possessive hug before leaving.

"She's nice," I said, lying.

Eric shrugged. "You'll get along soon enough," he said with an unconcerned air.

"Anyway, now that you're here, feel free to ask her any questions you want. I'll sign it to her. I can't guarantee the veracity of my responses if Diana here bad-mouths me, but . . ." He winked at me, an incongruous move on his part, and I laughed.

So the next hour flew by as Diana and I conversed with Eric as the middle man. It wasn't even strange, after a while. Mostly I watched them signing to each other. There was so much love in his face that it showed me a whole new, very desirable side to Eric Deng, a side I wished I could see more often, this vulnerability and openness. This Family Man side of him.

It's kind of hot.

8:30 p.m. When he suggested going to have dinner at a friend's restaurant, I told him that I didn't want dinner, which I must say is unusual for me. I placed my hand on his thigh and said I wanted to show him mine.

My room, that is.

"But you've never offered to show me your room before," he said, surprised. "You wouldn't even let me have a peek at your Fourth of July party."

"That's because back then, no man who'd seen the size of my closet would have wanted anything to do with me. But ever since Jason gave me a book by Marie Kondo, I've gotten much better with stuff. Besides"—I moved that hand all the way up, up—"I don't intend to spend a lot of time in the closet."

He floored that Maserati (as much as one can "floor" a Maserati in Singapore) and we were together alone chez moi for the first time since we started going out. I led him straight to my bedroom, where we did nothing new; yet, somehow, everything between us was different. Maybe because I didn't hold him at arms' length emotionally, maybe because I finally saw what kind of man Eric was—a lovely Shrek-y onion man made of layers of contradictions and complexity, but interlaced with tenderness. The physicality of the act was wrought not just out of mechanical passion, but tempered with new respect and understanding.

At the end of one particularly intense moment, he paused, looked deep into my eyes and asked me to say yes to being his forever.

"I'm yours," I said. And I meant it.

Sunday 25 September

7:30 p.m. Got a strange text from Suresh, who must be back in Jakarta by now. It said: **I miss you**. Surely he meant to send it to Anousha?

I deleted it.

9:30 p.m. Deleted Tinder and Sponk, both of which I'd been toying around with from time to time. Why was I looking at profiles and wasting time? I had already found my man. If I believed that, then I should act like it.

11:20 p.m. Deleted Candy Crush. Goodbye, old friend.

This deletion has nothing, of course, to do with the fact that I've belatedly discovered Angry Birds. Some millennial I'm turning out to be.

42

Monday 26 September

Dear Diary, something amazing happened today—a veritable partnership-saving miracle.

I was scrolling through *TLTS*'s Instagram when I got a message on LinkedIn from a stranger called Mohd Usman Ariff. Thinking it was someone from a recruitment agency or perhaps an admirer, I opened it.

It was my former classmate from law school, who'd gone by Uzi for most of uni (it was a different time back then, a simpler, less polarized time). I remembered Usman fondly because he graduated fifth in the year above me. And we might or might not have made out in some fresher's party. Whatever.

Saw your name in some of my files, brought back some good memories, just thought I'd say hi.

I smiled and replied:

Been a long time. Where're you slumming it now?

He replied:

Chapel Town.

Shit.

Listen, I just took over from the previous general counsel who left after the death of Charleston Sr., read up on the VizWare transaction (among others) as the boss is keen to examine all the loose ends from this year to see if he can salvage anything out of it, and the VizWare transaction is one he's particularly curious about. From what I can read and my recent chats with Langford-Bauer, Genevieve and Suresh—

Oh no, I thought.

—it seems like Chapel Town, under Charleston Sr., made a mistake in pulling out and icing the deal, which is an opinion Charleston Jr. and I appear to share. But we don't know the ins and outs of this deal entirely as there's been a mass defection since Charleston Sr. passed. So we'd like to speak to the lead coordinating counsel, i.e., you, to have a fuller picture, in person if you agree. Charleston Jr. insists on doing business in person. If he likes what he hears, the whole thing can move forward relatively quickly. It might not go anywhere on VizWare's side, but we're confident it will. The good thing is, last we heard, VizWare has not been courting anyone else, so there's hope yet. And vis-à-vis our friends at Sungguh, if they are keen to come on board again, I'm going to suggest to them that we prefer if you are put as lead coordinating counsel for the transaction instead of Genevieve, who's a li'l . . . erratic.

Wow, I typed, stunned. That's great. Of course I can fly over, if you sign an engagement letter.

Of course. Your time is valuable.

Thank you. You're the best.

No, *you* are.

I accept your deference, serf. But what I don't understand is—you wanted to reinstate me *after* speaking with all three of them?

Yes *wry face emoji* Genevieve and Langford-Bauer were royal pains in the butt, and bitched about you so thoroughly I felt ashamed on your behalf. As for Suresh—

I steeled myself. And tried to ignore the Kegel my heart just did at his name.

—Suresh told me, off the record, that you were the brains behind the whole operation. And that was why when they asked to take you off the file at Sungguh, he told them he would prefer to be taken off it as well.

Ah. That's. . . nice of him.

Anyway, that international tax colleague of yours, Langford-Bauer? He's going to have to come as well, as Charleston Jr. also wants a briefing on the appropriate structure for his investment in VizWare. He doesn't trust the old guard's recommendations.

A little shaken, I thanked Usman and said I would wait for his update.

So Suresh had never tried to usurp my place. He'd never even tried to backstab me. I had been the one projecting all those nasty impulses on him.

He couldn't help who his future wife is related to, and I should've given him the benefit of doubt when he asserted that he wasn't milking his ties with his future in-laws.

All of a sudden I felt like a giant Langford-Bauer myself. I wished Suresh was around so I could apologize to him for getting the situation completely wrong. Suresh was a decent guy—I'd met so few of those in my career that I'd missed the signs.

After I wrote a stiffly worded email to Mong (I was giving him the cold shoulder still, although I think he's mystified by the reason for it) to update him on this development, I dropped Suresh a text on his private number and apologized for thinking he'd backstabbed me, and that it had been a bit complicated between us after Luxembourg, for which I was sorry.

The response was swift:

This is Anousha. You stay away from Suresh if you know what's good for you.

43

Saturday 1 October

October. Blergh. Even the name sounds icky.

Ock-toh-ber.

Anyway, tonight is date night with Eric, who landed late last night from Paris. We were going to a new restaurant that his friend, a celebrity chef of some renown, had just opened.

I tried to get him to downgrade the meal (following that realization post-convo with Suresh that I really was being sugared, just a little) to hawker food, telling him about this *bak chor mee* place I'd heard my colleagues raving about, but he laughed in my face. "I don't eat hawker food, my dear," he said, waving off my protests.

He picked me up in a glossy midnight blue Rolls-Royce that I'd not seen before.

"New car?" I joked.

"Yes," he said, not joking. "I just picked it up this morning."

I didn't reply. Sometimes it was *so* hard to relate. "I have a surprise," Eric told me. "We're going to be joined by someone special." He picked up my right palm and squeezed it. "Don't, as you young people say, freak out."

My heart somersaulted. Was it another scary relative? Or maybe it was Diana again! As much as I could, I started tucking down my boobs, flattening them into my bra. I could tell Eric was amused, but I didn't care. Stepmothers didn't have boobs—they have bosoms, maternal ones that had no distinct personality, much like a gently used speedbump.

When we got to the restaurant, we were ushered into a corner booth. A tall, lithe woman with unnaturally pale skin and jet-black hair was already there, resplendent in a mauve sheath dress. She was sipping her tea and scrolling through her phone when she noticed our approach and stood up to greet us.

"Hello, you must be Andrea. My name is Esther," said the mystery woman, extending her hand for a handshake.

"Esther is, um, my lawyer," Eric said, a little sheepish.

"Oh," I said, instantly jealous.

Eric cleared his throat. "She's also my, ah, stepsister."

The relief I felt was palpable; I hoped it didn't show in my face. Of course. "Pleased to meet you," I said, shaking her hand. Esther grasped my hand with a viselike grip, her glittery rings digging into my flesh. Her eyes were hard, almost cold, even as her smile was wide. She was very attractive in a manicured, varnished way peculiar to many of the *Tatler* jet set: hair and makeup perfect; facial flaws buffed away by a careful surgeon; clothes discreetly luxurious and tailored almost to a fault. "So you're the woman my brother has been seeing," she said, giving me a swift once-over without blinking.

"Hmm," I replied noncommittally; conversely, I had not heard of her till today.

Eric cleared his throat and stood up. "I'll speak to Jack now," he said, referring to the celebrity chef. He left us in what he thought was a nonchalant manner, but I could see from his hurried footsteps that he was eager to give his sister room to do her thing. I steeled myself for what could only be an unpleasant fact-finding expedition.

"I'm sure you have questions for me," I said, as soon as Eric had left, cutting her off before she could speak. "Go ahead. I'm an open book."

She nodded approvingly. "I could see that you are a no-nonsense type of woman. That's good. Now, I know that things between you have progressed quite far; Eric tells me he is quite smitten with you and he wants to make the relationship official. He is even considering marrying you. Has he told you that?"

"N-not in those *exact* words," I hedged.

"Has Eric told you about his last . . . dalliance, and the arrangement he has with the woman?"

I nodded mutely.

"If you have children, you should know that Diana will still be treated like a legitimate child when it comes to matters of inheritance. She will be the firstborn, and your children, if you have any, will have to acknowledge her claim. You must agree to these terms before you can marry into our family. There will be an agreement you'll have to sign."

My face flushed. "I-I haven't even, I mean, this is . . ." I stood up. "Look, my relationship with Eric is still in its early days. I don't know why he felt it necessary to discuss this at this stage. This is ridiculous. Did he put you up to this? Well, if he did you should let him know in the future to discuss this with me first." I pushed my chair back and made to leave until she grabbed my wrist.

"Honey," Esther said, her voice softening, "I think it's because he wants to propose to you . . . tonight."

"What?" I said, just as the lights were dimmed and Sade's vocals boomed across the room. People whooped.

"Tonight . . . I celebrate my love for yoouuu," she sang, just as Eric walked out with a huge cake decorated with fabulous sugar peonies, lit with a gold candle. A waiter followed behind with a large bottle of champagne in a bucket and sparklers sending silvery flowers everywhere.

"Oh crap," I said, my voice faltering when I saw what was written on the cake.

It said, "Let's get married." (Yes, with a full stop.) A frisson of annoyance registered in my consciousness. It was so . . . presumptuous. He'd not even phrased it as a question; it was a statement at best, without even a "pretty please" to soften it. You could say it sounded like a command.

But then he was in front of me and he was holding a ring with what looked like a diamond as large as a thumbnail and my anger levels nosedived quite rapidly. People were clapping and cheering as he clasped me by my shoulders and kissed me deeply. In his deep, powerful voice, he asked, "Will you do me the honor of marrying me, Andrea Tang?"

And there it was. The romantic, public marriage proposal. Every woman's dream, right? Right? I hesitated, staring at the ridiculously large diamond. I could feel the tension rising in the room with every passing second in which nothing was said. I knew what was expected of me, but I couldn't do it. Was this really what I wanted? I closed my eyes and tried to shut out my audience.

For some strange reason, I saw Genevieve. She was smiling at me and mouthing something about the matrix. It was so freaky I opened my eyes and gave myself a shake.

"Will you marry me?" Eric said again, smiling, just the slightest steel underscoring his request. The hush that had fallen over the scene was almost unbearable. It carried in it the hope of every single ancestor watching over me at that instant. I could hear the sparklers fizzing in the silence. Someone's phone buzzed and it was silenced with a rapidity you would not get these days even during a funeral wake.

"Well? What will it be?" Eric said in a low voice, and, it must be said, not very romantically.

I took a deep breath and did the only thing I could under the circumstances: I said yes as loud as I could, then leaned over and said to Eric, sotto voce but very firmly, "I'll think about it."

Part IV

NO FLUKE

44

Sunday 2 October

9:50 a.m. "You'll *think* about it?" Linda shrieked. "That was your answer to a marriage proposal from Eric fucking *Deng*?"

"We're still in the early days of our relationship. Plus he ambushed me," I said between cool, calming gulps of bargain-bin Pinot Grigio. "It was the best I could do under the watchful eyes of thirty diners! Apparently some of them were his closest business partners!" I made a face.

"Well, I think it's brave," Jason said.

"Shut up, suck-up," Linda said, succinct in her meanness as always.

"Settle down, you two," I said companionably.

Jason and I were sprawled on the L-shaped couch, him with a glass of tap water, me with a bottle of Pinot Grigio that he had purchased from the local convenience store. Linda was on FaceTime with us from Lisbon; ostensibly she was there to meet with some clients, but really she was living it up with some Filipino jet-set friends of hers from boarding school. At least she was making every effort again to be there for me when I needed her: we had promised each other once upon a time that we would FaceTime whenever one of us sent out an emoji of a shark. A kind of Bat-Signal. I had sent one out as soon as I got home, but she was only able to reply to me six hours later to confirm that she could speak at 9:00 a.m. Singapore time, and now here we were. Neither Jason nor I had had much sleep (I'd put out an early-morning SOS for company at my place on the group chat and he'd come over with liquid breakfast, the doll), and we were now FaceTiming while (I was) drinking.

"All the same, although things are moving really fast, it *feels* natural. We seem to be in a good place, and I've already met his daughter."

"So, are you going to marry Eric or what?" Linda pressed. "And when are you expected to give an answer?"

"In two weeks, apparently."

"It doesn't seem right, to have to take two weeks to think over a marriage proposal."

"Touché, sister. But two weeks is all I could get."

"I meant, you shouldn't have to take so long, you dope."

"She's got a point," Jason said, making a face. "But, seriously, do you even love him?"

"I do love him," I said sincerely. "I could be happy with him."

"You could be happy with a vibrator, honey," Linda said. "That's how I get though my manless days."

I rolled my eyes.

"Anyway, I've got to go. We're attending a private after-party hosted by one of the Saudi princes, I believe. Someone told me David Guetta is spinning."

"Only David Guetta?" I said sarcastically.

"I think"—she was distractedly putting on mascara while FaceTiming me—"Rihanna's supposed to make an appearance as well, but the very *least* we can hope for is Maroon 5 minus Adam Levine."

After we had said our goodbyes and Jason left, I sat in the dark and watched YouTube videos of cats doing funny things while doing up a pros and cons list for marrying Eric so early in our relationship. Not that I could concentrate. I kept tweaking the list. Can't say I've found anything more gratifying in the pros column than "forever beating Helen."

11:05 p.m. Andrea Deng. Andrea Tang-Deng. Mrs. Deng.

11:47 p.m. It's just impossible to decide in two weeks. Mostly because this is so new. Normally couples date for at least a year, then they move in together, rough it for two years, then get engaged. That is the proper progression . . .

12:05 a.m. Oooh, knock on the door!

3:17 a.m. Was Eric in a suit. At first I was a little annoyed, since we were not supposed to see each other during these two weeks so I could have some space to think. Apparently a meeting in Jakarta had been canceled, so he'd decided to fly back to surprise me on his way to Malaysia. He'd come bearing a lush bouquet of dahlias, champagne, and a handwritten poem. It was all so sincere and romantic that I forgave the rule-breaking and spent a couple of hours just cozying up with him on the couch, drinking champagne while he caught me up on his admittedly complicated stepfamily tree.

"And speaking of family, here's one of the reasons I came back to Singapore today." He took something out of the pocket of his suit jacket. "Here," he said, handing it to me.

I looked down, stunned. It was my Cartier watch, my graduation gift from my parents, the one that Orson had filched. "I-I don't . . . I don't understand." I kept caressing the watch. "I mean, how?"

"I got it back for you from the . . . *boy* who'd stolen it from you."

Apparently not too long after I'd casually mentioned Orson at our first and only group date, he'd asked Linda for more details at the Fourth of July party, and used his contacts in the PI industry to track Orson using a photo that I had sent to our WhatsApp group at LGA and which Linda had forwarded. It had been difficult to track Orson, since he didn't really frequent the same spot twice, or at least he didn't follow any routine. "When my PI finally found him at one of the bars, he followed him to his HDB* flat, and—"

"Karate chopped him?" I interrupted eagerly.

He smiled, his eyes twinkling. "He took out his phone and threatened to start livestreaming unless he listened. He gave Orson an ultimatum. Either give back the watch or he would live broadcast his face and address on all the forums so all the women who he'd stolen from can take legal action—or otherwise." Now he was grinning.

"That is an awesome threat," I had to admit. "What did he say?"

"At first he didn't know which watch my PI was referring to. He was confused. Turns out this guy has been running love scams for some time. It was only when the PI told him the watch model and the inscription on the back that he remembered which one was yours. Said that he hadn't managed to pawn it because of that inscription, so he had been holding on to it. And now here it is."

I was so touched, not just by the lengths he went to to please me but by the level of attention he paid to the seemingly random things I said to him, that I started to cry. "Thank you. Thank you so much."

He kissed the top of my head. "You're welcome. Listen, I've been thinking about how I went about asking you to marry me. I'm sorry I sprung the whole engagement thing on you," he murmured in my hair. "I know it's fast, and we're supposed to do things a certain way, but I can't imagine waiting around two more years just so it's appropriate to pop the question. You know I'm a decisive person, and Andrea, I know it's you that I want."

I found it hard to speak, so I kissed him.

Since he had an early flight to Malaysia and I had to work in a few hours, he left sometime around three. His visit had left me

* HDB stands for Housing and Development Board, the statutory body responsible for Singapore's public housing, where the majority of Singaporeans live.

keyed up, so I eschewed sleep and decided to go for a rare jog, figuring that the exercise would help me think. I couldn't understand why I was on the fence about Eric—was it because it just felt too soon? That had to be it. Objectively speaking, Eric had so many good qualities it was hard to keep count: intelligent, caring, worldly, a good father, a family man, and, let's be honest, wealthy. And he was totally devoted to me.

The more I thought about it, the more it made sense to commit to Eric. The bird in the hand is worth none in the bush, obviously. And obviously I would win forever over Helen if I married Eric. Billionaire *and* of Chinese descent.

And if I could time it so I'd get pregnant immediately after the wedding, and announce it right before Helen's wedding . . .

Ahaha. Ahahaha!

Monday 3 October

7:08 a.m. Andrea Tang-Deng. Andrea Deng. Andrea Deng-Tang.

7:25 a.m. Let's try it out: Good morning, Mrs. Andrea Deng! Hmm. Has a nice ring to it.

8:35 a.m. OK, so if I'm going to say yes, then I guess I should consider myself engaged. Should I start planning the wedding already? Will just take a peek at some wedding sites. Also it might make sense to book Fullerton ASAP on the auspicious dates I'd like for the wedding, preferably before Helen's date.

8:37 a.m. Haha will get married two months before Helen hahahaha on 18th March hahahaa!

9:15 a.m. Shit, just got off the phone with the manager in charge of Fullerton's ballroom rental and, after an almost inaudible sniff, she told me 18th March is not available as it already has four weddings booked on that day. Apparently I should have booked a year ago if I wanted to get married on a particular date, especially one that was auspicious.

"Well," I said huffily to the girl at reception, "if I had known I'd be getting married a year ago, I'd not have gone to Auntie Wei Wei's CNY do with Linda, would I?"

Of course, the poor woman had no idea what I was on about,

but that's the kind of outburst you have to deal with when you man the friggin' reservations line for ballrooms.

9:20 a.m. Mrs. Andrea Deng. Mrs. Andrea Tang-Deng. Hmm. Maybe I'll just keep my maiden name. How will potential clients know that it is me, Andrea Tang of the "40 Most Influential Lawyers Under 40"?

OH SHIT! Am late for work!

9:57 a.m. Got to work late but no one was looking for me. The partners were on their annual partners' retreat, so the atmosphere in the office was relaxed.

10:05 a.m. Told Kai about my news. She shrieked and hugged me. I then put her on a mission to find me a suitable venue for five hundred guests on 18 March. #priorities

10:08 a.m. Hmm, just realized that Eric might want more than five hundred guests.

10:10 a.m. I literally have no idea what kind of wedding Eric would want. Not that he has a choice. Eric's a five-hundred-guests-or-more kind of guy, by default. It's a business wedding.

10:13 a.m. If I were marrying someone less impressive, I'd probably want only three hundred people at my wedding, if even. Less than one hundred if it had been strictly up to me. It would be held somewhere remote, on a beach; the vibe would be casual: cork sandals, floppy beach hats, linen suits; a softly beaded Claire Pettibone dress; my mother in restraints.

10:28 a.m. I should tell the girls. But I'm somehow very reluctant. I should wait. Tomorrow's Val's hen night. Seems a bit gauche to talk about my news. Yeah, that's right.

10:40 a.m. Called Melissa and Val and Jason and texted everyone else in my wider group of friends who hadn't heard about the proposal when I found out that Kai had basically told everyone on *all* her social media platforms (excluding LinkedIn, at least) that her boss was finally engaged (without naming names, but still, who else could it be—Suresh?), even when nothing is official yet. Honestly, is nothing sacred with Generation Z?

Hesitated in texting Suresh. Didn't. Figured he's already aware since he is friends with Kai on Facebook.

Everyone I contacted was apparently still unaware. Thank God for the social media digital divide. Means very likely older bosses will not know about the potential engagement until after the partnership decision is made, and will not be unfairly biased against my gender more than they already are (approximately 20 percent of the equity partners in my firm are women—it's pretty appalling).

6:00 p.m. Snuck out of the office early and went to the Dungeon (an underground bar/restaurant in the CBD favored by traders) to grab a couple of drinks with Linda, who just got back from Lisbon.

I love the Dungeon. The whole place was sweaty with testosterone and the sultry musk of successful people. I waded into the rich pheromone pond and sank into it blissfully, knowing I, too, would soon be spraying the scent of my success into the olfactory stew.

9:43 p.m. Drinkng wattrr v. slowly. Nce man holdifg straw to fface. Water cold. Must not ppuk

Oops. Toolate.

11:15 p.m. Will never drink again.

Tuesday 4 October

6:40 a.m. Must drink again. In twelve hours. Or bad friend. Urgh. Floor rushing up to face, must not—

Oopsie.

8:05 a.m. Am at work. Must not die.

9:11 a.m. Kai handed me a bottle of coconut water and what she says is "like a vitamin B pill, really." She gave me three others to take something or other blah blah urgh hungover.

10:05 a.m. Am feeling great! Listening to Bruno Mars on repeat! Am glad I have Spotify Premium!!

10:25 a.m. Mong opened the door to me doing a plank! Why not? Helps me think. Although he did not look too pleased. "Is health not part of work?" I asked him. He said yes, very hesitantly. To assure him, I told him I was still on the clock with one of our "favorite" clients. He chuckled and left me, still in plank. Boss Great!

2:07 p.m. Have had another two vitamin B pills twenty minutes ago and a Red Bull as energy was flagging! Kai said don't mix with caffeine, but she's an uptight Pilates vegan! Caffeine is legal drug, everyone knows!

4:00 p.m. Kai has no more pills. She said I was supposed to take one pill once every six hours, but how was I supposed to know?

4:57 p.m. Please let me die in peace, is all I ask.

10:45 p.m. Met at six p.m. at Le Luxe, a French fusion restaurant where we were supposed to celebrate Val's hen night. On a freaking Tuesday. WTF, I know.

One of Val's work friends, Jessie, a starched-face former beauty queen and bitter, broke divorcée of a casino tycoon, had been coerced into organizing the shindig for Valerie and a gang of ten girlfriends. The whole thing was a mess from start to finish, shambolic and flat. After a lackluster dinner, we went to K-Suites, a karaoke bar, and sang, well, attempted to sing because most of Val's friends (except Linda, myself, and another woman whose name I've forgotten) were all in their forties and fifties, rich (or pretending they were), and addicted to surgery; most of them had had so much work done to their faces it was like watching concrete stretch. They mimed singing as much as they could.

Linda should have organized it. She would have booked a table at some Les Amis restaurant, doused us in cocktails and champagne, then brought us out for a night of Ironic Clubbing à la Mambo Jumbo at Zouk. She would never have brought us to this place. But Linda was only a guest, and Jessie ruled iron-fisted over the proceedings, brooking no argument and allowing no deviations from her itinerary. She wanted bland rice pudding hen night, and we were going to get it no matter what.

But guess what? Valerie genuinely seemed not to care. She ate the bland food in that boring restaurant and she belted her off-key way over one Bublé song after another without holding back. This from the woman who was so careful and protective about her image that she once ex-communicated a friend who had let slip that she was Airbnb-ing her beautiful River Valley apartment (thus letting her other frenemies know that she needed the money). I watched her, and envied her. She had almost always believed in love despite all her odds, and she had finally been rewarded with her happily ever after. The only thing that would complete her world now was her getting pregnant, and at the rate she was going, who's to say it wasn't possible? She'd be the next Sophie B. Hawkins! And Linda, even Linda—Linda, the Lethargic in Love—had found her version of happiness. Whereas I—what was I destined for if I said yes to Eric Deng?

11:30 p.m. Despite Jessie's best attempts, we still had a decent night out and I was a little tipsy by ten p.m. (fine, very tipsy) and made my excuses to leave as I had a closing that week. I was struggling to open my door when I received a text from Suresh:

> **I'm back in town for a week, will be working from Singapore. Could we talk? Need your advice on something personal. It's urgent.**

And I thought, *Let's talk now, why not?* I told him to come over to my place, since I was the one living alone.

Alone. We would be alone in my place. The idea was oddly destabilizing, or maybe it was the alcohol.

My heart was pounding when I opened the door. "Hey there, stranger," I said. I beckoned him to come in. "You're up late."

"Sorry to have texted you at this hour, but I've got big news and I wanted to ask your opinion."

I trailed him to the living room in a semi-daze. He was dressed in a white singlet and a filmy, clingy pair of track pants. The effect was very arresting. I forced myself to stare at his chest. His very exposed chest. Come to think of it, I wasn't much better. I looked down and realized I was wearing a T-shirt and a pair of gym shorts, which showed a lot of leg.

We were both trying hard not to stare at each other's bodies in an Adam-and-Eve-post-forbidden-apple scene. But to admit to our uncomfortableness was to admit that we found each other's semi-nakedness affecting, and neither of us was willing to do that.

"So, what's up?" I said, casually placing my left hand against the counter to stabilize myself.

He caught sight of my engagement ring (I'd slipped it on at work before leaving, maybe because of *tai-tai* peer pressure or something—that rock is *huge*) and his lips thinned. "Are congrats in order?"

"On?" I asked, a little confused.

"Looks like someone proposed?" His face was expressionless. "Anyway—congrats."

I flushed. "Oh, erm, actually I haven't accepted his proposal, but, yes, he asked."

"Right," he said, pointedly looking at my ring.

"I was wearing the ring for fun. I meant to tell you about his proposal, but you weren't around. It just . . . felt inappropriate to tell you over WhatsApp or email, you know . . ." I was blabbering.

"So nothing is set in stone?" Suresh said, his lip twitching.

I laughed. "No, nothing is." We were smiling at each other now. I quickly changed the subject. "What did you come here to talk to me about? You said you needed advice."

"I do." He drew a shuddery breath and exhaled. "I've been offered representation!"

"What?"

"*TLTS!* Someone from a fancy literary agency DMed me and told me they love it, and I did some research on the agent, he's big and legit, so I signed with him. He and his team think *TLTS* is going to be big."

"Wow," I said, clapping excitedly. "Congratulations! You deserve it, you're so talented."

"Thank you," he said, his eyes shining but his voice serious.

Something else was up. "What is it?" I asked, a little afraid.

"They're saying that there's potential for it to be made into a series of books, web-toons, maybe even a movie, if we're lucky . . . but that I should take some time off to really work on the debut graphic novel." His eyes met mine. "And I'm really, really tempted. This is my chance—strike while the iron is hot, and all. So what I'm saying is . . . I-I think I should quit," he said.

"Wow." A bombshell. "This . . . this is great news," I said, my thoughts spinning.

"What do you think? Because Noush told me I was crazy for even thinking that. That I'd be stupid to quit. There's no guarantee I'd be making what I make now. Or that it'll turn out to be anything other than a flash in the pan. Maybe this is imposter syndrome talking, but . . . but I'm afraid I'm not as good as they think I am," he admitted quietly.

"What? You're being ridiculous. Of *course* you're as good as they say you are—better, even! And of course you should go for it—you'd be crazy not to! And not just because you're my competition. I think one of us should be happy in their career, at least."

He squinted at me. "Andrea, do you hear yourself? You just admitted that you are not happy."

I stared at him. "Yup. And?"

"If you're not happy, why continue being a lawyer? You should quit, too."

"That's ridiculous. Tons of people are in the same predicament, but we— I have no choice. You can afford to quit because you have options."

"You're the one who's super talented. And smart. And amazing," he said, his voice unsteady. "Andrea, I don't know how much clearer I can put it: you have all the choice. You're the better lawyer of the both of us."

As a response, I went to him and hugged him. Tightly. It was the first time I had actually had close, prolonged physical contact with him, after Luxembourg. He felt . . . warm. Safe. Muscular. He returned the hug and now we were completely enmeshed. I could smell the earthy cinnamon scent of his skin. Mmm. I locked eyes with him and flushed. He was so attractive with his velvet, honey-colored eyes and long Bambi lashes. And those soft, cotton-candy pink lips. Every neuron in my alcohol-addled brain was suddenly screaming at me to—

My stomach emitted a loud rumble.

—eat. Oh God, I was *so* hungry.

I let go of him and staggered to the kitchen. I found a bunch of half-black bananas and proceeded to peel one before smashing it, somewhat off target, into my mouth hole.

"You want one?" I said, making sure he had a good view of my mastication. All the better to turn him off so that I didn't have to deal with how much I wanted him right then and there.

"No thanks," he said evenly.

I opened the fridge door, took out a jar of possibly expired pickled onions, and began using my fingers to transfer them into my mouth. Regrettably, they did indeed taste like they had expired, which I visually confirmed when I looked into the jar and found the telltale film of mold.

I ran to the sink and began spitting the whole mess up.

"I really should go," Suresh said.

"Wait," I said, suddenly frantic. "Err, I . . ."

"Look, just get some rest. We'll talk some other time."

"Thanks," I said, curtly, extending my hand in a weirdly formal gesture.

"You're welcome," he said, shaking it.

We were both squeezing each other's hand so hard, it brought back memories of our first handshake, when we were each trying to show dominance over the other.

"Good night," he said, like a dog with a bone.

"Good night," I said through gritted teeth, not letting go.

"Count to three?" He gasped, as I increased pressure.

I winced and nodded. "On the count of three. One, two, three!"

We let go at the same time with simultaneous whooshes of relief.

"Well," he said.

"Good fight," I replied.

I was aware that we were both staring at each other in a very unkosher way. He took a hesitant step toward me. "Listen, Andrea, I've got something I need to confess."

"Can we talk tomorrow? It's late and I've got to, uh, go back to work," I babbled, skirting around the kitchen island. "I'm sorry, but it's this VizWare acquisition that's just restarted. There's still a chance I can salvage my shot at making partner, so . . . I really need to prepare my briefing for the general counsel as I'll be flying in to Omaha the day after, chop chop, hustle hustle."

He swore quietly. "You know what, I give up. Whatever. You do you." Then he strode out of the living room, uttered a curt "good night," and slammed the door to my apartment behind him.

Honestly! Some people are just so rude.

Wednesday 5 October

8:00 a.m. I will tell no one about what happened yesterday. It doesn't mean anything. And what we almost did, I think? What were we about to do?

8:05 a.m. OK, I'll just tell Linda.

8:08 a.m. Shit, I have a department meeting that's due to start at 8:30 a.m.! Shit! How could I have forgotten? My priorities are all over the place!

8:45 a.m. Arrived at the office after a surprisingly smooth MRT ride and ran to Resilience, the conference room where the meeting was being held. Saw through the frosted glass that the room was full and there was no way to slip in unnoticed. Panicked, before realizing my best defense would be to pretend I had an even more important meeting with a client. Ducked into the adjoining conference room (Dedication) and called Linda. She could be my alibi.

"You bunch of nerds. You guys are *so* into each other, just get it on already."

"No, we aren't."

"Yes, you are."

"No, we aren't."

Of course, this sophisticated exchange went on for some time, after which Linda, being completely shag-crazy, started egging me on to "jump Suresh's bones and taste the rainbow!"

Only Linda can pervert the tagline of Skittles.

But there will be no tasting of any candy. I must be strong. Back when I was sticking to the Life Plan, things were easy. Smooth-going. I didn't constantly doubt my every move. It was just when I started going off-piste that my life started coming off the rails. All Tiger Moms want and know what's best for their children. Look at the Kardashians. Everyone knows that Kris is the one conducting the orchestra so to speak, and look how successful they are. They might even be happy!

If I stick to my Life Plan, my life will be the best version of itself. And that is what I want.

10:10 a.m. Meeting next door is done. Saw my colleagues drift past my room. I stood up and made sure they saw me on the call through the unfrosted bits (I was still chatting with Linda), making threatening sounds and waving my arms. My junior, Xi Lin, flashed me a thumbs-up sign, which I returned. I should have been an actor, clearly.

10:45 a.m. A DEFCON 2 situation ("last bottle of water while stranded in the Sahara, with what could either be an oasis or a mirage one day's crawl away, and you have only one arm left, but at least you still have an arm" kind of catastrophe) has developed. Jin Li, Mong's secretary, called me in a panic.

"It's bad," she said, her anxiety mixing with her years of hardened PA professionalism in a disconcerting mash of cheery anguish. "He's got dengue—again."

"Aww fuck," I said, worried. I couldn't be mad at Mong anymore. "How *is* Mong?"

"You know that getting dengue for the second time can be deadly, right?"

"Yes," I said, full of contrition.

"Well, he's stable, but they are monitoring him closely, something about critical platelet counts and needing a transfusion and his rare blood type, but his helper is with him. She's taking good care of him." There was a loaded silence between us, before Jin Li said, almost apologetically, "His ex-wife and children are, well, indisposed."

"Right."

"But his parents are also with him."

"But they must be like . . . what, eighty?"

"Older," she said. "They had him when the mother was close to forty. He was the ninth child." She coughed and said, "Apparently she's volunteered to give blood, in case they run low."

Seems like Mong came from a line of fighters—he would make it through, right?

Right?

Come to think of it, there were no guarantees when it came to Mong. Who knows what other horrible chronic illnesses the man was hiding from us: he was the kind who would be perfectly capable of working through Ebola while ensconced in an isolation ward, just so he wouldn't infect the rest of the team, even as his brain started leaking through his nostrils . . .

"Can we do anything? Like run a blood donation drive?"

"It's OK, dear, the blood bank is good for now."

"Let me know when he's out of ICU so I can visit him, OK? Just . . . just keep me updated as to how he is," I said, trying to keep it together. I was this close to bawling: the man was family. He basically taught me almost everything I knew and made me the lawyer I was today. I'd spent more time with this man over the past few years than *any member of my biological family*—and it was the same for him.

If I ever got married, he would have to walk me down the aisle. He had no choice.

I realized that I was crying silently and held the phone at arm's length so I could blow my nose without giving my feelings away.

"I will," Jin Li said. "But, ah"—sounding embarrassed—"he told me that the only thing he cares about right now is the VizWare file. So . . . you know: close the deal. Make sure Charleston Jr. and, by extension, Chapel Town, are on board."

I did. I arranged with Chapel Town to get the return tickets to Omaha, where I would meet the elusive Charleston Wesley Jr., son of the founder of the coinvestor Chapel Town Investments, one of the largest family offices around. I would sign them just so Mong would get better. Even if it meant playing nice with goddamn Langford-Turdy-Bauer.

And maybe, just maybe, I could redeem myself and make partner. I still want that. Right?

Thursday 6 October

Landed in Omaha smoothly.

I was picked up at the airport by Charleston Wesley Jr.'s chauffeur, who drove . . . a Tesla Model S with the sticker "Say No to Fossil Fuels" emblazoned on it. So far, so good. As the housekeeper led me through the house to the living room, I noticed how homey and lived-in the house was: the leather couches were the kind you would be able to nap on; there was a large stone fireplace, over which were mounted several hunting trophies (mostly deer, one antelope, a buffalo); multicolored hand-knitted blankets and bean bags completed the décor along with several portraits of some dead (possibly related) people, a large Turner seascape, and a small mural of a soldier holding—oh dear—the head of a scalped Native American.

Ah. I knew there had to be a catch somewhere.

And there was the man himself. Slight, slope-shouldered, and white-haired, he was an Elmer Fuddish figure dressed in a thin white polo shirt and beige Dockers, sallow in complexion and altogether unimpressive in visage and bearing. He could have been cast as a hobbit. How was this man one of the Top 100 Richest Men in America?

Then he shook my hand with a perfectly calibrated handshake and I saw how shrewd his light blue eyes were. I stood up a little straighter.

He had noticed my gaze on the mural and apologized for it. "It belonged to my father, and even if the subject matter is rather abhorrent, I leave it there to remind myself that even the best of men have areas in their lives where they can make better choices. That's my motto in life and business, anyway. We're not bound by our past, you know."

I warmed to Charleston immediately. "I understand."

"I really appreciate you taking time out to fly here to allay my doubts about the closing. I have a lot of faith in your firm, because of what Usman told me. And I do prefer to do business in person."

"Of course," I said. He'd flown me business and put me in a suite in the local Hilton, so I was mollified.

"By the way"—he made a face—"your colleague Langford-Bauer is already here, along with Usman."

I fought the urge to groan audibly by doing a Kegel. "We won't take much of your time," I assured him.

"Oh, you can, my dear, but your colleague is a little bit of a—how shall I put it—a bit of a—"

Turd hillock? I said in my head. Out loud, "Challenge?"

"Yes," Charleston said.

"That's why he's the best, in London," I said, loyally. Firm first, personal animus second.

Over a sumptuous high tea spread of scones and other pastries, and delicious tea from a super isolated mountain plantation in China, we spent a pleasant, but intense, afternoon briefing Charleston and Usman on the situation. Langford-Bauer did his best to annoy me by constantly insinuating, in his subtle British way, that I was not as competent as him, but I kept it professional and classy, like Gong Li. Charleston seemed appeased by the explanation, considered the risks minimal, and agreed to go ahead with the closing. So long as VizWare said yes, it would be a win for me and the firm.

When we were done, he showed us around his ranch, where he kept a flock of champion fighting cocks (try saying that really fast) that he had bred out of some Mexican, Javanese, and Filipino stock. It was all quite fun, if only because Linda had an uncle who was a somewhat renowned breeder of gamecock in the Philippines, and I had visited a clandestine cockfight in a tobacco field in Cuba and had been shown how they were "outfitted" before the fight. The bloodlust, I told Charleston, reminded me of people queueing for Kanye's kicks.

"What?" Charleston said, coming to a stop and staring at me. "There are people who line up—to be kicked by something called Con Yay?"

I was struggling not to burst into laughter or pee. This was the point when Langford-Bauer said, in his supercilious voice, "She means 'shoes.' Kanye West has a range of sneakers, and they are very fashionable, these"—a wrinkle of his aristocratic nose—"*kicks*."

I wished, wished, wished that Suresh was with me right then.

I did find the time to complain about Langford-Bauer to Linda later that night over WhatsApp chat, once we'd gone back to our hotel after a full day of sightseeing in Omaha with Charleston Wesley.

"Tristan?" she said, surprised. "Tristan Langford-Bauer is your Singapore desk rep?"

"Yeah, why?"

"Oh," she said, giggling. "I know Tristan. He's a friend of a friend from London."

"Oh?"

"Yeah." Her voice was conspiratorial. "The next time he pisses you off, just say: 'Chicken of the Sea.' He'll know what it means."

"Tell me!" I said, practically foaming at the mouth. "Is he allergic to fish? Is that how I bring him down?"

"No, dummy, how amateur, and quite worrisome that you went straight to the option of murdering your nemesis, you psychopath.

Besides, ever heard of EpiPens? Chicken of the *C*, the letter *C*, *C* for . . . oh well. I've said too much," she said cheerfully, meaning she'd said exactly how much she wanted me to know.

I was dying of curiosity. "*C* for what?"

"Bye." The line went dead.

I typed some notes in My Cloud. Chicken of the *C*. *C* for "cocaine"? Or some kind of animal, even if that combination made less sense? Was Langford-Bauer involved in his own #PigGate? Hmmm.

The line rang again. I picked it up without screening for caller ID. "Linda, tell me—"

"Andy. Andy."

I tensed—only one person ever called me that, and it was my sister. "Melissa? What's up?"

Her voice was eerily calm. "I'm so, so sorry to tell you this over the phone, but . . . but Ma had a heart attack."

I gasped. "What? When?" I managed to ask.

"A few hours ago. You should come back as soon as you can."

48

Melissa was talking but through a fog of some kind. The sensation was one of tripping over a phantom step on a flight of stairs. I had a moment where I felt like the universe was tilting before the world righted itself on its axis. When the swoon had passed, I began to pack.

What had happened was my mother had had a heart attack in the wee hours of the morning. She'd been traveling back with a friend from Beijing; she'd landed in KLIA and taken a taxi when she started having bad cramps in her chest. It was lucky the taxi driver had recognized the symptoms and had brought her to the emergency room, or—

I shuddered.

The hospital had tried to call me, Melissa said, but couldn't reach me. So they had called her, the other emergency contact. It was the only good thing to come out of this, that my sister had been the one to be with my mother just before they had wheeled her into the operating room.

I told her I'd be there on the next flight out tomorrow morning, since it was already close to midnight Omahaian time, but that it would be difficult to know exactly what time I would land. Sometime Saturday night. After I had taken a Valium and waited for myself to calm down, I called Eric, who was in Hong Kong for a couple of board meetings, and he immediately offered to fly over.

"Thank you for offering," I said, touched. The grand opening of his new Lana hotel in Phu Quoc, Vietnam, his first eco-hotel in the region, was on Monday; I knew how important it was for him to open that hotel in person, since his family had fled China through Vietnam. "But don't change your plans; it's really not necessary."

"Of course it is. I'm coming over. You need support."

"No, it's really OK," I insisted. "She's stable for now. Please, stay, open the Dulit Lana Phu Quoc."

"You sure? I mean, it's fine. My deputy is here."

I laughed nervously. "Well, it's just . . . I haven't told her anything about your proposal."

"I see." I could hear the wry grin in his voice as he said, "Don't you think it'll make her recover faster if she hears your good news?"

"I think so," I said cautiously. "But my mother is unpredictable at best."

"I'll fly over after the opening. I know how to charm mothers," he said.

Says the man who's never been married.

After the call I got dressed in sweats and knocked on the door of Langford-Bauer's room, since I would need to leave earlier than expected, before the due diligence was completed. I prayed that he would be dressed so I wouldn't have to see his legs.

He was, in pajamas and a robe. I thanked God. It's hard to hate men with stick-thin, hairless legs.

Langford-Bauer was less than understanding. "What do you mean, you have a family emergency?" he said, having grown up never experiencing familial love. "Is anyone at death's door?"

"Actually," I said, squaring my shoulders, glad to be able to rub his face in my truth, "someone is at death's door. My mother . . . had a heart attack."

Langford-Bauer's face was a picture. "Oh my, this is unex— What I mean is . . . I'm, ah, dreadfully sorry," he stammered. "I didn't know, I mean . . . I'm so sorry, really." If he had pearls he'd be clutching them now, the bastard. "Are you two, ah, close?"

"How can you even ask me a question like that, at a time like this?" I said, disgusted. "So if I said no, that would make it OK?"

"No, no! That's not what I meant at all!" He blanched and actually started backing away from me. "You should, ah, definitely take some time off. Leave. Go. I'll take it from here."

"I will," I said. "And you'll just have to deal with the slack. You haven't had to deal with much of the slack so far because I've been an awesome, valuable team player." And then, fiercely: "And I'm an awesome, awesome woman."

"You certainly are." He cleared his throat, looking embarrassed. "You have been, of course, since the beginning. A strong . . . intelligent . . . team player, in spite, I mean, regardless of your, ah, gender." The way he was saying this you'd think I had just made him admit to the possession of a micropenis. "I, ah, I've always . . . admired your, ah, strong work ethic." I could see his eyes were crossing, so I let him off by waving his feeble compliments away.

"See that you do not text me during the next few days," I warned him. "Unless the sky is falling, and you're flat out of sky-umbrellas."

"Right," he said humbly.

I strode off to my room, booked the earliest flights back, and slept.

Friday 7 October

Early in the morning, I called to see how my mother was. Melissa assured me that she was stable, which was a huge weight off my shoulders, since I was so far away.

When Eric called to coordinate our schedules, I told him about the connecting flights I had to take.

"It's so complicated. You need to switch off and just relax in this difficult time. Why don't you let me fly you back?" he said.

"With what private jet?" I replied, halfheartedly teasing. "You told me you were too 'real' of a billionaire to have one."

He chuckled, sounding uncomfortable. "I do have a friend or two with idle jets who owe me favors. So, if you want . . ."

I rolled my eyes. "No, thank you, I'll take commercial. It's going to be tough, but I'll survive, even if I can only afford, horror of horrors, premium economy."

I could almost hear him flinch, even long distance. "When would you land?"

"In twenty-three hours. It's fine."

"I could get you back in almost half that time," he said.

Under the circumstances, it would not have been unreasonable to acquiesce. But his tone rubbed me the wrong way, for some reason. "She's stable, so I think we can afford to not take the private jet."

"Suit yourself," he said, sounding, to my ears, just a tad frosty.

I texted Linda to update her about the situation. And then I called the one person I knew would be able to sort everything out for me at work: Suresh. When I told him about my mother, he immediately assured me that he would handle it, since he was working from Singapore this week.

And this time, I trusted him whole-heartedly.

"Just send me your flight details and I'll sort everything out in the office."

"Thanks, Suresh, I—I really appreciate you." I swallowed hard. "Also for the honorable thing you did for me . . . with Sungguh."

A pause. "It's nothing, really. Is there anything else I can do for you?" he asked. His voice was soft, reassuring. "Name it."

I had a crazy urge to ask him to meet me in Kuala Lumpur—it was almost a physical craving. "No, thank you, just handle work and I'll be fine."

Work. It might seem insane to an outsider that I cared about work at a time like this, but they didn't get it. I'd been hardwired for too long to just throw everything aside even when my personal life was in chaos. Work had always been there for me, no matter how bad things were. Work was family, a drug. Work was life.

Saturday 8 October

Almost a whole day of traveling later, I landed in Kuala Lumpur, jet lagged and disoriented, and almost wishing I'd given in to Eric's private jet offer. Almost. I headed straight to the government hospital where my mother was recovering. The last thing I expected to see was Suresh and Linda, both standing awkwardly in the waiting lounge.

"Surprise!" Linda said. She threw her arms around me.

"You guys! You're both here!" I wheezed through a mouthful of Linda's hair.

"I think we got here on the same flight," Suresh said with a grin. "And we've had time to introduce ourselves and gossip about you, don't worry."

"Did you think I'd let you go through this alone, you dingbat?" Linda said, sniffling.

"No," I said, gratified. My eyes met Suresh's. *Thank you for being here*, I mouthed.

You're welcome, he mouthed back.

Melissa met us in the cafeteria, a coffee in her hand. If she was surprised to see Linda and Suresh, especially if she might have expected Eric in the latter's place, then she was too distraught to show it. Kamarul, her fiancé, had not stayed with Melissa after dropping her off at the hospital in order not to trigger my mother.

We took the elevator to the third floor, where my mother was resting in the coronary care unit of the ICU and under sedation. She had come through the emergency bypass surgery fine, but the attending cardiothoracic surgeon, Dr. Ng, a harried-looking woman in a severe bun who had seen far too many operating rooms and not enough sunlight, said that while the surgery had gone well, she was not yet out of the woods and they would have to monitor her for a few days. Going forward, we would have to take extra care to not upset her, and monitor her lifestyle and diet to manage her preexisting high blood pressure. "Don't stress her out," she admonished, like the heart attack had been our fault.

Don't stress her out? She was the person who stressed her children out, I almost shook my fist and shouted at her retreating back. Instead, I whispered this as the doctor strode off. Years of conditioning by Asian society had drilled into me a Buddhist reverence for medical authority.

"It's my fault," Melissa said, breathing hard. "I sent her an invite last week to our engagement party."

"It's not your fault," I said. "And let's not forget the real culprit: her diet of instant noodles, crackers, lard, and full-fat everything."

"Yeah, Auntie Jenny eats like she's a teenager," Linda chimed in. "Plus, Kamarul seems like the kind of guy any mother would have loved to have dating her daughter."

Suresh had been keeping a respectful distance in the waiting area so that we could have some family time. I motioned him over. "Suresh's one of the good guys I work with," I said, as he approached. "He's been a real rock."

Melissa eyed him shrewdly. "Where's Eric?" she asked in a low voice.

"In Hong Kong—or maybe Vietnam by now. He sends his regards," I said, offhandedly.

I introduced Suresh to Melissa.

"Any news?" Suresh asked, his brows furrowed.

I updated him, uncomfortably aware of how both Melissa and Linda were communicating furiously without speaking behind his back. There was a lot of lascivious winking on Linda's part.

"It's good that we got here in time," Suresh said, looking relieved that my mother was doing fine.

"Not too bored hanging out with us Tangs, Suresh?" Melissa teased, fluttering her tear-gunked eyelashes. Ah, the good ol' Suresh Effect. I rolled my eyes. Also, annoyingly enough Melissa always acted like she was the elder sister instead of me. I mean, just because she was in a functional relationship with a man and had money. But guess who was still on speaking terms with old Mumsie? That's right: *me.*

A wave of exhaustion hit me in the gut and I had to grab onto the back of a chair to steady myself.

"Whoa," Suresh said, grabbing me, "you OK?"

"I just need to rest. I think all the travel is starting to catch up with me," I said.

"Let's go find a hotel," Linda said. "The doctor did say she won't be able to receive visitors tonight, anyway."

"Don't be stupid, you guys can stay at our place. We have two spare rooms," Melissa exclaimed. She waved away our (admittedly feeble) protests. "You girls can share a room, and Suresh can take one. Or, you know." Now she was making weird facial expressions behind Suresh's back at me. I gave her the middle finger.

"Whoa, is that how you Tangs thank each other?" Suresh said.

"We have our ways," I said airily. Such as emotional blackmail, but still.

Melissa and Kamarul's home was a splendidly renovated, sleek and spartan three-bedder condo in Mont Kiara. It was the first time I was visiting their home since they had moved in together a few months ago. Kamarul showed us around while Melissa made us hot chocolate laced with a heavy dose of Amarula "to help with the nerves." Then the three of us girls hung out in the living room for an impromptu family reunion, catching up and trading Tang family gossip, Kamarul having shepherded Suresh to his man cave to play Counter-Strike. We finished chatting around 1:30 a.m., exhausted but feeling much more cheerful.

When everyone had gone to bed (Linda was snoring on the two-seater couch in the living room, passed out drunk), I hung out in the living room, drinking decaf coffee and scrolling through my Instagram. I was too hyped up to sleep.

I kept thinking, *What if?*

What if the heart attack had been more severe? What if it had debilitated or killed my mother? Despite how aggravating she could be, she was still my mother. I owed her, and my dad, everything I had in life. And I love her. I have to: she's my mother. She's sacrificed so much for me. If my mother wanted me to get married and have kids, and I could do that for her, why shouldn't I? It's not as though I was opposed to children and marriage. I wouldn't mind both. Actually, I'm not going to lie: I want both.

Eric wants to get married to me. Eric wants kids. Eric is at the right stage of his life. Eric and I were both cruising in the right direction.

After all, there was no such thing as a perfect partner. Even if I envied Melissa and Kamarul's easy way with each other, who's to say I would never have that with Eric one day? Why did we always assume that these things were supposed to just "come with the territory"? Didn't farmers have to, like, till the earth and fertilize it before they could get the soil to yield crops? Maybe my relationship with Eric was like that: a potato farm in the making. But scoff ye not at the humble potato, for were they not the most delicious tuber on God's green earth? I—

"Am I interrupting?" a voice said in the darkness, making me jump. It was Suresh.

"Not really, I was just stalking celebrities, no biggie," I said.

He sat down next to me on the couch. I was very aware that he was wearing only a pair of tartan boxer shorts and a thin white T-shirt that left little to the imagination.

Unfortunately, I had a very healthy imagination.

"Thanks for being here," I said, looking around him so as not to get distracted.

"Anything for you," he said softly. "How are you feeling?"

"Worried, but much better, thanks." I just noticed how golden brown his eyes were in the warm light. He had such soulful eyes. "Thanks for being here." I realized I was repeating myself.

"There was no question about me not coming over. I wanted to."

"You didn't need to, really. I have Linda."

We looked at Linda's prone figure on the couch, where she had passed out after the sixth Amarula hot chocolate. Actually, come to think of it, maybe the last two had just been straight-up mugs of Amarula.

"Does . . . does Anousha know you're here?"

Suresh shrugged. "Anousha and I had a fight. We're not speaking to each other."

"What about?" I asked. I wondered if it had been about me. Maybe it had been. There was, after all, that text that she had sent to me. She must suspect that we'd come close to crossing the line, once or twice.

"About my leaving the firm, actually."

Of course. What else would it have been about? I was being silly.

"What was her reaction?" I asked.

"She won't allow it. Her father is livid and—"

My phone buzzed and I started. An unidentified number—who could it be at this hour?

"Andrea, hey."

It was Eric. I excused myself and raised the phone to my ear. "Hello?"

"I just wanted to let you know I'm flying in from Vietnam. I've got the first flight out tomorrow morning. Where are you?" he said without preamble.

"At Melissa's," I said, a little surprised. "Wait . . . what? What about your hotel opening?"

He made an impatient noise. "Andrea, your mother had a heart attack. I bought a ticket as soon as I heard your message." He seemed bewildered that I would ask a question. "I am your man, am I not?" He said this without the least ring of irony.

Eric was at his most attractive when he was being authoritative. Suddenly there was no one else I wanted to see more. "Yes, you are. Where are you staying tomorrow?" I asked. I was vaguely aware that Suresh was gone.

"Park Suite at the Mandarin Oriental, where else?"

"I'll get my things and stay with you."

49

Sunday 9 October

The four of us, sans Kamarul for obvious reasons, arrived at the hospital just before noon, when visiting hours would start. I was surprised to see Eric already at the reception desk having an animated conversation with Dr. Ng and a distinguished-looking man in his fifties.

"Eric!" I said happily, giving him a bear hug.

"Nice reception!" He kissed the top of my head and nodded to Linda, who returned the nod. "And who are these lovely folks?"

"I'm Melissa, Andrea's younger sister," Melissa said. I could tell from the way she approached him with her hand half-extended that she was unsure of whether she should give him a handshake or a hug, to which Eric responded by gathering her in a warm hug. I smiled.

"And this is Suresh, my—" I turned toward Suresh, and suddenly my mind went blank.

"Colleague," Suresh said, giving Eric a handshake so firm I could feel it, standing beside Eric. And Eric was giving it right back: they were Power Moving each other. "It's nice to meet you. Andrea talks about you all the time."

"Likewise," Eric said, giving Suresh a thoughtful once-over. He was unsmiling. Then he turned toward me very pointedly, and said, "Is today the day I get to meet the future mother-in-law I've been hearing so much about?"

"Sorry, I'm just going to excuse myself to make a call," Suresh said, before leaving.

I shook my head, perplexed by Suresh's reaction and very aware of how Melissa and Linda were communicating behind Eric's back with a combination of unsubtle gestures and facial expressions. "Maybe we should wait to see if she's up to even receiving me." *And Melissa,* I didn't say.

Eric let me off the hook. "I suppose we shouldn't overwhelm her with news. Anyway, let me introduce you to a good friend, Dr. Caleb Foo. He's the chief of surgery at Pantai and a renowned cardiothoracic surgeon internationally." Pantai was a private hospital in Kuala Lumpur.

"Oh, uh, hi there," I said, confused. Dr. Foo nodded at me.

"This gentleman here wants me to discharge your mother and transfer her to Pantai for Dr. Foo to follow up, and I told him it was my professional opinion that she was too weak to be moved, not for another two to three days," Dr. Ng told me, her voice strained. "And in any case, it is the family's decision. Is that what you want?"

I looked at Eric. "What?"

"Yes." He beamed, misreading my response as being positive. He tucked a strand of loose hair behind my ear. "I wanted the best for your mother and you. Dr. Foo is the best." He said it in front of Dr. Ng, without a care for her feelings.

I exhaled sharply. "I appreciate your thoughtfulness, Eric, but Dr. Ng has been more than fine so far."

Dr. Ng threw me this little look of gratitude that somehow made her real to me for the first time.

"But Dr. Foo is the best," Eric insisted.

"Private hospitals are just so much better," Linda chimed in from behind Eric, where she'd been eavesdropping.

"I prefer that my mother stay here, thank you all," I said through gritted teeth.

Linda shrugged. “Told you she’s stubborn. I’m going to see if they have a Starbucks here.” Her talent for leaving when the shit got stirred was legendary.

Eric and I were now locked in a silent stare-down. Dr. Foo looked uncomfortable and made his excuses to leave.

“You’re not happy with my offer?”

“You’re being presumptuous,” I said slowly. “When have I ever said that I wanted my mother moved to a private facility?”

He frowned. “I was *being helpful*. Do you know how hard it is to get Dr. Foo to consult? He is the best and he came here on such short notice because he owes me a huge personal favor!”

“Nobody asked you for a new doctor. I prefer the current one we already have, my cranky, stone-faced doctor that you were rude to, thank you very much!”

Dr. Ng cleared her throat. “I’m going to, ah, check on Mrs. Tang.”

“Yes, please,” both of us said simultaneously. She hurried away.

“What gave you the impression that I would want you to do something like this without asking me?”

“Well, excuse me for trying to do something good for you.” He threw up his arms. “I don’t get you, Andrea. When you work, you constantly talk about rankings and reputation and how you’re the best at what you do, but when I try to get your mother, your *mother*, the greatest in health care that money can buy, you refuse me and dismiss my friend. Is that logical?”

I bit my lip. He made a lot of sense when he put it that way. “We can’t afford private hospitals,” I said, although that was only part of the reason I was miffed, and not even the most important one at that.

The frown on his face dissolved. “Is that why you were annoyed?” Eric folded me into his arms. “Oh sweetheart, I would have paid for everything. I wouldn’t have minded.”

I thawed a little, but something inside me rebelled. It wasn't so much what he wanted.

It was what I wanted, or didn't want.

But what was it that I wanted?

"Excuse me," a voice piped up.

We looked up. It was Dr. Ng again.

"Your mother is asking for you."

Seeing my mother on the bed brought home the gravity of the situation again. I sucked in my breath when I saw her. Her face was pale and her skin translucent as rice milk, stark against her dyed black hair, a bruise purpling across her face. She had hit her face against something in the taxi when the attack happened. An IV dripped.

Dr. Ng briefed the both of us on the root causes that had led to this heart attack. Aside from genetic predisposition, my mother's bad diet over the years had caused build up in her arteries and she'd need to change to a heart-healthy diet.

"I'm so glad you're here, Andrea," my mother wheezed, clutching my hand, once Dr. Ng had left. "Is . . . is your sister around?"

"Yes."

"Good."

"She wants to see you."

My mother exhaled sharply. "I . . . I suppose I should thank her. You can send her in afterward. Alone. There are some things I need to say to her."

That was a start. I was elated. "Thank you."

She smiled wanly in response.

"Ma, you heard what Dr. Ng said. Your diet is literally killing you. Why did you eat so much junk food and instant noodles, when you never let us do the same? It's a bit double standard, right?"

She avoided my eyes. "Well, how did you think your father

and I managed to save up enough money so you and your sister can go to university?" she said lightly.

I pictured the many times I saw my stay-at-home mother heating a bowl of instant noodles, throwing a couple handfuls of leftover green vegetables and cracking an egg into the MSG-ed broth while my sister and I ate rice with stir-fried beef or chicken and fried dumplings. She always made us take second, third helpings, and when we were done, she'd scoop our leftover meat and rice into her noodle bowl and chastise us for wasting food. I felt a rush of guilt. Even when it came to food, they'd always made sure we had the best they could afford.

"Of course, it wasn't just *savings,*" she acknowledged, "we carefully invested the money we saved as best as we could, otherwise inflation—"

"—*will take everything,*" I finished, trying to crack a joke by using an ominous voice.

"You young people these days, you don't even know how to save; once you get the money you spend spend spend. Why, when I was your age, I used to bring my own lunch to work, it was just white rice and *ikan bilis,* now everything is just avocado this and that and costs so much . . ." She rattled on and on in this manner, pausing only to draw breath, but instead of cutting her off or tuning her out, I kept quiet and listened. Maybe it was because she'd just had a close brush with death, but I took the sermonizing in stride. Glad to see her so verbose; glad to see her alive.

"Thank you for your sacrifices, Ma," I said quietly.

"It was never a sacrifice," she said quietly. "Sshhh, don't cry, Andrea. I'm tough. I'm not leaving you until I get grandchildren."

That again. I took a deep breath.

"Mom, there's someone I want to introduce you to."

"Oh?" she said.

I cracked a smile. "It's my fiancé, Eric."

My fiancé.

I had let the genie out of the bottle.

I opened the door and beckoned Eric into the room. Just before he entered, I said quietly, "I told her that I said yes."

He started, and clasped my hands. "That's wonderful," he said. "You've just made me the happiest man on earth!"

The happiest . . .

I walked in after him in a dream. I introduced him to my mother, who was practically hyperventilating with joy (or the tubes, it was hard to tell).

Eric and my mother barely had time to chat before a nurse came by to say visiting hours were up and kicked us out from our visit with my mom, who never stopped beaming. I noticed that Eric had taken to calling her "Mrs. Tang" without a hitch, even though they were closer in age than Eric was to me.

I felt guilty for introducing Eric and taking up Melissa's time with our mother, even if I'd been the one who brokered the truce. I made her promise to see Melissa tomorrow, first thing, and she was so thrilled she did so without a second thought. At least another good thing came out of this.

Eric and I left the hospital together in a limo. Once in, he pushed a button and the privacy screen came up with a soft *woosh* that used to make my pulse race because . . . well. You know.

Sure enough, he scooted over and drew me close. "I think a celebratory . . . dinner is in order, don't you?" he whispered in my ear.

"Uh, maybe another time," I said. "Everything with my mother has me pretty stressed out. Not to mention the partnership interviews."

"I can help with—"

"No," I said a little too quickly.

He drew back. There was hurt in his eyes, and something else. "I see."

I turned away from him and pulled out my work phone, pretending to scroll through emails. I felt numb. I had accepted his proposal—so why didn't I feel overjoyed?

I'd just secured my future, and my family's, no matter what happened at the partnership interview next week. So why didn't I feel like I'd done the right thing?

Worse still, I could feel the edges of a panic attack coming. I groped in my Mansur Gavriel tote for my inhaler, which I hadn't needed for months.

"Hey." He held me as I took several puffs. "What's the matter?"

I waved his concern away and wriggled out of his arms. I turned away from him and shut my eyes, trying to gain control over my breathing. Why was I having this reaction?

After my breathing had stabilized, he asked softly, "Is this about the private hospital thing?"

I could feel his eyes on me. "Maybe," I lied. In truth, I didn't know.

Suddenly he gripped me and swung me around to face him. "Andrea," he choked out. "Don't you know how much I care for you?"

I gaped at him, stunned by his passionate outburst. I realized I had never seen him lose control before. It was a little unnerving.

"I'm sorry you thought I was trying to control you. I had nothing but good intentions. You mean so much to me. Please believe me."

His sincerity was undeniable. I felt my anger and confusion ebb a little. How could I be mad at him for wanting the best for me? I tried to explain myself. "I get that, but it still doesn't change the fact you made me feel l-like I had no say in the matter because I don't have as much money as you."

His face twisted at the anger in my voice. "Andrea, I swear, I didn't mean to throw money at you in a disrespectful way . . . Not when— Not when I see you as my better half. I love you." He kissed my hands. "Please believe me. I would never, ever disrespect you like that."

I inhaled and exhaled shakily. "Look, I'm sorry I thought badly of your kind gesture. To me money is a form of control. My mother always kowtows to my aunt because she paid for my father's hospital bills, Linda has a bad habit of literally throwing money at me to win arguments—I just don't want to feel like I owe you. Even if we are"—I swallowed—"engaged."

There was a long silence in which I could hear the blood rushing in my ears. He cracked a rueful smile.

"Andrea, you are my future," he told me. "I just want the best for you. I'm sorry if that came off the wrong way."

"It's OK," I said, but when he reminded me I'd told him I'd come back with him to the Mandarin Oriental, I once again pleaded interview nerves. He was disappointed, but hey, we were going to be married, so we were going to be spending a lot of time together. What was the rush?

Monday 10 October

Linda flew home on the first flight this morning for work (and for Jason, of course).

I was alone in the living room, sitting on the couch, just staring at the wall. Kamarul and Melissa had gone to get brunch together, and, I suspect, to spend some time decompressing from our camping out at their place, the heart attack, and to mentally prepare for Melissa's first visit with our mother at noon.

I kept the news about my saying yes to Eric's proposal to myself; given the events of this weekend, it felt borderline inappropriate to spring this on them. Not now, anyway.

Not that that was stopping Eric, sweetness personified, from sending me pictures of ballrooms decorated in jaw-dropping lavishness and asking me what I thought of each. He was indeed thinking of inviting up to one thousand people to the wedding. He told me that I should start shopping for a wedding gown, or more, if I wished, having passed me one of his fancy-schmancy credit cards that had no limits.

"I know you're not profligate," he said, tenderly, to me, a person who'd always thought I was a spendthrift—but I guess we were measuring with different yardsticks now. "But darling—I want you to go all out."

This proclamation should, under normal circumstances, send me into a mindless buying frenzy, but lately I found myself deriving less and less satisfaction from shopping. So the credit card remained tucked in my work bag, a taupe Celine medium luggage tote that I had been coveting for some time and which Eric had had delivered to Melissa and Kamarul's yesterday night from the Mandarin Oriental as an impromptu "engagement gift."

A limitless credit card and I couldn't bring myself to use it. I wish I could tell you what's going on, dear Diary.

Suresh suddenly came out of his room and joined me on the couch with his bags. He was due back at the office and was taking a flight in less than three hours. We just sat there, side by side, not speaking, and for some reason my throat began to close up and I started to tremble. I was dangerously close to crying, or screaming. Or both.

"I'm going to leave Anousha," Suresh said quietly.

"What?" I said, shocked out of my own ennui. "How? Why?"

"I need to. I've changed. My feelings toward her have changed. I think I want . . . something else." He held my hand. Our eyes met, mine damp, his searching. "Andrea, I . . ."

"Don't," I said, withdrawing from him. "I can't . . . I can't."

"I think you can, if you allowed yourself to," he said sadly.

I shook my head, got up, and went to my room. Shut the door between us.

"Andrea," Suresh said, knocking insistently.

"No," I said. "This can't happen." I could hear him breathing as he stood outside the door, but I willed myself to remain motionless. After a while he slipped something under the door. A sealed brown envelope with my name written on it. I took it gingerly but did not open the door.

"Read it when you're ready," he said.

I waited till I heard him shut the front door behind him before I chucked the envelope into my work bag, unopened. I didn't trust myself around him. We were like the characters in that *TLTS* strip of his: a bad idea. Too alike, too unknown.

Tuesday 11 October

11:15 a.m. Home, reluctantly, at the insistence of my mother, who reminded me I had a wedding to plan and a promotion to secure. Melissa promised to keep me up to date on her recovery. Took today off. Suresh would be back in Jakarta and, I presume, is flying in again Thursday morning for the partnership interviews. I hadn't said goodbye before he left for the airport, but it can't be any other way. I must be strong.

10:20 p.m. Spent a couple of hours in the evening trying on wedding dresses in a bridal gown shop with Val, who was in for one of her fittings for her wedding gown (if ever there was a gown, it was hers)—I needed the distraction from the interviews, and what better way to kill two birds with one stone?

I'd heard of this store because of its reputation for stocking the most luxurious gowns, many of which cost the equivalent of a down payment for government housing in Singapore. Having never really fantasized about the details of my wedding day, I found the array of gowns daunting, but with Val's impeccable eye, soon found something pared-down and lovely, a pearl-white sheath gown with an off-the-shoulder neckline and softly draped skirt.

"Ohh," everyone said as soon as I stepped out onto the mini pedestal that all such stores have and faced myself in the mirror. I looked, well, stunning. What's more, I had a Pippa butt in that dress! It would have looked great at a garden or beach wedding . . . for someone else. I fingered the heavy fabric wistfully and told them I'd have to come back for my own appointment, and keep looking—for the kind of wedding Eric and I would be holding, I was going to have to go for the mother of all gowns.

Thursday 13 October

7:15 a.m. This is it.

8:20 a.m. Just saw a note on my desk from Kai:

Good luck with the final round of partnership interviews.

The note triggered fresh rounds of panic sweats, even though I sprayed layers of antiperspirant over whole body. Luckily I have two backup outfits.

8:55 a.m. Hmm, strange. Suresh isn't in his office (I walked by it to go to the loo—I mean, toilet—because the toilets on our floor were too busy). Kai can't get anything out of his stupidly loyal PA, Hong Lim. Goddamn principles.

10:30 a.m. Still not in.

11:45 a.m. Totally random that he's not at his desk. He's probably going through the interviews now. I wonder if he did break things off with Anousha. Not that it matters. Or maybe he'll wait till the interviews are over. If I'm being cynical and uncharitable, it would help his chances until he's secured partnership, then Inderjit can't touch him. Well, that's his business, on both fronts. Not mine.

11:50 a.m. Must not think of puking. Must not think of puking.

12:05 p.m. Thank goodness for second set of clothing.

2:30 p.m. Kai buzzed me and I went to Inspiration, the conference room where the senior partners making up the Partnership Committee (sans Mong, who was still in hospital) were gathered. Saw Genevieve exiting the room; she saw me and smiled her Wicked Witch of the East smile. Had no idea she was up for partnership. How is that even possible? She's been popping babies out like a Chiclets dispenser.

2:32 p.m. Must not be uncharitable toward another woman. Must not make it even more difficult for working women who choose to have one baby after another. Even if she is the Spawn of Medusa.

2:35 p.m. Urgh, am a terrible person—she is after all a member of the sisterhood. But still. Let's be honest: isn't something supposed to give? How is it Genevieve is the possessor of all I want in life? Isn't the myth of us career women being able to Have It All in life already dispelled? How is it she chose to get married and have babies while having a career, and I'm the single one, and I don't even get a clear shot at the one thing that's within my grasp?

Anyway. My turn now.

4:47 p.m. Done. Exhausted. Need vodka and sleep. Will find out if my whole life has been wasted or not in a few days.

It was a very disturbing interview. Evan Bilson, the managing partner with whom I have spoken twice in my life since he moved to Singapore to head the office ten months ago, was being oddly and openly hostile, asking me why I was only billing 2,210 hours this year instead of close to 2,460 hours as I did last year, a record for senior associates in the firm. He suggested that I was "coasting." When I mentioned we still had over two months to go till the year ended, he gave me this imperious stare and said, "Well, then how come some of your peers are billing more than you are, while spending time away from their desks?"

"Do you mean Suresh, future son-in-law of Inderjit Singh?" I wanted to shout, but didn't.

"Honestly," I said, with great feeling, "I don't know how anyone can put in more time than I do at the firm."

"But you nearly cost us Sungguh," he reminded me.

"I brought in Eric Deng. It's a small account of his, but still. And Chapel Town is in play again, which means VizWare—"

"That's not good enough, Andrea, to make up for Sungguh."

After which I think the rest of the interview went down the toilet, so to speak.

1:15 a.m. I;wm beingq silly am *vcleaarly* best choicec for partner-frr1@! Meritocrazcy shal triumpgh over neppooptism!!

Friday 14 October

7:20 a.m. Oh God. My eyes.

9:25 p.m. Am supposed to be working on a file but can't because I'm in physical agony, and not just because of my lingering hangover but also because I made the bad decision of buying half-price salad from the Viet deli for early dinner. (Why am I so cavalier about death by diarrhea? Why am I not so brave when it comes to matters of the heart?)

I've just received a text from Kai about the interviews. Apparently, Kai, who's friends with the chattier PAs working with some of the senior partners on the committee, had gotten wind that I had not been selected as one of the two final choices for the spot. Her sources were usually impeccable.

At first I was livid. I couldn't believe it. I wasn't even one of the final two? After everything I'd sacrificed for the firm?

What was the point of all those years of eating subpar food from the Viet deli, of chugging coffee and Red Bull (not at the same time, but sometimes yes?), of voluntarily not taking the annual leave dates I was entitled to, just to look like I was busy, even when I wasn't? What was the point of All. That. Fucking. Face Time? What did I have to show for it, except a whole closetful of barely used bags *and* actual eye bags?

And what's worse, my Work Dad didn't even believe in me.

I opened my secret stash of chocolate (hidden inside one of my gym bags) and took out the emergency tequila from my minifridge. Like an automaton, I started downing both.

Maybe it was the alcohol or the rage, but midway I got up, a hip flask full of whiskey in one hand, and made my way in a drunken weave to Mong's office, having a vague idea of letting him know what a jerk he'd been, to stab me in the back like that. Maybe I'd burn his precious law library. That'll show him!

Rage was making me talk out loud, but because it was a law firm and people mutter out loud all the time, like right nutters, not one single person I passed on my way to Mong's office gave me a second look, including a few of the more hard-core mouth breathers— I mean, juniors pretending to work.

I found myself standing outside his office, wild-eyed.

No one was in. It hit me that I had never seen it in its current state: pitch-dark, empty, its overlord away for the evening: Mong didn't exactly believe in personal time off, much less holidays. He was always working.

The door was ajar, so I slipped in to look around, curious, having never been in his office for more than a few minutes at a time and only to receive his instructions on a file. I turned on the antique brass reading lamp on his desk and lowered myself into the chair gingerly, almost as though I was afraid he would pop out from the shadows and say, in his laconic way, "Boo."

Mong's office was a study in minimalism. Behind him were the shelves of expensive books from the foremost legal experts, local and international, in different areas of law, that I'd fleetingly contemplated incinerating. The two framed pieces of art were Japanese wood-cut prints, of single men at study. His desk was conspicuously bare except for a few of his favorite awards, those chintzy crystal trophies that told the world how much he was worth, and a yellow legal pad with actual important words on them, not doodles. No pictures of his family, nothing remotely personal, although this was the one place he spent the most time and was probably the one place he felt truly at home. It wasn't because he was a private person, exactly. It was just a true reflection of who he was: married to his work, everything else second. This wasn't just his job—it was his identity.

I had a morbid image of Mong's funeral, and how everyone there was from the firm and, worse, dry-eyed. For some reason I'd been tasked to give a eulogy about Mong's life, and all I could do was read out a list of case law in which he'd triumphed over his opponents, and made his clients very happy and rich.

And what about me? How was I any different?

I didn't love the law, not this way. Yet I was spending almost as much time as he was at work. Perhaps, a voice inside me piped up hesitantly, I should take this as a sign that I had the wrong priorities?

"No," I whispered, shaking my head angrily. I deserved to be in that seat. It was the only thing I knew, and I was good at it. One of the best. And didn't Eric tell me that life was about compromises, that in the beginning he hadn't wanted to take over his family business, and now here he was molded to it and it to him, and he'd learned to accept his path, to make peace with his birthright, and now he was glad he did?

I called him and told him about what the firm had apparently decided.

"Honey," he said, "as soon as I'm back from Vietnam this weekend, I'm going to make things right."

"Whah you mean," I said, helping myself to the contents (emergency whiskey) of my hip flask.

"I'm going to take my business away. And I'm going to tell all my business partners to stop using your law firm, going forward. They aren't the only players in town." Steel entered his voice. "And then, we're going to launch an anti-discrimination lawsuit against them."

"Yeaaaaargh!" I said, excited and possibly drunk. "Sue them! Sue them!" (Even though there was a remote chance that there was another female candidate on that list, although I couldn't think of anyone else, male or female, who deserved this promotion more than me, if we were looking at merits.)

"And you can set up your own law firm with the business we'll channel to you. I'll make you managing partner of your own firm. How does that sound, my love?"

"Yas that shounds amazing," I slurred. "Are you sure about this?"

"Andrea, you are my future," he told me. "I want you to have everything, anything you've ever wanted. The world will be yours."

"You're the besht!"

"I love you," he said.

"I do you, too," I told him exuberantly. "I need a nap now."

So I took one.

12:30 a.m. Woke up, head throbbing, then the events of just now came rushing back. A sour mix of injustice, anger, bitterness, and the desire for revenge fizzed in my belly. I felt betrayed by the firm, which had dangled a promotion in front of me for two years.

But now, Eric was providing me with redemption, no matter what.

No matter—

"Ding!" A pop-up notification. A red-hot jolt of adrenaline: Suresh had just published another *TLTS* strip.

In a motel, Rhean and Water broke apart, naked, trembling, returning to themselves. Changing back. It's happening faster now.

The kills just keep them on a shorter and shorter leash.

There are two bodies on the floor beside their bed. A pimp and his business partner, their faces twisted. In horror. They were young, in their late twenties. Maybe they weren't even pimps. Water realizes he doesn't know anymore.

Water turned to Rhean. "I can't stop myself."

"Neither can I," she admits.

He knows this. This had gone on long enough.

He gets up, shaking, walks to his kill bag. Retrieves a syringe marked "W." With a swift jab to his thigh he injects himself with the lethal cocktail of drugs he'd concocted for this purpose. You die fast when that happens. Unless . . .

She cries out when she sees what he is about to do. Leaps off the bed and runs to him, too late.

He's already on the floor, already dying.

"Rhean," he says, with difficulty.

She's shaking her head, beating the floor, unable to hold him toward the end. "Why?" she asks, even though she knows.

"My North Star . . . ," he whispered. His nickname for her. "Do you remember w-why I chose it for you?"

Rheans nods, weeping. Between tears, she manages to finish his words for him. "You don't have to be the brightest star in the sky, but you're the one I look to when I need direction."

"I love you, Louise," he says, fading. He remembers everything now.

All of a sudden a dam inside me burst. I couldn't stop crying. From exhaustion, from confusion, the gnawing realisation that I was stagnating even as I was moving, from the shape of things unknown in my new future. But it was time to move on from the ill-fitting life I'd made my own for too long. I needed to redeem my own true self, whomever she was, and Eric could not be part of that journey. I would never have to ask the hard questions in the life Eric envisaged for me, a life where all the texture and sharp edges would be sanded away by money and privilege. That was not a life, at least not one I wanted to live. The time for safety nets was over.

"YOLO," I whispered, blowing my nose with pieces of Mong's legal pad. The snowflakes had it right, after all.

Part V

THE LAST TRUE SELF

Saturday 15 October

1:20 a.m. Just checked *TLTS*. Suresh is now at 718K followers on Insta! And there's a heap of reaction videos on YouTube of people crying and most of it is of the positive kind where no one threatens the creator of *TLTS* for ending Water.

It's official—Suresh's bold move to kill Water has broken the internet—ish.

Visited Mong at the hospital. He was asleep, which was good. For lack of a good gift idea, I wrote him a card and told him that Viz-Ware was in play again. Usman had written in to tell me this morning.

Also brought him a super boring new edition of some collection of essays from a super boring constitutional law expert from America, so he'd have something light to read.

Then I called Eric.

He met me at Les Deux, the very first restaurant we ever dined at together ("first date" seemed too juvenile a way to put it when it came to Eric). I wouldn't let him pick me up from my place, preferring to meet him there directly.

There was champagne, a vintage bottle, chilling in a bucket, and dozens of red roses. He was sipping a glass of his favorite Burgundy red. I sat down and refused the menu when offered—I wouldn't be staying.

"So, here we are," he said.

I bit my lip and said nothing; I literally could not speak, so clenched was my jaw.

"I think I already know what this is about," he said after several uncomfortable moments had passed; his tone was cool, his face expressionless.

I slid the beautiful ring in its box back to him. "I'm sorry, Eric. I just . . . I really thought I could, but I can't. I'm so, so sorry." I looked at him and looked away. The words were trivial compared to the visible impact it had on him.

He pocketed the box and gave me a small, sad smile. "It's fine. I was afraid that was what you were going to say the moment you told me you wanted to meet in public. But I was hoping"—gesturing at the champagne, roses—"that my instincts would turn out wrong this time."

"I wanted so much to mean yes," I said, feeling worse and worse. "But I would have been making a big mistake. You are a good man—just not for me. I'm so, so sorry, Eric—for taking it back." I tried to return the Charles Bukowski book, even if it had become such a prized possession to me in such a short time.

He flinched and pushed it back to me. "Please keep that—it was a gift. It's fine, really. I knew this was the likelier outcome from the moment I saw you hesitate when I proposed. When a woman tells you she needs time to mull over her reply to your marriage proposal . . . well, the odds are definitely not in your favor. Even when you said yes to me in front of your mother, I thought you . . . you seemed . . . unsure."

"Why did you agree to wait, then?"

He held my hand and gave it a squeeze. "I guess I wanted some more time to endear myself to you, in hopes that one day you'd be convinced to keep me by your side." He lifted my hand to his lips and kissed it. Then he placed it gently on the table. "Goodbye, Andrea."

"Goodbye, Eric." It was taking all my willpower not to burst into tears at the wounded look in his eyes. I stood and walked away, but not before I paid the tab on our table (an eye-watering sum for his wine and the uncorked champagne). It was not a Power Move, but it was the right thing to do.

Monday 17 October

8:30 a.m. Went to work and put in the Face Time. There's still a chance Kai's spies are wrong. It ain't over till the fat lady sings.

Still . . . what a chore.

Sunday 30 October

5:30 p.m. Just came back from KL after visiting my mom over the weekend. She's recovered remarkably quickly, even if the heart attack had been a minor one. Turns out Eric was right: finding out that I was engaged had indeed hastened her recovery.

I did try to tell her, really; I had it all written down. How I recognized what a good man Eric was and how wonderful our life would be, but one without the surprises, the discovery, and yes, even the struggle, that make life *Life*. Choosing Eric meant choosing to study medicine when I really wanted to study pharmacy, however ridiculous that analogy was. Choosing Eric meant not ultimately choosing Me.

But I still couldn't. I saw her wan face light up whenever she talked about wedding venues and dates, and I couldn't do it. She may end up waiting on the longest engagement ever.

1:05 a.m. OMG. What will happen to me when she finally finds out? When Auntie Wei Wei and the whole clan find out??? Will never hear the end of it. I'll have to change my name and move to Japan, where people have given up on reproducing and have turned to much more enlightened, spiritually renewing social activities, like viewing blooming sakuras, bathing in *onsens*, etc. And maybe at one of the *onsens* I will, while in top physical shape, run into the divine, utterly age-appropriate Takeshi Kaneshiro, who is still, as far as I can google, single, and we shall fall hopelessly in love.

Mmm. Takeshi Kaneshiro.

1:35 a.m. Texted Linda about possibly moving to Japan.

1:45 a.m. She texts back: **Try learning kanji then tell me how you feel about Japan in an hour.**

I rolled my eyes. I speak Mandarin, bahasa Indonesia, English, two Chinese dialects, and Spanish at B2 level. How difficult can Japanese be? Challenge accepted.

3:05 a.m. Forget Japan.

Monday 31 October

7:15 a.m. Terrible MRT ride. Blond cyborg cyclist was back and weirder than ever. Why, God, why, are men not arrested on public indecency if they wear Lycra suits? Why? It's *so* unfair!

9:20 a.m. Must . . . not . . . hurl . . . myself . . . out . . . of . . . building . . .

10:15 a.m. Ooh croissants!

1:20 p.m. Have decided to embark on a self-imposed season of sobriety. Much as I hated to admit it, I think I drink a bit too much. I have to stop using (so much) alcohol and Angry Birds/Candy Crush as ways to self-medicate. Abusing alcohol and mobile phone games is not allowing me space to develop the clarity of mind needed to identify and understand the root cause(s) of my problems so that I could truly solve them, according to a listicle I found on a mental health website today.

3:15 p.m. OK, it's maybe premature to lump mobile phone games with alcohol. Angry Birds, for example, promotes problem-solving skills and hand-eye coordination. It's the key to keeping the brain young, unlike alcohol, ruiner of brains.

7:05 p.m. Maybe will just have a wee bit of Malbec.

1:03 a.m. Oof.

Saturday 5 November

Exercised today. Ran 3 km on a treadmill.
Fine, power walked.
Fine, walked.
But still—it's a start.

52

Saturday 12 November

Today is Valerie's Big Day!

I got ready with the enthusiasm of a detainee going to a forced labor camp. This wedding was going to be an extravagant snore fest. Valerie's friends were super boring *tai-tais*, the kind that had been so successfully declawed by their ceaselessly unsurprising life of comfort and luxury that the only thing that stimulated them was the consumption of luxury goods and being profiled by one society magazine or the other. I could only hope that Ralph Kang's friends turned out to be raging drunks, professional clowns, or charming intellectuals.

Ralph's friends . . .

The blood drained from my face. I had totally forgotten that Eric would be attending the wedding!

I contemplated flinging myself off a tall building but then reality reasserted itself and I sighed. I would likely see Eric again eventually so why not now in the civilized setting of five hundred of society's Who's Who. I would be like the Dude in *The Big Lebowski*, Zen as a Japanese zephyr on Valium.

By the time I arrived at One Fullerton I was sweating so hard that I was worried it was showing through all the gold lace of my favorite (and only) Valentino gown, a vintage piece I had chanced upon one day in a boutique in Chelsea, London. But I needn't have worried because the sheer amount of bling on display (and the concentrated glory emanating from such a tight clutch of egos) was far more distracting than my sweat stains, plus the lighting was flattering. I downed a couple of glasses of vintage champagne, breaking my season— I mean, week of sobriety, alas, and immediately felt better, so that by the time Linda arrived, herself plus-one-less (Jason, who had been invited, was down with flu), I was in a significantly upbeat mood. As usual, she looked amazing; she wore a fitted mermaid gown in a deep oxblood red satin that set off her fair skin and jet black hair to maximum advantage. She wouldn't be dancing alone later, that much was for sure.

She gave me a hug as soon as she saw me and said, "You're lucky I've got spare deodorant. Come with me."

I looked at her tiny cigarette clutch and said, "How—"

"It's best you don't ask too many questions," was her cryptic reply.

Fifteen minutes later she had fixed me and the cocktail hour was drawing to a close. We were escorted to our seats right next to the bridal table. I was gratified to see that Valerie, thoughtful even in the face of her general flightiness, had made sure that Eric and I were no longer seated at the same table. I did however have the company of La Linda, which made it more bearable; she was the only one at the table I knew aside from two women from Valerie's hen night coterie, and they were far too busy networking with other more important people than me and chatting with their plus-ones.

Someone rang a gong and everyone else drifted to their respective tables, decorated in the autumnal white-and-gold color scheme of the wedding with centerpieces of faceted crystal vases filled with sprays of white ostrich feathers, gold branches, and soft white flowers. I glanced around to see who else I knew in the crowd, and had to stop myself from bolting when I saw Anousha, seated at a table nearby with the managing partner of my firm, Evan Bilson, along with a few of the senior partners and their plus-ones. I had almost forgotten that the firm had been invited, Ralph being a long-standing client; I guess Anousha and Evan must know each other from before, some London connection perhaps. I found myself wishing Suresh was there, but I knew he was still in Jakarta.

I was just morosely thinking to myself that the wedding couldn't get any worse when Eric made his appearance, dashing in a black tux as he entered the ballroom with his arm around the waist of none other than Anne, Diana's mom. They made a splash as they wove their regal way to their table; Anne's one-shouldered canary yellow gown stood out from the crowd. She looked fabulous, but I had a feeling that her smug smile had more to do with her society debut on the arm of Eric Deng, who had hitherto kept her existence hush-hush, than her exquisite dress.

The release of emotions upon actually seeing him, them, even though I had known that he would be there, hit me suddenly and hard. I gasped.

"Oh, sweetie," Linda whispered, gripping my hand tightly under the table. She, too, had seen Eric.

I watched him like a hawk. At one point they walked past our table, and our eyes met. I nodded at him and gave him a tight smile. A barely perceptible tightening of the lips was the only acknowledgment I got. Then he looked away, expressionless, as though he hadn't seen me, or worse, he had seen me but deemed me unworthy of recognition. As though I was a stranger.

Anne looked my way and gifted me with a life-sapping glare. You'd think she'd be more grateful, considering how quickly she had risen up the ranks of his affection. Eric Deng, notorious for his reserve and protective of his privacy, could not be making a bigger statement than his public parade with her on his arm in that dress.

Just like when he popped the question to a roomful of his closest friends and family, and then you dropped him like a hot stone and humiliated him, a voice reminded me in my head. I felt worse and worse. I downed two glasses of champagne in quick succession before asking the server for another. Linda tried to get me to slow down without drawing attention to my drinking, but she needn't have worried—there was serious shoulder-rubbing going on at our table, which had a deputy minister, a Mediacorp star, and a successful Austrian tech entrepreneur in his early forties, good-looking and obviously interested in Linda, but who Linda was steadfastly ignoring; the old Linda would have encouraged and toyed with him, even if she weren't interested. Nobody except Linda cared that I was drinking myself to oblivion, or why. I was suddenly glad I knew no one at the wedding.

By the time Valerie and Ralph made their grand entrance, waving and smiling, I was quite tipsy. Ralph was wearing a sharp black tuxedo that flattered his tall but slightly portly frame; Valerie was stunning in a champagne gold Inbal Dror gown that I had till then only seen photos of; it was a long-sleeved, lacy beaded number with a plunging V-neckline in gold braid and a daring front slit, showcasing Valerie's svelte and toned body to honeyed perfection. She was radiant in her happiness. Even Ralph looked radiant, literally and figuratively.

Valerie had obviously started him on a course of very ablative laser therapy, because he looked like he'd been Photoshopped—in person. He looked only a few years older than his real age.

The festivities continued with the usual speeches and performances while dinner was being served. Midway between the fourth and fifth courses, as people began to mingle again while the band started to play, I stood up.

"Where are you going?" Linda asked.

"To the toilet," I stage-whispered to everyone.

"I'm coming with you." Linda stood up and held my elbow, but I shook her off.

"I am *fine*," I hissed. Then I clattered my way to the ladies', where, mercifully, there was no queue and only two ladies powdering their noses to hear me gagging over the toilet bowl as I struggled to empty the contents of my stomach. I knelt there on the luxurious toilet floor in my luxurious gown with tears and snot running down my face, feeling sorry for myself, until my knees began to protest. I looked at my watch and realized I had been gone for less than five minutes. Great, even my body was betraying me.

I opened the stall door to find Linda waiting for me. She was holding a tall glass of warm water with a few slices of lemon in it. “Drink it,” she ordered. I drank it.

“Take this,” she said, handing me a pill. She made a face when she saw my hesitation. “Trust me, it’s going to make your nausea go away and it’s totally safe with alcohol. This was my lifesaver in Cannes.”

I took the pill with a glass of tap water. Don’t argue with the experts.

“You’re on the verge of ruining this night by making a scene. Are you going to stop drinking for the rest of the evening or what?” she said sternly.

“Yes,” I said in a small voice.

“Promise me.” Linda can be very scary when she’s standing over you eight inches taller thanks to a combination of superior genes and sky-high heels.

“Yes,” I squeaked.

“Good.” She relaxed and went back to Friend Mode. “Now I’m going back to my seat. You’re going to wait two minutes, fixing your makeup and hair in the meantime, then return to your seat, *tu comprends*?”

I nodded.

But the night was not slated to go my way. As I was walking back to the ballroom, who should I see but the hatchet-faced and much older, very married-with-sprogs Evan, locked in a passionate liplock in a shadowy alcove . . . *with Anousha!*

“Ahhh!” I screamed.

“Ahhh!” Anousha screamed, pushing Evan away like he was a diseased leper. But Evan was built like a former rugby player and barely juddered on the spot. He blearily locked eyes with me—and belched.

I ran. This evening was definitely on a highway to hell. Could it get any worse?

It could, apparently. Anousha cornered me sometime during the eighth course, sans Evan.

"We need to talk," she hissed in my ear after smiling and greeting everyone at the table. Then she led me outdoors, lit a cigarette, and offered me one, which I accepted.

"So, you saw me and Evan . . . having, ah, a moment just now." Jumping right into it.

"Yes," I said. Alcohol-composed. Since witnessing that disturbing clinch, I had totally ignored Linda's evil eye and downed two glasses of white wine successively.

"I think you know that you owe me one. The great Andrea Tang. I've heard so much about you from my fiancé. Can't say I'm a fan, especially after Suresh told me that you guys kissed on the plane, after Luxembourg. He told me before he left for Jakarta."

"Oh?" I said, serene, not bothering to correct her that it had been more of a lip-brush than a lip-lock. I was in a very Zen place right now. She didn't scare me at all. I knew then that that was some next-level shit that Linda had given me. I made a mental note to request some more pills once this nightmare of an evening was over.

"Don't act coy," Anousha said, her eyes narrowing as she stubbed out the cigarette, along with some of my toes, with her shoe. I felt the grinding from a faraway, untouchable cloud. I smiled at her and saw the first flicker of uncertainty in her eyes.

"What do you want?" I asked quietly.

She smiled her anaconda smile. "What happened out there . . . was a one-time, drunken mistake. I want you to keep what you saw to yourself, if you want to keep your job, that is."

"Bullshit. How long has this been going on?" I said. I knew a first-time clinch when I saw one—the way they were prodding tongues was too familiar, too honest.

"None of your fucking business." Her defensive tone told me everything I needed to know. "You kissed Suresh first, and now he's lost the plot. I'm merely setting things right again."

I had no idea what she was talking about, so I just raised my eyebrow, Linda-style. I felt sorry for Suresh, whose fiancée was on some twisted revenge mission.

She confirmed my suspicions. "I told Evan that I strongly preferred, and that my father would agree with me if I asked him, if you were not made partner this year. Just as a little reminder to know your place. A little probation. Maybe some time spent being seconded in Myanmar. I heard it's just full of eligible human rights violators—right up your alley, isn't it?" She smirked. "And who knows, if you are good, in one year, two years down the road . . . you'll be back on partner track. If you are behaved. And you stay away from Suresh—he's mine."

So he never broke up with her, despite what he'd said. Somehow that revelation hurt me more than it should.

"So let me get this straight: you're boning a married man old enough to be your dad, just so you can get back at me? That's pathetic. And super unfeminist."

"I always get what I want," she said in response, though her confident mask was slipping. Now I knew for sure that the partnership was secondary: she had mainly hooked Evan to hurt Suresh, to hurt me. She thought that my career was all I had. She wasn't wrong—it used to be; in fact, until recently it had been everything to me—but it would no longer be. Maybe it was the drugs talking, or maybe it was the magic of the Gomez-Kang union, but suddenly I realized that the job that I was clinging to, my shitty, life-sucking job that paid me so well to afford things I didn't need, didn't matter in the grand scheme of things. And I was tired of having other people's decisions dictate the course of my life.

"Fuck you, fuck partnership, fuck the law firm. Tell *Evan* that he doesn't have to worry about me—I'm resigning *right now.*" (Loud, unladylike belch.) "I'll have a letter on his desk first thing Monday; oh, and by the way, tell *Evan* that I'll serve my three months' notice in absentia, as garden leave, you got that? And don't worry"—I looked deep into her eyes, feeling sober and in control for the first time in a long time—"I have other more important things in my life to concern myself with than which limp wick you're burning. I'll keep your and Evan's goddamn secret for all your sakes. You disgust me, you know that? I pity Suresh; I pity *you* most of all." I stubbed out the cigarette on her clutch and she yelped. "Have a nice life, Anousha."

I stumbled away with as much dignity as I could. Drunken walk-offs are not easy.

I told Linda what had happened (we don't keep secrets from each other, and she could be trusted to keep this to herself—and maybe Jason; but it stops at Jason, for sure). The news of Anousha's infidelity she greeted with indifference ("Their relationship is toast anyway," was her reasoning). She congratulated me on finally shaking off the corporate shackles and asked me what I was going to do with my time. I realized I didn't know. Despite how much I bitched and moaned about work, I did enjoy aspects of it; working as a lawyer had given me a very comfortable salary, for one. I just hadn't taken a break in the last two years as I raced to become a partner, and now I was adrift. All I knew was I needed a breather from work and corporate life, and that meant I should not be job-hunting or odd-jobbing, just "resting" or "pursuing leisure activities," whatever those were. I was however acutely aware that my new hobbies were going to have to be cheap, since I still had a mortgage to pay and somewhat limited savings. Maybe I could learn to crochet? Lawn bowl? Join a church choir?

The trouble was everything I could think of that seemed cheap as an activity just seemed so . . . so . . . boring.

Valerie and Ralph began making the rounds in the ballroom to greet the guests. When they finally reached our table, she promised to have a cigarette together with me before the night was over. Sure enough, just as the dessert was being served, Valerie tapped me on the shoulder and we managed to evade well-wishers to duck outside to the same spot where Anousha and I had had our earlier spat. I quickly caught her up on the situation (Valerie was trustworthy).

"This is fate," Valerie said emphatically. She gripped my bare shoulders. "This, darling, is an opportunity. You have no job."

"Right."

"No life."

"Yep."

"Nothing to lose."

"Thanks," I said sarcastically.

"You know what I mean"—she waved the air dismissively—"so focus on the important message behind my words: you have to live your life. Take up golfing! Join a new book club! Life waits for no one! Car-pay dee-em!"

"Right," I said, touched. Valerie might throw clichés out every other sentence or so, but at least they were always apropos to the situation at hand. I gave her an impulsive hug once again. "That certainly worked well for you. Congrats, babe. You deserve every happiness in the world." Oddly enough, tears pricked my eyes. "You're a good friend, you know that?"

"That goes both ways, Andrea," Valerie replied, pleased with my compliment: it was the first time she had ever heard me refer to her as such. "Well, if I'm a good friend, then for goodness' sake tell me the truth: you care for Suresh, don't you?"

I swallowed. "I mean, I think if things had been different, and we'd both been single, I *could* perhaps see myself caring for him."

Valerie made an impatient noise. "If you want to be happy, you have to start being honest with yourself. So *when* you've decided to admit to yourself that you do care for Suresh, don't wait around for him to return from his secondment before telling him how you feel. Don't use Anousha as an excuse any longer. Go to Jakarta and surprise him." She started fishing around in her clutch. "Now, if you want to find him without going through your law firm or Kai, here's the number of a private investigator/psychic I used when I was still married to my first husband. He's very good. He'll find Suresh even if he's in a body bag at the bottom of the Pacific!"

"Er, thanks," I said, pocketing the card she had just handed me. Her actions raised a legitimate, worrying question: why was she carrying around the business card of a private investigator/psychic at her wedding?

Alas, before I could ask, she was swallowed by a mob of socialites wishing to take a "we-fie" with her. Then I saw her no more till she was waving at us as she and Ralph "left" for their honeymoon, i.e., went to their bridal suite at the hotel.

Start being honest with yourself about how you feel, Valerie's voice echoed in my head.

How did I feel?

I took a deep breath and let it out. If I were being honest, I did know. I just wasn't sure how Suresh felt about it. But I resolved to tell him the next time I saw him.

As for my job, it was high time to cut *those* puppet strings. Let them try to find some other dedicated, attractive, intelligent lawyer who would sacrifice everything for her job, and see if they have luck with that!

Now that I had made up my mind on my next steps, I went home to work on them. As in, I went to sleep. Hey, it had been a long day.

53

Sunday 13 November

Even though I had a lot of things to say to Suresh in person, I didn't use Valerie's PI. That's just not how I roll. But I did tender my resignation, as promised, via email.

Then all hell broke loose. But thanks to the wonders of technology, I muted all the hysterical texters. I turned on Netflix, and I literally, not euphemistically, chilled.

I felt great.

Monday 14 November

Went to the office to collect my personal items, as requested by HR. My garden leave of three months had been approved by, you guessed it, Evan himself.

Three months. That is almost unheard of in this part of the world and in this sector. I was almost feeling guilty for the firm when I remembered all the long hours of overtime I'd sacrificed to these ungrateful bastards in the hope of making partner, and all the guilt evaporated in a jiffy.

Got in around 4:00 p.m. to complete my exit interview with a skinnier Mong, back from his second dengue scare and who couldn't stop blinking away tears during that one hour, bless him, and the stony-faced HR manager.

When the HR manager had gone, I pulled out my phone to ask Mong about the email I had seen. I needed the closure.

"Did you really think Suresh was the better candidate for partner this year?"

He did a double-take. "Suresh? What are you talking about?"

Wordlessly, I showed him the screenshot of his email.

Mong read what was on the screen and looked a bit shocked. "Andrea, honestly, that's not what happened. Here's the actual email I sent."

He showed me his phone. "Read it," he said quietly.

Dear partners,

In terms of both candidates, Suresh and Andrea, I do think that Suresh is the better candidate on paper . . . but Andrea is the better candidate overall. She is a fighter. She will never give up. That's what I think if you asked me to choose between these two excellent candidates.

Best, Sim Mong

"I chose you," he said. "I will always choose you, my Work Daughter. Besides, you do get that you saw a *draft* email, right? Did you really think that I would miss a full stop? Me?"

"I didn't know what to think, I was so shocked," I admitted. A tear came to my eye. "But I suppose I should have known better than to think the legendary Toh Sim Mong would commit a typo."

"Amen." He hugged me, tight. "Dear God, I'll miss you. I wish you the very best in the next stage of your career. I have no doubt you will be a star, no matter where you end up . . . just as long as it's not with a competitor."

"It won't be," I assured him, sniffling.

"Right-o, my love."

Then he left me to go back to work, indubitably.

I entered my office and saw my team—Kai; my juniors, Josiah

and Xi Lin; the associates I was friendly with: Carla, Pei Lynn, Dina, and Wai Seng—gathered inside with a farewell cake and gifts, including a beautiful ink-black Chanel 19 maxi flap bag from Mong (thanks to Kai's guidance, no doubt). I was so touched.

When the eating, singing, and speeches were done and everyone had left, I started to pack my belongings into the large Ikea plastic crates and several cardboard boxes that Kai had prepared for me. I heard a knock on the door and said absently, "Come in."

"It's me," Suresh said, looking dapper in a sharp dove-gray suit and a turquoise tie. He shut the door behind him.

I pretended to be busy, riffling through an open box I'd just packed, consisting mostly of, surprise surprise, old sports bras and leggings. "Can I help you with something?" I said stiffly.

He picked up a business card (Langford-Bauer's) from the "dump" pile on my table and studied it intently, maybe because I'd crossed out his name and scrawled "Satan's spawn" on it. "I heard yesterday that you're leaving the firm from Anousha, who heard it from Evan. Obviously I was the last to know. Just like when Eric proposed to you."

His tone was prickly, and I felt my hackles rising. "Well, it's not like we've been communicating much since Anousha came back," I said.

"And now you're leaving the firm, I'm guessing to become Mrs. Deng?" His tone was cutting. "I don't blame you: you've always hated your job, and now here's your gilded exit strategy."

So Suresh still thought I was engaged to Eric, and that little barb, from him of all people . . .

"Well, I'm glad I'm not stuck in a dead relationship where my partner treats my career as being more important than the man himself," I blurted, too hurt to correct him about Eric.

He was bemused. "What the hell does that mean?"

"Why don't you ask Anousha, who you never broke up with," I replied, ducking my head and picking up the box before he could see the tears welling in my eyes. "Well, no worries. With me out of the running you'll definitely have a clear shot at being made partner next year."

He threw up his arms. "Andrea, what are you *talking* about? I quit. Almost a month ago. And I've negotiated an early exit from my notice period. *That's* what I've been trying to tell you."

"What, because even Anousha couldn't make you partner?" I said.

"Andrea, I've *never* been in serious contention for partnership, not this year anyway, even if I'm eligible for it. My move to Singapore was in reality a self-inflicted demotion because, and you should have known this, there was no way I could have built up my network and brought in enough business this year in time for the partnership rounds. That's why Inderjit's been so adamant about buying us a house in London. He wanted me back in the partnership saddle—*in London*."

"But you kept talking about it!"

"I was still halfheartedly working toward it, but only because Anoush wanted an expensive wedding. Then somewhere along the line, in Jakarta, when I had a lot of time to think, it became abundantly clear I didn't care about being partner or even being a lawyer at all. Plus I liked needling you. You seemed so obsessed with it, so I thought I'd play along."

"B-but . . ." My thoughts were speeding in every direction; I was gobsmacked. "So . . . so . . . so who got made partner?" It was the only question I trusted myself to ask without bursting in to tears. All this while I'd been beefing with him over the stupid partnership—and he hadn't even been in contention?

He pressed his lips into a pale line. "It was Genevieve. Haven't you heard? They just announced it over email."

I couldn't believe it. I had ruined *everything* because of Genevieve. No, I corrected mentally, because of my stupid ego, because I was so obsessed with being the best. I was furious.

"But what . . . what will you do next?"

"My comic. I'm going to try to turn it into a graphic novel, like that agent suggested."

"Congrats," I said.

"But enough about me, what about you and Eric? What's next?"

"We're buying a castle together," I lashed out.

"Good for you," he said tonelessly. "I broke up with Anousha yesterday, by the way, when she got back from her one-month observership in Seattle."

"Good for you," I said, equally tonelessly, even though I felt as though someone had sucker punched me. So that's why he took so long to do it. He was consistent in being a gentleman, at least.

Then I bolted with the half-packed box of stuff I'd been working on before he came in. Despite my recent journey of self-improvement, I'm still at heart afraid of confrontation; I wanted to resolve the misunderstanding, but I was terrified he'd laugh at me and say that I'd just been a distraction at work, and now that he wasn't gunning for partner, now that he'd broken up with the woman he'd been with for over a decade, he'd want to be single or date someone hotter and more successful than me.

So while I still had several boxes in my office, I would get Kai to retrieve them for me later. I just had to get away.

I ran to the toilet, found an empty stall, and shut myself in there. I tried to stem the rising tide of tears by thinking about the spring collection of Louis Vuitton bags, but that backfired since I wouldn't be able to afford them anymore. Shit. Then I thought about the chaos that would hit my least favorite clients, what with me and Suresh leaving, the two best hustlers in the firm, and someone subpar like Genevieve being made partner, and like magic all my tears and regrets about leaving died away.

Every dark cloud has a silver lining—but theirs wouldn't.

All's well that ends well—except for them.

Good things come to those who wait—and they will wait forever.

(OK, OK, I'll stop.)

I stayed in there longer than I should admit, not wanting to run into Suresh again on my way out. Finally I got myself together, gathered my things, left the toilet with my head held high, and got into the elevator, where I promptly bumped into Genevieve, who'd been on maternity leave till a couple of weeks ago and had returned looking svelte and well rested, everything a mother with a newborn wouldn't usually be. I savored the small happiness of knowing I'd never have to see her or smell her again. When the doors opened to the building lobby, I was about to breeze past her (as fast as I could, considering I was carrying a box of books and other trinkets), when she piped up in a conversational voice all the while side-eyeing me, "Isn't it a shame when people leave? Especially when they know they can't go further in a firm?"

Something in me detonated. Maybe it was yesterday's shrimp curry. I didn't linger to investigate. "I wouldn't be so smug: your husband is on TINDER, and WE MATCHED!" I shouted, as the elevator doors closed on her surprised, and grossed-out, face before she could make her own exit. And I know it was childish, dear Diary, but by golly, it felt good.

I can't believe I used to care about what she thought about my choices in life.

I placed the box on the floor and fished in the packed Celine bag for some tissues to plug my running nose (allergies triggered by Genevieve's ridiculous fragrance) when I realized there was something else in there that I'd managed to forget about: Suresh's letter.

My heart hammering, I tore it open with trembling hands. Read the handwritten words, again and again, until my vision swam with it.

And then I began to run.

I ran all over the lobby like a loon and finally out of the building, scanning the taxi queue, hoping in vain to catch Suresh somehow, but he was nowhere to be found. Dammit. I decided to take a taxi to his place right away; I couldn't let off now or I'd chicken out as usual. I needed to find him.

It was time to let him know that things between Eric and me were over and that he was the reason why, to apologize for always assuming the worst of him and clear the air, to kiss the heck out of him if he'd allow it, basically. In the cab, I read his note once more:

Andrea, I'm not sure how to tell you this, since we're both with other people, but I've fallen for you and if you'll give me a chance I would like to show you what you mean to me. I have to leave for New York on Monday 14 November for the next six months and I don't know what's going to happen, but I think we have what it takes to make it work, no matter what.
You're my North Star, Andrea.

When I got to Suresh's, I was so eager to see him again that I didn't even care that I was raising a ruckus; I just started banging on the door.

The door flew open and a bleary-eyed, unshaven, and wild-haired face that belonged to neither Suresh nor Anousha peered at me. "Who the fuck?" the man said. "What do you want? Whatever it is you're selling, Auntie, I'm not buying!"

I squinted at the degenerate still in bed so late on a Monday afternoon. He looked vaguely familiar. It took me a few moments to realize where I'd seen him before. "Chandran? It's me, Andrea. From Catan with Suresh a few months ago."

"Oh." Chandran squinted at me. "Sorry. I thought I'd seen you before, somewhere. Wait, let me put in my contact lenses. Come in."

I waited in the living room, wondering what was going on. What was Chandran doing at home? And where was Suresh? I'd assume he'd come straight home with his stuff from work. But the house was strangely still, and when I peeked into Suresh's study, his personal laptop and all his inks were gone.

When Chandran came back I begged him to tell me where Suresh was.

"I don't know, man," Chandran said. "He didn't say. I just got here two nights ago and the place was already like this, all packed up. I have the *worst* headache. It must be the jet lag. Y'know, I was in San Francisco for a Catan championship and . . ."

I tuned out as he droned on and on about a new point system or something, and tried calling Suresh; no luck, it kept going to voicemail. I texted him, the same "We need to talk" pleas, the same "It's important" platitudes, to WhatsApp and all the other platforms we used. None of the messages were read. I checked the Read receipts and realized he hadn't actually looked at his phone in over an hour.

Shit . . . could he have left for New York already?

". . . And my sponsors are saying I'll need to stay in the global leagues if I wa—"

I blew up. "Enough with the Catan already, Chandran! The world doesn't revolve around your dumb board game! This is important." I grabbed his shoulders and shook him. "Tell me the truth, you human wombat! Where is Suresh?!" I released him, panting.

Chandran sulked. "I told you, *I don't know*. I have a spare key. I always crash here when I'm in town." He brightened. "Didn't you know I moved to Estonia two months ago? It's great, it's like, there's a whole community of Catan and Dominion and Minecraft players there, including a Church of Catan, haha . . ."

I left this font of information.

I asked the others to call him: Linda, Valerie, his friends from work (Mong, Kai), Ray, Chandran, Faisal. Nothing. It was as though Suresh had dropped off the face of the earth. I checked his personal Facebook, his personal Instagram, Twitter, even his LinkedIn, for traces of his hide. Nothing. Not that I had expected much, as he didn't really have an active presence . . . except . . .

"Ping!" I looked at my phone. A notification from Instagram—and a post from *The Last True Self*!

Suresh had uploaded a photo of himself (his face obscured by a smiley-face emoji) on a plane:

> **On my way to the Big Apple. One step closer to TLTS graphic novel! See you in New York. #midcareergapyear #crushingit**

Suresh was already gone. Can't believe he was already on his way to America. I imagined him at Comic Con being surrounded by adoring comic book groupies, some of whom had to be hot Brahmin women from the right families. And maybe they played Catan.

I dashed away the tears falling down my face. I had lost: it was too late.

Friday 18 November

7:00 a.m. Woken up by alarm and was confused until I recalled that I was due to fly to KL in less than two hours to visit my mom so that I can reveal how far I'd chosen to fall from her ideals. Oh God.

12:35 p.m. Arrived at my mother's condo in Bangsar and knocked on the door, having discovered I'd forgotten my keys. She answered, dressed in a sleek long-sleeved jade cotton-silk top on gray linen slacks, looking fully operational, even if she still had a sallow undertone to her skin.

I decided to dive right in. "Hi, Ma, don't yell, but I've resigned and I'm not getting married," I said in a rush. Why not just face the music all at once? I would no longer be a prisoner of the tyranny of anyone's expectations, even if it meant I might not live to see another day.

She surprisingly refrained from yelling at me. "So I can see," was all she had to say.

I slumped onto a bar stool at the kitchen island and waited for her to begin the onslaught.

She stood and looked at me for a long time while I avoided her gaze. I felt her taking in the state of my unkempt hair, my bloodshot eyes, the cloud of tobacco and alcohol stink that must emanate from my pores, the weight I had gained from McDonald's and Nando's deliveries.

"You don't look too good," she observed in less harsh terms than she would normally use. "What's wrong?"

"I've made a mistake," I began. I looked at the countertop, biting my lip as I fought to control a surge of tears. "I've made many mistakes, and now I think I've lost the one good thing in my life."

"You're not talking about Eric Deng," my mother stated matter-of-factly. It was her way of asking an open-ended question.

I took a deep breath and plunged right in. I told her about Suresh: who he was, where he was from, and what had happened between us; I didn't hold back on the details. It was the first conversation that we'd ever had about a love interest of mine, and when I was done I was both elated at the disclosure and scared of her response. I could already hear her thoughts: *My daughter, the one I raised with milk from my own breasts, the last of my single children, rejected a billionaire . . . for an Indian comic artist/former lawyer?*

"Oh dear, *what* a mess," she said with a sigh as she wearily took a seat at the bar. Suddenly she looked much older than her age, and I felt guilty for unloading my troubles on her so soon after her health scare. "Why are all my children insisting on sending me to my grave early?"

"Mom, why do you always want us to suffer just to make you happy?" I cried, hurt by her response.

"What are you talking about? I don't *want* my children to suffer for my sake," she said, affronted. "How can you say that? Do you even know what goes on in a mother's heart when she sees her children running toward a cliff with only rocks to greet them below?"

She reached for the pitcher of water and poured herself a glass. "On the contrary, I only want my children to have the best, and to make the choices that save them from suffering. When you told me about Eric, I was so happy for you; I could see he was mature, he had made it in life, he was stable, and he really cared about you. These are all the qualities of a sensible choice. Plus I didn't even know there was someone else. But I'll be honest, Andrea, even if

I'd known that you were in love with this Suresh person, I would probably still have advocated for Eric because when you reach my age you will know that love doesn't conquer everything, and that someone you respect and honor, who respects and honors you back, can bring you more long-term happiness than a hot, sweaty affair." She made a moue of distaste, as though sexual attraction was merely a good-for-nothing afterthought.

"Suresh is a good man," I said defensively. He might be in New York and out of my reach, but that didn't mean I'd sit by and let my mother malign him.

"Maybe," my mother said. "I judge on the overall facts presented to me. Young people are always so ruled by their passion that they forget the realities of life. You can't live in a couple bubble forever. We grow, we age, and sometimes we grow apart. Don't forget I was one of those young people, too, once upon a time, believing that love was all I needed. And look where it got me and your father." Her eyes clouded over. "There was love between us, once. You know that we met at university, don't you?"

"Yes," I said. I had the vaguest recollection of some political rally or something that they attended for the heck of it; I was ashamed I knew little else, mostly because when I was younger it had seemed a little obscene to me to ask my parents how they met and fell in love, when all they did was hurt each other.

"We were introduced by mutual friends and became sweethearts at university, although we were an odd pairing even in the beginning. My family was quite comfortable, respected, politically connected. I was raised in comfort, if not luxury, while he was a transplant from Kedah, a scholarship kid with little money of his own, an orphan raised by his uncle and aunt. But he was smart and I liked the way his hair fell into his eyes; we dated other people but always came back to each other; I couldn't imagine my life without him, and he thought I was the only woman for him. So what if my family hated him? So what if my father threatened to cut me out of his will?

Your father and I were in love. And for some time, it was enough. We were so happy in the beginning I couldn't imagine it being any other way. I never thought that one day, twenty years later, he would cheat on me several times, the so-called love of my life."

"What?" I was incredulous. I had not known this. I had just assumed that they were wrong from the beginning—and when he got cancer, my mother had just accepted him, to care for him, until he'd passed on . . . "Why didn't you say anything to us?"

"It doesn't matter anymore, and what happened between your father and me is our business, that's the way it is with our generation—I saw it as my burden to carry," my mother said heavily. She sighed. "And then our friends, those that 'settled' because they made sensible, family-approved choices, they're still married, still together. So can you blame me when I hope my children make better, safer choices in life? Especially your sister, who, once married to a Muslim Malaysian, has to convert, and has to be OK with the fact that, in Malaysia, he can legally take a second, third, fourth wife if he wishes, without consulting her?"

I had never thought of it that way; I had always assumed that my mother had just been, well, racist. "I see your point, Ma. But maybe these are the things you need to tell Melissa, so she can assure you that Kamarul is the kind of man who would never do that to her. And maybe spend some time with Kamarul before you condemn him. You and Melissa have made such progress since your heart attack, after all. I mean, you're actually answering her texts!"

She bowed her head and was silent for some time. "I'll need to think about this," she said at last.

I hugged her. That was progress, it really was. "He's a solid guy, Ma. Don't let prejudice kill off any hope of reconciling this family."

She held up her hand. "Baby steps, Andrea, baby steps. But coming back to you and Suresh, you're right. What happened between me and your father isn't the rule for all love marriages. I won't let my bitterness cloud your decisions anymore. I've had a lot of time to think about what's important after the heart attack, and I've changed my position on some things. I loved your father, and we were so happy once. Maybe that kind of love is worth all the potential pain you open yourself to? Maybe . . . Ooh, I was young once, and I would have chosen a chance at love over anything"—her voice grew pensive; she was thinking of my father—"so I'll say this, darling: if Suresh makes you happy, then I'll step aside."

"Thanks, Ma," I said, awkwardly giving her a hug. I didn't have the heart to tell her it was likely too late for me and Suresh; it was enough, for now, to know that she believed in my ability to make good choices. She patted me briskly on the back but didn't pull away from my embrace. We weren't a very expressive family, usually. But if my mom can change . . .

"Anyway, what do I know, he might be the best thing ever and you might turn out to be the *Titanic*. I mean, the things I found in that underwear drawer of yours . . ."

I released her at once. "Thank you for your vote of confidence," I said through gritted teeth.

"Just promise me one thing."

"What, that I'll look for a job?"

"Well, yes, that is still very important, but what I wanted to say is: go after what you want. I support you."

I made a noncommittal noise. If only it could be that easy.

Friday 2 December

My sister called with good news: she's pregnant, all of ten weeks! And she and Kamarul went over to my mother's, told her the news, and everyone involved is still alive! In fact, Ma is over the moon, although she wants them to get married ASAP, which means there will be a big, fat, multicultural, multiracial wedding on the horizon, with lots of color and potential for drama and, more important, it will be held *before* Helen and Magnus's: in short, the perfect wedding to kick-start next year.

Can't say what the aunties will think about this, but, dear Diary, that's my mother's problem, not mine, mwuahahahahahahah!

The only low point in all of this is the fact that once again, Linda will be my plus-one.

Friday 9 December

Amazing news! *wipes tears of joy and snot, the latter which incidentally sounds way better than *nasal mucus,* its proper term, from face* Water is NOT dead! Or at least he has revived! Suresh just teased a strip where Rhean, in embracing a dead Water, discharges a blast of energy through her touch. And a finger twitches . . .

Is it weird that I'm so invested in a couple that exists only on paper?

Saturday 10 December

12:00 p.m. Another beautiful morning of me waking up to a Saturday that is entirely mine. No law firm. No man. No Hunger Games to win.

Paradise.

I can't explain how good it feels to be the boss of me, myself, and I, living on my own terms, my mother having been muzzled by news of my sister's pregnancy, so am now totally, utterly free to pursue my passions and my hobbies (whatever they may be) with no job to cushion me and my ass, my soon-to-be-thirty-four-year-old ass that is still as soft as an old pillow, even with all this free time on my hands where I could be working out.

Oh God.

It's OK, it's OK, need to learn to take it easy, #YOLO, otherwise what kind of millennial am I if I can't take a career sabbatical? Also I've managed to sell almost all of my bags, which netted me a small fortune, and am renting out my spare room on Airbnb. Val helped me with the pictures and everything, incorporating filters that make my apartment exude a *hygge* vibe (i.e., the kind of apartment where Danish uber-waifs would prance around making cloudberry waffles with Stevia sprinkles while yodeling), which I am told is very in and ill, all at the same time, which explains the 80 percent occupancy rate, so I'm not *totally* adrift. Le mortgage is covered and all.

Am also interviewing for a job as head of legal at an international nonprofit working with urban refugees in Kuala Lumpur. The work is meaningful and interesting, exactly the kind I'd gotten into the legal profession to pursue. I've done two rounds of interviews and the chances are looking good. If I get it, I will have to move back to the motherland, something I'm apprehensive about; it's been a while since I've lived there. To relearn the serpentine roads and the fractal skyline, snarling traffic jams, raintrees, and roadside vendors; the snatch-thieves, hawkers, buskers, beggars; the smog, heat, bustle, and wet chaotic beauty of KL—it should be interesting.

At least I will be close to family.

Family is, after all, almost everything. But not quite.

Friday 16 December

Linda and I were scheduled to fly to Chiang Mai for a Tang family hen party/retreat for Helen, sponsored by Auntie Wei Wei (Helen's wedding registration is scheduled for 31 December). Linda had volunteered to organize it, promising that it would be a whole bunch of fun but which Linda had, for some unfathomable reason, booked at a silent retreat. A luxury, six-star silent retreat, but still: no alcohol, no tech, no talking. And she was going to spring this fact upon the unsuspecting bride-to-be and the wedding party (three other cousins we didn't like, no Melissa because she's still so early in the pregnancy) at the last minute (when we arrived, essentially).

"Revenge," Linda said when I questioned her motives. "For when she called us a bunch of loser spinsters."

"She never said that," I told her.

"Her eyes did."

"It was Auntie Wei Wei. And I'm pretty sure she didn't say it in those exact words, either."

"Same thing. The sins of the parent shall be visited upon their children, haven't you learned anything from *Game of Thrones*? The other Tangs will just have to be collateral damage."

Dear God, Linda was a right nutter.

"Besides, this way we won't have to talk to any of them. *En plus*, I got a sweet discount for the trip through my connection, and you, my dear, will not have to pay a single cent. Consider it an advance birthday gift. Well, except for the 'respect' deposit, you're on the hook for that. But that's for your own good, since we do need some way to rein in your destructive tendencies."

I gave her a hug. Linda was many things—but she was mostly my dearest, kindest girlfriend.

After a turbulent flight, am now in Chiang Mai surrounded by dejected or wild-eyed corporate types in a silent retreat. The resort looked like something out of a Condé Nast feature, all wooden-villas-in-the-middle-of-a-decorative(?)-paddy-field pretty, and posh to boot. How posh, you ask? The girls and I were issued pure linen resort wear (as standard uniform), pure organic cotton pajamas; everything was organic and locally sourced; the drinking water was "energized" with semiprecious stones and infused with herbs and flowers; proper king-size beds in every room, complete with a heated hot tub in each bathroom for "reflective evening soaks"; there was a resident yogi who was of some international renown; and every evening, angels were summoned to bless the dreams of the residents. Linda did not slum it, even when she was on a revenge mission.

Unfortunately, despite its twelve-hundred-thread-count Egyptian cotton luxury, it was also one of the stricter retreats, where guests were supposed to spend *ten days* in "blissful," strict silence, practicing yoga, meditating, staring blankly into space while composing haikus/bucket lists, the like. There were some group meditations and yoga sessions, but we were not even allowed to interact then, as eye and any other form of contact between guests was strictly prohibited. Writing notes to the staff was allowed, but that was it. Breaking the vow of silence had expensive consequences: you could have your "respect" deposit forfeited—something I couldn't afford. To nip any temptation to reach out to the evil modern world, there was zero tech on the compound, unless you count the stupid old-school phone at the reception that was only to be used in case of an emergency. No modems, no Wi-Fi, no mobiles, not even any books or music, just our naked thoughts, desires, dreams, bodies, merging with the universe.

Fuck. That.

Helen and the other cousins quit after the second night and presumably flew home, or so the note from the reception said. I laughed—silently. Until I remembered that I was still stuck on the resort.

By the fourth day I was ready to escape the compound or pay good money for ten minutes on the internet. I was even willing to use dial-up internet. Anything!

By the fifth day I was literally shaking with desire whenever I thought of my phone, even my work phone. I couldn't remember why I had quit the firm if it meant I couldn't type on that lovely, tactile keypad. I missed my phones. I mean, I couldn't even play Candy Crush (which I am by no means re-addicted to).

By the sixth day I was begging Linda, who was oddly enough serene in the absence of all tech, to take me home, in sign language, whenever we were alone in a community room. She would give me her Evil Eye but keep mum, not because she was afraid of losing the deposit but because the rest of the guests were pretty hard-core. I had seen them gang up on another woman who, on the third day, had started muttering at the portrait of the venerated guru, shushing her so vigorously (and perhaps releasing their own pent-up frustrations) that she burst into tears and was escorted off the premises, presumably never to see her deposit again.

So far, so bad: Linda wasn't caving in, and I couldn't afford to crumble.

Here's what was happening chez moi. We were supposed to meditate and keep a journal of our thoughts at the end of the day, to catalog them, which apparently helps clarify them and thus nudge our brains into resolving emotional conflicts. In reality I found myself doodling and composing long, rambling poems to Suresh. In the poems I would explain how I really felt about him, how I regretted pushing him away every time he tried to make a move, until it was too late. Then at the end of the night I would mouth the words before I'd shred them methodically into long strips, deriving a kind of weird satisfaction from the destruction of my truest thoughts, my innermost feelings, in such a tangible way.

Not that I would ever show Suresh those poems anyway: they were terrible. Most of them rhymed.

On the seventh night, desperate, I ignored house rules and rapped on Linda's door, shaking with the need to talk to someone.

She opened the door in what was most definitely not standard issue silent retreat wear: a racy black silk negligee. Not surprisingly she was holding a smartphone, and the screen was showing a semi-naked Jason modeling equally racy boy thongs. I was too far gone to bother quizzing her how she had managed to smuggle these things to her room—instead, I lunged.

"Gimme," I rasped, my first word to another human in days. She raised the phone high, grabbed me by my robe, and pulled me into the room as I flailed for the phone.

"Gimme," I moaned, scrabbling for the phone in desperation.

"Keep your voice down," she hissed, "or we'll get caught."

"I'm out," Jason said, above my head. "Call me when you're alone again, lovebug."

Linda shoved me onto the bed. "Stay there or I'm throwing the phone down the toilet bowl and you won't get to use the phone at all."

"You wouldn't dare," I breathed, winded and incredulous. But of course she would: it was an Android. Plus she probably could get a replacement at the snap of her imperious fingers, no problem, no consequences. I stayed down.

"What do you want with the phone?" she said pleasantly.

"Suresh. Call!" Apparently I'd forgotten how to string sentences together out loud.

"Nope, no can do." She waggled her finger at me. "Remember you're here to detox, to figure out what you want. You have to go through the program, stay off-grid, be silent." Said the woman having FaceTime sex!

I grabbed her arm. "Not leaving till I speak to Suresh. It's important. Wanna tell him, *now*, how I feel about him."

She studied me, arms akimbo and frowning. "Are you sure you know what you want? You just rejected a marriage proposal after seriously considering it."

I nodded and forced myself to enunciate every syllable. "I want to speak to— I want Suresh. I've never been surer of anything else in my life—I've just spent a week meditating on it, for the love of sake." Fat tears pricked my eyes and dripped down my face. They dislodged the ice pick up her ass.

"All right, if you feel so strongly about it, I'll sort something out for you, but not tonight. Wait for my Bat-Signal." She shooed me out of the room. "Now get going before they do the night rounds and we get caught together. My reputation will never live that down."

And with those parting words, I found myself out in the corridor and staring at her locked door, wondering how it was that I wanted to punch her in the mouth and hug her at the same time. There was poetry in that tension.

I padded back to my room, the beginnings of a limerick brewing in my head.

The next day I was clearing up the dining room after breakfast (we all have chores here. How could I have forgotten to mention this? Posh people paying for the privilege to serve their equals—there was nothing posher than that) when one of the orderlies, I mean, male attendants came up behind me and whispered, "Follow me to the New Awakening Meditation Courtyard," before walking away. I turned and saw Arjun, the resident palm and aura reader (yes, I know, it's a thing), who, upon catching my eye, winked at me.

I briefly toyed with the possibility that he had been soliciting a sexy encounter before dismissing it outright. Arjun was close to ninety. He would probably dislocate a hip. But what could he want to say to me so badly that he would break the sacred vow of silence? Maybe I had a moldy aura or a misaligned chakra that he hadn't wanted to point out in front of the others. Or he had looked into my future, seen something disastrous, and needed to warn me about it.

I am a very positive, glass-half-full person, obviously.

I stepped into the courtyard and drew a sharp breath.

There, standing in the dappled shade of a copse of mango trees, half-hidden by a tree trunk, was Suresh, dressed in beige chinos and white polo shirt, which left nothing to my imagination (I was already starved from all stimuli). He looked lotus-flower fresh. In contrast, I looked like I had been living under a bridge, having not used a hairbrush or makeup or deodorant since the moment I entered this hellhole retreat.

Then I recalled that I used to work in the same office as him and he'd seen me take cookie crumbs out of my bra. My sports bra. The one I would wear whenever I ran out of proper bras. So . . .

I shrugged and approached Suresh's hiding spot, stopping a few feet away out of respect for the resort rules and his olfactory faculties.

"Enjoy," Arjun said before skipping away. The crafty, limber old sprite!

"Hi," I said after a long pause where we drank each other in. "What brings you here?" Ever the elegant, subtle one I was.

"You," he said simply, ever succinct.

"How did you find me? I went off-grid. This place is unlisted. Only my mother and sister know where I am!"

"And that's exactly how I knew where to find you. Your mom, she DMed me, via Instagram."

"What?"

"Yup, she told me she was a big fan of *TLTS*, which she discovered while she was performing her due diligence on me"—a pointed look in my direction, to which I responded with an innocent *Who, me?* shrug—"but that she had a daughter who was an even bigger fan of mine, and that she was with a bunch of ladies in a silent retreat in Chiang Mai with Linda and I should go find her and be happy. So here I am."

I couldn't believe it—my mother was on Instagram? Also she was *helping* me and Suresh get together—so that I would be *happy*? Was this the Upside Down?

"So you didn't come because of Linda?" I said faintly, trying to make sense of my off-kilter world.

"Nah. She texted me yesterday around midnight, but that was after I'd arrived at my hotel here. Her text said that you had something you needed to tell me in person, though." He cleared his throat. "So here I am, Andrea—what did you need to tell me?"

"Ah, well, you see, I had this case I needed to discuss . . ."

Good Lord, I just couldn't help joking even at this pivotal moment. I tried again. "It's, y'know, about us." I was blushing up a storm.

So was he. "Just so you know, even if you hadn't contacted me I would have sought you out anyway. I'm sorry for the radio silence after the last time we saw each other in the office. I was really hurt by your accusations and I thought you were engaged to Eric, and as soon as I got to the States, I'd blocked you on all the channels, changed my number, etc., hoping to erase you from my life."

I nodded. I completely understood why he'd blanked me. "And did it work?"

"Yes, it did, at least in the beginning. I threw myself into the editorial process of the graphic novel, but as much as I love *TLTS*, I couldn't concentrate. I kept thinking about how we left things. Finally it became clear to me that I needed to see you, to straighten things out between us, or nothing I do will ever be right."

"Why?" I said, needing to hear it from him.

"You know why—I like you."

"Since when? And how?" He'd hinted in his note, but I was in full lawyer mode: I mean, I'd seen Anousha's butt in a tight dress.

Suresh's gaze was on the mango tree behind me. "I know this sounds lame, but I've had feelings for you for some time now," he confessed. He turned his gaze on me. "Something about the way you type, slightly cross-eyed and the top of your tongue sticking out—it's sexy." He shuffled closer. "On a more serious note, the more time I spent with you, the more convinced I was that you were the person I wanted to end up with, because you challenge me, you keep me on my toes, and you make me miss you when you're not around. You're my North Star."

Oh my God, this is the kind of nerd romance stuff I never thought I'd be swayed by, but here I was, tears in my eyes like a proper sap.

We'd been inching closer and closer to each other the whole time, and suddenly my nose was touching his chest and his arms were around me.

"So your Eric phase is officially over?" he whispered into my ear.

I nodded. Every fiber in my being nodded. "Completely over," I whispered in the direction of his shoulder.

"Who ended it?"

"I did."

"Why?" He drew back and looked me in the eyes. He was very beautiful in the soft morning light; I couldn't believe he was mine.

"Because I have feelings for you, too," I told him, blushing as I said it. Funny how the simplest words become so hard when you're afraid of being rejected.

"Is that so."

I nodded, very nonchalant, very Catwoman-esque. "Yup."

"Double confirm?" he teased, lapsing into Singlish.

"Shut up," I said. And by way of shutting him up, I leaned over and kissed him. There was a moment of hesitancy as our lips touched; he pulled back and whispered my name like he couldn't believe we were finally doing this, but then I tugged him back and kissed him with the entire force of my being until I felt him give in, returning the kiss with an intensity that matched mine. We wrapped our arms around each other, the kissing getting more frantic with every second, our lips—

"Andrea!" someone screeched. "You won't believe this, but I'm—we're—getting kicked out of the resort!"

"What?" I said, shoving Suresh away guiltily. Was (silent) kissing allowed on silent retreats?

It was Linda, being frog-marched down the path by two male attendants and a porter following behind with what looked like the entire luggage collection by Louis Vuitton.

"Phones are not permitted on the retreat, Miss Andrea. Not only did we catch her with one, she was conducting a lewd FaceTime conversation on it," one of the attendants said, looking hassled, "and right in the middle of the Serenity Yoga room and right under the gaze of our guru!"

I groaned. "Linda, for fuck's sake! Could you not keep it in your pants?"

"It was just a nipple, the uptight bastard," Linda shouted, waving her right fist, which was clutching a mini bottle of rum.

"It was an entire breast," the man said, looking like he was close to tears.

"I'm going to sue!" Linda shouted, as she was escorted off the premises by browbeaten employees. "I want my money back. I don't feel any more energized and look how downtrodden my friend still looks!"

"Wait a second, this man is not from the retreat," said one of the attendants, the larger one built like a tank, pointing at Suresh. It wasn't a difficult deduction, since Suresh was wearing "outside world" clothes. The attendant let go of one of Linda's arms and ambled toward us with a snarl. "Hey! You there! You're trespassing!"

"Oh shit, let's get out of here," Suresh said, grabbing my hand and tugging me down the driveway, trailing the still struggling and shouting Linda and her band of orderlies. I fought to contain my giggles—who the hell gets booted off a silent retreat?

But first—

"Kiss me, Suresh Aditparan."

He smiled, drew me close, and we kissed again. And Diary, it felt just right.

Acknowledgments

There comes a time, and that time comes for every soon-to-be published author, when they've read their book for the gazillionth time and they are torn—*torn*—between setting themselves or the book on fire, or both; and then they find out they have to write the acknowledgments, and they have literally run out of words, coherent thought, or brain matter and all is lost, and they should take their emergency zombie apocalypse bug-out bag and run screaming into the night.

Thankfully, I am not that author, because I've long prepared for this, perhaps even before the book was done. Ah, the foresight. The hubris. The time-wasting. But mostly the foresight.

Anyway, here goes:

I want to thank my husband, Olivier Too, who told me that I should finish this manuscript instead of palavering on and on about one day being a published author. Your loving encouragement, chocolate, boba and wine runs, superior legal and plotting skills, and—most important—co-parenting skills have helped make this book what it is today.

And then there's my wonderful, super-diligent, and on-fire agenting team (and savvy beta readers), Allison Hunter and Clare Mao, at Janklow & Nesbit—thank you for taking a chance on me, and for helping me shape this novel to what it is today.

My editors, Margo Lipschultz and Ore Agbaje-Williams—I'm so glad to be working with you both. Your patience, skill, support, and enthusiasm made this journey such a joy. Thank you for taking me on. And this goes for all the great folks at both Putnam and HarperFiction who've helped make this book a beautiful reality—all my heartfelt thanks.

My alpha readers: Jie and my sister, Rae, for being so generous with your time and love in reading and brainstorming along with me. Especially you, Rae: you always were so encouraging when we were kids and you had to read some of my early work, some of which, in retrospect, I seriously doubt was age-appropriate—thanks for the sisterly support.

My brother, James, who's always been my cheerleader in all my writing endeavors and in life, thanks for your love.

I am also indebted to the following busy people who've read parts of my book and offered constructive criticism: comics Dan McG, Pete Johannsson, Kok Wei Liang; or advised me on aspects of law/taxation/medicine for this novel: Laurent Henneresse, Leong Chuo Ming, Ivan Lu, Sophie Tan, Lynn Koh, YW Lum—all mistakes or creative deviations are mine alone. Friends who've offered me advice or help in their own way throughout this process: Seng Bee, Wayne Cheong, YL Lum, Nadya, and somewhat belatedly, my high school English teacher Ms. Lina Lee of Catholic High School, who spurred me to write better by giving me the occasional A minus in composition.

My dearest friends Serena, Laura, and Meera, whose friendships over the years have fortified me in myriad ways. Friends in Luxembourg: Claire, Pit, Iya, Laurent, Gina, Jeanne, who were always there for me. My SP friends and cheerleaders, especially Lina, Caren, Chelsea, Jacyln, and Lynn; Hanna and all the lovely writer friends in the @2020Debuts group for being so supportive and helpful, online and in person. Thank you.

The showrunners of the superb amateur stand-up comedy scene in Singapore (hey Sam! Eugene! Heazry!) and my fellow comics of the 2015–2017 vintage: thanks for the laughs and the friendships. If it weren't for stand-up, I wouldn't have developed the thick skin needed to survive the submission process. Hugs!

Anyone who's ever told me I could write and who encouraged me (even if you lied through your teeth) and/or gave me constructive feedback—thank you.

The Wohls (epecially Michele and Benoit), Toos (Kevin), and other Hos—mega props for always loving me, feeding me, and bearing with me, especially when I'm hangry and grumpy from the work. And for having a poker face when I first told you about my ambition to be a published author.

My darling Sophie for your patience when I wrote instead of hanging with you, as much as you deserved.

Ah Poh, in heaven: I love you, I miss you.

Last but not least, my parents, who loved me enough to encourage me to pursue my dreams, and who did so unconditionally. Thank you for everything. I promise I used at least 2 percent of the knowledge gained from my law degrees to write this book.